Henry Dircks

Naturalistic Poetry, Selected from Psalms and Hymns

Of the Last three Centuries

Henry Dircks

Naturalistic Poetry, Selected from Psalms and Hymns
Of the Last three Centuries

ISBN/EAN: 9783744770019

Printed in Europe, USA, Canada, Australia, Japan

Cover: Foto ©Andreas Hilbeck / pixelio.de

More available books at **www.hansebooks.com**

NATURALISTIC POETRY,

SELECTED FROM

Psalms and Hymns of the last Three Centuries.

IN

FOUR ESSAYS,

DEVELOPING THE

PROGRESS OF NATURE-STUDY,

IN CONNECTION WITH

Sacred Song.

BY

HENRY DIRCKS, LL.D.; M.R.S.L., Etc.

AUTHOR OF " THE LIFE OF THE MARQUIS OF WORCESTER," ETC. ETC.

Nec sum animi dubius, verbis ea vincere magnum
Quàm sit, et angustis hunc addere rebus honorem:
Sed me Parnassi deserta per ardua dulcis
Raptat amor : juvat ire jugis quà nulla priorum
Castaliam molli devertitur orbita clivo.
VIRGIL.

LONDON:
SIMPKIN, MARSHALL & COMPANY;
EDINBURGH: WILLIAM P. NIMMO.
1872.

PREFACE.

THE reader, if unacquainted with the author's treatise on NATURE-STUDY, *as applicable to the purposes of Poetry and Eloquence,* published in 1869, will require to be informed that the present critical essays are based on the principle of the system therein developed. As respects that highly interesting and important subject, the work in question traces from the most simple to the most complex forms of language, how the rudest as well as the most enlightened and polished speakers and writers are more or less indebted to external Nature for particular modes of expression prefiguring some object, or its qualities, or phenomena connected therewith. The style that thus gives figurative expression to our ordinary discourse, to proverbial sayings, and to many popular songs, is usually, in its higher flights, but in no other, attributed to immediate *inspiration* for its origin; but whether such " inspiration " is real or only imaginary has always, apparently, been considered too sacred to be called in question. Now, although most assuredly Nature-Study demands genius to eliminate excellence in its performances, still we may reasonably doubt whether those poetical beauties which commend themselves alike to all readers when referring to peculiar phases of Nature, are not oftener traceable to the results of premeditated study, or to the realities of actual occurrences, than to any mysterious spiritual influence, such as by common consent we designate " inspiration."

But be this as it may, on one point all critical inquirers must be agreed, that there is much attainable excellence connected with Nature-Study, if search be made for it ; and that if its sublimities are, after all, due to actual inspiration, its multitudinous lesser excellences remain to be gathered up by those who will patiently plod through this pursuit, securing what they can thus assuredly attain, and leaving the richer harvest of rare productions to the happy influences of possible inspiration.

Although we cannot track the precise methods by which particular poets have actually studied the great world of animate and inanimate Nature, yet, by taking the collective results of such study, by whatever diversity of methods obtained, we can form a pretty accurate conception of the result as a whole ; that is, for example, we trace the natural history of one poet, or one class of poets, chiefly to biblical history ; of another to knowledge gained from Buffon, Cuvier, or Linnæus ; other poets again dwell on human nature, almost to the exclusion of all other animate objects, and of scenery; again, we have poets who revel in astronomy; others in botany, and so on, as may be most agreeable to their peculiar tastes and studies, and their advantages for obtaining information.

Our present business, however, is to discover by the standard of our own system, as developed in NATURE-STUDY, before-named, what progress has been made in this particular study during the last three centuries, as exemplified in Sacred Poetry, taking for this purpose THE BOOK OF PRAISE, a collection of "the best English Hymn Writers, selected and arranged" by Sir Roundell Palmer, Bart., 8vo. 1864. The reader will thus have comparatively easy access to the authorities herein quoted; and it may be confidently stated, that neither the editor of that work, nor the authors of the poems it contains, had the subject-matter of this essay present to their minds while engaged in preparing their publications.

Criticism, hitherto, so far as it could pretend to discourse on *Nature-Study*, has invariably treated of "Descriptive Poetry" as alone worthy of any notice. And it invariably classes "Human Nature" as distinct from "Nature," the latter being only appreciated as *scenery*, or the picturesque.

As already stated and explained in NATURE-STUDY, we only distinguish in the world around us the works of God, or of Man; that is, NATURE, and ART; and, therefore, *what is not Nature must be Art.* These distinctions serve every necessary purpose for classifi-cation ; and the present notice will prepare the reader for finding among the selections hereafter quoted, pieces which he might otherwise consider somewhat misplaced.

The author, if he may judge by the tone of the numerous critics of his treatise on this subject, perso-nal as well as public, has good reason to believe that few readers fully realize the scope and design of his Grammar of Study. They seem to understand it for all that the work itself contains, but appear to be cog-nizant of nothing beyond ; whereas the sole aim of the book is, by showing what has been done in Nature-Study, and in what manner such labour has been per-formed, to direct and point out progression in the same direction, on the same principle or system, so as to avoid mere repetitions of the same subject under different shades of form and character ; urging to find out something new, and therefore state something original. A Grammar of Language is not intended to teach the simple repetition of its exercises, however good in themselves, but rather to inform mankind how to speak and write correctly on whatever they shall have to communicate. Yet there are not a few critics who point to the exercises in the Grammar of Nature-Study as though they were the limits to the design of the work !   But the strangest view taken of the Grammar of Nature-Study is that enunciated in the

Dublin Review, January, 1872, which declares that its author " is making a bold attempt to ' secularize ' not only poetry, but Nature itself,"—and that, " to try and sever the poet's study of Nature from those religious aspirations for which Dr. Dircks has *so much disrelish* is something like an attempt to sever light from the sun" (page 28). We have heard of a political grammar of the English language, but a religious *grammar* of Nature would, we think, be a novelty. As if to show what the author overlooks in consequence of this "*materializing*," as it is called, we are informed that—"Dr. Newman, whose acuteness is beyond the questioning of criticism [?], has always believed and taught that visible phenomena are a mere cloak hiding the invisible agency of Angelic spirits. In his Anglican sermon on ' The Powers of Nature,' he speaks thus :—' I do not pretend to say that we are told in Scripture what Matter is, but I affirm that as our souls move our bodies, be our bodies what they may, so there are Spiritual Intelligences that move those wonderful and vast portions of the Natural World which seem to be inanimate ; and as the gestures, speech, and expressive countenances of our friends around us enable us to hold intercourse with them, so in the motions of universal Nature, in the interchange of day and night, summer and winter, wind and storm fulfilling His word, we are reminded of the blessed and dutiful angels . . . . . Every breath of air and ray of light and heat, every beautiful prospect, is, as it were, the skirts of their garments, the waving of the robes of those whose faces see God in heaven.' "

If this be the critic's as well as Dr. Newman's style of Nature-Study, we unhesitatingly assure both that it is a most fanciful piece of religious romantic word-painting. The latter carefully shields himself by such remarks as—'I do not pretend to say;' his taking on himself to 'affirm;' hinting that 'we are reminded;' and that his fanciful penetration 'is, as it were;' and so on. We cannot but enter our protest against this extravagant attempt at untruthful teachings pretending to have their source in Nature. Religious instruction is *not* promoted by the most poetical prose fancies of a morbid imagination, or by the substitution of such frothy nothings for the Sacred Scriptures. There is no end to the marvels which heated imaginations can produce, based on the wildest fancies, without a shadow of Nature's truthfulness. The style thus adopted by Dr. Newman may be produced *ad libitum*. In like manner, from the 4th vol. of his *Parochial Sermons,* he is quoted as observing, that:—" Above and below, the clouds of air, the trees of the field, the waters of the great deep will be found *impregnated with the forms of everlasting spirits,* the servants of God which do his pleasure." And it is acknowledged of him, by Sir Francis Doyle, that:—

" He scarce believes in any rose, in any actual rainbow; the stars themselves are little better than phantom lights, visionary flashings of that great dream, woven between the soul and God, which men agree here to call, for the moment, our visible and material universe."

What there is of religion in all this wild romantic invention we are at a loss to conceive. Nature it is not, and Spiritual it is not; but dreaming it may be; and that too, of a poetic mind 'in a fine frenzy,' straining to attain the infinite. The moment man falls away from Nature he becomes the creature of intolerable folly. It never seems to have occurred to Dr. Newman or his critics (but, by the way, he "is beyond the questioning of criticism "), that he renders to us Nature unnatural, and Angels as domestics, alluding to " the skirts of their garments," and " the waving of the robes " of the " blessed and dutiful angels." By means of this interchange he brings, or tries to bring Heaven to earth; but as a set-off he transfers our earth to Heaven. What he knows of the earthly we can understand; but what intelligence he can have of the spiritual more than other learned men we are at a loss to comprehend, nor are we aware that he has ever laid claim to any other than the substitution of his fruitful poetical imaginings, the ingenious fancies of a heated and over-wrought brain, for actual spiritual insight into futurity. Without his seemingly being aware of the fact, strange interminglings are made of the natural and unnatural, of the spiritual and the material, and of the religious and the romantic. It is a law of Nature, that Nature is alike to all men; whereas Nature as employed by Dr. Newman, displays the stars as the ornaments of angelic robing; while to others they may be the lights of the New Jerusalem; and to a third spiritual poetizer of Nature after this fashion, they may be wandering spirits moving heaven-ward, or whatever the next fabulist may choose to depict them. But again, inexhaustible as Nature evidently appears to be, Dr. Newman makes such grasping appropriations of the sublimities of Nature for the mere furbishing up of gorgeous apparel, that precious metals and stones become less than dust under the feet of such an assumed-to-be spiritual investigator of the universe. It is a strange doctrine that attempts the teaching of things that are spiritual, by mystifying even our daily experiences. But is mystifying, spiritualizing? Is it sufficient to make everything on earth, or in and around it matters of mystification, to prove that anything whatever of a truly spiritual character has been elicited? Are then all the myths of a fruitfully fanciful head of necessity spiritual? How can it be shown to prove any thing when this spiritualizing spirit practises with like effect on fables—such as dragons, salamanders, phœnixes, and similar monstrosities, as it does when dealing with the plainest facts ? For the purposes of Poetry and Eloquence it is found that figurative language must be sternly true to Nature, and comprehensible to all minds. To hope to instruct by rendering the visible invisible, by cloaking truths in mystery, by substituting conditions that are spiritual to take the place of material matter, is an evident perversion of common sense, of refined taste, and of cultivated judgment. Prismatic frothiness, however beautiful and satisfying to the eye, and however spiritual its semblance, is unsatisfying for our edification and instruction in any one practical sense affecting the welfare of human society; and such is the character of all those feverish fancies, with whatever fervour accomplished, that perpetually substitute for truth unintelligible airy nothings, leading to nothing, because based on nothing within the range of human comprehension. Such reveries, if seriously entertained, might go far to finding in the Earthly a substitution for that which is Heavenly, and might with little apparent difficulty or absurdity be worked up into proving that man ought to respect, yea, even to worship, stocks and stones ! Fortunately this is but the feeble fabric of a flimsy and transparent superstition, encouraged only by those who "love darkness rather than light"—the light of common sense, of reason, and of a sound (not a sickly, sentimental) religion.

We have hitherto spoken of Nature-Study as invaluable to the Poet, the Prose Writer, and the Orator; we are now about to adduce practical evidence of its value in Literary Criticism. The subject chosen is, perhaps, one of the least promising in general literature, being Sacred Poetry, which has never had a reputation for either appealing to Nature or in any way being much indebted to it, and principally because it derives little or no aid from merely Descriptive Poetry. But, when Nature is viewed with the wider range given to it in Nature-Study, we find that its operation on the minds of different poets presents marked differences of influence and treatment. This does not at first sight appear so striking in individual cases as in groups. Thus, for example, we more readily see the gradations in the 17th, 18th, and 19th centuries contrasted one with the other, than between any two individual poets. This selection, therefore, forms the First Essay.

From poets considered collectively we come next to examine what we may term representative poets, that is, such as have obtained distinction characteristic of the age. Thus we have selected GEORGE HERBERT for the 17th, Dr. ISAAC WATTS for the 18th, and JOHN KEBLE for the 19th century, affording the matter of the 2nd, 3rd, and 4th Essays.

It is intended by means of these Essays to lay more clearly open to view the scope and aim of Nature-Study than has yet, perhaps, been attained through the medium of the Grammar on the subject. The study is a novel one; and may probably be supposed by some readers to require too much thought and investigation, and too much labour to repay any process of deep research or much painstaking. When it is seen, however, what can be done to develope the genius of a poet even in the dryest and most unpromising occupations of the muse, that fact alone should suffice to startle lethargy into activity and stimulate inquiry. We consider, (we think with some reason) that we have here opened to view an entirely new field of criticism in a department fruitful in results, and promising to be attended with a decidedly beneficial influence on the poetry and the general literature of the future.

H. D.

WHITEHALL CLUB,
  WESTMINSTER, 1st *July*, 1872.

CONTENTS.

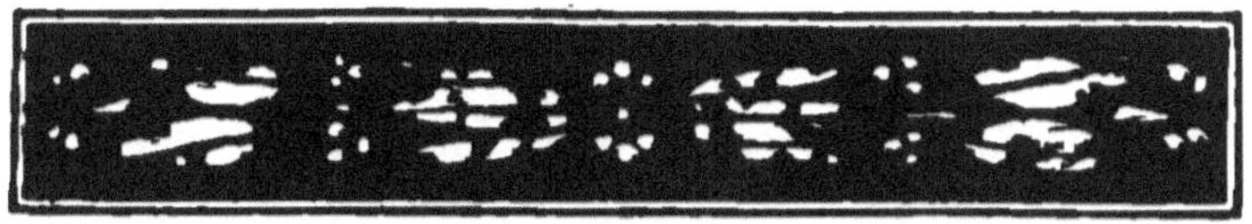

AN ESSAY

ON

THE PROGRESS OF NATURE-STUDY,

AS EXEMPLIFIED IN THE

SACRED POETRY

OF THE LAST THREE CENTURIES.

THE light in which we are about to examine the composition of certain Psalms and Hymns, pertaining to the last three centuries, is so entirely without precedent that it will be necessary to offer a few preliminary observations in explanation. We do not propose anything in the character of a retrospective review of the literary merits of writers of Sacred Song generally, but shall solely endeavour to show the evidence which Poetry of this class affords of the progress made in that particular pursuit, which we may denominate—Nature-Study. This limitation will be better understood if the reader bears in mind that literary compositions can only deal with objects of the material world as belonging either to Nature or Art. But it may be said : " This surely omits the Spiritual and Intellectual ;" and yet, as the latter have reference to, and concern MAN only, even these become, through him, but a department of Nature: a subdivision of the subject upon which we have no intention to enter. If we exclude *Art*, and confine our attention to *Nature*, then everything by which we are surrounded, belonging to Creation, forms a subject for Nature-Study;—all phenomena, all tangible objects, all we see, and assign to the animal, vegetable, or mineral kingdom, are of, and belonging to NATURE. All that is of Man's invention, does, in its widest sense, and in contradistinction to Nature, appertain to ART. We have, therefore, to discard the usually accepted idea of *Nature* meaning only the material world, and of *Art* having reference only to the Fine Arts. When we find in Sacred Poems such terms as Angels, Anointed, Armies, Battles, Bands, Books, Bulwarks, Chains, Chariot, Church, City, Conqueror, Courts, Cross, Crown, Debt, Diadem, Dominion, Empire, Feast, Fight, Footstool, Fold, Fount, Garden, Garments, Gates, Grave, Hall, Harps, Heathen, Hosts, Idols, Image, Jerusalem, Kingdom, Legions, Mansions, Manger, Nail, Paradise, Pastures, Pinnacles, Ploughshares, Pruning-hooks, Raiment, Robes, Room, Sacrifice, Seat, Seal, Sepulchre, Sceptre, Shield, Slain, Spear, Squadron, Stable, Street, Temple, Tenement, Tent, Throne, Tomb, Towers, Triumphs, Trumpets, Unguents, Walks, Walls, Wheels, Zion, and the like; such Poems will usually partake more of Art than of Nature, unless the composition be of sufficient length to admit of their being combined.

The examination we are about to enter upon, is consequently of a purely intellectual and literary character; it remains unaffected by the subject or sentiments adopted by the Poet, and has, therefore, no respect for sect or party. Like the Sun, it shines on all alike,—the evil and the good. It is of little consequence, with respect to results, what class of Poetry we subject to an enquiry like the present, but it ought to interest us in no small degree to be now first informed of the progress made in this important study by Christian Poets, from the 17th to the 19th century, especially when we bear in mind that Dr. Johnson, in his Life of the Poet Waller (1605-1687), expressed it as his opinion, that—" The essence of Poetry is invention : such invention as, by producing something unexpected, surprises and delights. The topics of devotion are few, and being few, are universally known ;—but few as they are, they can be made no more : they can receive no grace from novelty of sentiment, and very little from novelty of expression ;" adding : " From poetry, the reader justly expects, and from good poetry always obtains, the enlargement of his comprehension and the elevation of his fancy; *but this is rarely to be hoped by Christians from metrical devotion.*" And why not ? Because, says our great moralist : " Omnipotence cannot be exalted ; Infinity cannot be amplified ; Perfection cannot be improved." A conclusion which, as applied to the " Supreme Being," is incontrovertible, but the Infinity and Perfection of Nature remain to us for research, meditation, and constant delight and instruction. No doubt, however, the author of Rasselas shared with his own Imlac in despairing of ever being able to cope with a subject so vast, sublime, and apparently incomprehensible as animate and inanimate Nature.

To bring a subject of such magnitude as that afforded by the productions of the Poets of three centuries, within reasonable bounds, it has been considered sufficient not only for the purposes of the present Essay, but likewise as furnishing a satisfactory answer to the enquiry,—What progress has been made in Nature-Study by the Poets of Sacred Poetry during the last three centuries?—to derive all our authorities from " THE BOOK OF PRAISE, *from the best English Hymn writers*,"—selected and arranged by Sir Roundell Palmer, 1864, whereby we obtain ready reference to more than 140 poets, and above 200 hymns, all of which we have here arranged in the order of date, century by century. As stars of the first magnitude, we have GEORGE HERBERT in the 17th, WATTS, and the brothers WESLEY in the 18th, and KEBLE (who has been styled " pre-eminently the Christian interpreter of Nature,") in the 19th century.

To avoid misconception of our design, let it not be supposed that we are attempting any more than an exact and faithful representation of the knowledge and use made of Nature by the various poets of the different periods named. We have nothing to advise or denounce, we simply show what has been done, and how it has been performed; and it is for poets themselves to adopt, or discard, or improve what we thus lay before them. And readers at large will, for the first time, become acquainted with the extent to which Nature can be made available in every variety of solemn, serious, and truly sacred poetical effusions. The learned editor of the work just named, remarks that: " A good hymn should have simplicity, freshness, and reality of feeling; a consistent elevation of tone, and a rhythm easy and harmonious, but not jingling or trivial. Its language may be homely; but should not be slovenly or mean. Affectation or visible artifice is worse than excess of homeliness." Some hymns do not admit of either direct or indirect allusions to Nature, which happens when they are strictly devotional, or when they relate to subjects whose sublimity rises above all sublunary considerations; it is only when the poet finds some phase of Nature serve his fancy and imagination that we select his hymn for special notice. Or it may happen that his language is so suggestive of Nature's influences on a warm imagination, that we see HER reflected as in a mirror, even in a hymn which is neither professedly descriptive of Nature itself, nor having any direct allusion to an actual object or natural occurrence. We now proceed to the examples themselves, and shall conclude with a summary of such observations, in reference to their various treatment of Nature, as may be considered necessary for exemplifying a progressive process in that particular study.

WITH these brief introductory remarks, we shall now consider in order the Hymns of the 17th, 18th, and 19th centuries, with reference to this speciality, to show what has been effected so far, and how it has been executed, in the absence of definite rules of art. We commence then with the

SEVENTEENTH CENTURY.

Anonymous, 1616.

1. A hymn appeared by F. B. P., which we principally notice here to show what we mean by Art in criticism of the present character, when referring solely to poetical compositions: a restriction which the reader will be pleased to bear in mind throughout. It commences:—

> Jerusalem, my happy home,
> When shall I come to thee ?

The poet designates the city of the blessed a "happy harbour," a " pleasant soil," where "lust and lucre cannot dwell;" and then, in a quaint style proceeds :—

> Thy walls are made of precious stones,
> Thy bulwarks diamonds square ;
> Thy gates are of right orient pearl,
> Exceeding rich and rare.
>
> Thy turrets and thy pinnacles
> With carbuncles do shine ;
> Thy very streets are paved with gold,
> Surpassing clear and fine.

This concludes with a dash of Nature, of the most sketchy character possible :—

> Thy gardens and thy gallant walks
> Continually are green,
> There grow such sweet and pleasant flowers
> As nowhere else are seen.
>
> Quite through the streets, with silver sound,
> The flood of Life doth flow ;
> Upon whose banks on every side
> The wood of Life doth grow.
>
> There trees for evermore bear fruit,
> And evermore do spring ;
> There evermore the angels sit,
> And evermore do sing.

GEORGE HERBERT, 1632.

2. Among his Poems, *The Temple*, we find that hymn—

> Let all the world in every corner sing
>   My God and King !
> The heavens are not too high ;
> His praise may thither fly :
> The earth is not too low ;
> His praises there may grow.

    .   .   .   .

As it consists of only two verses it does not, however, allow him the scope of which he might have availed himself in a longer one on *The Lord's Day*, commencing :—

> O day most calm, most bright !
> The fruit of this, the next world's bud ;

> The week were dark, but for thy light.

Most part of the remaining verses are quaintly artificial ; thus Sundays are " the pillars ;" or are " Threaded together on Time's string."

GEORGE WITHER, 1641.

3. We next come to consider this poet, the first of whose hymns treats of *God the Creator*. He sings, calling for universal praise :—

> Strike the viol, touch the lute,
> Let not tongue or string be mute ;
> Nor a creature dumb be found
> That hath either voice or sound.

The " creatures," &c. summoned are thus addressed :—

> Lowly pipe, ye worms that creep
> On the earth or in the deep:
> Loud aloft your voices strain,
> Beasts and monsters of the main;
> Birds, your warbling treble sing;
> Clouds, your peals of thunder ring;
> Sun and moon, exalted higher,
> And bright stars, augment the choir.

> Come, ye sons of human race,
> In this chorus take your place,
>
> .   .   .   .   .
>
> Seas and floods, from shore to shore,
> Shall their counter-tenors roar:
> To this concert, when we sing,
> Whistling winds your descants bring ;
>
> .   .   .   .
>
> Then, O come, in pious lays
> Sound we God Almighty's praise !

Here we have a lengthened example of broad generalization, such as (even when Nature is elaborately introduced) is common to the sterile style of the period. The next piece by this Poet that we shall notice refers to *Morning*, which might be expected to have moral and religious sentiments presented to us in a frame-work rich in Nature-Study ; but out of six verses we cannot extract a single line for our purpose. Another, however, on *Evening*, commences thus :—

> Behold the sun, that seem'd but now
>   Enthronèd overhead,
> Beginneth to decline below
>   The globe whereon we tread ;
>
> .   .   .   .
>
> Thus time, unheeded, steals away
>   The life which Nature gave ;
> Thus are our bodies every day
>   Declining to the grave.
>
> .   .   .   .

In the next and last piece by this author, the subject relates to *Childhood*, and consists of twelve verses of six lines each. It begins :—

> Sweet baby, sleep! what ails my dear,
>   What ails my darling thus to cry ?
> Be still, my child, and lend thine ear,
>   To hear me sing thy lullaby.

SAMUEL CROSSMAN, 1664.

4. This poet is the author of thirteen verses on *The*

Holy Catholic Church, which from the solemnity of the subject and its mode of treatment offers little or no opportunity for reference to worldly objects, except in one verse where they are negatively referred to, not for description, but by way of affording a striking contrast between the Heavenly City, and our earthly existence, thus :—

> No sun by day shines there,
> Nor moon by silent night ;
> Oh no ! these needless are ;
> The Lamb's the City's Light :
> O happy place !

Another of his hymns on *Resurrection and Eternal Life* is of much the same character, being wholly and simply devotional.

JOHN AUSTIN, 1668.

5. A hymn was composed by Austin, treating of *God the Creator* in eight verses, one-half is allusive to Nature, while the remainder is occupied with reflections consequent thereon; the former are as follows :—

> Hark, my soul, how every thing
> Strives to serve our bounteous King;
> Each a double tribute pays,
> Sings its part, and then obeys.
>
> Nature's chief and sweetest quire
> Him with cheerful notes admire ;
> Chanting every day their lauds,
> While the grove their song applauds.
>
> Though their voices lower be,
> Streams have too their melody ;
> Night and day they warbling run,
> Never pause, but still sing on.
>
> All the flowers that gild the spring
> Hither their still music bring ;
> If Heaven bless them, thankful they
> Smell more sweet, and look more gay.

He then calls on his "sluggish heart" to—

> Learn of birds, and springs, and flowers,
> How to use thy nobler powers.

Another of his hymns on *Christ Ascended*, which was altered by John Wesley in 1739, is cast in a different strain; as is also his variation of one of Richard Crashaw's hymns, composed in 1646, on *Holy Communion;* the same remarks apply to his hymn on *Hope* in nine verses, expressive of humility, and offering a prayer for guidance,

> That every step, or swift, or slow,
> Still to Thyself may tend !

RICHARD BAXTER, 1681.

6. We can only quote one verse in one of his hymns, illustrating "Thy will be done," namely :—

> If death shall bruise this springing seed
>   Before it come to fruit,
> The will with Thee goes for the deed,
>   Thy life was in the root.

Like most poets of this period he is apt to go almost out of his way to adopt objects of sense in every-day life, as when in the same piece he says :—

> Christ leads me through no darker *rooms*
> Than He went through before.

JOHN MASON, 1683.

7. Mason, in a hymn addressing *God the Holy Ghost,* sings :—

> There is a Stream, which issues forth
>   From God's eternal Throne,
> And from the Lamb, a living stream
>   Clear as the crystal stone.

> The stream doth water Paradise;
>   It makes the angels sing ;
> One cordial drop revives my heart;
>   Hence all my joys do spring.

The seven verses only afford these two for our purpose. In another of his productions, consisting of three verses of six lines each, addressed to *The Lord's Day*, he seems not to have found scope for the exercise of any similar display of poetically imaginative power.

BISHOP THOMAS KEN, 1697—1712.

8. We have next to direct attention to four hymns by Bishop Thomas Ken, written between the years 1697 and 1712 ; three of them relate to periods of the day, the first being *Morning*, which commences :—

> Awake, my soul, and with the sun
> Thy daily stage of duty run;

> .   .   .   .

In the third verse we find the simile—

> In conversation be sincere;
> Keep conscience as the noontide clear.

And the soul is admonished—

> By influence of the light Divine
> Let thy own light to others shine.

Addressing the " heavenly choir," the poet sings :—

> Had I your wings, to Heaven I'd fly;
> But God shall that defect supply;
> And my soul, wing'd with warm desire,
> Shall all day long to Heaven aspire.

Another simile simply expresses—

> Lord, I my vows to Thee renew;
> Disperse my sins as morning dew.

And thus we close our selection, from the poet's fourteen verses. The next is his well-known *Evening Hymn* :—

> All praise to Thee, my God, this night :

and his third hymn concludes the series with *Midnight,*

bnt these two are wholly spiritual and devotional. The
last of his hymns is on the *Holy Communion*, soaring high
above all mundane affairs.

MISCELLANEOUS, 1646—1662.

The following poets and their poems are inadmissible
from their dealing more with *Art* than *Nature* :—RICHARD
CRASHAW, 1646,—" With all the powers my poor soul
hath." JOHN QUARLES, 1654,—" O King of kings, before
whose throne." BISHOP JEREMY TAYLOR, 1655,—" Lord!
come away !"—and an Anonymous poet, 1662,—" Come,
Holy Ghost, our souls inspire."

Our selections in illustration of the seventeenth century
end here.   They all evince a certain degree of hardness and
harshness of outline when dealing with Creation, partaking
more of the indications of carvings than of pictures from
green and gay and genial Nature. We now proceed to
examine in like manner the—

EIGHTEENTH CENTURY.

ISAAC WATTS, 1700—1720.

9. We commence this century with various hymns from
the prolific pen of Isaac Watts, passing over the first, " I
give immortal praise." In his version of the 100th Psalm,
the following lines occur—

> Before Jehovah's awful throne,
>   Ye nations, bow with sacred joy;
>
> His sov'reign power, without our aid,
>   Made us of clay, and formed us men ;
>
> We'll crowd Thy gates with thankful songs,
>   High as the heavens our voices raise;
> And earth, with her ten thousand tongues,
>   Shall fill thy courts with sounding praise.

> Wide as the world is Thy command;
> Vast as eternity Thy love;
> Firm as a rock Thy truth shall stand,
> When rolling years shall cease to move.

This is given as altered by Charles Wesley, in 1741; but to Watts is due the merit of its design, and for elevation of thought and language it ranks as one of his best compositions. It may not be out of place here to direct attention to a certain difficulty that frequently occurs in separating what essentially belongs to Art from that which is entirely of Nature. The critical reader will observe in the few foregoing lines "throne," "sov'reign power," "gates," "courts"—all traceable to Art alone, yet so intermingled with what is derived solely from Nature as to defy their disjunction in a readable extract. This remark applies with equal force to Watts's version of the 93rd Psalm, in which appears "royal state," "robes," "sovereign might," "majesty," &c. He proceeds—

> In vain the noisy crowd,
> Like billows fierce and loud,
> Against Thine empire rage and roar:
> In vain, with angry spite,
> The surly nations fight,
> And dash like waves against the shore.

The 146th Psalm opens thus—

> Happy the man, whose hopes rely
> On Israel's God; He made the sky,
> And earth and seas with all their train.

In quoting his rendering of the 65th Psalm, we can only do the poet justice by giving it entire—

> On God the race of man depends,
> Far as the earth's remotest ends,
> Where the Creator's name is known
> By Nature's feeble light alone.
>
> He bids the noisy tempests cease;
> He calms the raging crowd to peace,

> When a tumultuous nation raves
> Wild as the winds, and loud as waves.
>
> Whole kingdoms, shaken by the storm,
> He settles in a peaceful form;
> Mountains, establish'd by His hand,
> Firm on their old foundations stand.
>
> Behold, His ensigns sweep the sky;
> New comets blaze, and lightnings fly!
> The heathen lands, with swift surprise,
> From the bright horrors turn their eyes.
>
> At His command the morning ray
> Smiles in the east, and leads the day;
> He guides the sun's declining wheels
> Over the tops of western hills.
>
> Seasons and times obey His voice;
> The evening and the morn rejoice
> To see the earth made soft with showers,
> Laden with fruit, and drest in flowers.
>
> 'Tis from His watery stores on high
> He gives the thirsty ground supply;
> He walks upon the clouds, and thence
> Doth His enriching drops dispense.
>
> The desert grows a fruitful field,
> Abundant food the valleys yield;
> The valleys shout with cheerful voice,
> And neighbouring hills repeat their joys.
>
> Thy works pronounce Thy power divine;
> O'er every field Thy glories shine;
> Through every month Thy gifts appear;
> Great God! Thy goodness crowns the year!—1719.

In the last verse but one we have an example of the non-natural, or negative view of Nature, affording a bold hyperbolical figure, as—

> The valleys shout with cheerful voice,
> And neighbouring hills repeat their joys.

This is a happy poetical rendering of the Psalmist's language. In 1720 Watts wrote—

> I sing th' almighty power of God,
> That made the mountains rise,
> That spread the flowing seas abroad,
> And built the lofty skies.

> I sing the wisdom that ordain'd
>   The sun to rule the day:
> The moon shines full at His command,
>   And all the stars obey.
>
> .   .   .   .
>
> There's not a plant or flower below,
>   But makes Thy glories known;
> And clouds arise, and tempests blow,
>   By order from Thy throne.

His 98th Psalm does not admit of this style, neither do his hymns commencing, "When I survey the wondrous cross"—"Not all the blood of beasts, on Jewish altars;" nor "Plunged in a gulf of dark despair"—with the exception of a couplet in the fourth verse of this last:—

> Oh! for this love, let rocks and hills
>   Their lasting silence break.

We must also exclude the hymn, "Come, let us join our cheerful songs with angels round the throne,"—likewise, "Salvation! oh! the joyful sound!" and "Join all the glorious names" (consisting of twelve verses); to which we may add—"Now is the hour of darkness past." His 72nd Psalm, dated 1719, affords us only the first out of six verses—

> Jesus shall reign where'er the sun
> Does his successive journeys run;
> His kingdom stretch from shore to shore,
> Till moons shall wax and wane no more.

And from the second and third verses of another application of the same Psalm we quote—

> As rain on meadows newly mown,
> So shall He send His influence down;
> His grace on fainting souls distils
> Like heavenly dew on thirsty hills.
>
> The heathen lands, that lie beneath
> The shade of overspreading death,
> Revive at His first dawning light,
> And deserts blossom at the sight.

Such pieces as the following, however, do not admit of this peculiar treatment, as :—" Come, Holy Spirit, heavenly Dove;" "Lord of the worlds above;" "Why do we mourn departing friends?" "My God, my King, Thy various praise;" "Blest are the humble souls that see;" "My Shepherd will supply my need;" "The Lord my Shepherd is;" "Almighty God, Thy piercing eye;" "Up to the hills I lift mine eyes;" "From all that dwell below the skies;" "Accept, my God, my evening song;" "Must friends and kindred droop and die;" "O happy soul, that lives on high;" "My God, the Spring of all my joys;" "How vast the treasure we possess;" and lastly, "Early, my God, without delay."

In the 19th Psalm "the gospel" is placed in contrast with "the sun," commencing with the latter :—

> Behold, the morning sun
> Begins his glorious way;
> His beams through all the nations run
> And light and life convey.

Treating of the *Holy Catholic Church*, an application is made of Nature-Study to render the heavenly state comprehensible to ordinary understandings, in the hymn— "Come, we that love the Lord," thus :—

> The men of grace have found
> Glory begun below;
> Celestial fruits on earthly ground
> From faith and hope may grow.
>
> The hill of Zion yields
> A thousand sacred sweets,
> Before we reach the heavenly fields,
> Or walk the golden streets.
>
> .   .   .   .
>
> We're marching through Emmanuel's ground,
> To fairer worlds on high.

From his 103rd Psalm we select the fifth out of six verses, for the following reading of the scriptural simile :—

> Our days are as the grass,
> Or like the morning flower;
> If one sharp blast sweep o'er the field,
> It withers in an hour.

One of his hymns, consisting of four verses, commences :—

> The waves of trouble, how they rise,
> How loud the tempests roar!
> But death shall land our weary souls
> Safe on the heavenly shore.

Commemorating the *Resurrection and Eternal Life*, Watts passionately and yet tastefully sings :—

> There is a land of pure delight,
> Where saints immortal reign,
> Infinite day excludes the night,
> And pleasures banish pain.
>
> There everlasting spring abides,
> And never withering flowers;
> Death, like a narrow sea, divides
> This heavenly land from ours.
>
> Sweet fields beyond the swelling flood
> Stand dress'd in living green:
> So to the Jews old Canaan stood,
> While Jordan roll'd between.
>
> .   .   .   .
>
> Could we but climb where Moses stood,
> And view the landscape o'er;
> Not Jordan's stream, nor death's cold flood,
> Should fright us from the shore.

The poet has here availed himself of that scope which such a remote scene affords for the fullest possible play of imagination and fancy, introducing a touch of the negative view of things in our present mundane state of being, for there :—

> Infinite day excludes the night.

There are " everlasting springs"—

> And never withering flowers.

The last verse but one of the 90th Psalm, " Our God, our Help in ages past," solemnly and happily expresses an old theme—

> Time, like an ever-rolling stream,
>   Bears all its sons away ;
> They fly forgotten, as a dream
>   Dies at the opening day.

In a hymn to *Morning*, Watts describes the sun's regular, continuous course, " without weariness or rest," which he would fain emulate :—

> God of the morning, at whose voice
>   The cheerful sun makes haste to rise,
> And, like a giant. doth rejoice
>   To run his journey through the skies;
> From the fair chambers of the east
>   The circuit of his race begins;
> And, without weariness or rest,
>   Round the whole earth he flies and shines.

.   .   .   .

The 92nd Psalm is paraphrased in seven verses, the fourth of which gives us that phase of Human Nature which unluckily for the public weal preponderates in society of every class. The Psalmist declares—" My heart shall triumph in my Lord," but—

> Fools never raise their thoughts so high,
> Like brutes they live, like brutes they die;
> Like grass they flourish, till Thy breath
> Blast them in everlasting death.

His hymn in praise of *Divine Love*, begins—" Go worship at Immanuel's feet." From this piece, of eighteen verses, we select the following passages :—

.   .   .   .

> Earth is too narrow to express
> His worth, His glory, or His grace!
> The whole creation can afford
> But some faint shadows of my Lord;
> Nature, to make His beauties known,
> Must mingle colours not her own.

Is He compared to Wine or Bread?

.　　　　.　　　　.　　　　.

Is He a Tree?　The world receives
Salvation from His healing leaves:
That righteous Branch, that fruitful bough,
Is David's root, and offspring too.

Is He a Rose?　Not Sharon yields
Such fragrancy in all her fields;
Or if the Lily He assume,
The valleys bless the rich perfume.

Is He a Vine?　His heavenly root
Supplies the boughs with life and fruit :

.　　　　.　　　　.　　　　.

Is He the Head?　Each member lives,
And owns the vital power He gives;

.　　　　.　　　　.　　　　.

Is He a Fountain?　　　.　　　　.

.　　　　.　　　　.　　　　.

Is He a Fire?　He'll purge my dross;
But the true gold sustains no loss:

.　　　　.　　　.　　　　.

Is He a Rock?　How firm He proves!
The Rock of Ages never moves.

.　　　　.　　　　.　　　　.

The next inquiries answered are :—" Is He a Way ?" " a
Door," " a Corner-stone," " a Temple,"—followed by :—

Is He a Star?　He breaks the night,
Piercing the shades with dawning light;

.　　　　.　　　　.　　　　.

I know the bright, the Morning Star!

Is He a Sun?　His beams are grace,
His course is joy and righteousness:

Oh! let me climb those higher skies
Where storms and darkness never rise!

.　　　　.　　　　.　　　　.

Nor earth, nor seas, nor sun, nor stars,
Nor heaven His full resemblance bears:
His beauties we can never trace
Till we behold Him face to face.

In a production of this character the negative or non-natural view of Nature has been ably employed by the poet to ennoble his subject, so far as it lies within the limited powers of human intelligence to foreshadow (however faintly and imperfectly) the loftiest spiritual aspirations; for, as he states of the Christian's hope, in his hymn, "O happy soul, that lives on high:"—

> His pleasures rise from things unseen,
>   Beyond this world and time,
> Where neither ears nor eyes have been,
>   Nor thoughts of sinners climb.

A hymn of five verses, beginning, "When Christ, with all His graces crown'd," concludes:—

> Up to the fields above the skies
>   My hasty feet would go;
> There everlasting flowers arise,
>   And joys unwithering grow.

The entire hymn partakes of Nature's influence, as shown in the expressions—"Sheds his kind beams—a young Heaven on earthly ground—glory in the bud—a blooming paradise—wild desert—the shining day—clouds of sin,"&c.; and with these observations we conclude for the present our remarks on the preceding selected compositions.

Simon Browne, 1720.

10. Of four hymns by this poet, the first is an appeal to the "Holy Spirit" for guidance in a right course and conduct of life; the second is addressed to *Evening*, being a variation on one by Watts; it is a prayer, or evening song of thanksgiving for protection—"Through all the dangers of the day." The third commemorates *The Lord's Day*, when his only desire is that he may:—

> On wings of strong devotion rise,
> Pass every cloud, pass all the skies,
>   And leave beneath Thy feet the stars.

In the last, on *Divine Love*, ranked by his editor among " Songs of the Heart," he makes a peculiar use of the negative, when, allusive to the Almighty's glory, he observes—

> Thy presence makes celestial day,
>   And fills each raptur'd soul with bliss;
> Night would prevail were God away,
>   And spirits pine in Paradise !

But hymns of this class afford little material in furtherance of our present enquiry.

John Christian Jacobi, 1722.

11. " Holy Ghost, dispel our sadness," as here given, is a variation by Toplady, 1776, from Jacobi. In the third verse the omniscience of the Deity is thus expressed :—

> Known to Thee are all recesses
>   Of the earth and spreading skies;
> Every sand the shore possesses
>   Thy Omniscient Mind descries.

A second hymn, from J. C. Ruben, " Sleep well, my dear," is a happy and beautiful comparison between the infant Saviour and the babe cradled " in down, soft every way."

Joseph Addison, 1728.

12. He first published in the *Spectator* of 1728, without any special acknowledgment of its authorship, his widely and justly celebrated paraphrase of the 19th Psalm, addressed to *God the Creator :*—

> The spacious firmament on high,
> With all the blue ethereal sky,
> And spangled heavens, a shining frame,
> Their great Original proclaim.

> The unwearied sun, from day to day,
> Does his Creator's power display,
> And publishes to every land
> The work of an Almighty hand.
>
> Soon as the evening shades prevail,
> The moon takes up the wondrous tale,
> And nightly to the listening earth
> Repeats the story of her birth;
> Whilst all the stars that round her burn,
> And all the planets in their turn,
> Confirm the tidings, as they roll,
> And spread the truth from pole to pole.
>
> What, though in solemn silence all
> Move round the dark terrestrial ball;
> What, though no real voice or sound
> Amidst their radiant orbs be found;
> In reason's ear they all rejoice,
> And utter forth a glorious voice,
> For ever singing as they shine,
> ' The hand that made us is Divine.'

His hymn—

> When all Thy mercies, O my God,
>   My rising soul surveys,

touches on the everchanging phases of human life and experience, from childhood to manhood, and its final issue: helpless "infancy," "the slippery paths of youth," "the pleasing snares of vice," "sickness," and "death."   But the treatment of these is broad and general, and, therefore, though in a merely literary point of view, it is less striking as a poetical composition, in all other respects it is singularly happy, polished, and charmingly simple and effective. His rendering of the 23rd Psalm is justly popular :—

> The Lord my pasture shall prepare.
>
> .　　　　.　　　　.　　　　.
>
> When in the sultry glebe I faint,
> Or on the thirsty mountain pant,
> To fertile vales and dewy meads
> My weary, wandering steps He leads,

> Where peaceful rivers, soft and slow,
> Amid the verdant landscape flow.
>
> .　　　　.　　　　.　　　　.
>
> Though in a bare and rugged way,
> Through devious lonely wilds I stray,
> Thy bounty shall my wants beguile ;
> The barren wilderness shall smile,
> With sudden greens and herbage crown'd,
> And streams shall murmur all around.

His prayer for forgiveness of trespasses—" When rising from the bed of death," composed in 1719, is throughout in keeping with the solemn appeal for pardon of sins by one—

> Who knows Thy only Son has died
> To make that pardon sure.

John Wesley, 1739-1743.

13. Of four hymns in this selection, one is a variation from John Austin, 1668 ; the second, and the last from the German ; and the third from J. H. Rothe.   The hymn :—

> O Thou, to whose all-searching sight
> The darkness shineth as the light,

presents us with but slight allusions to external Nature, figuratively applied, in such lines as :—

> If in this darksome wild I stray,
> Be Thou my Light, be Thou my Way ;
>
> .　　　.　　　.　　　.
>
> When rising floods my soul o'erflow,
> When sinks my heart in waves of woe,
>
> .　　　.　　　.　　　.
>
> If rough and thorny be the way,
> My strength proportion to my day.

The hymn from Paul Gerhardt—" Commit thou all thy griefs"—consisting of 16 verses of four lines each, alludes to the Almighty :—

> Who earth and Heaven commands,
> Who points the clouds their course,
> Whom winds and seas obey.

The Christian is advised :—

> Give to the winds thy fears ;

being assured of the " King of kings " that—

> Through waves and clouds and storms,
>   He gently clears thy way ;
> Wait thou His time ; so shall this night
>   Soon end in joyous day.

The hymn by Rothe, six verses of six lines each, is not redeemed for the purpose of this essay by the single line :—

> Though waves and storms go o'er my head ;

but may prove a useful study of that style over which Nature has no influence whatever, but which nevertheless may bear the undoubted marks of many excellencies.

Charles Wesley, 1739-1762.

14. We have now to examine 26 psalms and hymns by this eminent Christian Poet. The collection also contains one altered from Watts, another to which Wesley added the last verse ; and a third which he wrote in 1758, but we have here only Madan's variation in 1760 ; and lastly the hymn " Lo ! God is here !"—from Gerhard Tersteegen.

His first hymn :—

> Hark ! how all the welkin rings
>
> .   .   .   .
>
> Joyful, all ye nations, rise,
> Join the triumph of the skies ;
> Universal Nature say,
> Christ the Lord is born to-day !

throughout forty lines contains no nearer approach to

Nature than is here supplied. Similar in this respect are the hymns—"O for a thousand tongues to sing;" and "Blow ye the trumpet," announcing "the year of Jubilee;" also, "Christ the Lord is risen to-day," eleven verses, which truly—

> 'Scarce on earth a thought bestow ;'

—likewise—"Rejoice, the Lord is King"—which treats solely of His kingdom and rule; of the same class are—"Thou Judge of quick and dead,"—"Come, let us join our friends above,"—"Jesu, Thou art my Righteousness,"—"God of my salvation, hear,"—"Happy soul! thy days are ended ;" and thus in like manner we might proceed with no less than thirteen other hymns; but their further enumeration could serve no useful purpose, although reference to the whole series may prove instructive to the Nature-student by satisfying him of the wide difference existing between a style which discards, and one that judiciously adopts such language and figurative expression, as cannot fail to occasion vivid associations with Nature to arise in the minds of intelligent readers.

His hymn from the German—"Lo! God is here! Let us adore," has only one simile (which occurs in the last verse) :—

> As flowers their opening leaves display,
> And glad drink in the solar fire,
> So may we catch Thy every ray.

In the fourth verse of his hymn, "Eternal Beam of Light Divine," we find the common simile :—

> Be Thou, O Rock of Ages, nigh !
>
> .   .   .   .
>
> And grief, and fear, and care shall fly
> As clouds before the mid-day sun.

The hymn of all others which might have proved an exception to this barrenness of associations with the living and the inanimate kingdoms of Nature is addressed to *Morning*—" Christ, whose glory fills the skies,"—and is occupied with such generalizations as :—" The skies, Light, Sun, shadows of night, Day-spring, Day-star,"—

> Dark and cheerless is the morn
>
> .   .   .   .
>
> More and more Thyself display
> Shining to the perfect day !

While another poem to *Night* is even more strangely sterile in figurative expressions.

The next we shall notice—" Come, O thou Traveller unknown," the longest of the series, consisting of 14 verses of six lines each, participates in this general dearth of Nature's loveliness and its manifold applications ; while the last we have to consider—" Christ, my hidden Life, appear," is only noticeable for the couplet :—

> Never in the whirlwind found,
> Or where earthquakes rock the place.

Uninviting as this critique appears, and disappointing as it certainly must prove to a numerous class of the poet's ardent and devout admirers, it is none the less rigidly correct, and beyond being gainsaid. If any one of the foregoing productions more than another admitted of different treatment, surely we may point to his *Morning* and his *Evening* hymns, which, whatever may be advanced in favour of the style of his other productions, admitted of a closer association with Nature than we can find in either of those poems.

From the entire selection we are obliged to exclude no

less than 23 hymns, none of which display the slightest indebtedness to universal Nature. This peculiarity in Charles Wesley's sacred poetry has never before come under remark, nor could it be expected to excite any especial attention as criticism is usually conducted, that is, with an almost total omission of attention to this obvious beauty in all metrical compositions that employ the more delicate colourings of Nature; not but that some of the finest hymns are strictly spiritual, devotional, and meditative without possessing any other symbolic expressions than such as from their being entirely Scriptural elevate the mind far above all considerations connected with this weary work-a-day world. However, we are not even advocating the employment of Nature-Study in Sacred Poems, but only showing how it has been used, and what progress poets have made in that special pursuit during the last three centuries. It is clear that this particular poetical enrichment of spiritual and ethical writings has Scriptural usage for its authority; and its propriety and usefulness, therefore, cannot be called in question, considered, as it ever should be, in connexion with its familiarizing to our minds the great, glorious and ineffably beautiful and marvellous designs and works of the Almighty Creator—

> Whose works we cannot count, yet dimly trace
> Some millions, whelmed in magnitude of space.

John Cennick, 1742-1752.

15. Author of that grand hymn :—

> Lo ! He comes with clouds descending,
> Once for favoured sinners slain.

in 1752, of which a variation was executed by Charles Wesley in 1758 and M. Madan in 1760. The third verse begins :—

> Every island, sea, and mountain,
> Heaven and earth shall flee away ;

and the whole hymn is exceedingly elevated in tone and sentiment.

His two other hymns in this collection, "Children of the Heavenly King ;" and "Jesus, my all, to Heaven is gone," are admirable compositions; the last presents a brief negative allusion to "The way the holy Prophets went," as a path in which—

> No lion, no devouring care,
> No ravenous tiger shall be there.

Robert Seagrave, 1748.

16. We have only his hymn—"Rise, my soul, and stretch thy wings," which, as having reference to the *Resurrection and Eternal Life*, might not be expected to touch on the "transitory things" of earth. The following approaches the negative style in viewing Nature :—

> Sun, and moon and stars decay;
> Time shall soon this earth remove ;

—but not so the lines :—

> Rivers to the ocean run,
>   Nor stay in all their course ;
> Fire ascending seeks the sun ;
>   Both speed them to their source :

—the next are of a mixed character :—

> Fly me Riches, fly me Cares,
>   Whilst I that coast explore ;
> Flattering world, with all thy snares,
>   Solicit me no more !

Dr. Philip Doddridge, 1755.

17. An examination of sixteen specimens of his hymns shows that only one-half of them come within the limits of our strictures ; these we shall find are the following :—

> How rich Thy favours, God of grace,
>   How various and Divine !
> Full as the ocean they are pour'd,
>   And bright as Heaven they shine.

The next—" Ye golden lamps of heaven, farewell," has the following :—

> .   .   .   .
>
> Farewell, thou ever-changing moon,
>   Pale empress of the night.
>
> And thou, refulgent orb of day,
>   In brighter flames array'd ;
>
> .   .   .   .
>
> Ye stars are but the shining dust
>   Of my divine abode.

From the 17 verses of his Hymn to *Night*, beginning :—

> Interval of grateful shade,
> Welcome to my weary head :
> Welcome, slumber, to mine eyes,
> Tired with glaring vanities.

We select as follows, commencing at the fifth verse :—

> What though downy slumbers flee,
> Strangers to my couch and me ?
>
> .   .   .   .
>
> While the empress of the night
> Scatters mild her silver light,
> While the vivid planets stray
> Various through their mystic way,
>
> While the stars unnumbered roll
> Round the ever constant pole,
> Far above these spangled skies
> All my soul to God shall rise.

Omitting tho next two verses, we proceed :—

. . . .

> And His Spirit doth diffuse
> Sweeter far than midnight dews.

Again, after six verses, which also we omit, the hymn concludes—

> With Thy heavenly presence blest,
> Death is life, and labour rest ;
> Welcome sleep or death to me,
> Still secure, for still with Thee !

Relating to *Seed Time and Harvest* we have his hymn— "Eternal source of every joy," from which we shall quote the 2nd, 3rd, and 4th verses :—

> The flowery spring at Thy command
> Embalms the air and paints the land ;
> The summer rays with vigour shine,
> To raise the corn, and cheer the vine.
>
> Thy hand in autumn richly pours
> Through all our coasts redundant stores,
> And winters, soften'd by Thy care,
> No more a face of horror wear.
>
> Seasons and months and weeks and days
> Demand successive songs of praise ;
> Still be the cheerful homage paid
> With opening light and evening shade !

On the *Old and New Year*, his hymn—"Awake, ye saints, and raise your eyes"—has for its closing verse :—

> Ye wheels of Nature, speed your course !
>   Ye mortal powers, decay !
> Fast as ye bring the night of death,
>   Ye bring eternal day!

We shall also quote for the sake of one line the concluding verse of the hymn— " To-morrow, Lord, is Thine"—

> To Jesus may we fly,
> Swift as the morning light;
> Lest life's young golden beams should die
> In sudden endless night!

In the hymn commemorating *The Lord's Day*, " Lord of

the Sabbath ! hear our vows," the fourth verse offers an example of the application of a negative view of Nature, thus :—

> No rude alarms of raging foes;
> No cares to break the long repose;
> No midnight shade, no clouded sun,
> But sacred, high, eternal noon.

The hymn, " Let Jacob to his Maker sing," employs natural objects figuratively, as " rivers swell — rising floods"—

> Then let the fires their rage display,
> And flaming terrors bar the way.

Next follows the negative employment of these figures—

> Unburnt, unsing'd, He leads them through,
> And makes the flames refreshing too.
>
> The fires but on their bonds shall prey ;
> And floods but wash their stains away.

We pass over eight of the poet's hymns from their proving unsuitable for illustrating the subject under consideration, as must inevitably be the case when the hymnist is restricted by paraphrasing particular texts of Scripture, certain forms of prayer, praise, and similar exercises, requiring conformity to some Scripture text, or a strict simplicity of thought and language.

Thomas Olivers, 1757—1772.

18. He was author of the hymn, commencing like one by Cennick (*see* p. 27) :—

> Lo ! He comes with clouds descending !
> Hark ! the trump of God is blown :

from which, however, we can only quote an idea borrowed from Nature's phenomena, and thus expressed—

> Hear His voice, as mighty thunder
> Sounding in eternal roar,

> While its echo rends in sunder
> Rocks and mountains, sea and shore :
> Hark! His accents
> Through th' unfathom'd deep resound!

His hymn, "The God of Abraham praise," was published in 1772. It consists of twelve verses of eight lines each, composed in language finely conceived, but not having any direct application to our purpose. We may take the present occasion, however, to remark on the absolute impossibility of conceiving the nature of the supernatural as other than in keeping with our common sense and cultivated mental attainments. Thus considered in the present instance, the poet not inconsistently sings—

> I shall. on eagle's wings upborne,
> To Heaven ascend.

And thus conveyed, proceeds :—

> The goodly land I see,
> With peace and plenty blest,
> A land of sacred liberty,
> And endless rest:
> There milk and honey flow,
> And oil and wine abound,
> And trees of life for ever grow,
> With Mercy crown'd.

Then follows the negative application :—

> The listening spheres attend
> And swell the growing fame,
> And sing, in songs which never end,
> The wondrous Name !

For, as Addison sang, a quarter of a century earlier :—

> ' In reason's ear they all rejoice.'

ANNE STEELE, 1760.

19. She composed four hymns included in this collection, from which we can only take the following :—

> Far from these narrow scenes of night
>
> .   .   .   .
>
> Fair distant land ; could mortal eyes
>   But half its joys explore,
> How would our spirits long to rise,
>   And dwell on earth no more!

Then follow three verses of the usual negative bearing, no "sickness, grief, or cloud," but " immortal bloom ;" " no alternate night," for all is " glory."   She also wrote :—

> When I survey life's varied scene,
>   Amid the darkest hours
> Sweet rays of comfort shine between,
>   And thorns are mix'd with flowers.

MICHAEL BRUCE, 1768.

20. The author of :—

> Behold! the mountain of the Lord
>   In latter days shall rise
> On mountain tops, above the hills,
>   And draw the wondering eyes.
>
> .   .   .   .
>
> The beam that shines from Zion's hill
>   Shall lighten every land;
>
> .   .   .   .

Its six verses, however, display no peculiarity beyond what appears slightly in the foregoing lines.

JOHN MORRISON, 1770.

21. Of two of his hymns—the first, " The race that long in darkness pined"—presents no noticeable figure ; and the second, " Come, let us to the Lord our God," is only distinguished by the following lines :—

> His voice commands the tempest forth,
>   And stills the stormy wave;
>
> .   .   .   .

> Long hath the night of sorrow reign'd;
> The dawn shall bring us light;
>
> .   .   .   .
>
> His coming like the morn shall be,
> Like morning songs His voice.
>
> As dew upon the tender herb,
> Diffusing fragrance round;
> As showers that usher in the spring,
> And cheer the thirsty ground.
>
> .   .   .   .

ANNA LÆTITIA BARBAULD, 1773.

22. The first of four hymns by this eminent poetess commences :—

> Again the Lord of Life and Light
> Awakes the kindling ray,
> Unseals the eyelids of the morn,
> And pours increasing day.
>
> O what a night was that which wrapt
> The heathen world in gloom!
> O what a Sun, which broke this day
> Triumphant from the tomb!

But the remaining seven do not maintain this elevated strain. The hymn, "How blest the sacred tie that binds, in union sweet, according minds," has reference solely to the *Communion of Saints*, and is composed in an accordant simple style of thought and expression. Her next, " Praise to God, immortal praise," contains the lines following :—

> For the blessings of the field,
> For the stores the gardens yield;
> For the vine's exalted juice,
> For the generous olive's use:
>
> Flocks that whiten all the plain;
> Yellow sheaves of ripen'd grain;
> Clouds that drop their fattening dews;
> Suns that temperate warmth diffuse:

> All that Spring, with bounteous hand
> Scatters o'er the smiling land;
> All that liberal Autumn pours
> From her rich o'erflowing stores:
>
>   .   .   .   .
>
> Yet, should rising whirlwinds tear
> From its stem the ripening ear;
> Should the fig-tree's blasted shoot
> Drop her green untimely fruit ;

And though all should thus in succession fail, yet we should raise " Grateful vows and solemn praise."

The hymn, " Awake, my soul! lift up thine eyes," presents us with touches of Human Nature :—

> Here giant Danger threatening stands,
> Mustering his pale terrific bands;
> There Pleasure's silken banners spread,
> And willing souls are captive led.
>
> See where rebellious passions rage,
> And fierce desires and lusts engage;
> The meanest foe of all the train
> Has thousands and ten thousands slain.
>
> Thou tread'st upon enchanted ground,
> Perils and snares beset thee round;
> Beware of all, guard every part,
> But most, the traitor in thy heart.

  .   .   .   .

John Newton, 1779.

23. It is rather disappointing to find that of seventeen of his hymns, only two afford materials for this essay. The first three have for their subjects : *Christ Incarnate,—Crucified,*—and *Ascended.* The fourth, " He, Who on earth as man was known," has the following verses :—

> His hands the wheels of Nature guide
>   With an unerring skill,
> And countless worlds, extended wide,
>   Obey His sovereign will.

  .   .   .   .

> When troubles, like a burning sun,
>   Beat heavy on their head,
> To this Almighty Rock they run,
>   And find a pleasing shade.

.   .   .   .

In the hymn—"While with ceaseless course the sun," occurs the common simile—

> As the lightning from the skies
>   Darts, and leaves no trace behind ;
> Swiftly thus our fleeting days
>   Bear us down life's rapid stream :

.   .   .   .

The remaining fifteen hymns by this poet owe their inspiration, style, and language to other than Nature's outward influences. Not all sacred poets have an eye for Nature; some have that pleasing possession in but a moderate degree, while in a chosen few it is overflowing as the swollen stream; and its seasons are ever-returning Springs and Summers. Indeed why not, so often as opportunity favours, "look through Nature up to Nature's God?"

William Cowper, 1779.

24. Of this distinguished poet's hymns only seven out of twelve in this selection claim our attention. The parable of the sower—"Ye sons of earth, prepare the plough," in six verses, presenting but slight variations on the words of the second verse :—

> The seed that finds a stony soil
>   Shoots forth a hasty blade ;
> But ill repays the sower's toil,
>   Soon wither'd, scorch'd, and dead.
>
> The thorny ground is sure to balk
>   All hopes of harvest there ;
> We find a tall and sickly stalk,
>   But not the fruitful ear.

The first line of a hymn of four verses is—"For mercies, countless as the sands;" another of eight verses begins with the simile—

> Fierce passions discompose the mind,
>   As tempests vex the sea ;

while another, "Far from the world, O Lord, I flee," desires for prayer—

> That calm retreat, the silent shade,

The fourth verse, alluding to "the soul," declares :—

> There, like the nightingale, she pours
>   Her solitary lays,
> Nor asks a witness of her song,
>   Nor thirsts for human praise.

A fourth hymn of four verses, each containing eight lines, "Sometimes a light surprises," concludes "I cannot but rejoice :"—

> Though vine nor fig-tree neither
>   Their wonted fruit shall bear ;
> Though all the field should wither,
>   Nor flocks nor herds be there.

We next have that fine, impassioned production, unsurpassed perhaps by any composition within the range of modern sacred poetry—

> God moves in a mysterious way
>   His wonders to perform ;
> He plants His footsteps in the sea,
>   And rides upon the storm.
>
> Deep in unfathomable mines
>   Of never-failing skill,
> He treasures up His bright designs,
>   And works His sovereign will.
>
> Ye fearful saints, fresh courage take ;
>   The clouds ye so much dread
> Are big with mercy, and shall break
>   In blessings on your head.

> Judge not the Lord by feeble sense,
> 　But trust Him for His grace ;
> Behind a frowning Providence
> 　He hides a smiling face.
>
> His purposes will ripen fast,
> 　Unfolding every hour ;
> The bud may have a bitter taste,
> 　But sweet will be the flower.
>
> Blind unbelief is sure to err,
> 　And scan His work in vain ;
> God is His own interpreter,
> 　And He will make it plain.

The last of his hymns that we shall have occasion to refer to has for its first verse—

> The billows swell, the winds are high,
> Clouds overcast my wintry sky ;
> Out of the depths to Thee I call,
> My fears are great, my strength is small.

The remaining five hymns are not to our purpose for their style and matter. With the single happy exception just named, these hymns disappoint us when we consider the ability of the poet, and the unquestionable fact of his having been a warm lover of Nature, keenly alive to its unbounded beauties and sublimities.

Thomas Gibbons, 1784.

25. He was the author of the following hymn, in which we have an excellent example of the poet's command of a pleasing imagination, and ability to infuse into a sacred poem certain influences of Nature without any absolute descriptive effort :—

> Thy goodness, Lord, our souls confess,
> 　Thy goodness we adore ;
> A spring, whose blessings never fail,
> 　A sea without a shore.

> Sun, moon, and stars, Thy love attest
>   In every cheerful ray ;
> Love draws the curtains of the night,
>   And love restores the day.
>
> Thy bounty every season crowns
>   With all the bliss it yields ;
> With joyful clusters bend the vines,
>   With harvest wave the fields.
>
> But chiefly Thy compassions, Lord,
>   Are in the Gospel seen ;
> There, like the Sun, Thy mercy shines
>   Without a cloud between.

There are here only four lines which might have been omitted, but with no advantage to this polished composition. His next and last hymn is—"To Thee, my God, whose Presence fills"—which we shall not quote beyond the following expressions referring to Nature—"The earth, and seas, and skies,—Wave rushes upon wave—Bid the roaring tempest cease." He describes God's throne to be firm—

> Though oft Thy ways are wrapt in clouds,
>   Mysterious and unknown.

Philip Skelton, 1784.

26. He composed a hymn addressed to *God the Creator*, commencing "To God, ye choir above, begin," in thirteen verses of four lines each, which teems with the objects of external Nature; thus:—

> Praise Him, thou sun, Who dwells unseen
>   Amidst transcendent light,
> Where thy refulgent orb would seem
>   A spot as dark as night.
>
> Thou silver moon, ye host of stars,
>   The universal song
> Through the serene and silent night
>   To listening worlds prolong.

Sing Him, ye distant worlds and suns,
  From whence no travelling ray
Hath yet to us, through ages past,
  Had time to make its way.

Assist, ye raging storms, and bear
  On rapid wings His praise,
From north to south, from east to west,
  Through heaven, and earth, and seas.

Exert your voice, ye furious fires
  That rend the watery cloud,
And thunder to this nether world
  Your Maker's words aloud.

Ye works of God, that dwell unknown
  Beneath the rolling main ;
Ye birds, that sing among the groves,
  And sweep the azure plain ;

Ye stately hills, that rear your heads,
  And towering pierce the sky ;
Ye clouds, that with an awful pace
  Majestic roll on high ;

Ye insects small, to which one leaf
  Within its narrow sides
A vast extended world displays,
  And spacious realms provides ;

Ye race, still less than these, with which
  The stagnant water teems,
To which one drop, however small,
  A boundless ocean seems.

The three remaining verses are reflective, and offer the
exhortation—

Loud send, ye wondrous works of God,
  The grateful concert round.

This is the first hymn of the foregoing series to which we
can point as going beyond the Natural History of the Bible,
and the ordinary information of Sacred Poets generally ;
as when in the third verse, above, allusion is made to those
immensely remote planets to which it may be supposed that
the light of the sun has not yet travelled ; in the sixth

verse to the wonders of ocean's depths; and in the eighth and ninth, allusion to insects and to animalculæ.

JAMES FANCH AND DANIEL TURNER, 1791,

27. Are the joint composers of a hymn of twenty-three verses on *Christ Ascended*, commencing:—

> Beyond the glittering starry globe
>   Far as th' eternal hills,
> There, in the boundless worlds of light,
>   Our great Redeemer dwells.
>
> .   .   .   .
>
> Blest Angels,
>
> .   .   .   .
>
> Ye saw Him, when the heavens and earth,
>   A chaos first, He made,
> And night involved the formless deep
>   In her tremendous shade.
>
> And when, amidst the darksome void,
>   He bade the light arise,
> And kindled up those shining orbs
>   That now adorn the skies.

The remaining portions concerning the life, death, and resurrection of Christ are in chaste keeping with such a solemn narrative.

MISCELLANEOUS, 1703-1792.

We regret being obliged, by the limits our subject entails on us, to omit all comment on the following poets and their hymns. NAHUM TATE, 1703,—" While shepherds watched their flocks by night." RALPH ERSKINE, 1734,— " O send me down a draught of love, or take me hence to drink above!" THOMAS HASTINGS, 1742,—" Child of sin and sorrow;" and—" Return, O wanderer, to thy home." WILLIAM HAMMOND, 1745,—" Holy Spirit,

gently come ;" and "O Lord, how little do we know."
Joseph Hart, 1759,—" Come, Holy Spirit, come." Au-
gustus M. Toplady,—who between 1759 and 1777
published seven hymns of some length and various degrees
of merit. His " Rock of Ages, cleft for me," is justly es-
teemed ; and another—" I saw, and lo ! a countless throng,"
in seven verses comprising ninety-three lines, suggests :—

> Soften my passage through the wilderness ;
> And vines, nectareous, spring where briers grew :
>
> .   .   .   .   .
>
> But soon the clouds return ; my triumph dies ;
>   Damp vapours from the valley rise,
> And hide the hill of Sion from my view.

John Bakewell, 1760,—" Hail, Thou once despisèd Jesus."
An anonymous poet, 1762,—" Jesus Christ is risen to-day,
Hallelujah !" Joseph Grigg, 1765,—" Behold ! a Stranger's at the door !" William Cameron, 1770,—who
wrote a variation on one of Watts's hymns, 1709,—" How
bright these glorious spirits shine." William Williams,
1759 to 1774, the author of three hymns. John Byrom,
1773,—" My spirit longeth for Thee." John Ryland,
1777,—whose hymns—" Sovereign Ruler of the skies ;" and
" O Lord, I would delight in Thee," offer pious ejaculations,
with every thought directed heavenwards, independent of all
earthly reflections ; (all these, like many similar instances
of grave and solemn poetry, have their own intrinsic merits,
irrespective of all mere meretricious ornament.) Selina,
Countess of Huntingdon, 1780—" The world can neither
give nor take." Rowland Hill, 1783 and 1796,—" Exalted
high at God's right hand ;" and " We sing His love, Who
once was slain." John Berridge, 1785,—" O happy saints,

who dwell in light,"—and the 131st Psalm —" Jesus, cast a look on me." SAMUEL MEDLEY, 1789 and 1800,—"Hear, gracious God! a sinner's cry," and "Dearest of names, our Lord our King!" JOSEPH SWAIN, 1792,—" 'Tis Heaven begun below," so that we shall be filled "with everlasting joy" :—

Bright as meridian day,
Calm as the evening ray,
Full as a sea without a shore.

And lastly, THOMAS HAWEIS, 1792,—" O Thou, from whom all goodness flows."

We thus bring to a close our observations on Sacred Poetry belonging to the 18th century, and proceed to consider that of the—

NINETEENTH CENTURY.

THOMAS KELLY, 1802-1836.

28. We have sixteen specimens of this poet's hymns, but from these we can only select two examples ; the first being—" Lo! He comes! let all adore Him!" commencing at the second verse with—

Let the valleys all be raisèd ;
  Go, and make the crooked straight ;
Let the mountains be abasèd ;
  Let all Nature change its state ;

   .   .   .   .

Through the desert God is going,
  Through the desert waste and wild,
Where no goodly plant is growing,
  Where no verdure ever smiled ;
But the desert shall be glad,
And with verdure soon be clad.

Where the thorn and brier flourish'd,
  Trees shall there be seen to grow,

Planted by the Lord and nourish'd.
　Stately, fair, and fruitful too ;
They shall rise on every side,
They shall spread their branches wide.

From the hills and lofty mountains
　Rivers shall be seen to flow,
There the Lord will open fountains,
　Thence supply the plains below.

．　　　．　　　．　　　．

The hymn, "Thus saith God of His Anointed," although on the same subject, yet, like the first in the selection, "We'll sing, in spite of scorn," it does not approach the style of the foregoing composition. The hymn, "Jesus, the Shepherd of the sheep," need scarcely be quoted for the single line—

O guard Thy sheep from beasts of prey,

nor others in a similar strain, naturally associated with the Shepherd's care of his straying flock. Equally slight are the references to Nature in "We're bound for yonder land," in which occur :—

The perils of the sea,
The rocks, the waves, the wind,

．　　　．　　　．　　　．

Then let the tempests roar,
　The billows heave and swell ;
We trust to reach the peaceful shore
　Where all the ransom'd dwell.

THOMAS GISBORNE, 1803.

29. His hymn, composed in reference to the *Holy Catholic Church*, "A soldier's course, from battles won," portrays the land, "Where soldiers war no more," as :—

The land, where, (suns and moons unknown,
And night's alternate sway,)

> Jehovah's ever-burning throne
>   Upholds unbroken day:
> The land, (for Heaven its bliss unseen
>   Bids earthly types suggest,)
> Where healing leaves and fadeless green
>   Fruit-laden groves invest :
> Where founts of life their treasures yield
>   In streams that never cease ;
> Where everlasting mountains shield
>   Vales of eternal peace.

.   .   .   .

Such is the only Paradise that man does or can mentally realize, for in very truth—

> . . . . Heaven, its bliss unseen,
>   Bids earthly types suggest,

and by no effort of genius, no stretch of the most comprehensive, refined, and fruitful powers of imagination has man ever been enabled to grasp ideas that go beyond evident associations with the objects of sense and with home experiences.

James Montgomery, 1803—1853.

30. Out of nineteen specimens of this author's hymns and versions of Psalms, only seven of them will answer as illustrative examples for our present purpose; of these we shall commence with the third verse of the 72nd Psalm, in seven verses of eight lines each, "Hail to the Lord's Anointed :"—

> He shall come down like showers
>   Upon the fruitful earth,
> And love, joy, hope, like flowers,
>   Spring in His path to birth ;
> Before Him on the mountains,
>   Shall peace, the herald, go,
> And righteousness, in fountains,
>   From hill to valley flow.

> Arabia's desert-ranger
>   To Him shall bow the knee;
> The Ethiopian stranger
>   His glory come to see:
>
>   .   .   .
>
> For He shall have dominion
>   O'er river, sea, and shore,
> Far as the eagle's pinion,
>   Or dove's light wing, can soar.
>
>   .   .   .
>
> The mountain-dews shall nourish
>   A seed, in weakness sown,
> Whose fruit shall spread and flourish,
>   And shake like Lebanon.
>
>   .   .   .
>
> The tide of time shall never
>   His covenant remove.
>
>   .   .   .

In the hymn, "Lord God the Holy Ghost," occurs the simile:—

> Like mighty rushing wind
> Upon the waves beneath,
> Move with one impulse every mind,
> One soul, one feeling breathe.

And in another, "What are these in bright array," negatively:—

> Hunger, thirst, disease unknown,
> On immortal fruits they feed.

Also, in like manner, we find another negative adaptation in the second verse of the hymn, "Friend after friend departs," thus:—

> Beyond the flight of time,
>   Beyond this vale of death,
> There surely is some blessed clime,
>   Where life is not a breath,
> Nor life's affections transient fire,
> Whose sparks fly upwards to expire.

The hymn, "There is a calm for those who weep," concludes:—

> The sun is but a spark of fire,
> A transient meteor in the sky;
> The Soul, immortal as its Sire,
> Shall never die !

Among the editor's selection of *Songs of the Heart* is a hymn by Montgomery, " A poor wayfaring man of grief," from which we make the following scanty extracts :—

> I spied him, where a fountain burst
> Clear from the rock.
>
> .   .   .   .
>
> 'Twas night ; the floods were out ; it blew
> A winter hurricane aloof.

And from another, " For ever with the Lord !" namely :—

> Yet clouds will intervene,
> And all my prospect flies ;
> Like Noah's dove, I flit between
> Rough seas and stormy skies.

HENRY MOORE, 1806.

31. His hymn in reference to *Hope* is largely imbued with touches affecting Human Nature, thus :—

> Our life is but an idle play,
> And various as the wind ;
> We laugh and sport our hours away,
> Nor think of woes behind.
>
> See the fair cheek of beauty fade,
> Frail glory of an hour ;
> And blooming youth, with sickening head,
> Droops like the dying flower.
>
> Our pleasures, like the morning sun,
> Diffuse a flattering light ;
> But gloomy clouds obscure their noon,
> And soon they sink in night.
>
> Wealth, pomp, and honour, we behold
> With an admiring eye ;
> Like summer insects, drest in gold,
> That flutter, shine, and die.

> One little moment can destroy
>   Our vast laborious schemes ;
> And all our hopes of solid joy
>   Are sweet deceitful dreams.

.　　　.　　　.　　　.

The remaining two verses amplify the consequent advice to soar " Above the thoughtless crowd."

WILLIAM BENGO COLLYER, 1812 and 1829.

32. His first hymn, " Great God, what do I hear !" is literally governed by a couplet in the last verse :—

> Stay, fancy, stay, and close thy wings,
>   Repress thy flight too daring !

It differs widely from his second, " Haste, traveller, haste ! the night comes on," which has the following verse :—

> The rising tempest sweeps the sky;
> The rains descend, the winds are high ;
> The waters swell, and death and fear
> Beset thy path, nor refuge near;
>   Haste, traveller, haste !

Its seven verses conclude, " There yet is hope ;—in Christ is all ! Haste to Him, haste !"

WILLIAM HURN, 1813.

33. Of his two hymns, " O house of Jacob, come," and " There is a River deep and broad," we can only cull one verse from the latter poem :—

> Clearer than crystal is the stream,
>   And bright with endless day;
> The waves with every blessing teem,
>   And life and health convey.

John Bowdler, 1814.

34. It is rare to meet with such delicate and chaste treatment of Nature in a class of poetry, from which it might seem almost prudent to exclude it, as we find in the following exceedingly beautiful specimen. It opens thus :—

> Sing to the Lord with cheerful voice,
>> From realm to realm the notes shall sound ;
> And Heaven's exulting sons rejoice
>> To bear the full Hosanna round.

Then follow five verses unsurpassed for their treatment of Nature inferentially, without the introduction of any allusion that does not rather enliven than distract the singers of such a hymn :—

> When, starting from *the shades of night,*
>> At dread Jehovah's high behest,
> *The Sun arrayed his limbs in light,*
>> *And Earth her virgin beauty drest ;*
> Thy praise *transported Nature sung*
>> *In pealing chorus loud and far ;*
> *The echoing vault with rapture rung,*
>> *And shouted every morning star.*
> When, bending from His native sky,*
>> The Lord of Life in mercy came,
> And laid His bright effulgence by,
>> *To bear on earth a human name ;*
> *The song,* by cherub voices raised.
>> *Roll'd through the dark blue depths above ;*
> And Israel's shepherds heard amazed
>> The seraph notes of peace and love.
> And shall not *man* the concert join,
>> *For whom this bright creation rose ;*
> *For whom the fires of morning shine,*
>> *And eve's still lamps, that woo repose?*

The hymn concludes, " Thy praise shall fill each grateful voice :"—

> Long as yon glittering arch shall bend,
>> Long as yon orbs in glory roll,
> Long as the streams of life descend
>> To cheer with hope the fainting soul.

---

* " When the Eternal bows the skies."—*Watts.*

We have here what we may truly esteem as a pure emanation from unconscious genius. Can anything be more refreshing than thus to escape from the turgid, dry, formal, and artificial style of the Elizabethan period? The personification, together with the negative use of Nature here employed, cannot but be admired.

In Bowdler's hymn, "To Heaven I lift mine eye," we find an application of the negative view of Nature in speaking of the Saviour :—

> For Him no weary hours assail,
> Nor evening darkness spreads her veil
>   O'er His eternal day.

Where—

> The sun with milder beams shall shine,
> And eve's still queen her lamp incline
>   Benignant from above.

JOHN MARRIOTT, 1816.

35. His hymn, "Thou, whose almighty word," in four verses of seven lines each, concludes thus :—

> Boundless as ocean's tide
> Rolling in fullest pride,
> Through the earth, far and wide,
>   Let there be light !

JAMES EDMESTON, 1820.

36. He wrote the hymn—

> Lead us, heavenly Father, lead us
>   O'er the world's tempestuous sea ;

composed without any further reference to the objects of Nature ; but in another, "Why should I in vain repining," we find the following simply figurative applications :—

> Why should I,　　.　　.　　.
> 　　Mourn the clouds that cross my way;
> Since my Saviour's Presence shining
> 　　Turns my darkness into day ?
>
> Earthly honour, earthly treasure,
>
> 　.　　　.　　　.　　　.
> And the silken wings of pleasure
> 　　Only waft us on to sin.
>
> But, within the vale of sorrow,
> 　　All with tempests overblown,
> Purer light and joy we borrow
> 　　From the face of God alone.

Henry Hart Milman, 1822—1827.

37. Such subjects as *The Crucifixion, Prayer,* and the
Burial of the Dead, give no scope for poetic treatment of
Nature, and this may account for the four specimens of
hymns by this accomplished poet failing in passages for
quotation.　The first is " Ride on ! ride on in majesty ;"
the next, " Bound upon the accursèd tree ;" the third, " Oh
help us, Lord ! each hour of need ;" and the last, " Brother, thou art gone before us."

As studies of our subject, we may notice, that the first
of these poems merely alludes to " palms," and to " The
wingèd squadrons of the sky ;" but the burden of the song
is the riding in " lowly pomp," " in majesty," and alludes
to " His sapphire throne."　The second asks :—

> 　.　　.　　＊　　.　　.　　Who is He ?
> By the sun at noonday pale,
> Shivering rocks, and rending veil.

The whole effect being more that of an altar-piece than
an ordinary work of Nature-Study, as indeed it ought to
be, always avoiding irrelevant and distracting objects calculated to destroy the awful solemnity that it is the main

feature of such a composition to command. The same
feeling actuates the composer of prayers and kindred effusions in a metrical form, however impassioned in tone and
sentiment.

William Ball, 1825.

38. He is the author of the subjoined hymn, in which
he has touched on Nature sufficiently to exhibit the
slightest possible tinge, as garments are impregnated with
the perfume of the flowers and herbs over which they have
passed :—

> There is a pure and tranquil wave,
>
> Whose waters gladden as they lave
> The peaceful shores above.
>
> While streams, which on that tide depend,
> Steal from those heavenly shores away,
> And on this desert world descend
> O'er weary lands to stray.
>
> The Pilgrim faint, ...
>
> Refresh'd beside their verdant brink,
> Rejoices in their flow.
>
> And feed by those still streams, that rise
> Beneath the Tree of Life !
>
> It may be that the breath of love
> Some leaves on their pure tide have driven,
> Which, passing from the shores above,
> Have floated down from Heaven.

Samuel Rickards, 1825.

39. In the *Book of Praise*, the editor has arranged in
the first part or division of its subjects, no less than twenty
hymns relating to *Christ Incarnate*, the productions of
J. Williams, J. Keble, T. Grinfield, N. Tate, C. Wesley, T.

Kelly, J. Montgomery, J. Anstice, E. H. Sears, J. Morrison, Bishop Heber, Harriet Auber, W. C. Dix, Dr. Doddridge, Dr. Watts, J. Newton, and Rickards. The last stands alone amidst this array of talent; when examined in the manner here adopted, thus affording strong evidence that, even the most solemn and sacred subjects are not wholly incompatible with certain associations derived from Nature, under the careful management of a refined and correct taste and judgment. What can be more judicious and chaste than the following?—

> Though rude winds usher thee, sweet day,
>   Though clouds thy face deform,
> Though Nature's grace is swept away
>   Before thy sleety storm ;
> Ev'n in thy sombrest wintry vest,
> Of blessed days thou art most blest.
>
> Nor frigid air nor gloomy morn
>   Shall check thy jubilee ;
> Bright is the day when Christ was born,
>   No sun need shine but He ;
> Let roughest storms their coldest blow,
> With love of Him our hearts shall glow.
>
> Inspired with high and holy thought,
>   Fancy is on the wing ;
> It seems as to mine ear It brought
>   Those voices carolling,
>
> .   .   .   .

The conclusion of this, and the whole of the remaining five verses we omit as being irrelevant here ; and the last verse is only a repetition of the first. It is seldom, however, that the sacred poets of this period or their predecessors indulge the taste for Nature-Study, which we cannot but admire in the foregoing lines. To our thinking this style serves appropriately to enhance the solemnity of all that follows regarding " the shepherds," the " manger," and the birth of " creation's Heir."

BISHOP REGINALD HEBER, 1827.

40. Of the fourteen hymns in this selection we have only
to examine five, the remainder being unsuitable, although
in all other respects they are highly finished compositions.
The first of these begins :—

> Brightest and best of the sons of the morning !
>   Dawn on our darkness, and lend us Thine aid !
> Star of the East, the horizon adorning,
>   Guide where our infant Redeemer is laid !
>
> Cold on His cradle the dew-drops are shining ;
>   .   .   .   .
>
> Say, shall we yield Him .   .   .
>   Odours of Edom .   .   .   .
> Gems of the mountain, and pearls of the ocean,
>   Myrrh from the forest, or gold from the mine ?

Of *Christ's Kingdom and Judgment* he sings :—

> From Greenland's icy mountains,
>   From India's coral strand,
> Where Afric's sunny fountains
>   Roll down their golden sand,
> From many an ancient river,
>   From many a palmy plain,
> They call us to deliver
>   Their land from error's chain.
>
> What though the spicy breezes
>   Blow soft o'er Ceylon's isle ;
> Though every prospect pleases,
>   And only man is vile ;
> In vain with lavish kindness
>   The gifts of God are strown ;
> The heathen in his blindness
>   Bows down to wood and stone.
>
>   .   .   .   .
>
>   Messiah's Name.
> Waft, waft, ye winds, His story,
>   And you, ye waters, roll,
> Till like a sea of glory
>   It spreads from pole to pole ;
>   .   .   .   .

Another hymn commences :—

> O King of earth, and air, and sea !
> The hnngry ravens cry to Thee;
> To Thee the scaly tribes, that sweep
> The bosom of the boundless deep :
> To Thee the lions roaring call.

. . . .

A hymn of ten verses, *The Call*, opens with the couplet :—

> The winds were howling o'er the deep,
> Each wave a watery hill ;

but the poet is not further tempted to apply, even figuratively, any of Nature's manifold aspects and phenomena. Another to *Hope* is more diffuse :—

> I praised the earth, in beauty seen
> With garlands gay of various green ;
> I praised the sea, whose ample field
> Shone glorious as a silver shield ;
> And earth and ocean seem'd to say,
> " Our beauties are but for a day."
>
> I praised the sun, whose chariot roll'd
> On wheels of amber and of gold ;
> I praised the moon, whose softer eye
> Gleam'd sweetly through the summer sky;
> And moon and sun in answer said,
> " Our days of light are numberèd."

. . . .

Although the " chariot" of the " sun" is here referable to Art, its omission would have weakened the sense of the remaining lines. And for the same reason single words or lines are elsewhere occasionally admitted to sustain the poet's meaning, where otherwise confusion might follow.

JOHN KEBLE, 1827—1857.

41. We are now arrived at that period in our critical history which is rendered memorable by the publication of our author's celebrated work, *The Christian Year*, a produc-

tion which possesses a world-wide reputation. In the present instance our attention is directed to seven examples of his sacred poems, among which only three will come under our immediate consideration. The first of these is for " Septuagesima Sunday :"—

There is a book, who runs may read,

The works of God, above, below,
  Within us and around,
Are pages in that book, to show
  How God Himself is found.
The glorious sky, embracing all,
  Is like the Maker's love,

The moon above, the Church below,
  A wondrous race they run ;
But all their radiance, all their glow,
  Each borrows of its sun.

The Saviour lends the light and heat
  That crowns His holy hill ;
The saints, like stars, around His seat
  Perform their courses still.

The saints above are stars in Heaven ;
  What are the saints on earth ?
Like trees they stand, whom God has given,
  Our Eden's happy birth.

Faith is their fix'd unswerving root,
  Hope their unfading flower ;
Fair deeds of charity their fruit,
  The glory of their bower.

The dew* of heaven is like Thy grace ;
  It steals in silence down ;
But, where it lights, the favoured place
  By richest fruits is known.

The raging fire, the roaring wind,
  Thy boundless power display;
But in the gentler breeze we find
  Thy Spirit's viewless way.

---

* This line of the eighth verse, " The dew of heaven," &c., reminds us of Shakspeare's beautiful allusion to *Mercy* as dropping like " The gentle rain from Heaven," &c.

> Two worlds* are ours : 'tis only sin
>   Forbids us to descry,
> The mystic heaven and earth within,
>   Plain as the sea and sky.

.   .   .   .

The favourite comparison of Nature to a Book is reproduced here, much in the style adopted in Sylvester's translation of Du Bartas' *Divine Weeks and Works.* His second hymn† in the selection is :—

> What sudden blaze of song
>   Spreads o'er the expanse of Heaven ?
> In waves of light it thrills along,
>   Th' angelic signal given :

.   .   .   .

> Like circles widening round
>   Upon a clear blue river,
> Orb after orb, the wondrous sound
>   Is echoed on for ever.

.   .   .   .

In the perusal of Keble's poetry it frequently happens that some thought, figure, word, line, or expression, reminds us of the influence which the works of other poets must have had on his mind and compositions. In the foregoing extract our attention is involuntarily called to Tennyson's Idyl, *The Brook*, in which he employs the oft repeated line, " But I run on for ever."   And certainly the reference to " circles widening" on the brook is a striking reflex of Shakespeare's employment of the same figure in Henry VI., as characteristic of *Glory.*

The third hymn,‡ " When God of old came down from Heaven," is composed in that more sober and subdued style which its solemnity and the sacredness of its subject

---

* " Oh mighty Love ! Man is one world, and hath
  Another to attend him."—*Herbert.*

† For *Christmas Day.* See " The Christian Year."

‡ For *Whit Sunday.* See Ibid.

seem usually to demand, as being more in unison than any other with the grand and sublime.

The fourth and fifth hymns of the selection consist respectively of twelve out of sixteen stanzas of the first, and twelve out of fourteen stanzas of the second of the first two poems of *The Christian Year.*[*]

The remaining two hymns of this selected series are taken from Lord Nelson's *Salisbury Hymnal.* The first of these commemorates *Seed Time and Harvest*, with the slightest possible allusion to Nature in extremely broad and general terms:—

> Our hope, when autumn winds blew wild,
>   We trusted, Lord, with Thee ;
>
> .   .   .   .
>
> The former and the latter rain,
>   The summer sun and air,
> The green ear, and the golden grain,
>   All Thine, are ours by prayer.

The last, *Holy Communion*, is wholly spiritual in its sentiments and language.

Anonymous, 1832.

42. If the subjects of some hymns may be adduced as fully justifying abstinence from allusions to objects of external Nature, surely others that call up associations with the shepherd, his flock, and their pastures, might be made, by judicious treatment, vehicles for some pic-

---

* The portions omitted (referring principally to Nature) will be found in the Essay on Keble's *Christian Year.* In these poems " Morning" commences—
> Hues of the rich unfolding morn,

And " Evening" begins—
> 'Tis gone, that bright and orbèd blaze.

We thus lose four introductory stanzas in the first, and two in the second, which in some measure, perhaps, enhances the gravity of the language employed in the remaining verses. See *Book of Praise*, pp. 278, 293.

turesqueness of arrangement and language. Take, for instance, the present poem, consisting of four verses, "Saviour, who Thy flock art feeding," and it would not be too much to expect something beyond such barren expressions as :—

> Never, from Thy pastures roving,
> Let them be the lion's prey,

entreating that "the lambs" may :—

> Feed in pastures ever vernal,
> Drink the rivers of Thy grace!

This is hardly doing justice to such a subject, or making an effort to employ the most elevated style of expression to the highest aspirations of human intellect. In attempting simplicity of thought, style, and delivery, the poet has carefully to avoid the extreme of adopting that strain which is little, mean, and puerile; so difficult is it in seeking simplicity to steer between and find the precise middle course that separates the child-like from the merely childish in word, thought, and action. Wordsworth's poems afford abundant examples of such attempted simplicity, with varied success; but the effort is more to be commended than the examples themselves which he generally supplies. In Nature, the extreme beauty of its pervading simplicity, whether in forms, materials, or adaptations, is marvellous beyond all human conception. What can appear more common, and yet more simple, than the air we breathe, the water we drink, the earth on which we tread, yet are they all bound up in mysteries that eye hath never seen, nor mind ever communicated to mind. We may discover that we have to deal with gas, or light, or heat; but having gone thus far, we can proceed no farther. The

poet cannot do better than always to bear in mind, as
emblems for his conduct, the simplicity of the child—the
whiteness of the snow—the verdure of the fields—and the
deep blue of the heavens.

JULIA ANNE ELLIOTT, 1833.

43. Her hymn, commemorating *The Lord's Day*, consists
of seven verses of six lines each, and begins :—

> Hail, thou bright and sacred morn,
>   Risen with gladness in thy beams !
> Light, which not of earth is born,
>   From thy dawn in glory streams :

beyond which we do not find a single illustrative line.

DR. JOHN HENRY NEWMAN, 1833.

44. This distinguished theologian is the author of " *The
Dream of Gerontius*," and other Poems. As a poet, Sir
Francis Doyle, in his lectures at Oxford, declared of him
that :—" He scarce believes in any rose, in any actual rainbow ; the stars themselves are little better than phantom
lights, visionary flashings of that great dream, woven between the soul and God, which men agree here to call, for
the moment, our visible and material universe." And so
long as men prefer to sleep and to dream away their days as
well as their nights, this kind of romance may be extended
indefinitely. The less we know of anything the more we
may easily say and write about it. A world of books would
not suffice to theorize upon the idea whether the moon is
or is not inhabited ! But sober-thinking men will ever
prefer something more tangible and comprehensible than

the most brilliant visionary can ever pen or sing. An admiring critic, in an article in the *Dublin Review*, for January, 1872, treating of " Nature and the Poets," quotes from Dr. Newman's *Parochial Sermons*, and says of their author that " he has always believed and taught that visible phenomena are a mere cloak, hiding the invisible agency of angelic spirits." Such guessing no one can gainsay. But who can accept it as truth, or even as a reasonable approach to the truth, derivable from any analogy in Nature ? Certainly no man living. Speaking of " the blessed and dutiful angels," Dr. Newman arrives at this conclusion in repect to the " motions of universal Nature," that :—" Every breath of air and ray of light and heat, every beautiful prospect is, *as it were*, the skirts of their garments, the waving of the robes of those whose faces see God in heaven." How has he arrived at this guess ? How does he even know that angels have garments at all ? He even surmises as a possibility that—" when examining a flower, or a herb, or a pebble, or a ray of light"—these may actually be no other than " the visible things" belonging to " some powerful being"—" whose robe and ornaments" were constituted of " these wondrous objects." This is very ritualistic, to say the least of it ; robed and jewelled angels is a truly human fancy, and though the whole is put as a mere imaginary picture, it is easy in the next stage of this process to conclude and assert that such dreams are facts.

This is a sickly misuse of Nature. Nature is mystical and mysterious enough in itself, without the meretricious aid of man's puny fictions to enhance its character and importance. Nature is so stupendous in its grandeur and magnificence, and so lovely, beautiful, and wondrous in its minutest details, that the mystifications of the highest human genius, even when beautiful as prismatic bubbles, are not more important or significant than they are. All attempts to soar to the infinite fail miserably; and if Dr. Newman, in this respect, falls no lower than others have fallen before him in attempting such god-like flights, he has a happy advantage which is always accorded to truly imaginative poets. If the world receives his poetical fancies, recorded in homely prose, for prophetic second-sight, we would suggest that the fault is probably more with the deluded readers than with him, or any such modern seers. In simple truth we may pursue with advantage the study of much in Nature that is within the power of our cultured capacity to cope with, and thence gradually proceed to attempt the development of remoter facts. But to commence our pursuit with that which is loftiest and beyond human comprehension and to study Nature through a descending scale, is as hopeless in this as in any other achievement to which we might apply our mental energies. But, alas! on the subject of Nature, there is an intolerable weight of learned ignorance and trifling in the world, and would-be philosophers, looking sky-ward, invariably find their path suddenly terminating in a dreary slough of interminable difficulties.

After this long digression, it is time we proceeded to consider this poet's address to *Patience*, which affords some few touches of Human Nature :—

> Lead, kindly Light, amid th' encircling gloom,
>   Lead Thou me on ;
> The night is dark, and I am far from home ;
>   Lead Thou me on ;

> Keep Thou my feet; I do not ask to see
> The distant scene; one step enough for me.
>
> .   .   .   .
>
> I loved the garish day, and, spite of fears,
> Pride ruled my will :   .   .   .
>   lead me on,
> O'er moor and fen, o'er crag and torrent, till
>   The night is gone.
>
> .   .   .   .

Henry Francis Lyte, 1833—1847.

45. Only four out of his sixteen psalms and hymns call for any especial notice. His style is singularly deficient of figurative expressions traceable to Nature. He sings in the 8th Psalm :—

> When glorious in the nightly sky
>   Thy moon and stars I see,
> O what is man ! I wondering cry.

But his subject inspires him no farther; and in the 74th Psalm, he has not a flight beyond :—

> Happy birds that sing and fly
> Round Thy altars, O Most High !

In the 11th Psalm, "My trust is in the Lord," he rises to :—

> Why bid me like a bird
> Before the fowler flee ?
>
> .   .   .   .
>
> The wicked may assail
>
> .   .   .   .
>
> All earth's foundation fail,
> All Nature's springs be dry ;
> Yet God is in His holy shrine.
>
> .   .   .   .
>
> While like the sun, His saints shall rise,
> And shine with Him above the skies.

The 46th Psalm opens with :—

> God is our Refuge, tried and proved,
>   Amid a stormy world ;

> We will not fear, though earth be moved,
>   And hills in ocean hurled.
>
> The waves may roar, the mountains shake,
>   Our comfort shall not cease.

> .   .   .   .

Even the 137th Psalm fails to win from him anything more appertaining to Nature than :—

> Upon the willows long
> My harp has silent hung :

> When shall I pass the wilderness,

> O guide me through the desert here.

A hymn of six verses, of eight lines each, " Jesus, I my cross have taken," offers only the couplet :—

> Storms may howl, and clouds may gather,
> All must work for good to me.

This is almost sufficient evidence in itself of the exceedingly unambitious character of his poetry.

In the hymn, " Long did I toil, and knew no earthly rest," he employs the symbolic language :—

> Whate'er may change, in Him no change is seen ;
> A glorious Sun, that wanes not nor declines ;
> Above the clouds and storms He walks serene,
> And sweetly on his people's darkness shines :

but this is all we can glean from six verses, of six lines each.

Human Nature, in a supplicating attitude, is slightly touched in the following hymn :—

> Abide with me ! fast falls the even-tide ;
> The darkness deepens ; Lord, with me abide !

> Swift to its close ebbs out life's little day ;
> Earth's joys grow dim ; its glories pass away ;
> Change and decay in all around I see ;

> Thou on my head in early youth didst smile ;
> —— though rebellious and perverse meanwhile,

Through cloud and sunshine, O abide with me !

Heaven's morning breaks, and earth's vain shadows flee ;
In life and death, O Lord, abide with me !

WILLIAM WORDSWORTH, 1834.

46. The Poet of Nature is here represented by only one hymn, "Up to the throne of God is borne," consisting of eight verses, of eight lines each, in which we find but one verse to present to the reader, though it contains the ordinary epithets, "as the light of day grows dim—noontide—from morn to night—the mid-day hour—one hour of rest — each field — every grove—in the east — this day's course." The verse selected runs thus :—

> Look up to Heaven ! the industrious sun
> Already half his race hath run ;
> He cannot halt nor go astray ;
> But our immortal Spirits may.

MISCELLANEOUS, 1830—1836.

Some instruction in Nature-Study (differing, however, in importance) may be obtained from what we omit as well as from what we review. We shall here have to pass over no less than four poets, the authors of twelve hymns, namely :—

GEORGE MOGRIDGE, 1830 ; hymn on page 72.

CHARLOTTE ELLIOTT, 1834—1837 ; pages 175, 224, 374, 400, 401, and 427.

THOMAS GRINFIELD, 1836 ; pages 36, 241, and 338.

EDWARD OSLER, 1836 ; pages 272, 320, and 335.

Reference to these will make it evident that they contain little or nothing as regards elementary Nature to call for especial notice ; they are correct, and commendable as compositions expressive of Christian feeling and sentiment, but are enunciated in a strain that never attains to any true association with the objects, phases, and phenomena of external Nature.　These examples show as clearly how Nature may be dissociated from meditative, religious, and moral or serious topics, as the general purport of this Essay affords illustrative examples of a totally opposite mode of treatment.　Both being correct, both possessing many excellencies, and both demanding equal talent in their conception and management as poetical compositions.　We are not arguing more for the one style than for the other, considering each correct and just in its place, but we are especially desirous to call attention to the fact of the growing influence of Nature on sacred as well as on all other classes of poetry ; and likewise to offer incontestable proofs that such influence of Nature is not limited (as critics seem hitherto to have imagined) to descriptive poetry, but permeates thoughts, sentiments, and expressions of the most simple as well as of the most complex character, a fact pre-eminently illustrated by the productions of our immortal bard, whose distinguished peculiarities in this respect gave birth to the system of investigation and study now advocated.*

JOHN CHANDLER, 1837.

47. He is the composer of a hymn addressed to *Morn-*

---

* See NATURE-STUDY, as applicable to the purposes of Poetry and Eloquence.　First edition, 8vo.　Moxon.　1869.　And the same, second edition, 12mo.　Nimmo, Edinburgh.　1870.

ing, "O Jesu, Lord of heavenly grace," concluding in the figurative language :—

> O hallowed be the approaching day !
> Let meekness be our morning ray ;
> And faithful love our noonday light ;
> And hope our sunset calm and bright !

Three other hymns by the same poet adopt a different strain of expression, in accordance with their subjects, *The Communion of Saints* and *Church Dedication.*

John S. B. Monsell, 1837—1850.

48. Of his two hymns, we can only quote from the second, relating to *Discipline* :—

> The spring-tide hour
> Brings leaf and flower
> With songs of life and love ;
> And many a lay
> Wears out the day
> In many a leafy grove.
> Bird, flower, and tree
> Seem to agree
> Their choicest gifts to bring ;
> But this poor heart
> Bears not its part,
> In it there is no spring.
>
> Dews fall apace,
> The dews of grace,
> Upon this soul of sin ;
>
> Yet, year by year,
> Fruits, flowers, appear,
> And birds their praises sing ;
> But this poor heart
> Bears not its part,
> Its winter has no spring.
>
> Lord, let Thy love,
> Fresh from above,
> Soft as the south wind blow ;
> Call forth its bloom,
> Wake its perfume,
> And bid its spices flow !

And when Thy voice
Makes earth rejoice,
And the hills laugh and sing,
Lord ! make this heart
To bear its part,
And join the praise of spring !

ISAAC WILLIAMS, 1838—1842.

49. Omitting two out of five of his hymns, we shall commence with :—

Morning lifts her dewy veil
  With new-born blessings crown'd ;
Let us haste her light to hail
.   .   .   .

Christ hath shed a fairer morn,
  From darkness rising free ;
.   .   .   .

From the swaddling bands of night
  When sprang the world so fair,
Putting on her robes of light,
  O what a power was there !
.   .   .   .

When from the Eternal's hand
  The earth in beauty stood,
Deck'd in light at His command,
  He saw, and called it good.
.   .   .   .

His last hymn we quote entire :—

The child leans on its parent's breast,
Leaves there its cares, and is at rest ;
The bird sits singing by his nest,
        And tells aloud
His trust in God, and so is blest
        'Neath every cloud.

He has no store, he sows no seed ;
Yet sings aloud, and doth not heed ;
By flowing stream or grassy mead
        He sings to shame
Men, who forget, in fear of need,
        A Father's Name.

> The heart that trusts for ever sings,
> And feels as light as it had wings ;
> A well of peace within it springs ;
>   Come good or ill,
> Whate'er to-day, to-morrow brings,
>   It is His will !

JOHN HAMPDEN GURNEY, 1838—1851.

50. Out of five specimens of his hymns, we commence with the first :—

> Yes, God is good ; in earth and sky,
> From ocean-depths and spreading wood,
>
>   .   .   .   .
>
> The sun that keeps his trackless way,
>   And downward pours his golden flood,
> Night's sparkling hosts, all seem to say
>   In accents clear, that God is good.
>
> The merry birds prolong the strain,
>   Their song with every spring renewed ;
> And balmy air, and falling rain,
>   Each softly whisper, " God is good."
>
> I hear it in the rushing breeze ;
>   The hills that have for ages stood,
> The echoing sky and roaring seas,
>   All swell the chorus, " God is good."
>
> Yes, God is good, all Nature says,
>   By God's own hand with speech endued ;
> And man, in louder notes of praise,
>   Should sing for joy, that God is good.
>
>   .   .   .   .

The second hymn has reference to the *Resurrection* and *Eternal Life* :—

> Earth to earth, and dust to dust,
>   .   .   .   .
>
> Like the seed in spring-time sown,
> Like the leaves in autumn strown,
> Low these goodly frames must lie,
> All our pomp and glory die ;
>
>   .   .   .   .
>
> Yet the seed, upraised again,
> Clothes with green the smiling plain ;

Onward as the seasons move,
Leaves and blossoms deck the grove ;

Lord, from Nature's gloomy night
Turn we to the Gospel's light.

The two next hymns are of an entirely spiritual character ; so we quote from the last of the series, " Lord of
the harvest ! Thee we hail :"—

The varying seasons haste their round,

If Spring doth wake the song of mirth ;
If Summer warms the cheerful earth ;
When Winter sweeps the naked plain,
Or Autumn yields its ripen'd grain ;
  Still do we sing

—————— ———— Thou dost reign.

Lord of the harvest ! all is Thine !
The rains that fall, the suns that shine,
The seed once hidden in the ground,
The skill that makes our fruits abound !
  New, every year,
  Thy gifts appear ;
New praises from our lips shall sound !

Robert Allan Scott, 1839.

51. In the Psalm, " Lord, Thou hast formed my every
part," we find only such lines as—

Though I should seek the shades of night,

To Thee the darkness seems as light,
  The midnight as the noonday clear.
The heavens, the earth, the sea, the sky,
  All own Thee ever present there.

Sir Robert Grant, 1839.

52. He wrote a version of the 104th Psalm in six verses, of eight lines each, "O worship the King." Commencing with the second verse, he sings :—

> O tell of His might,
>   O sing of His grace,
> Whose robe is the light,
>   Whose canopy space ;
> His chariots of wrath
>   Deep thunder-clouds form,
> And dark is His path
>   On the wings of the storm.
>
> The earth with its store
>   Of wonders untold,
> Almighty, Thy power
>   Hath founded of old,
> Hath stablish'd it fast
>   By a changeless decree,
> And round it hath cast,
>   Like a mantle, the sea.
>
> Thy bountiful care,
>   What tongue can recite ?
> It breathes in the air,
>   It shines in the light ;
> It streams from the hills,
>   It descends to the plain,
> And sweetly distils
>   In the dew and the rain.

.   .   .   .

The 19th Psalm is not so fully imbued with Nature's influences. The opening couplet—

> The starry firmament on high,
> And all the glories of the sky,

reminds us of Addison's lines, "The spacious firmament on high." In the third verse he proceeds :—

> The heart, in sensual fetters bound,
> And barren as the wintry ground,
> Confesses, Lord, Thy quickening ray

> Thy word ——————————————
> With genial influence can beguile
> The frozen wilderness to smile ;
> Bid living waters o'er it flow,
> And all be paradise below.

The last verse commences with an example of the negative view of Nature, thus :—

> Almighty Lord, the sun shall fail,
> The moon forget her nightly tale,[*]
> And deepest silence[*] hush on high
> The radiant chorus[*] of the sky ;
> But, fix'd for everlasting years,
> Unmoved amid the wreck of spheres,
> Thy word shall shine in cloudless day,
> When heaven and earth have pass'd away.

In this hymn :—

> When gathering clouds around I view,
> And days are dark and friends are few,

the following lines refer to Human Nature :—

> When sorrowing o'er some stone I bend,
> Which covers what was once a friend,
> And from his voice, his hand, his smile,
> Divides me for a little while ;
> Thou, Saviour, mark'st the tears I shed,
> For Thou didst weep o'er Lazarus dead !

His only remaining hymn, " Saviour, when in dust to Thee," is in a strain that does not admit of any similarly figurative expression.

Sarah Flower Adams, 1840.

53. In a hymn on *Patience*, consisting of five verses, of seven lines each, the last of these introduces the following lines, partaking of the negative style in alluding to Nature :—

---

[*] " Nightly tale," " silence," and " radiant chorus," are evidently suggested by Addison's hymn to *Creation*.

> Or if on joyful wing
>   Cleaving the sky,
> Sun, moon, and stars forgot,
>   Upwards I fly,
> Still all my song shall be,
> Nearer, my God, to Thee,
>   Nearer to Thee !

BAPTIST WRIOTHESLEY NOEL, 1841.

54. His hymn to *Joy*, in seven verses of four lines each, commences :—

> There's not a bird, with lonely nest
> In pathless wood or mountain crest,
> Nor meaner thing, which does not share,
> O God ! in Thy paternal care !
>
> .   .   .   .

The third verse begins :—

> Each barren crag, each desert rude,
> Holds Thee within its solitude;
>
> .   .   .   .

The fifth declaring :—

> And every moment still doth bring
> Thy blessings on its loaded wing;
> Widely they spread through earth and sky,
> And last to all eternity.

JOSEPH ANSTICE, 1841.

55. Among six specimens of his sacred poems, only the one allusive to *Seed Time and Harvest* satisfactorily offers itself to our notice :—

> Lord of the harvest! once again
> We thank Thee for the ripen'd grain;
>
> .   .   .   .
>
> For all sweet holy thoughts supplied
> By seed-time, and by harvest tide.
>
> The bare dead grain, in autumn sown,
> Its robe of vernal green puts on;

> Glad from its wintry grave it springs,
> Fresh garnish'd by the King of kings :
>
> .   .   .   .
>
> So shall Thine angels issue forth;
> The tares be burnt; the just of earth,
> Playthings of sun and storms no more,
> Be gather'd to their Father's store.
>
> .   .   .   .

The fourth of these specimens commences with a faint touch of Nature in the lines :—

> Father! by Thy love and power,
> Comes again the evening hour :
> Light has vanished, labours cease,
> Weary creatures rest in peace.
> Thou, whose genial dews distil
>   On the lowliest weed that grows,
> Father! guard our couch from ill,
>   Lull thy children to repose.

We are obliged to omit all notice of " When Thou, O Lord, in flesh wert drest," " Thou the cup of death didst drain," " When came in flesh th' Incarnate Lord," and " Sweet is the Spirit's strain."

T. B. BROWNE, 1844.

56. He composed the following version of the 148th Psalm, which is wholly negative as regards its reference to Nature :—

> Praise the Lord of Heaven, praise Him in the height,
> Praise Him, all ye angels, praise Him, stars and light ;
> Praise Him, skies, and waters, which above the skies,
> When His word commanded, 'stablished did arise.
>
> Praise the Lord, ye fountains of the deeps and seas,
> Rocks and hills and mountains, cedars and all trees;
> Praise Him, clouds and vapours, snow, and hail, and fire,
> Stormy wind, fulfilling only His desire.

> Praise Him, fowls and cattle,———
> ——————— men and maidens, all created things;
> For the Name of God is excellent alone;
> Over earth His footstool, over heaven His throne.

HENRY ALFORD, 1845.

57. From five specimens of his hymns we make the following selection, commemorating *Seed Time and Harvest*, commencing with the third:—

> Come, ye thankful people, come,
> Raise the song of Harvest-Home!
> All is safely gather'd in,
> Ere the winter-storms begin ;
>
> .   .   .   .
>
> We ourselves are God's own field,
> Fruit unto His praise to yield;
> Wheat and tares together sown,
>
> .   .   .   .
>
> First the blade, and then the ear,
> Then the full corn shall appear:
>
> .   .   .   .
>
> In the fire the tares to cast,
> But the fruitful ears to store
> In His garner evermore.
>
> .   .   .   .

The next relating to *Church Dedication*, begins:—

> The lovely form of God's own Church,
> It riseth in all lands ;
> On mountain sides, in wooded vales,
> And by the desert sands—

which is but a meagre contribution from eight verses of four lines each.

MISCELLANEOUS, 1847—1851.

Again we have to notice an interregnum in the production of naturalistic sacred poetry, so far as specimens before us, from the following poets, afford evidence of this singular falling off in production. For instance, we have in succession :—

> Mary Bowley, 1847, a hymn on page 467
> Sir Edward Denny, 1848　　　ditto　　　208
> James Elwin Millard, 1848　ditto　　　3
> Anna L. Waring, 1850-1860　ditto　　　230
> Emma Toke, 1851　　　　　　ditto　　　75
> Arthur Tozer Russell, 1851 ditto　　　77, 259, 314,
> 　　　　　　　　　　　　　　　　　　　　and 409
> Henry Downton, 1851　　　　ditto　　　315 and 317

We have here no less than eleven hymns, the compositions of seven writers of sacred song, not one of whose poems is marked by any indebtedness to Nature, and yet each is un-exceptionable in its own particular manner. Thus the first hymn on this list has "Patience" for its subject, and treats of the love of the Saviour, upholding and urging reliance on Him. The second is a prayerful appeal that "all our griefs" may be swept away. The third is a solemn address to "The Holy Trinity." The fourth amplifies "Thy will be done," and so on of the rest, which afford little or no scope for other than the treatment which is here, and in all such compositions, judiciously adopted. In the present instance, it is only remarkable that four years should elapse without furnishing examples where, in some application or other of Nature, its propriety, fitness, and excellence might have been abundantly set forth. The next author we shall examine is—

JOHN MASON NEALE, 1851.

58. In the hymn "The strain upraise of joy and praise,"
full scope is afforded for a display of negative views of
Nature :—

    The planets glittering on their heavenly way,
    The shifting constellations, join and say,
                    Alleluia !

      Ye clouds that onward sweep,
      Ye winds on pinions light,
    Ye thunders, echoing loud and deep,
      Ye lightnings, wildly bright
  In sweet consent unite your Alleluia !
      Ye floods and ocean billows,
      Ye storms and winter snow,
      Ye days of cloudless beauty,
      Hoar frost and summer glow;
      Ye groves that wave in spring,
      And glorious forests, sing
                    Alleluia !
First let the birds, with painted plumage gay,
Exalt their great Creator's praise, and say
                    Alleluia !
Then let the beasts of earth, with varying strain,
Join in creation's hymn, and cry again,
                    Alleluia !
Here let the mountains thunder forth sonorous,
                    Alleluia !
There let the valleys sing in gentler chorus,
                    Alleluia !
Thou jubilant abyss of ocean, cry
                    Alleluia !
Ye tracts of earth and continents reply
                    Alleluia !

   .   .   .   .   .

Another hymn commencing :—

      Jerusalem the golden,
        With milk and honey blest,

declares in the fourth verse—

      The pastures of the Blessèd
        Are decked in glorious sheen:

neither in the above nor his three other hymns do we find
any further matter for quotation.

JOHN HUNT, 1853.

59. His hymn treating of *Creation*, opens with :—

> Let all the world rejoice,
> The great Jehovah reigns;
> The thunders are His awful voice;
> Our life His will ordains;
> The glories of His Name
> The lightnings, floods, and hail proclaim.

The succeeding four verses we shall give for their excellence in bold and graphic generalization :—

> He rules by sea the land,
> O'er boundless realms he sways;
> He holds the oceans in His hand,
> And mighty mountains weighs:
> Unequalled and alone
> In majesty He fills His throne.
>
> The universe He made
> By his prevailing might;
> The earth's foundations He hath laid,
> And scattered ancient night;
> When heaven, and earth, and sea,
> Proclaimed His awful majesty.
>
> When the bright orb of day
> First gleamed with ruddy light,
> And yonder moon, with silver ray,
> Marched up the vault of night;
> And stars bedecked the skies,
> That seemed creation's thousand eyes;
>
> And earth's fair form was seen,
> With flowers and blossoms drest;
> And trees, and fields, and meadows green,
> Adorned her youthful breast,
> Hung out in boundless space,
> Amid the ocean's cool embrace;

The next verse proclaims the singing of the "angel throng," and proceeds to reflect on the instability of matter, adopting a negative view of Nature, thus :—

> But this fair world shall die,
>
> .   .   .   .
>
> In ashes and in ruin lie,
>
> .   .   .   .

> Soon shall the day be o'er
> Of yonder brilliant sun;
> And he shall set to rise no more,
> .   .   .   .
> .   .   all soon
> Shall fade the stars, and yon pale moon.

The application of which view then naturally follows by contrast, the throne of the Eternal One alone possessing stability.

Anonymous, 1853.

60. The author of four hymns, of which we can only give the last, commencing :—

> Rejoice, though storms assail thee;
>   Rejoice, when skies are bright;
> Rejoice, though round thy pathway
>   Is spread the gloom of night:
>
> .   .   .   .
>
> Look back on youth's gay visions
>   When life one glory seem'd:
> Who pour'd those rays of gladness
>   Which on thy prospect beam'd?
>
> Recall the hours of anguish,
>   And let thy soul rejoice,
> Though wave on wave of sorrow
>   Rush on with fearful noise :
>
> .   .   .   .
>
> For silently and swiftly
>   The wheels of time roll on.

Cecil Frances Alexander, 1853—1858.

61. Of two poems by this author, the second begins :—

> The roseate hues of early dawn,
>   The brightness of the day,
> The crimson of the sunset sky,
>   How fast they fade away !
>
> .   .   .   .

THOMAS TOKE LYNCH, 1855.

62. In his hymn, "Gracious Spirit, dwell with me," he employs the figures—

> Shut my heart up like a flower
> At temptation's darksome hour,
> Open it when shines the sun,
> And His love by fragrance own.

Again —

> Silent Spirit, dwell with me;
> I myself would quiet be,
> Quiet as the growing blade
> Which through earth its way has made,
> Silently, like morning light,
> Putting mists and chills to flight.

But this style is not sustained in the remaining four verses, all of six lines each.

HARRIETT PARR, 1856.

63. Her hymn addressed to *Night*, "Hear my prayer, O heavenly Father," in five verses of four lines each, only claims notice here for the couplets :—

> Keep me, through this night of peril,
> Underneath its boundless shade:

And—

> None shall measure out Thy patience
> By the span of human thought.

JAMES FORD, 1856.

64. Of his two hymns, the first to *Noonday*, "When at my mid-day task I ply," consisting of twenty-two verses of

four lines each, is but slightly tinged with any of the influences of animate or inanimate Nature. We have the
simile regarding Human Nature :—

> For see, in all this noon-tide heat,
> How worldlings labour for the meat
> That perishes and comes to nought,
> Like shadow, when we think 'tis caught.

Then as to the Light :—

> The sun has his meridian past;
> Soon will its beams oblique be cast;
> And twilight pale will rise t' enshroud
> Their radiance in the western cloud.

These are followed by religious reflections and applications. His hymn to *Midnight*, "Awake, my soul, awake to
prayer," is somewhat similar, throughout nineteen verses.
In the second verse occurs :—

> Hush'd is the world's external din.

But the general tenor of the hymn is devotional.

Horatius Bonar, 1856.

65. His five hymns merely supply us with the last verse
from, "Calm me, my God, and keep me calm" :—

> Calm as the ray of sun or star
>   Which storms assail in vain,
> Moving unruffled through earth's war
>   Th' eternal calm to gain !

Sir Henry Baker, 1857—1861.

66. Only one out of his three hymns has the slightest
possible allusion to Nature. It begins, " Praise, O praise

our God and King," and five verses have as many couplets
presenting subjects for praise, as :—

> Praise Him that He made the sun
> Day by day his course to run,
>
> .　　　.　　　　.　　　.
>
> And the silver moon by night,
> Shining with her gentle light,
>
> .　　　.　　　.　　　.
>
> .　.　.　. He gave the rain
> To mature the swelling grain,
>
> .　　　.　　　.　　　.
>
> And hath bid the fruitful field
> Crops of precious increase yield;
>
> .　　　.　　　.　　　.
>
> Praise Him for our harvest-store ;
> He hath fill'd the garner-floor.

Thomas Davis, 1859, 1860.

67.　Out of five verses of his hymn, "Fearless, calm, and
strong in love," we can only offer the following verse :—

> Like the fisher, patient be;
> Try at morn, and try at even,
> Hope, where thou canst nothing see;
> 　And still trust in Heaven.

His hymn to *Joy*, in eight verses of six lines each, is,
however, redolent of Nature :—

> Why comes this fragrance on the summer breeze,
> 　The blended tribute of ten thousand flowers,
> To me, a frequent wanderer 'mid the trees
> 　That form these gay, though solitary bowers?
>
> .　　　.　　　.　　　.
>
> Why bursts such melody from tree and bush,
> 　The overflowing of each songster's heart,

So filling mine, that it can scarcely hush
  Awhile to listen, but would take its part?

    .   .   .   .

Why leaps the streamlet down the mountain's side,
  Hastening so swiftly to the vale beneath,
To cheer the shepherd's thirsty flock, or glide
  Where the hot sun has left a faded wreath,
Or, rippling, aid the music of the grove?
Its own glad voice replies, that God is Love!

In starry heavens, at the midnight hour,
  In ever-varying hues at morning's dawn,
In the fair bow athwart the falling shower,
  In forest, river, lake, rock, hill, and lawn.

    .   .   .   .

Nor less this pulse of health, far-glancing eye,
  And heart so moved with beauty, perfume, song,
This spirit, soaring through a gorgeous sky,
  Or diving ocean's coral caves among,
Fleeter than darting fish or startled dove,
All, all declare the same, that God is Love!

The concluding three verses are the application and the prayer to —

  Proclaim for evermore, that God is Love!

His third and last hymn, of four verses, on the same theme, proceeds:—

Shall I fear, O Earth, thy bosom?
  Shrink and faint to lay me there,
Whence the fragrant lovely blossom
  Springs to gladden earth and air?

Whence the tree, the brook, the river,
  Soft clouds floating in the sky,
All fair things come, whispering ever
  Of the love Divine on high?

    .   .   .   .

We have here, indeed, an oasis in the desert, as compared with the dry, hard, unattractive style but too common with many of our hymn writers, who write as if they carefully eschewed the examples set before them in the pages of Holy Writ.

Miscellaneous, 1801—1862.

We have in conclusion to add the following to the list of authors already given, the insertion of whose hymns we have found incompatible with our design in the present criticism.

An anonymous poet, who, in 1801, wrote "Jerusalem, my happy home." HENRY KIRKE WHITE, 1803 and 1806, two hymns, "O Lord, another day is flown;" and "Much in sorrow, oft in woe." SIR WALTER SCOTT, 1803, "That day of wrath, that dreadful day." THOMAS COTTERILL, 1810, "Thee we adore, eternal Lord!" ANNE FLOWER-DEW, 1811, "Fountain of mercy! God of Love!" in which "the sower—spring's influence—suns—dew—yellow harvest," and the like expressions, scarcely admit of being extracted in illustration of Nature-Study applied to poetical compositions. WILLIAM DRENNAN, 1815, "The heaven of heavens cannot contain." JOHN CAWOOD, 1816, "Almighty God! Thy word is cast." CHARLES DYSON, 1816, "O Lamp of Life! that on the bloody Cross." BENJAMIN BEDDOME, 1818, "And shall I sit alone." HARRIET AUBER, 1819, "Bright was the guiding star that led." SAMUEL M. WARING, 1827, "Now to Him, who loved us, gave us." FANNY F. MAITLAND, 1827, a fragmentary hymn by H. Kirke White, completed by her. WILLIAM H. BATHURST, 1831, four hymns. BISHOP T. F. MIDDLE-TON, 1831, "As o'er the past my memory strays." BISHOP R. MANT, 1831—1837, four hymns. MRS. DANIEL WILSON, 1830, "O Lord, Thy heavenly grace impart." An anonymous writer, M. G. T., 1831, "Saviour, I lift my trembling eyes." JOSIAH ·CONDER, 1837 to 1856, three hymns. ALGERNON HERBERT, 1839, "Though, by sorrows overtaken." SUSAN L. MILES, 1840, "Thou, who didst stoop below." RAY PALMER, 1840, two hymns. F. ELIZABETH COX, 1841, "A thousand years have fleeted." An anonymous writer, 1841, "Ere another Sabbath's close." ANDREW REED, 1842, "There is an hour, when I must part." Two anonymous writers, one wrote in 1842, "Hosanna! raise the pealing hymn;" the other, in 1843, "In memory of the Saviour's love." WILLIAM J. IRONS, 1853, "Father of Love, our Guide and Friend." WILLIAM W. How, 1854, "O Holy Lord, content to live." RICHARD MASSIE, 1854,—his hymn, "Source of good, whose power controls," composed in five verses of eight lines each, has only the following lines which we can extract:—

> As the hart, with longing looks
> For refreshing water-brooks,
> Heated in the burning chace ;
> So my soul desires Thy grace.

An anonymous poet, 1855, "Thou God of Love! beneath Thy sheltering wings." JAMES D. BURNS, 1855, "O time of tranquil joy and holy feeling!" ROBERT C. CHAPMAN, 1857, "My soul, amid this stormy world." A variation from John Quarles by THOMAS DARLING, 1857, "O King of kings, before whose throne." ELIZA F. MORRIS, 1858, "Poor child of sin and woe." EDWARD H. BICKERSTETH, 1858, "Mercy alone can meet my case." CATHERINE WINKWORTH, 1858, "Whate'er my God ordains is right." An anonymous writer, H. L. L., 1859, whose only conspicuous line is :—

> In the green pastures of the heavenly shore,

which occurs in the hymn, "Rest, weary soul!" JOHN B. TOMALIN, 1860, "Saviour, who didst from Heaven come down." EDMUND H. SEARS, 1860, "It came upon the midnight clear"—a hymn in which the poet would almost seem to have aimed at avoiding the association of anything earthly with heavenly aspirations, beyond the bald expressions, "the midnight clear; earth; solemn stillness; the cloven skies; the weary world; sad and lowly plains; men at war with men; ever-circling years; the whole world"—all highly suggestive, yet never showing the slightest flight of imagination in the treatment of the poem. JOHN E. BODE, 1860, two hymns. WILLIAM C. DIX, 1861, "As with gladness men of old." FRANCIS T. PALGRAVE, 1862, two hymns. ROBERT SMITH, 1862, "Come, take my yoke, the Saviour said." And an anonymous writer, 1862, "Just as thou art, without one trace."

We have thus passed in rather rapid review the spiritual metrical labours of no less than sixty-seven hymnists, dating from the year 1616 to 1860, comprising a period of nearly three centuries, and affording fair average examples of meritorious psalms, hymns, and other sacred songs. Of these we have taken only a partial view, partial because we pronounce upon them in reference to only one particular quality which these compositions exhibit, omitting to notice in them many qualities that recommend these, and others that have been wholly omitted: when considered critically as poetical compositions, or regarded as works of a highly meritorious Christian character.

But the reader has been apprised from the commencement of this Essay, that our strictures would be rigidly confined to the selecting and commenting upon only such passages in these Songs of Praise as bore directly or indirectly on those influences of Nature which comprise a system of Nature-Study.

In the first place, then, we shall call attention to the first obvious result of this investigation, which plainly points to the difference in the style of the hymns placed before us, century by century. 1. In the seventeenth century, the most conspicuous poets under review are Herbert, Wither, and Baxter, but we peruse them in vain for other than the most artificial strains, amounting almost to an avoidance of every other accessory than such as daily life afforded in manners; customs; and habitations, with all their ornamentation and furniture; nothing belonging to these seems to have appeared undignified, conceited, or extravagant. By such means, rather than by direct applications to external Nature, the poet seems to have gained the public ear, because such was the public taste. The poems of Herbert sold by tens of thousands, and Quarles was a universal favourite with the religious world. 2. In the eighteenth century the public taste indicated a slight change; we begin to observe more of the freshness and fragrance of Nature, and less of cabinet-work and cupboards. Nature begins to associate with Art, and poets enter into descriptions, employ metaphors, and speak typically, under the direct inspiration of universal Nature. Watts, in particular, led the way, pointing out the propriety of' thus imitating and enlarging the figurative style of pictorial Scripture passages. Addison too, followed in taking this enlarged view of sacred poetry, and though not aided by Wesley, yet the productions of Cowper, Mrs. Barbauld, and other composers of poems devoted to sacred, moral, and didactic subjects, show the advance made during this century in attempts to ennoble psalmody by a larger infusion of allusive and direct applications of Nature than the examples of their predecessors warranted : although quite in accordance with Human Nature and Divine authority.

3. In the present century the change is no less curious than it is obvious and gratifying ; indeed, we appear to be lost in surprise that poetical taste could have pursued any other than this natural course, although not strictly allied to a classical understanding of the matter. But poets, like painters, had much to learn with respect to Nature, and it was not until a poet took the subject seriously into hand, and made it the study of a long life, that Nature in all its greatness, extent, and variety, assumed a goodly and manageable form in verse. Wordsworth must ever be considered Nature's High Priest ; he did more than any other of his tribe to open the eyes of the purblind public, and to elevate and ennoble the tastes of other poets. However, this is no mere theory, we have here the plain fact before us, that whereas of yore the sacred poetry of centuries has been remarkable for its sterility in Nature's influences in one way or another, the present century not only emulates but far exceeds the two preceding it, in its many adaptations of the kingdoms of Nature, and of natural phenomena, to the ennobling religious poetical effusions : by giving vividness to expressions of a pious and moral bearing, and beautifying the language of sacred songs ;

adorning whatever relates to the Creator with the nearest possible semblance and reflection to which human intellect can attain of His own sublime works.

Let us now proceed to examine the nature and quality of the use made by these several poets taken in succession irrespective of all other considerations; because we have to show the precise character of their adaptations of Nature in some of its multitudinous phases. To bring these within reasonable compass, we shall consider them under the several classes of—1. Description; 2. Figurative language generally; 3. Similes in particular; 4. That which is principally due to imagination and fancy; 5. Direct applications to Human Nature; 6. The strictly spiritual, relating to Almighty power, greatness, and goodness; together with the moral, meditative, and religious expression of sentiments and feelings; and 7. Negative views of Nature, affording hyperbolical and other figurative expressions relative to things and matters beyond human comprehension, otherwise than as thus brought home to the common understanding of mankind.

1. Description.

Descriptive poetry has, strictly speaking, little, if anything, to do with sacred metrical compositions. Its aspirations being heavenward, are spiritual, and partake so little of that which is earthly, that it almost appears repugnant to Christian feeling to consider psalmody and hymnody as other than the result of direct divine inspiration; yet the sacred poet can, when occasion demands, tread terra firma with a sure footing; but we may rely on it that the muse will bound thence with lightning-speed to worlds beyond the skies. Our first illustrative example (by an anonymous poet, in 1616) very placidly describes gardens with flowers, streets beautified with trees, and fruit, and stream;—but there also angels sit and sing. WATTS, as we have seen, (page 18), exactly describes the early dawn of a bright sunny morning, the sun rising until—

> Round the whole earth he flies and shines.

In like manner ADDISON, page 21, affords us a noble picture of the sun by day, and the moon and starry firmament by night, making universally known—

> The work of an Almighty hand.

Sometimes, however, the poet is not so lavish; nothing can be more curt than those lines of SEAGRAVE's, page 28, "Rivers to the ocean run," "Fire ascending seeks the sun." To this extent many Christian poets indulge in description, but mostly to enforce the truth of some moral or religious truth. DR. DODDRIDGE, page 29, beautifully bids farewell to the sun and moon, as "refulgent orb of day," "pale empress of night." His address to *Night* is also very fine :—

> While the vivid planets stray
> Various through their mystic way.

Again, his hymn for *Seed Time and Harvest*, allusive to "the flowery spring," is charmingly descriptive throughout three verses, (page 30.) He enthusiastically sings :—

> Seasons and months, and weeks and days,
> Demand successive songs of praise.

Here then we have the apology for making better known to the vulgar that which we praise, by entering upon some vivid description of its naturally prominent features, but still the sacred muse, it must be allowed, has usually shown itself chary in this indulgence of anything approaching to what seems to be considered too close an association with merely material matters, as too grovelling, too earthly; and this too, although not relating to the meretricious works of man, but to the wonderful provisions of the Almighty for man's well-being in his present precarious state of existence. Hence *descriptions* of visible Nature are very restricted in their scope and subjects, just as we find in such an example of condensation as that afforded by MONTGOMERY, at page 47 :—

> 'Twas night; the floods were out; it blew
> A winter hurricane aloof.

What profane poet would not have amplified these two lines to as many pages, at least?

COLLYER has indulged some little in description, page 48, in his hymn, "Great God, what do I hear!" but not nearly to the extent which his subject, "The rising tempest," would have afforded under other circumstances.

BOWDLER, in a hymn, page 49, remarkable for the play of imagination and fancy, affords evidence of powerful and picturesque descriptive talent. Under his treatment *Creation* is all animate and ecstatic, when, "shouted every morning star." The cherub song—

> Roll'd through the dark blue depths above.

The poet who wrote thus could have given us more from the same fount.

So solemn a subject as that of *Christ Incarnate* restricts the poet to very limited descriptive efforts, and yet RICKARDS has shown a masterly exercise of his ability in graphic sketching, page 53—

> **Though Nature's grace is swept away,**

through "rude winds, clouds, and sleety storm."

It is rare to find in sacred song such express names as "Greenland, India, Africa, Ceylon," and yet BISHOP HEBER, page 54, has succeeded in delicate descriptive etching and in tinting with decidedly good effect, informing us of lands whose "sunny fountains"—

> **Roll down their golden sand,**

an El Dorado, however, amazingly inferior to that haven to which the heathen is directed, he who—

> ——— —— **in his blindness**
> **Bows down to wood and stone.**

"The spring-tide hour," page 67, by MONSELL, is a delicious morsel of word-painting, rich in all the glories of summer, with its birds, and flowers, and fruits; zephyrs skimming the groves—

> **Soft as the south winds blow,**

calling forth a profusion of rich and spicy bloom. And all this luscious song was written to teach us *Discipline*.

The descriptive vein frequently shows itself, although not immediately called into activity by the subject. GURNEY, communicating the fact that "God is good," chooses a pleasant rural picture to enforce this truth, page 69, "Yes, God is good"—

> **From ocean-depths and spreading wood.**

That hint suffices, and we have a fine panorama of " the sun, the stars, the birds, the air, the rain, the hills, sky, sea," and finally " all Nature." This is skilful, but only an artist would seize upon it. Equally happy is he in warbling—

> The varying seasons haste their round.

Spring, summer, autumn, and winter successively call forth the promise that—

> New praises from our lips shall sound !

We trust this absence of asceticism in piety will not be deemed irreverent, but make many proselytes.

Seed Time is so suggestive of coming *Harvest*, that it is gratifying to find ANSTICE, page 73, devoting a hymn really touching on topics associated with them :—

> The bare dead grain, in autumn sown,
> Its robe of vernal green puts on ;

and most agreeably and appropriately associated with suitable expressions of thankfulness to the " Lord of the harvest !"

On the same subject, but in high relief by way of contrast, we have a hymn by ALFORD, page 75, in which every opportunity for being truthful and graceful in description is neglected. We are called to sing " the song of Harvest Home" in a most common-place and comfortless manner. In another of his poems, not even—

> The lovely form of God's own Church,

carries him beyond the dry catalogue of " all lands, mountain sides, wooded vales"—

> And by the desert sands.

Desert indeed ! without a breath of air, a ripple of water,

or the least show of vegetable or animal life. So difficult
does it appear to be to some minds, to soar beyond the
dust, and cobwebs, and black-letter of their own libraries.

HUNT indulges in graphic generalizations (page 78) very
happily and pleasantly, creation being the burden of his
song; we have, therefore, "boundless realms, the oceans,
mighty mountains, the universe, the earth's foundations,
the bright orb of day, and moon, and night, stars"—

> That seemed creation's thousand eyes.
> And earth's fair form was seen,
> With flowers and blossoms drest ;
> And trees, and fields, and meadows green.

Very pretty and truthful, but, after all, not grasping much
of this grand and gorgeous *Cosmos*.

JAMES FORD, in a single verse of four lines, page 81,
depicts sunset and twilight; but in this, as in many
similar instances, the poet satisfies himself rather with the
naming a fact than making an effort at definite description. There is consequently in all such compositions
a preponderance of dull, doubtful, hard outline, which
readers are left to fill up and enliven agreeably to their
own tastes and fancies, or knowledge and experience.
On the other hand, the true master of descriptive poetry
thinks out every trifle for his readers, and leaves little to
their mere imagination ; because he depicts scenes and
situations of no ordinary conception, and gratifies and
delights by constant surprises where least expected, or
seeming least likely to be accomplished.

We have thus brought to a close our examination of
examples selected from sacred poets of the last three centu-

ries so far only as Descriptive Poetry is concerned. And here it is important to dwell awhile in order to direct the Nature-student's attention to the singular but irrefragable fact, that hitherto Nature-Study has been limited by the universal consent and practice of all literary critics to this particular class of poetry. Refer to the interminable volumes and pages of learned reviews and miscellaneous critical works and essays touching this subject, and it will be found throughout that the poet or prose writer is estimated for his love of and acquaintance with Nature by his compositions of a *descriptive* character. If not characterized by word-painting the author was at once doubted, or peremptorily declared to afford no evidence of his observance of Nature. Of such poets would be Shelley, Keats, and even Burns, Byron, and Moore. Although we have here given "Description" first in order, we consider it as being far from first in importance; but this view, hitherto, has not obtained with critical writers, particularly when examining and arranging poetical productions. Even so lately as 1871, in M. Taine's elaborate and excellent *History of English Literature*, this universal feeling on the subject shows no appearance of giving way; for he observes with respect to the poets of the eighteenth century, particularly Pope, that "Every aspect of Nature was observed; a sunrise, a landscape reflected in the water, a breeze amid the foliage, and so forth." (P. 207.) It is the same wherever we turn for information, hoping in our simplicity that, from the heavens above to the earth beneath, and the waters surrounding it, something beyond this " cribbed, cabined, and confined" influence of Nature on man's intelligence, sentiments, and feelings might be even darkly discovered. But our researches end in absolute discomfiture. The great world of Nature may have its portraiture limned by artists, cut in marble by sculptors, or *described* by poets, but there the matter ends. It is all the work of the eye; nothing passes through the intellectual alembic of the mind to escape etherealized, or other than a mere word-painted picture. How strange it now appears that Nature, in the critical estimation of so many writers, should have been so long and persistently limited and abridged; with, at the same time, abundant evidence to the contrary in the poems and dramas of Shakspeare alone. We trust to make it apparent that Nature-Study is of far wider range and far greater in its importance than has ever hitherto been shown.

2. FIGURATIVE LANGUAGE GENERALLY.

We find in HERBERT, author of *The Temple*, instances of very dissimilar and unequal poetical compositions. One of his best poems is an address to *The Lord's Day*, " O day most calm, most bright!" page 7, in which he ventures on such figurative expressions as :—

> The fruit of this [world], the next world's bud.

But the furniture and ornament of a mansion or cabinet, museum or wardrobe, would appear to interest him infinitely more than the buds, leaves, blossoms, and fruits of Nature. In this respect he closely resembled Quarles, who died in 1644.

BAXTER alludes to death figuratively, page 10, as bruising

the " springing seed" ere it " come to fruit ;" but spiritual life was there " in the root."   Unfortunately he adopted the vicious, artificial style of the age.

BISHOP KEN's poetry is not particularly ambitious. He admonishes the Christian to have a care that his soul, by the influence of " light Divine" shall let its " own.light to others shine."

But we must turn to WATTS for variety in figurative language.   He describes, page 15, Jesus' reign as being wherever " the sun" journeys ; and his " kingdom" as stretching " from shore to shore"—

Till moons shall wax and wane no more.

" Trouble" has its " waves" which " rise," and like " the tempests roar !"   But "Death" at last lands " weary souls"—

Safe on the heavenly shore.

" Death" being but as " a narrow sea" dividing it " from ours," as declared in another hymn.

The Christian's hope, page 20, partakes of " pleasures" in " things unseen :"—

Beyond this world and time,

and unattained by ears, eyes, or even the very thoughts of sinners.

J. WESLEY, page 23, presents us with little material for remark.   In figurative expression he is very brief; the Lord is appealed to for " Light," and to become the suppliant's " way" against " rising floods"—

When sinks my heart in waves of woe.

The Christian, page 24, is to give his fears " to the

II

winds," assured that through "waves, and clouds, and storms," God will clear his way, and so shall his "night" end in "joyous day."

CHARLES WESLEY, page 26, is even less disposed to launch out in flowery epithets, for we have only one illustration derived from twenty-six of his poems. Although his subject is *Morning*, he merely generalizes on the objects of Nature, and expresses his feeling that the intellectual morn is "dark and cheerless," without the full influence of Christ's glory—

> Shining to the perfect day !

MICHAEL BRUCE, page 33, sings of "the mountain of the Lord," which "in latter days" is to draw "wondering eyes;" and that "The beam that shines from Zion's hill" shall in effect, "lighten every land."

The following stanza by COWPER, page 38, is wholly metaphorical :—

> The billows swell, the winds are high,
> Clouds overcast my wintry sky ;
> Out of the depths to Thee I call,
> My fears are great, my strength is small.

In the parable of "The Sower," he does but paraphrase the style and language of the original. And this is all we glean from twelve hymns by a poet eminent for his love of home and rustic Nature ; yet these would appear to have had but slight effect on the inspiration of his muse : so true is it that without previous study and a world of information we look on and may even live among the brightest and sublimest scenes of Nature without their ever thoroughly entering and influencing the heart and mind of the poet whose attention has not been closely and continuously directed to the consideration of her many moral and mental influences; that is, when applied under the judicious management of the poet, the fabulist, the orator, and all classes of writers, whether for amusement or instruction, whether grave or gay, simple or florid.

KELLY is figuratively expressive in his hymn, page 43, "Lo! He comes! let all adore Him!" and in another, "We're bound for yonder land;" a heritage "Where all the ransom'd dwell."

MONTGOMERY could not be otherwise than associated in this category, see pages 45 to 47. Man's short-lived hopes and natural decay are graphically depicted, page 47; he "droops like the dying flower," and all his prospects and pursuits—

> Are sweet deceitful dreams.

In highly impassioned language BOWDLER, page 49, calls for universal praise from Inorganic as well as Organic Nature—

> Long as the streams of life descend.

In a like manner, EDMESTON, page 51, expresses a sense of the vanity of repining; why—

> Mourn the clouds that cross my way;

although "within the vale of sorrow," with "tempest overblown."

As might be expected, we turn to KEBLE's poems to find redundant examples of figurative expression, although he is frequently wanting in originality. In his hymn for "Septuagesima Sunday," the sky—

> Is like the Maker's love.

The " church" and the " moon"—
> Each borrows of the Sun.

Dr. Newman finds the stars to be brilliants on the robes of the blessed angels, Keble gratifies us more by imagining—
> The saints above are stars in Heaven.

They stand " like trees"—
> Faith is their fix'd unswerving root.

CHANDLER, page 67, prays that our hope may be " our sunset calm and bright."

In a pleasing hymn by MONSELL, page 67, he regrets that his heart, unlike all other things in Nature,—
> Bears not its part,
> Its winter has no spring.

WILLIAMS, page 69, declares that the trusting heart sings,—
> And feels as light as it had wings.

On the *Resurrection* and *Eternal Life*, GURNEY has a hymn, page 69, in which man's state is set forth as " like the seed," and autumn " leaves :"—
> Yet the seed, upraised again,
> Clothes with green the smiling plain.

He has also another in a like strain, dedicated to *Harvest*.

The bountiful care of the Almighty is the subject of one of GRANT's hymns, page 71 ; it appears everywhere alike :—
> And sweetly distils
> In the dew and the rain.

ANSTICE, treating of *Seed Time and Harvest*, page 73, alludes to the time when the just shall be—
> Playthings of sun and storms no more.

ALFORD, page 75, on the same topic, does not rise above the "wheat and tares," and the one being garnered and the other burnt.

An anonymous poet, in 1853, page 79, wrote, "Rejoice, though storms assail thee;" proceeding with this recommendation also "when skies are bright," and though encompassed with "the gloom of night;" calling to rememberance "youth's gay visions," and anguish with "wave on wave of sorrow"—

> For silently and swiftly
> The wheels of time roll on.

In this division of our subject we frequently approach the Religious, Reflective, and Moral; or even the Imaginative and Fanciful. But we have adduced examples sufficient to show how largely Nature assists in developing a particular style without trenching on either of the foregoing divisions, which we shall notice separately hereafter. By "Nature" it has hitherto been customary to conceive that Human Nature was to be understood, all other Nature being either Inanimate, or otherwise Animal and Vegetable Nature. The idea of Nature as a whole, and as at the head of a system, simplifies and systematizes our views and expressions. The poet sees in Nature at large many features and phenomena which he adroitly and happily applies to human action and sentiments, and the invisible in Nature is brought home to our intelligence by reference to and association with objects ever present to our observation; Man's life is like a flower—time, a stream—the seasons, the ages of man; seed time and harvest, his life and death; the one takes place of the other and figurative

expression ensues. We may obtain this style by education, conversation, reading, and particularly by studying
the poets. But the best objects of study are the
actual fields, floods, products, and goodly atmosphere
of productive and reproductive Nature itself, should the
desire be to add vigour, freshness, and originality of expression to our utterances, whether in speaking or writing.
We may study ART and derive a collateral advantage from
that source, but art is liable to constant change, to become
old fashioned, and even obsolete. In the study of NATURE,
however, the student has the advantage of a most paradoxical model, one of antique yet virgin beauty; unchang-
ing, and unchangeable, yet ever varying; affecting alike
the minds of all nations of every clime and country; no-
where differing, but appealing in one unvarying tone and
spirit to all classes of the human race.

3. SIMILES.

All the hymns we have examined, as well in the present
collection as in others, strike the mind as being remarkably deficient in the style and matter of their similes.
We find endless repetitions of the same thought without
even any apparent attempt to set it forth in better language, or in any way to render it more than usually
attractive. Our present examples are not characterised by
any elevation of thought, or much dignity of language.
WITHER alludes to the setting sun, page 8, and its " declining " which suggests that in the same way, time and
our lives are daily—

Declining to the grave.

Noon, and noon-tide are common in similes referring to purity and clearness, Bishop Ken recommends us, page 11, to—

Keep conscience as the noontide clear;

and he is not more happy in illustration when he prays :—

Disperse my sins as morning dew.

These instances will exemplify what is meant by poverty of invention in this department of poetry, which it would appear has been thought unworthy of any study to improve it, although Nature-Study abundantly supplies the means of novel illustration on all subjects. The fair inference to be drawn from the fact before us, however, would be, that Similes are figures of such difficult invention, that there is nothing left for the poet but to polish obsolete ones when he can find them, or to repeat to the best of his ability even those which are the most common, and the most threadbare with use. It cannot be that they are so easy of accomplishment as not to be worth looking after; the only just conclusion to be drawn from actual poetical practice, is that, they challenge the inventive powers of most of our poets. If similes are easy to accomplish, it is unpardonable to neglect studying grace and novelty in them; if difficult they are the more deserving of study, for whatsoever is ornamental should be highly finished, correct, and beautiful, as in the minutest particle of animate or inanimate matter. Thus Nature-study steps in at every point to admonish the poet, and to assure him that nothing in his divine art is poor, mean, or worthless. Religious feeling has called into exercise the finest genius in every department of the Fine Arts, in architecture, statuary, painting, music, oratory; why then should there be any less ambitious efforts to be exact, and at the same time elevated and original in songs of adoration, prayer, praise, and thanksgiving addressed to the Almighty as we reverently bow—

> Before Jehovah's awful throne.

WATTS, page 13, represents the Divine command, " Wide as the world;" His love, " vast as eternity;" His truth, " Firm as a rock." The crowd are " like billows;" surly warlike nations, " dash like waves;" God's influence on fainting souls is,—

> As rain on meadows newly mown,

and " dew on thirsty hills." The gospel, like the sunbeams, "light and life convey." Our days, page 17, are as grass, as the flower:—

> If one sharp blast sweep o'er the field,
> It withers in an hour.

Time is likened to "an ever-rolling stream;" and the human race die, "forgotten as a dream"—

> Dies at the opening day.

Here we see how Watts ingeniously gives some slight turn or another to dignify similes even when drawn from books in place of being sought for in the fields, gardens, hills, and dales of Nature itself; but such efforts are of the study, and too often are feeble and effete.

In CHARLES WESLEY's hymn from the German, page 25, we find the patient Christian waiting and watching for Divine influence,—

> As flowers their opening leaves display,
> And glad drink in the solar fire.

Here the German hymnist escapes the musty literature that furnishes most of the similes of sacred song, and the result will, we trust, induce other poets to follow in the same healthy direction. But Wesley, singing of Divine Light, shows its power to dispel grief, so that it shall fly, " As clouds before the mid-day sun." When we obtain nothing beyond these two examples from twenty-six poems, their dearth of ornament in this respect becomes singularly significant.

Dr. Doddridge, page 29, compares God's fulness of favours as equalling " the ocean ;" fleetness is, " as the morning light ;" but to find even these we have searched sixteen hymns.

Morrison sings that, the coming of the Lord shall be " like the morn," page 34 ; and as " dew upon the tender herb," and as Spring " showers " that " cheer the thirsty ground." Newton, the author of seventeen hymns, has only two affording such similes, as comparing troubles to " a burning sun," page 36, and our fleeting days, which for their evanescence are—

> As the lightning from the skies
> Darts, and leaves no trace behind.

Although we have here twelve hymns by Cowper, page 37, they present us simply with one common-place simile, that " passions discompose the mind, as tempests vex the sea." It seems incredible that any such number of his poems could have been selected, showing the almost total absence of this figure of speech : and in him it is the more distinguishable, because assuredly he was a passionate lover of Nature.

Gibbons, page 39, in a hymn of considerable excellence

introduces the single simile relating to "the Gospel" wherein, "like the Sun," divine mercy shines, "without a cloud between." It is rather singular that a poet like JAMES MONTGOMERY, could compose nine hymns, employing no more than two similes. He prays the Lord, page 46, that He would,—

> Like mighty rushing wind
> Upon the waves beneath,
> Move with one impulse every mind,
> One soul, one feeling breathe.

In comparing the heavenly with our earthly state, he says that in the latter "life's affections," like "sparks fly upwards to expire."

One hymn by HENRY MOORE, contains no less than five similes, but all are expressive of the one favourite topic with poets, namely the instability of all things appertaining to this world; evanescence is the common theme of humanity, the shortness of time, the uncertainty of life, the perishing and passing away of all our brightest hopes and treasured possessions. Thus again, page 47, we are told that "life" is "an idle play;" that it is "various as the wind," even "beauty fades," and "glory" has "an hour;" human "pleasures" are but as "the morning sun," which "clouds," and "night" obscure; "wealth" too, with its attendant "pomp and honour," are but,—

> Like summer insects, drest in gold,
> That flutter, shine, and die.

In short, from birth to death, our lives verily,—

> Are sweet deceitful dreams.

Passing over thirteen hymn writers, we come next to LYTE, who simply applies the figure of sunrise, page 63:—

> Like the sun the saints shall rise.

And GURNEY, page 69, makes ordinary applications of seed sowing, in reference to the *Resurrection* :—

> Like the seed in spring-time sown,
> Like the leaves in autumn strown.

The twelfth poet after him that comes under our notice, is LYNCH, who, on page 80, has :—

> Shut my heart up like a flower
> At temptation's darksome hour.

Also, addressing the "Silent Spirit," he solicits to dwell with it, for—

> I myself would quiet be,
> Quiet as the growing blade.

Which growth, he beautifully suggests, proceeds,—

> Silently, like morning light.

These are among the most poetical of this entire group.

We conclude with DAVIS, page 82, who associates patience with the operation of fishing, advising,—

> Like the fisher, patient be,
> Try at morn, and try at even,
> Hope, where thou canst nothing see.

Of all figures one might have reasonably expected a redundancy of Similes rather than this evident deficiency; and being so few, we regret the more their poverty of ingenuity. Why this should be the case it is difficult to surmise. Man is so associated with Nature, and Nature supplies such abundant, pleasing, poetical, and apt applications, that this absence of supply appears more like studied indifference, than ordinary neglect.

With Scripture before him as his guide for imitation, and inspiration, it is surprising that any poet, much less the sacred poet, should miss those useful similitudes that tend so greatly to impress on every mind moral and religious sentiments.

It may be of service to some readers to direct their attention to the perusal of Spencer's "Storehouse of Similes," 1658, reprinted 1868 ; and "Flowers of Fancy ; a collection of Similes," by Henry Schultes, 8vo. 1829. We recommend these as being suggestive, and as guides for avoiding what has been done, rather than for imitation ; for that which was supposed to be original may thus be discovered to be old, if not hackneyed. "But amongst all the writings which tend to replenish and illuminate the human mind with sublime ideas the Sacred Volume, *velut inter ignes Luna minores*, stands transcendent, and will be found best adapted to ennoble our conceptions."

4. Imagination and Fancy.

That which is purely fanciful plays but a small part in sacred poetry, there is frequently much, however, that draws on the imaginative powers of the poet in his day-dreams of Paradise, of almighty power, of the future state of happy or unhappy spirits, and an endless variety of other and contingent topics. But there are lighter touches than such subjects call for, in which the imagination and fancy perform an agreeable and essential part in giving beauty and interest to what might otherwise be bald, dry, hard, and distasteful. Herbert ingeniously declares, page 7 :—

> The heavens are not too high ;
>   .   .   .   .   .
> The earth is not too low,

for man's praises of his Maker to reach Him. The commencement of his poem on *The Lord's Day* is absolutely delicious—

> O day most calm, most bright !

And from such a poet this is truly a surprise, a burst of inspiration, after the artificial illustrations that disfigure too many of his other pieces. WITHER shows almost a frenzy of delight, page 7, calling for universal praise—

> Strike the viol, touch the lute,
> Let no tongue or string be mute.

In another hymn, page 8, we have the sun "Enthronèd overhead." A poem that relates to the infant Christ, page 8, delicately begins :—

> Sweet baby, sleep ! what ails my dear,
> What ails my darling thus to cry ?

Thus, as it were, associating the infant of to-day with a story of antiquity and world-wide interest.

MASON, page 10, attempts a glimpse of Paradise, whose stream of waters is—

> .   .   .   a living stream
> Clear as the crystal stone.

WATTS, who was one of the first sacred poets to introduce an improved strain in the language of our hymns, displays more imagination and fancy than is usually found among hymn writers. His version of the 100th Psalm is of this character, page 12 ; the "nations" bow—

> Before Jehovah's awful throne.

It is declared of the millions—

> We'll crowd Thy gates with thankful songs,
> High as the heavens our voices raise.

And it concludes by declaring the stability of His truth, even—

> When rolling years shall cease to move.

Allusive to the love of the Prince of Grace for his

creatures, page 15, he would, to proclaim it, have "rocks and hills"—

<blockquote>Their lasting silence break.</blockquote>

Nothing can be more truly naturalistic than this appeal to that appallingly solemn and indefinite awe engendered by Alpine and other mountain stillness and silence, terrible without being ghastly, and creating a feeling more nearly allied to horror than to pleasure. A hymn to *Morning*, page 18, commences by announcing that at God's voice—

<blockquote>The cheerful sun makes haste to rise,
And, like a giant, doth rejoice
To run his journey through the skies.</blockquote>

Another hymn, calling us to "worship at Immanuel's feet," declares—

<blockquote>Earth is too narrow to express
His worth, His glory, or His grace !</blockquote>

Nay, further—

<blockquote>Nature, to make His beauties known,
Must mingle colours not her own.</blockquote>

So that of course they can alone be sought for by "angel minds," and not by man in this nether world.

Simon Browne, commemorating *The Lord's Day*, enthusiastically rises " on wings of strong devotion," soaring beyond every cloud, passing " all the skies," to worship—

<blockquote>And leave beneath Thy feet the stars.</blockquote>

As might be expected from Addison, we find in his paraphrase of the 19th Psalm, page 21, that exercise of poetical licence which is not so readily accorded to the general order of hymn writers, who appear to consider that solemnity and seriousness require a certain style of stern sterility; as rocky peaks are grand and sublime, and vast sandy plains have still a thrilling interest, although barren of sustenance to the human race; so too are wastes of waters, and the fathomless aerial ocean surrounding this " dark terrestrial ball."   With Addison, these,—

> And spangled heavens, a shining frame,
> Their great Original proclaim.

All around and beyond us is equally sublime and past our finite comprehension; but let us look at home, and within, and we shall still find abundant material for specution, much that is beautiful beyond conception or imitation, and look where we will and as minutely as we please, perfection and accumulated marvels of exquisite forms and singular adaptations of parts to serve their intended purposes meet our eyes and senses in every animate and inanimate substance, and in all their attendant phenomena, whether of light, life, or motion, throughout the universe of water, earth, and air.   According to Addison's poem, the Moon relates its tale to the earth, which the Stars confirm, and the heavenly host are, with " a glorious voice "—

> For ever singing as they shine
> " The hand that made us is Divine."

The longest of Addison's pieces, showing his fertility of imaginative power is the 23rd Psalm—"The Lord my pasture shall prepare," page 23, with its " fertile vales, dewy meads, peaceful rivers, verdant landscape, rugged way, barren wilderness, sudden greens and herbage, and murmuring streams."   All this, it is true, is but fancy's sketch, but it is as delightfully rural as though it were fresh from the ready pencil of Gainsborough.

Dr. Doddridge, page 30, recommends the sinner's flight to Jesus :—

> Lest life's young golden beams should die
> In sudden endless night !

OLIVERS, page 32, in attempting to convey a glimpse of the "goodly land" of "endless rest," takes flight on "eagle's wings."

COWPER, in happier mood, page 37, prayerfully aspires to the finding of the "silent shade," where his "soul"—

> There, like the nightingale, she pours
> Her solitary lays.

In that fine hymn—"God moves in a mysterious way," the author advises "fearful saints" to take courage, for—

> The clouds ye so much dread
> Are big with mercy, and shall break
> In blessings on your head.

He also reminds us as to the purposes of Divine Providence, which "ripen fast" that—

> The bud may have a bitter taste,
> But sweet will be the flower.

GIBBONS displays much command of fancifully imaginative power, judging from the two specimens before us; in the latter of which, page 89, he employs the noble thought in reference to God's throne, as being firm—

> Though oft Thy ways are wrapt in clouds,
> Mysterious and unknown.

FANCH and TURNER, page 41, in their hymn on *Christ Ascended* speak happily of the heavenly home, as—

> Beyond the glittering starry globe,
> Far as th' eternal hills.

And say of the blessed angels,—

> Ye saw Him, when the heavens and earth,
> A chaos, first, He made.

Although we have sixteen hymns by KELLY before us, only one, the hymn, at page 43, "Lo! He comes! let all adore Him!" is distinguished for flights of fancy, announcing that,—

> Through the desert God is going,
> Through the desert waste and wild,

where grows "no goodly plant," nor "verdure ever smiled." But the "thorn" shall be supplemented by "trees"—all "stately, fair, and fruitful;" and from the mountains, "rivers shall be seen to flow." Pleasant indeed to us is this glimpse of the picturesque after perusing scores of dull, dry, monotonous compositions in which prosiness would almost appear to be considered the necessary accompaniment of piety.

What sacred poet is there who has not tested the powers of his imagination and fancy to depict Paradise with effective and graphic fervency? GISBORNE, among many in the the same path, has tried his pen in describing the land "Where soldiers war no more." It is without "suns and moons," and night. "Unbroken day" proceeds from the "ever-burning throne." But the poet stays his flight to warn us that he can only proceed as aided by "earthly types;" such as, for example: "healing leaves," with "fadeless green," abundant fruit, never-ceasing founts and streams, and—

> Where everlasting mountains shield
> Vales of eternal peace.

This happy and delightful desire to escape beyond the known into realms of infinite space, and realize an elysium beyond our starry sphere, is as universal among poets as it is unsuccessful in its issue. Every attempt is a flight with waxen wings, although often the failure is a noble one, including the fall of many mighty monarchs of the muse's hierarchy. We have made a point of dwelling on this matter at this juncture, because it opens a wide field for the poet's serious consideration, whether by a closer attention to Nature-Study, he might not rise higher, proceed farther, and succeed better than has hitherto been the fate of all poets the instant their subject takes such heavenward flights. So long as poets only copy poets, or are solely inspired by each other's inspirations, there must of necessity be a certain mannerism distinguishable in all their paradisaical pictures. POLLOK, than whom few men in this walk of sacred poetry have risen higher in the sublime of religious aspirations, has evidently attempted to soar beyond the ordinary style of such conceptions in his dissertation on Desert Solitude, where, contemplating a primeval landscape, he sings—

> . . . . Nature showed, herself,
> And reaped her crops ; whose garments were the clouds ;
> Whose minstrels, brooks ; whose lamps, the moon and stars ;
> Whose organ-choir, the voice of many waters ;
> Whose banquets, morning dews ; whose heroes, storms ;
> Whose warriors, mighty winds ; whose lovers, flowers ;
> Whose orators. the thunderbolts of God ;
> Whose palaces, the everlasting hills ;
> Whose ceiling, heaven's unfathomable blue ;
> And from whose rocky turrets, battled high,
> Prospect immense spread out on all sides round,
> Lost now between the welkin and the main,
> Now walled with hills that slept above the storm.

Few poets have attained to such rapturous expression with all heaven and its untold host and glories before them in visionary prospect ; it is a " fine frenzy" indeed that can dream thus of this earthly paradise, and may well shame all who set limits to the land of promise almost as though it were an island of the Atlantic.

We have nineteen psalms and hymns by MONTGOMERY, page 45, but unexpectedly his, like too many other spiritual songs, evince the accustomed deficiency in imagination.

The Lord's coming down to his chosen people he compares to the descent of "showers" on the earth, and the attendant fruition. But there is little force or ingenuity in adding—

> Arabia's desert-ranger
>   To Him shall bow the knee ;
> The Ethiopian stranger
>   His glory come to see.

He makes a fanciful application of the negative, or non-natural, in comparing "the sun" to "a spark of fire," for, being but a *spark* what untold millions of millions must be beyond its remotest ken! And what indeed, we may ask, is man, or the mote in the sunbeam of the world which he now inhabits? Scarcely the shadow of a shade.

HURN's hymn, page 48, "There is a river deep and broad," is sunny with endless day, refreshing with its "crystal stream," and promising in "life and health."

We find more satisfactory examples in BOWDLER's hymns, page 49, particularly the one, "When starting from the shades of night," which has been already fully noticed for its peculiar excellencies. It contains the fine personification—

> The Sun arrayed his limbs in light,
>   And Earth her virgin beauty drest.

All join in Nature's transport of song—

> And shouted every morning star.

The pealing chorus of unbounded adoration—

> Roll'd through the dark blue depths above.

Amidst the universal rapture can man be silent? He—

> For whom the bright creation rose ;
> For whom the fires of morning shine,
>   And eve's still lamps, that woo repose ?

It is, however, not in portions alone, but as a whole that we consider this to be a highly finished and masterly production, full to repletion of fire, spirit, and energy, yet not in the least overstrained.

The hymn, page 52, "There is a pure and tranquil wave," a commencement which of itself is one of promise, has several happy touches. The heavenly streams are supposed to visit " this desert world," and to refresh the faint " Pilgrim," in sight of " the Tree of Life." This suggests—

> It may be that the breath of love
> Some leaves on their pure tide have driven,
> Which passing from the shores above,
> Have floated down from Heaven.

How superior are such thoughts and expressions to the common dry-as-dust style of too many of our well-intentioned but unimpassioned hymnists.

RICKARDS is chastely descriptive in his hymn, page 53, " Bright is the day when Christ was born," which concludes with the verse :—

> Inspired with hope and holy thought,
> Fancy is on the wing ;
> It seems as to my ear is brought
> Those voices carolling.

Among fourteen hymns by Bishop HEBER, page 54, we have only to notice one line in his " Brightest and best of the sons of the morning !" praying for guidance to " where our infant Redeemer is laid !"—

> Cold on his cradle the dew-drops are shining."

The style reminds us of Moore's melodies ; but how differently would he have treated this and other hymns ; and that too without in the slightest degree overstepping the strictest bounds prescribed by the sacredness and solemnity of their subjects. Another of Heber's poems commences, " From Greenland's icy mountains," and desires the spread of the " Messiah's name :"—

> Waft, waft, ye winds, His story,
>   And you, ye waters, roll,
> Till, like a sea of glory,
>   It spreads from pole to pole.

This is certainly not making the most of the opportunity, and the figures presented to the mind in the trilling of such a song, jubilant with the desire for the widespreading of the Gospel.

In his hymn, " O King of earth, and air, and sea !" his imagination carries him to notice the universal cry for protecting care, not to " hungry ravens" alone, but likewise to

> —— the scaly tribes, that sweep
> The bosom of the boundless deep.

Another hymn, *The Call*, has the couplet :—

> The winds are howling o'er the deep,
>   Each wave a watery hill.

The last of this selection, addressed to *Hope*, is also characterized by several pleasing figures ; the earth —

> With garlands gay of various green.

To a common observer of Nature, green is green, while the truly poetical and artistic observer finds greens of every variety of shade, from the almost white or yellow to that which approaches black. We see in the " greens" of Nature one simple but strikingly illustrative instance of Nature's boundless variety ; and, in this instance, not in colour alone, but in form, size, texture, and every conceivable attribute of vegetable production. But still there is a

limit; Nature has reserved its green for other objects than
for its full-blown flowers and blossoms; and it is only occasionally that we observe a pale apple-green sky.

We have now arrived at the hymns of that eminent
sacred poet, KEBLE, but the specimens are few and insufficient, being, indeed, partly incomplete; in a separate
essay, however, we shall endeavour to repair this deficiency.
Adopting the idea of Nature being " a book," he suggests
that " the works of God" are " pages" in that book. The
Moon and the Church are each represented as borrowing
light " of its sun." The saints are " like stars" around
the Saviour's throne; the saints on earth—

> Like trees they stand, whom God has given,
> Our Eden's happy birth.

Then it follows that—

> Faith is their fix'd unswerving root,
> Hope their unfading flower;
> Fair deeds of charity their fruit,
> The glory of their bower.

He is very happy in expressing himself in the couplet—

> But in the gentler breeze we find
> Thy Spirit's viewless way.

LYTE, page 64, gives bold illustrations of fearlessness in
remaining calm " though earth be moved," and although
even hills be " in ocean hurled," for it requires superhuman
strength of mind to remain stoical amid the commotion
and upheavings of an earthquake.

The unchangeable Deity is represented as—

> A glorious Sun, that wanes not nor declines;
> Above the clouds and storms He walks serene.

The astronomical theory that our sun is the centre only

of our own system, but dependent on another centre, greater, and possibly more luminous, in a system of which we form but a small part, appears to be the nearest approach to the idea of such a sun as that which the poet may have had in his mind when he penned the foregoing couplet. Herein we reach the truly sublime without the slightest chance of failure.

His hymn, " Abide with me! fast falls the even-tide," commences in a strain which does not disappoint us; the approach of death is finely expressed :—

> Heaven's morning breaks, and earth's vain shadows flee.

We might quote MONSELL's hymn on page 67 entire, " The spring-tide hour," but shall only refer to it; it is full of instances of rural felicity to express that all rejoice :—

> But this poor heart
> Bears not its part,
> In it there is no Spring.

The contrast thus presented is exceedingly appropriate and picturesque.

" Morning lifts her dewy veil," commences a hymn, page 68, by WILLIAMS, in which he sings that,—

> When from the Eternal's hand
> The earth in beauty stood,
> Deck'd in light at His command,
> He saw, and called it good.

This is exceedingly graphic generalization; we see the glorious orb at a glance, and vouch for the verdict passed.

Another of his hymns illustrates " trust in God," by similar trust on the part of " the child," and " the bird;" the latter :—

> —— has no store, he sows no seed ;
> Yet sings aloud, and doth not heed ;

> By flowing stream or grassy mead,
>   He sings to shame
> Men, who forget, in fear of need,
>   A father's Name.

If this specimen were characteristic of our sacred melodies generally, we doubt not they would have a far greater popularity than they have ever yet enjoyed.

The hymns by GURNEY, page 69, present more than usual variety in thought and expression. The Creator's goodness is variously exemplified " in earth and sky :"—

> From ocean-depths and spreading wood.

This is very noble generalization. Then follow " the sun" that " pours his golden flood ;" and " Night's sparkling hosts." Nor does he omit the " merry birds"—

> And balmy air and falling rain.

The " rushing breeze" too has a word of thanksgiving; as also—

> The hills that have for ages stood,
> The echoing sky, and roaring sea.

This is all in good keeping, and possesses much that is truly grand—

> And man, in louder notes of praise,
> Should sing for joy that God is good.

We thus see by what accessories a song of this nature, which in other hands would appear barren, cold, and unimpassioned, acquires beauty, strength, and vitality.

Referring to the *Resurrection*, appropriate allusions are made to seed sowing and spring ; then—

> Onward as the Seasons move,
> Leaves and blossoms deck the grove.

A psalm by GRANT, page 71, has several impressive lines; as—

> Whose robe is the light,
> Whose canopy space.

This is a version of the 104th Psalm, "Who coverest thyself with light as with a garment: who stretchest out the heavens like a curtain." The poet has judiciously substituted "space" for "the heavens;" the latter we are apt to conceive as referring to our own limited atmosphere; whereas "space" is limitless, for who can conceive the possibility of limit to infinite space, boundless beyond the possibility of having any barrier? "His chariots"—

> Deep thunder-clouds form,
> And dark is His path
> On the wings of the storm.

The "bountiful care" of the Lord—

> It breathes in the air,
>   It shines in the light !
> It streams from the hills,
>   It descends to the plain.

A hymn to *Joy* by NOEL, page 73, presents us with only two lines :—

> And every moment still doth bring
> Thy blessings on its loaded wing.

Another by ANSTICE, page 74, has the couplet :—

> Thou, whose genial dews distil
>   On the lowliest weed that grows.

The negative style of NEALE's hymn of universal praise, page 77, affords scope in its treatment for some display of imagination and fancy, although used with studied brevity; thus :—

> The planets glittering on their heavenly way,
> The shifting constellations,—

are lines possessing much sublimity of conception. And beautiful are—

> Ye groves that wave in spring,
> And glorious forests——

Next we find the feathered tribe, " the birds with painted plumage gay." But it seems a curious anomaly in Nature that the choicest songsters in the grove are birds of plainest plumage ; and we trace something assimilating to this fact in the circumstance that not the gayest and gaudiest blossoms present us with the finest fruits, but that, on the contrary, they are generally, as compared to the wide field of floral beauty, simple almost to insignificance.

A hymn by HUNT, page 77, treating of *Creation*, represents the Almighty by observing—

> He holds the oceans in His hand,
> And mighty mountains weighs.

This is truly sublime, without the slightest turgidity. It is a grand figure, simply and sensibly expressed, incapable of offending the most fastidious taste. The stars, the poet fancifully considers, " seemed creation's thousand eyes." The newly created world is seen in all the luxury of spring, while flowers, trees, and meadows—

> Adorned her youthful breast,
> Hung out in boundless space,
> Amid the ocean's cool embrace.

The constant and natural effort of every poet, as in the foregoing instance, is to soar amid remote realms of light and glory, looking down on all below and all around with sublime dignity. But these intellectual flights are almost as difficult of realization as are the oft-tried physical efforts to outvie the flight of birds. Man is wedded and bound to earth to a degree almost beyond belief. His thoughts are trammelled by what he knows at home, and his home-thoughts, as we have already observed, travel with him even heavenward. This struggle of the imagination to rise superior to mundane affairs and associations affects equally the painter with the poet; and thus it is that while most artists would require an acre of canvas to depict a sublime scene, a really highly gifted genius would accomplish more on a single square foot. This gift of realizing extended mental vision is a distinguished characteristic of every great poet.

Evanescence is a favourite theme with nearly all poets, and particularly concerns all who dwell on sacred subjects. ALEXANDER, page 79, tastefully pictures to us—

> The roseate hues of early dawn,
> The brightness of the day,
> The crimson of the sunset sky,
> How fast they fade away !

We almost fancy we are perusing some poem by Keble, the style is so like his, indeed, his manner may have influenced in some degree the composition of this hymn.

LYNCH is especially deserving of notice for what appears to be quite original in its application, page 80, when in his hymn, " Gracious Spirit, dwell with me," he employs the figure—

> Shut my heart up like a flower
> At temptation's darksome hour.

Then as to perfect rest, quietude—

> I myself would quiet be,
> Quiet as the growing blade
> Which through earth its way has made.

And noiselessly, yea—

> Silently, like morning light.

Examples such as these cheer like those discoveries that occasionally reward the botanizing traveller on his way through a bleak unpromising champaign country.

Bonar approaches the foregoing strain in his hymn, page 81, "Calm me, my God, and keep me calm :"—

> Calm as the ray of sun or star,
> Which storms assail in vain.

There is a magnificence as well as a striking propriety in such associations with the sublimities of Nature.

We shall conclude with the hymn, pages 82, 83, of a true lover of Nature, and one possessing the will and power to express his love. Davis, addressing *Joy*, thus delightfully expresses himself :—

> Why comes this fragrance on the summer breeze,
> The blended tribute of ten thousand flowers ?

And again :—

> Why bursts such melody from tree and bush,
> The overflowing of each songster's heart ?

We might quote farther but this must suffice. Taken altogether the ground we have traversed is not quite barren, yet we cannot call it fruitful. We may be charged with accepting too much ; but we prefer such a charge to that of omitting the smallest contribution, for it is only by bringing together all we can find that the quality of the whole can be estimated.

5. Human Nature.

It will doubtless excite much surprise that sacred poems like those under notice, affecting man's welfare in his present, and his happiness in a future state of being, should be so slightly impressed with characteristics of human nature itself. But that this is really the case will appear from the poverty of illustration afforded by the entire series of psalms and hymns, although we have selected from them all we can find on this subject.

In poems as in pictures, the history of the Holy Family has perpetuated many lovely sketches of domestic felicity. Father, mother, and child, in a variety of forms and fashions, and variously engaged and domiciliated, crowd on our memory as gathered from books, prints, paintings, and statuary. The hymnist has not been behindhand in producing imitative poems. WITHER's poem, page 8, "Sweet baby, sleep! what ails my dear?" allies modern with ancient affection and solicitude; but while the former has every solace and comfort, the infant Christ on the contrary,—

> The King of Kings, when He was born,
> Had not so much for outward ease.

Forty-two poems by WATTS are strangely enough all but totally deficient in those delineations that tell of sinful man in his motley moods and his various stations in society. There is in this respect a peculiar absence of dramatic effect. It seems strange that this can be true, it looks and sounds so incredible. But so it is. Man is lost in the crowd. We hear of "nations," of "fierceness and rage," and "surliness." We hear of "man," and his "race" generally, and his being "made of clay." He is "happy," or "miserable," or "sinful," or "foolish," and "wicked," and "heathenish." We are also told of "men of grace."　　" Fools " live " like brutes," and flourish " like grass," as set forth in the 92nd Psalm.　The general terms " Sinner," or the " Christian," preclude all distinctness; *man* is a continual *we* and *he ;* it matters not whether he is Solomon or Lazarus ; wealth, wisdom, and station make no modifications, call forth no distinctions, and neither greatly raise nor depress the theme.　The interest is not in the relations between man and man, or man and woman, but mankind and heaven, or its dread reverse of deathless doom.

We pass without remark no less than twelve poets and their productions, to notice Mrs. BARBAULD's hymn, page 35, " Awake, my soul! lift up thine eyes," a warning against a host of spiritual foes, leading necessarily to sketchy touches of human nature.　There is " great danger," followed by " Pleasure's silken banners," led on by " rebellious passions," treading a path beset with " perils and snares,"—

But most, the traitor heart.

Against these " the Man of Calvary," with armour and shield, is to wage valiant warfare, defiant of sin and death.

No less than eight other hymn-writers escape our observations from the same dearth of human interest in their compositions, which are intended more for congregational singing than closet meditation, and are not therefore addressed to, nor do they specially single out prince or peasant, the good or the bad steward, the bountiful, merciful or miserly man, the soldier, murderer, thief, liar, or any dangerous member of society.　The human family is good or bad, and there are no degrees of distinc-

tion between saints and sinners that demand selection.
It is this absolute generalization that occasions the uni-
formity especially observable in hymns, and which tend
in a great measure, to enfeeble them in the estimation of
those who delight in graphic characteristic sketches of the
male and female character, in all their diversities of situa-
tion and modes of thought and action.

HENRY MOORE, in his hymn, page 47, " Our life is but
an idle play," taking this line for his text, proceeds to
note,—

> We laugh and sport our hours away ;

meanwhile " beauty fades," youth sickens, pleasures have
their sunshine and gloom, " wealth, pomp, and honour,"
are admired, all our schemes are but dreams ; but beyond
this sublunary scene all is blooming and divine, boundless
in wealth, and endless in glory.

Dr. NEWMAN, addressing *Patience,* page 63, and pleading
for Divine assistance, describes the applicant's early
state :—

> I loved the garish day, and spite of fears,
> Pride ruled my will.   *   *   *

LYTE, page 64, simply declares,—

> Thou on my head in early youth didst smile,
> —— though rebellious and perverse meanwhile.

GRANT, page 72, is not more diffuse, all we obtain of a
personal character is :—

> When gathering clouds around I view,
> And days are dark and friends are few.

The anonymous poet of 1853, reflectively observes :—

> Look back on youth's gay visions,
> When life one glory seem'd.
> .   .   .   .
> Recall the hours of anguish.

And lastly, we have the remarks of FORD, page 81, on mankind generally, and are required to see :—

> How worldlings labour for the meat
> That perishes and comes to nought.

So far and no farther do we find Human Nature in these hymns presented to our observation as being individual, or characteristic of classes of the human family at large.	In short, hymns are not sacred dramas.

6. RELIGIOUS, MORAL, MEDITATIVE EXPRESSIONS OF SENTIMENT AND FEELING.

The Poems of GEORGE HERBERT, page 7, although occasionally injured by the admission of mean images and fantastical expressions, have always been the delight of those readers who can appreciate noble thoughts proceeding from a pure mind.	They have circulated by tens of thousands, and their popularity rather increases than diminishes as years roll on.	Among those of his compositions which are most free from blemish, his hymn, " Let all the world in every corner sing," maintains the same tone throughout; and this sustained spirit is still more observable in, " O day, most calm, most bright," a charming hymn, some few lines excepted, as for example his uncouth allusion :—

> That as each beast his manger knows,
> Man might not of his fodder miss.

AUSTIN appeals to his soul to mark how everything strives to serve his Maker, page 9,—

> Nature's chief and sweetest quire,
> Him with cheerful notes admire.

And he commends his " sluggish heart," to observe and be instructed by the " birds, springs, and flowers."

Baxter's hymn, page 10, "Now it belongs not to my care," illustrating "Thy will be done," is composed in a very meditative and prayerful tone. He inquires,—

> For, if Thy work on earth be sweet,
> What will Thy glory be ?

Bishop Ken's poem to *Morning*, page 11, rich in many beauties, is a luminous example of the style under consideration, as are also his *Midnight*, and his *Evening Hymn*.

Dr. Watts's poems afford abundant specimens of all styles and classes of spiritual songs, although among those before us, page 12, such as are associated with Nature-Study occur rather by accident than otherwise. "Before Jehovah's awful throne;" the 65th Psalm, "On God the race of man depends;" "I sing th' almighty power of God;" his 92nd Psalm; also, "Come, we that love the Lord;" and others on pages 17 to 20 are all equally prominent for either their strikingly religious, meditative, or didactic character. No preceding Christian Poet surpasses him for variety, and solid, sound good sense, free from all the narrowness, harshness, and bigotry of a sour sectarianism. He "would be measured by his soul," and it is to his noble Christian spirit, combined with high intellectual attainments, that we are to attribute the elevated tone and generous sentiments of most of his psalms, hymns and other poems. He is particularly effective in expressing Almighty might, power, and goodness. At page 13, is the couplet,—

> On Israel's God ; He made the sky,
> And earth and seas with all their train.

He calms "the noisy tempests," he appeases "whole kingdoms," at his will the "mountains" are established,

" comets blaze," the " sun " rises and sets ; " seasons and times " obey Him, and he supplies the earth with fruitful showers, causing deserts and valleys to flourish.

SIMON BROWNE, page 20, wrote several hymns which are of a solemn and meditative character.

ADDISON'S muse, page 21, could not be otherwise than nobly abstracted, soaring aloft, communing with those bright intelligences, or whatever they are, for—
<blockquote>In reason's ear they all rejoice,</blockquote>
and picturing to our minds an infinity of bespangled firmament, carrying on an interchange of spiritual communications between our earth and its satellite.

Equally enchanting are his poem, " When all thy mercies, O my God," and his Psalm, " The Lord my pasture shall prepare."   How solemn too, is his prayer, " When rising from the bed of death."

The hymns of CHARLES WESLEY, from which we have had to quote for other characteristics, are not remarkable in the class which now claims our attention. His hymn, page 26, " Christ, my hidden Life appears," declares that Christ's " comfortable voice" is—
<blockquote>Never in the whirlwind found,
Or where earthquakes rock the place,</blockquote>
—the whisper of His grace being at all times " still and silent."   Although we have carefully examined the twenty-six poems by him, contained in this collection, we have been unable to trace any more intimate connection between the subjects of them and Nature than is here given ; and as a matter of course it is only where some such association shows itself that our present remarks apply. This partial view is, therefore, so far disadvantageous to this exceedingly worthy and decidedly eminent clergyman and hymn writer.

SEAGRAVE, page 28, abandons "riches" and a "flattering world," to explore heavenly regions. DR. DODDRIDGE has a pleasing hymn to *Night*, page 29, "tired with glaring vanities," which is thoroughly reflective throughout; and he is extremely eloquent on *Seed Time and Harvest*, to which he pays "cheerful homage." His hymn, "Awake, ye saints," is short and mellifluous. OLIVERS' hymn of twelve verses, "The God of Abraham praise," is a truly solemn spiritual song, giving "thanks to God on high."

ANNE STEELE's hymn, page 33, "When I survey life's varied scene," is a metrical version of the prayer, "Lord, teach me to adore Thy hand," composed in the spirit of fervent solicitude for Divine help throughout until life has "its happy end." Her poem on *Creation** is, however, a highly superior composition to these.

---

* Her hymn *On Creation and Providence*, is not included in this series; it consists of fourteen verses, of which the following are the second and third:—

> Where'er I turn my gazing eyes,
>   Thy radiant footsteps shine;
> Ten thousand pleasing wonders rise,
>   And speak their source divine.
>
> The living tribes of countless forms,
>   In earth, and sea, and air;
> The meanest flies, the smallest worms,
>   Almighty power declare.

The fifth and sixth verses run:—

> The meads array'd in smiling green,
>   With wholesome herbage crown'd;
> The fields with corn, a richer scene,
>   Spread thy full bounties round.
>
> The fruitful tree, the blooming flower,
>   In varied charms appear;
> Their varied charms display Thy power,
>   Thy goodness all declare.

Morrison, pages 33, 34, dwells on the goodness, greatness, and grandeur of God; who commands the tempests, stills the seas, and whose coming shall be like " the morn,"—

Like morning songs His voice;

yea as " dew " and as " showers on the thirsty ground."

Mrs. Barbauld's song of praise " for the blessings of the field," and all the bounties of spring, page 34, as also her hymn, " Awake, my soul! " are the immediate result of deep religious sentiment and reverent meditation. The latter depicts the weaknesses and foibles of Human Nature, with a well sustained warning of caution against " the traitor in thy heart."

Newton, affirming the Creator's power and might, page 35, alludes to His sovereignty over this and " countless worlds." In Him the sinner finds the shade and shelter of an " Almighty Rock."

The twelve poems by Cowper in this selection, are by no means conspicuous in this department of our strictures, taken in connection with evidences of Nature-Study; which is all the more remarkable, as his very name as a poet reminds the reader of his preference for rural life and scenery. Here we have twelve of his hymns affording only one example of a direct application of Nature to the figurative or any other illustrative enforcement or embellishment of religious or moral sentiments. His poem of the Sower, follows the Scripture text; the hymn, page 37, " Sometimes a light surprises," commends a spirit of con-

---

Concluding with references to the sun, moon, stars and their influences, followed by the creation of man,—

Of reason's light possess'd;

and the creature of God's constant providential care.

stant rejoicing, although vine, or fig, or field should prove unproductive. His splendid hymn, "God moves in a mysterious way," is throughout grand and majestic, winning the hearts and commendations of all sects and parties. But we are in this critique looking for precise language, precise natural objects, precise typical or symbolical applications and uses of the matter and objects of this world, adopted for mental purposes. It is not enough for us, in this Essay, that certain points are implied, are matters of course, are something that no Christian reader can misunderstand; the philologist can only be satisfied by the exact examples themselves; that which is merely inferred but not expressed, will not always suffice as in the present instance, for Nature-Study assumes an actual acquaintance not only with this earth itself, but with all its animate creatures and products, and all their attendant phenomena of life, light, heat, and other characteristics.

GIBBONS, is entirely meditative, in his hymn, page 38, "Thy goodness, Lord;" as are also SKELTON, in his address to *The Creator*, page 39; and FANCH and TURNER, page 41, on *Christ Ascended*. TOPLADY, although the author of several long pieces, is not conspicuous in the adoption of figures derived from universal Nature; these appear slightly in his hymn, "I saw, and lo! a countless throng." In his melancholy, he sees clouds and vapours rise from the valley, "and hide the hill of Sion" from his view.

KELLY, page 43, has several excellent hymns of this class, particularly, "Lo! He comes!" and, "We're bound for yonder land," although his language is not quite so definite as could be desired.

GISBORNE, in a truly meditative mood, gives a type of Paradise, page 45; and MONTGOMERY has several hymns deserving of special notice; as, the 72nd Psalm, page 45, and his hymn, "For ever with the Lord;" but still they do not fully illustrate our subject. HENRY MOORE affords a better example, page 47, in his hymn to *Hope*, which is largely imbued with touches of Human Nature, advising us to soar "Above the thoughtless crowd." COLLYER, page 48, is to be commended for his hymn, "Haste, traveller, haste!" containing seven truly spirited verses, warning the supine and negligent sinner, that "the night comes on, thy footsteps stray,—pursue thy way—shelter (gain)—linger not," but still—

> There yet is hope; hear mercy's call.

DR. NEWMAN, in the single hymn by him which we have to notice, page 63, prays:—

> Keep Thou my feet; I do not ask to see
> The distant scene; one step enough for me,
>
> Lead me on,
> O'er moor and fen, o'er crag and torrent, till
> The night is gone.

There is here all the gloom of Dante, and the reader cannot fail to imagine that he has stumbled on a page of the *Inferno*.

LYTE, page 63, has a version of the 8th Psalm, in which occur the lines:—

> When glorious in the mighty sky
> The moon and stars I see,
> O what is man! I wandering cry.

And in the 11th Psalm:—

> Like the sun, His saints shall rise,
> And shine with Him above the skies.

In a hymn, " Jesus, I my cross have taken," occurs :—

> Storms may howl and clouds may gather
> All must work for good to me.

But he makes no further allusion to Nature thoughout 48 lines.   In another hymn he reflects :—

> Change and decay in all around I see.

We have only one hymn, page 65, by WORDSWORTH, to remark upon, and that only for one line ; after alluding to the sun, which cannot " halt or go astray," he remarks :—

> But our immortal spirits may.

This poet was so observant of Nature through the period of a long life that it becomes us to study almost every word and stanza he wrote. We have already, however, ex-pressed our doubts whether he had arrived at any method in his study ; or whether, as seems most likely, he took Nature as occasion presented, and his own temperament suited with times and seasons. One pictures him as a dreamy student, a wanderer among mountains, moors, and streams, amidst sunshine, showers, and mists, at all seasons ; and courting even the wildest features of wintry hail, snow, and storm ; observing the mildest and wildest appearances of Nature, and all to which it gives birth in animal and vege-table creation ; but specially man in all his relations and concerns in this life. What Wordsworth saw he describes, and he is throughout, the artist, depicting every possible phase of Nature, within the reach of his personal knowledge. But we cannot see that he has attempted anything beyond that can enrich our language with any new figures of speech, any similes, proverbs, metaphors, or symbolical expressions of any kind whatever. But in poetry he is the undoubted pioneer in Nature-Study by giving an importance to it that was previously wanting; although he confined himself only to a branch of the subject, without attempting to form an entire system, by which he might not only have vied with Nature in its own beautiful and wonderful variety, but also have shown how this very peculiarity may be taken advantage of for the purposes of poetry and eloquence, in symbolical and metaphorical forms of composition and delivery.

CHANDLER, in his poetical address to *Morning*, page 67, energetically urges:—

> Let meekness be our morning ray;
> And faithful love our noonday light;
> And hope our sunset calm and bright!

ISAAC WILLIAMS, illustrates, page 68, from the acts of a child, and the singing of a bird—"trust in God." The latter, he says:—

>   sings to shame
> Men, who forget, in fear of need,
>   A father's name.
> The heart that trusts for ever sings,
> And feels as light as it had wings;
> A well of peace within it springs;
>   Come good or ill.

GURNEY, page 69, in his hymn, "Yes, God is good," throughout the universe, and through all His creatures—

> Yes, God is good, all Nature says,
>   By God's own hand, with speech endued;
> And man, in louder notes of praise,
>   Should sing for joy, that God is good.

Seed-time occasions the reflection:—

> Low these goodly frames must lie,
> And all our pomp and glory die;
>
> Lord, from Nature's gloomy night
> Turn me to the Gospel light.

The "varying seasons" in like manner suggest :—

> New every year
> Thy gifts appear ;
> New praises from our lips shall sound.

GRANT, in a very pleasing hymn, page 71, "O worship the King," commences :—

> O tell of His might,
> O sing of His grace,
> Whose robe is the light.

The remaining verses express the Almighty's majesty, power, and "bountiful care."

Grant's version of the 19th Psalm has :—

> The heart, in sensual fetters bound,
> And barren as the wintry ground,
> Confesses, Lord, Thy quickening ray ;

and in the last verse :—

> Unmov'd amid the wreck of spheres,
> Thy word shall shine in cloudless day,
> When heaven and earth have passed away.

Sorrowing over a deceased friend's tomb, he cries :—

> Thou, Saviour, mark'st the tears I shed,
> For Thou didst weep o'er Lazarus dead !

NOEL, page 73, in a hymn to *Joy*, reflects that there is neither "a bird"—

> Nor meaner thing, which does not share,
> O God ! in Thy paternal care !

Also that :—

> Each barren crag, each desert rude,
> Holds Thee within its solitude.

And in the fifth verse :—

> And every moment still doth bring
> Thy blessings on its loaded wing ;
> Widely they spread through earth and sky,
> And last to all eternity.

Anstice, alluding to *Harvest*, page 74, sings :—

> So shall Thine angels issue forth ;
> The tares be burnt ; the just of earth,
>
> Be gather'd to their Father's store.

Another hymn on the same subject by Alford, page 75, has the verse :—

> We ourselves are God's own field
> Fruit unto His praise we yield ;
> Wheat and tares together sown,
>
> In the fire the tares to cast,
> But the fruitful ears to store
> In His garner evermore.

Hymns like these afford more scope for effective displays of Nature-Study than hymnists seem disposed to exercise in such compositions ; we find in them a prevailing tameness, from their being all cast in the same mould, as though there were an imperative necessity for an unvarying, dead, dry treatment. Nature-Study happily teaches, not only by positive material objects, but likewise by plain, indisputable and applicable characteristics ; thus, in the present instance we might urge on the student's attention that the beauty and simplicity of Nature is not deteriorated by sunshine, rainbows, or the gay colouring of clouds, plumage, flowers, or the other abundant examples of variety of every conceivable complexion. There is a simplicity devoid of nakedness, and a charm in chastely appropriate ornament ; but barrenness and tastelessness go hand in hand.

An anonymous poet, 1853, author of the hymn, page 79, urges the Christian :

> Rejoice, though storms assail thee ;

as also "when skies are bright," or amid "the gloom of night," and—

> Though wave on wave of sorrow
> Rush on with fearful noise.

Lynch, page 80, in a beautiful hymn, prays for protection—

> At temptation's darksome hour.

His language is exquisitely figurative and appropriate, as we have already shown.

Harriett Parr's address to *Night*, page 80, is a hymn by no means enriched by figurative expressions, and is only noticeable for the following couplets :—

> Keep me through this night of peril,
> Underneath its boundless shade.

And in reference to the Lord's patience—

> None shall measure out Thy patience
> By the span of human thought.

In his hymn, " Praise, O praise our God and King," Sir Henry Baker commences :—

> Praise Him that He made the sun,

and so on for the "moon, rain, grain, crops, and harvest."

Dyce, composed the beautiful hymn to *Joy*, pages 82, 83, the burden of which is to declare, that, " Summer, songsters, streamlet, heavens,"—

> —— Forest, river, lake, rock, hill, and lawn,
>
> All, all declare that God is Love !

A third hymn by the same poet offers comfort to the dying :—

> Shall I fear, O Earth, thy bosom ?
> Shrink and faint to lay me there,
> Whence the fragrant lovely blossom
> Springs to gladden earth and air ?

Also spring " the tree, brook, river, and soft clouds :"—

> All fair things come, whispering ever
> Of the love Divine on high.

If this division of our critique appears short, considering that all hymns have a religious and moral tendency,
it must be remembered that we can only quote such
as are associated with Nature ;   and although this
character might be easily and happily communicated to
all hymns, it is almost surprising how much more general
it has been to prefer associations with *Art*, using that
term in the wide sense in which we claim to apply it in
treating of Nature-Study. As this has never hitherto
been remarked, much less ascertained and demonstrated
as has been done in this Essay; we may expect that future
poets will avail themselves of the obvious improvement
which consequently suggests itself to every ingenious and
reflective mind imbued with sensibility to the grace and
grandeur of Nature.

7. Negative Views of Nature.

Most of the sublime passages in the Bible, as in
Job, Solomon's Song, the Psalms, Isaiah, Revelation,
&c., afford evidence of the employment of the non-
natural estimates of Nature, such as might justly be called
exaggerations of the boldest kind possible, and not surpassed by the fabled influence of Orpheus' lute. Indeed
the style · is not only a concomitant of the sublime and
solemn, but equally so of fable, satire, and sheer bombast,
under slightly modified treatment. This distinction in the
poetical adaptation of distorted, magnified, and perverted
Nature has never before been noticed, and yet its presence
or absence goes far to mark sensibly distinguishing traits
in the style of poetical compositions ; thus we find it

largely adopted by Shakspeare, less by Milton, and scarcely
at all by Wordsworth, a circumstance in itself sufficiently
remarkable with respect to the latter, to whose muse we
should otherwise have been inclined to ascribe every possible investigation of the great field of widespread Nature,
during a life terminating at a patriarchal age.

Sacred Melody, having Sacred Writ for its source,
abounds less than might be expected with figures of this
character, and adds less from the Orientalist or from surrounding Nature to call forth our eulogy; hence, no
doubt, arises much of that appearance of turgidity and
absence of warm adulation and ecstatic enthusiam for
which other and calmer expressions are substituted by the
Northern muse. Such examples as we can find we shall
now proceed to string together.

WITHER issues a summons to all creatures and inanimate objects, page 7, to sound "God Almighty's praise."
First, "ye worms"—

> Loud aloft your voices strain,

—then marine "beasts and monsters," also "birds," and—

> Clouds, your peals of thunder ring;

likewise "sun and moon," with "bright stars," yea "seas
and floods,"—

> Whistling winds your descants bring.

The Heavenly City is variously pourtrayed. CROSSMAN,
page 9, takes the usual view of negativing all our ordinary
experiences. Just what we possess we shall *not* find there,
"no sun by day"—

> Nor moon by silent night.

We return to Creation, in a hymn by AUSTIN, page 9, demanding universal praise from all animate and inanimate creation. The groves, the streams, and the very flowers unite in varied praise, while the latter—

> Smell more sweet, and look more gay.

MASON, page 10, rather suggests than describes Paradise, with its stream, clear as " crystal stone," and its cordial influences.

BISHOP KEN, in his *Morning* hymn, page 11, makes the usual application, addressing the "heavenly choir"—

> Had I your wings, to Heaven I'd fly.

WATTS has been more successful than most hymnists in deriving sublimity of metaphorical expression from absolute Nature. The external sovereignty of Jehovah, combined with greatness and goodness are drawn with consummate skill, page 13—

> Wide as the world is Thy command ;
>   Vast as eternity Thy love ;
> Firm as a rock Thy truth shall stand,
>   When rolling years shall cease to move.

Compared to these lines, how cold, hard, heavy, and dull appear many others by not less aspiring writers of Christian minstrelsy, well meaning, but tame, vapid versifiers in all they produce, the result of being mere copyists of copyists who, excluding Nature, revel in books, and mistake in believing that good intentions, unaided by appropriate studies, are and must be all sufficient.

Following the language of the 65th Psalm, Watts sings :—

> He walks upon the clouds, and thence
> Doth His enriching drops dispense.

And in the next verse—

> The valleys shout with cheerful voice,
> And neighbouring hills repeat their joys.

His hymn, " Plung'd in a gulf of dark despair," page 15, has a grand idea conveyed in the couplet—

> . . . . . let rocks and hills
> Their lasting silence break.

A request which would seem to require in its fulfilment either an earthquake or a volcanic eruption!

Paradise, " Emmanuel's ground," is more than once sketched by Watts, and always with his wonted ability in such high-wrought imaginings. Here, page 16, allusion is made to its " celestial fruits," " heavenly fields," and " golden streets." In another draught it is represented as " a land of pure delight," with "infinite day," and boundless " pleasures," " everlasting springs," non-"withering flowers," green " fields," and "swelling flood."

Watts's hymn, in eighteen verses, ."Go, worship at Immanuel's feet," is suggestive of the style of Wither, Quarles, and Herbert, and has several allusions of a negative character while endeavouring to find expression for God's worth, glory, and grace, under the several inquiries, " Is He a tree?" a rose, a vine, the head, and so forth, page 18; finally declaring—

> Nor earth, nor seas, nor sun, nor stars,
> Nor heaven, His full resemblance bears.

Our examples of this poet being limited by the specimens before us, we refer to a separate essay on other pieces by him for farther and different illustrations of this among his other styles of interweaving Nature with his sacred poetry.

Simon Browne, in a hymn commemorating the Sabbath, allegorically alludes to the soul's elevation in prayer, page 21, and thus he would—

> On wings of strong devotion rise,
> Pass every cloud, pass all the skies,
>   And leave beneath Thy feet the stars.

This is very nobly and gracefully expressed, producing an effect of sublimity seldom surpassed.

Addison's version of the 19th Psalm, page 22, sets before us the Moon relating to the planets and the stars her "wondrous tale," while in their turn they—

> Confirm the tidings as they roll.

And the mystery of this is explained, because—

> In reason's ear they all rejoice.

The whole piece is a gem of most dignified and harmonious melody.

There are many common-place approaches to the Negative style, scarcely worth noticing, such as Seagrave's allusion, page 28, to planetary decay, and—

> Time shall soon this earth remove.

It is in the very nature of Negative applications that the poet should be in constant danger of making a false step, and so approaching, if not wholly sinking into either bathos or bombast. Dr. Doddridge, page 29, has doubtfully expressed himself, we think, in depicting the future :—

> Ye stars are but the shining dust
>   Of my divine abode.

They surely deserve a worthier estimate of the object of their creation !

His view of Heaven, page 31, presents, "No rude alarms—no cares—no midnight—no clouded sun"—

> But sacred, high, eternal noon.

His hymn, "Let Jacob to his Maker sing," has negatives relating to passing through the fire "unburnt," the flames are described as "refreshing," and the "bonds" alone are burnt.

OLIVER sings in Addisonian strains, page 32, of "listening spheres" which "sing in songs that never end."

ANNE STEELE treats of Heaven, page 33, as a "fair distant land," a stranger to "sickness, grief, or cloud," with, in lieu thereof, "immortal bloom" and constant light.

COWPER stands prominent in this department for his exquisite hymn, page 37, "God moves in a mysterious way;" we come upon it among a collection of hymns as an emerald oasis in the desert of such rhymes as are there but too profusely spread.   What but the poet's pen could convey a grander idea of Divine majesty, than the couplet—

> He plants His footsteps in the sea,
> And rides upon the storm.

What concentration of thought! what a conception of the nobility of greatness and Almighty power!

SKELTON has given us, page 39, a remarkable hymn* with respect to its Negative side of Nature;—here, as in our early notice of Wither, we have a response to the call on all Nature to rejoice and praise its Creator, but in far superior language and imagery.   Sun, moon, stars, storms,

---

* There is sufficient similarity between this and Wither's hymn, pages 7, 8, to consider that the latter may have suggested Skelton's poem.

clouds, fish and birds, and insects, animalculæ, and last and least, the race—

> Still less than these, with which
> The stagnant water teems,
> To which, one drop, however small,
> A boundless ocean seems.

The poet has here taken advantage of modern science, and treats of remote planets whose light has not yet—

> Had time to make its way

to our globe, and remote oceanic organizations,

> Beneath the rolling main,

Montgomery, like all other poets similarly engaged, supplies his estimate of a state of future bliss, through the medium of Negative views of our present existence, page 46, therefore we find of the angelic host that,—

> Hunger, thirst, disease unknown,
> On immortal fruits they feed.

And afterwards, in another hymn, he suggests that there is some " blesséd clime "—

> Where life is not a breath,

nor " affection transient," expiring like the sparks that " fly upwards."

In his hymn, " There is a calm for those who weep," he has a rather extravagant attempt at sublimity in the line,—

> The sun is but a spark of fire.

If this is not bombast, it is at all events very like it, because as proportioned to such a spark, what becomes of the " great globe itself," and " all that it inherit?"

Hurn has a hymn of six verses, page 48, from which we

have selected one for the object of this essay, but this specimen displays much excellence in execution; it gives a sketch of Paradise, with its clear stream, dispensing "life and health." The fourth and sixth verses run thus :—

> Along the shores, angelic bands
>   Watch every moving wave;
> With holy joy their breast expands,
>   When men the waters crave.
>
>   .   .   .   .
>
> Flow on, sweet Stream, more largely flow,
>   The earth with glory fill;
> Flow on, till all the Saviour know,
>   And all obey His will.

Only a deeply meditative and imaginative mind, largely imbued with true religious feeling could write thus. · But as affecting Nature-Study, these stanzas have nothing in them to which we can direct the student's attention, beyond the evidence which they afford of a transfusion of Nature's influences into the very thoughts and expressions employed by the poet. They might have been written, we may surmise, on a sunny day in some secluded and almost rural nook, overlooking the sea coast, without a single thought about ancient, or classic, or musty gothic literature; the poet's only book being Nature's self, the poet's eye and mind the while glancing from this earthly to a heavenly habitation.

Bowdler, in his very spirited hymn, page 49, "Sing to the Lord with cheerful voice," calls for an universal concert in praise of the Creator, and most by Man—

> For whom the bright creation rose;
> For whom the fires of morning shine,
> And eve's still lamps, that woo repose.

And this expression of joy and thanksgiving is to continue,—

> Long as yon glittering arch shall bend,
>   Long as yon orbs in glory roll,
> Long as the streams of life descend,
>   To cheer with hope the fainting soul.

There is nothing here of the dull, dry, ascetic tone which many persons conceive to be a necessary consequence of such themes, but which we ascribe to native inability, and lifelessness of imagination.

In the same hymn occurs the following example of personification :—

> The Sun arrayed his limbs in light,
>   And Earth her virgin beauty drest.

This is in every way noble and magnificent, a flight beyond the ordinary stretch of modern naturalistic sacred poetry. All creation is represented here as animate,—

> Thy praise transported Nature sung,
>
> And shouted every morning star.

Such language calls forth an irresistible thrill of surprise and delight.

In treating of the Godhead the poet calls into exercise his highest aspirations, bounded alone by the confines of human thought :—

> For Him no weary hours assail,
> Nor evening darkness spreads her veil
> O'er His eternal day.

To Him the night is clear as the day, and thousands of years are less than a moment of time.

As we devote an essay to the poems of KEBLE, we shall only remark here, that his sacred pieces are replete with apposite allusions to Nature which enforce, illustrate, and ornament whatever he advances; we have here, page 56, such examples, as—

> The saints, like stars, around His seat,
> Perform their courses still.

The "saints on earth,"—

> Like trees they stand, whom God has given,
> Our Eden's happy birth.

And they flourish with,—

> Hope their unfading flower;
> Fair deeds of charity, their fruit.

In his version of the 46th Psalm, LYTE, page 64, employs the figures :—

> We will not fear, though earth be moved,
> And hills in ocean hurled.

Nor shall "comfort" cease, though—

> The waves may roar, the mountains shake.

In this narrative of mundane commotions we find there is the mixed character of the natural with the non-natural. But we must seek in the text for the true source of the poet's inspiration :—"Therefore will not we fear, though the earth be removed, and though the mountains be carried into the midst of the sea."

In a hymn he declares of the Almighty :—

> ———— In Him no change is seen ;
> A glorious sun, that wanes not nor declines ;
> Above the clouds and storms He walks serene.

GURNEY, represents all Nature as rejoicing, page 69 :—

> Yes, God is good, all Nature says.

All without respect, inanimate as well as animate ; mineral, vegetable, and animal, progressing onwards to "man in louder notes of praise."

The 19th Psalm—"The heavens declare the glory of God, and the firmament showeth his handywork. Day unto day uttereth speech, and night unto night showeth knowledge"—offers a favourite theme for poetic treatment. GRANT, page 72, would seem to emulate Addison, but with too evident an approximation not only to his figures, but also to his precise language :—

> Almighty Lord, the sun shall fail,
> The moon forget her nightly tale.

These and other lines merely reverse the style of address. One represents the moon rehearsing her tale, the other her forgetfulness of it.

The 148th Psalm, affords T. B. BROWNE, page 74, ample latitude for negative figures from Nature. Heaven, earth, and all things on and under the earth, and its waters are exuberantly jubilant :—

> Praise Him, clouds and vapours, snow, and hail, and fire,
> Stormy wind, fulfilling only His desire.

But throughout the poet limits himself to the precise features of his text, generalizing where others might have been disposed to enter into particular descriptions.

Very similar is a hymn, page 77, by NEALE, all Creation being called on to—

> Exalt their great Creator's praise, and say Alleluia !

Nor are " planets, clouds, winds, thunders, floods, storm, or frost," exempt.

In his hymn, " Jerusalem the golden," we learn of Paradise :—

> The pastures of the blessèd,
> Are decked in glorious sheen.

HUNT, page 78, treating of Creation, declares that the glories of Jehovah's name—

> The lightning, floods, and hail proclaim.

The hymn concludes : —

> But this fair world shall die.

> Soon shall the day be o'er
> Of yonder brilliant sun.
>
> .   .   .   .   .
> .   .   .   all soon,
> Shall fade the stars, and you pale moon.

This specimen closes our examples in this particular class, and it will no doubt be a matter of general surprise that they are so few and so deficient in originality of conception. It is a common piece of advice to us in every important endeavour to aim high, as the most likely means to approach success. But here we discover no such ambitious aims.

Let us turn to such a poet as Pollok to illustrate our meaning, and show what can be wrought out where will and power unite. He describes the war of elements :—

> Overhead,
> And all around, wind warred with wind, storm howled
> To storm, and lightning forkèd lightning crossed,
> And thunder answered thunder, muttering sounds
> Of sullen wrath ; . . . .

Showing that "natural or mental wealth" alone neither delighted God, nor secured peace ; and that it was impossible—

> With aught but moral excellence, truth and love,
> To satisfy and fill the immortal soul !
> Attempt, vain inconceivably ! attempt,
> To satisfy the Ocean with a drop,
> To marry Immortality with Death,
> And with the unsubstantial Shade of Time,
> To fill the embrace of all Eternity !

This style indicates true largeness of mind and mighty expressive power. Where do we find anything approaching this strain throughout the entire volume of " The Book of Praise" ? Even Sternhold was fired with greater enthusiasm when he wrote the not unexceptionable verses :—

> The Lord descended from above,
> And bowed the heavens high,
> And underneath His feet He cast
> The darkness of the sky.
>
> On cherubs and on cherubims
> Full royally He rode,
> And on the wings of mighty winds
> Came flying all abroad.

POPE, too, in a similar style, has :—

> Not God alone in the still calm we find,
> He mounts the storm and rides upon the wind.

But the Psalms, and many portions of the Sacred Writings, abound with figures which owe their sublimity to Negative views of Nature. Indeed, it is only by such aid that the poet can represent the objects of sense, so as to place them before the mind's eye, and bring them (even then somewhat mistily) before the mental vision of the illiterate millions. The poet who does not avail himself of this advantage of magnifying to majestic proportions whatever he desires to render specially prominent is like a wanderer through mines of wealth, who nevertheless returns home in a state of abject penury. The poet has all imaginable treasures within his reach, and it rests entirely with himself to labour as one that sees no task in his labour, or to fall asleep and slumber on with listless satisfaction while others reap the treasures of which he hopelessly neglects to avail himself. What others have done he might effect or approach ; but what is not in the soul can never reach the surface. Except only in poetry, humility is highly commendable ; in that walk of literature it can only mean being satisfied with mediocrity, with not falling below predecessors, and implies the total absence of ambition to excel others in giving satisfaction to the students of verse.

But let it not be supposed that we are advocating the obtrusion of figures, although drawn from Nature, without inculcating strict attention to propriety. Forced metaphors and so-called "flowery language" are our aversion; they merely serve to display a total absence of taste and judgment, and render a poem which might be tolerable under more simple and judicious treatment, vulgar, offensive, and irritating. Wherever the proper figure is required, the great secret for its development is to apply to it the artlessness and beauty or sublimity of universal Nature, in a manner suitable to its express department.

CONCLUSION.—We have thus shown by examples how a knowledge of NATURE-STUDY may be applied to the critical examination, not only of sacred poetry, but poetry of every description. We have chosen the present branch, as the least promising and least understood, to prove the advantage of a study that can find so much matter among poems having no express tendency to illustrate Nature. If so much may be done in this line, how much more may be expected from dramatic and other poetry?

NATURE-STUDY has yet to be learnt; it is a novel and untried study, and its various advantages are not so much as suspected. It applies to prose as well as to poetry, especially fiction, as in novels and romances, where word-painting has considerable scope, and where variety of character is a chief ingredient in the narratives. The writer, the reader, and the professional critic are all equally benefited by a knowledge of Nature-Study, as it facilitates composition in that particular ; and when what is written is read with understanding, the pleasure of perusal is greatly enhanced, and fairer criticism must follow as a natural consequence.

So long as Nature-Study was supposed to be restricted to the province of Descriptive Poetry, the poet of Nature could only be considered as an artist allied to the painter, but using a pen instead of a pencil, and words instead of colours. But when the wide range of Nature in literature is thoroughly understood, its study will no longer require argument or apology. It leads to originality and novelty of conception ; without it the poet is wholly dependent on inspiration (whatever that may mean), that something which aids him just when he is least prepared or thinking of the subject. The student of Nature, by means of country rambles and suitable observation of the Universe, can collect illustrations of every conceivable variety, including numbers which have never before been thought of. Instead of twisting and turning what has been said by others a thousand times, into some other mode of expression, he may strike out entirely new ideas He may even chance to become a plagiarist of some poem of Oriental origin, from following the path of Eastern poets at the hallowed shrine of glorious Nature itself. There are Natural Histories — Biblical, classical, and modern. We can detect in a poet from which of these sources he draws his information. Truth or falsehood, if we admit the fable, will serve us for similitudes. It is thus with the Sphinx, the Phœnix, or the Salamander. The natural, or imaginative, object only serves as a picture to impress us, and to imprint some truth on our minds. The similitude proves nothing. *Art* will serve quite as well as *Nature* for precisely the same purpose; and it is a mere matter of taste which we shall choose, but we should recommend Nature as speaking a universal and unchangeable language, appealing to all hearts alike.

Let the reader peruse "The spiritual use of an Orchard or Garden of fruit trees; set forth in divers similitudes between natural and scriptural fruit trees, according to scripture and experience," by Ralph Austen, 1657; reprinted in 1847. The wonderful ductility of Nature, as it may be called, is fully exemplified in this amusing and instructive work; it abounds in examples of similarity without actuality. For instance:—

"There are many wild Fruit-trees in the woods, waste grounds and hedges, that have fair and beautiful fruits to look upon, both for bulk and colour, and yet are very harsh, sour, unpleasant fruits," &c. &c.

This similitude our author considers to shadow forth:—

"That many spiritual fruit trees bring forth fair and specious fruits to observation which yet are unpleasant to the Husbandman."

He makes a hundred observations after this manner, with comments thereon, just as if he had discovered the true interpretation of fruit-trees. This emblematic style of writing is accepted as the unsealing of a great mystery, by those who forget that our language abounds with proverbs and similes quite as recondite, derived solely from manners, customs, habits, food, dress, furniture, and mechanical and other arts with equal truth, justice, and resemblance between them and maxims of thrift, morals, and religion.

NATURE-STUDY, then, opens to us a wide field for exer-

cisc and investigation. If the first published treatise, or
Grammar, on this subject has not been clearly compre-
hended in regard to its scope and object, it is to be hoped
that this critique will afford a good and practical illustration of one at least of its great and important advantages
as applied to the criticism of our Poetical Literature.

ESSAY II.

GEORGE HERBERT,

17TH CENTURY.

And there were, too,—Harp! lift thy voice on high,
And run in rapid numbers o'er the face
Of Nature's scenery,—and there were day
And night, and rising suns and setting suns,
And clouds that seemed like chariots of saints,
By fiery coursers drawn, as brightly hued,
As if the glorious, bushy, golden locks
Of thousand cherubim, had been shorn off,
And on the temples hung of Morn and Even.
And there were moons, and stars, and darkness streaked
With light and voice ; and tempest heard secure,
And there were seasons coming evermore,
And going still, all fair, and always new,
With bloom, and fruit, and fields of hoary grain.

Pollok.

ESSAY II.

ON THE DEFECTIVE STATE OF NATURE-STUDY IN THE 17TH CENTURY, AS EXHIBITED IN THE SACRED POETRY OF GEORGE HERBERT.

The "Sacred Poems and Private Ejaculations," under the general title of *The Temple*, by George Herbert, "late Orator of the University of Cambridge," 1632, have gone through many editions, of which the 12th, dated 1703, is now before us. He was contemporaneous with many poets of distinction, Marlowe, Raleigh, Ben Jonson, Beaumont, Sir H. Wotton, Carew, the Fletchers, Wither, W. Browne, Quarles, Habington, Suckling, Izaak Walton, and others, whose works must have in some measure influenced his genius, although evidently without enriching and refining his taste, or sobering his judgment.

Herbert was not only a man of the most pure and saint-like character, but also a Poet of no mean order, yet in dealing with his poetical effusions for the object of the present work, we feel ourselves under the disadvantage of being reminded at every page more of Quarles' quaintly conceited *Emblems*, than of Nature's handyworks in firmament, field, and flood, they are so overrun with Art, and Art too of the most grotesque features, and the more grotesque because associated with the most serious, solemn and sacred subjects; so that we smile when we ought to be grave, and are often displeased when the direct purpose of the Poet is evidently to convey to the mind important moral truths and religious impressions. In this respect we acknowledge Herbert's shortcomings to be such as belong not to him alone, but to the entire period in which he flourished. Instead of antique simplicity, the age appears to have assumed a species of domestic classicality, if we may so term its strange assemblage of high and low, ornamental and grotesque, in interminable disorder and entanglement. The poet adopted anything and everything indiscriminately that came in his way, without forethought or selection, as it would appear, for in no other way can we account for the discordant admixture of heterogeneous materials, mingled in a single serious metrical composition. The prevailing taste of the period was for oddity of conception and grotesqueness of combination and execution, and the pleasure must have arisen from finding that sense, though partly concealed under rubbish, could nevertheless be brought to light by a slight touch of refinement; thus many a poem, unintelligible if judged by its introduction, might yet possibly terminate unexceptionably. Herbert seems to have inherited many of the excellencies mingled with the weaknesses of the poets of his age. On the latter deficiency we have no desire to dwell, and shall therefore rest satisfied with comparatively few examples, such as his comparing Death to " darkness " and proceeding :—

> Thus in thy Ebony box
> Thou dost enclose us, till the day
> Put our amendment in our way,
> And give new wheels to our disorder'd clocks.

In his third poem on *Affliction* he declares:—

> My thoughts are all à case of knives,
> Wounding my heart
> With scatter'd smart;
> As wat'ring-pots give flowers their lives.

In some lines on *Unkindness*, its reverse is expressed by—

> My friend may spit upon my curious floor.

A poem of thirteen verses on *Misery*, is designed to show that "Man is a foolish thing," and is followed by reflections on "his game, his drink, pollutions, actions, follies, sloth," &c.

> Indeed at first Man was a treasure,
> A box of jewels, shop of rarities,
> A ring, whose posy was, *My Pleasure:*
> He was a garden in a Paradise:
> Glory and grace
> Did crown his heart and face.

We have a strange example of an Anagram, in ten lines, which reads very like trifling with the idea of the "sacred Name" of Jesu being "deeply carved" on the heart, after which the poet tells us that:—

> A great affliction broke the little frame,
> Even all to pieces; which I went to seek:
> And first I found the corner where was J,
> After, where ES, and next where U was graved.

These put together were made out to spell "*I ease you*," and "Jesu."

Herbert's sentiments as a poet, may be partly gathered from some of his own verses. Of *A true Hymn*, he says:—

> The fineness which a Hymn or Psalm affords,
> Is, when the soul unto the lines accords.

And he comes to the conclusion that:—

M

> —— if the Heart be moved,
> Although the verse be somewhat scant,
>   God doth supply the want.
> As when the heart says (sighing to be approved)
> *Oh, could I love !* and stops; God writeth, *Loved.*

It must be in this spirit that at the very *Church-porch* we are met by the request to—

> Hearken unto a Verser, who may chance
> Rhyme thee to good, and make a bait of pleasure :
>   A verse may find him, who a Sermon flies,
>   And turn delight into a Sacrifice.

His whole desire was to please God not man, and never was there a poet less fearing critics than the author of *The Temple.* In the second verse of his *Forerunners,* he makes a clean breast of his determination :—

> So, *Thou art still my God,* be out of fear.
>   He will be pleased with that ditty !
> And if I please him, I write fine and witty.

And commences the verse following, with the line :—

> Farewell, sweet phrases, lovely Metaphors.

Including,—

> Lovely enchanting language, sugar-cane,
> Honey of Roses—

And so truly does he adhere to his purpose that, we lament to say we cannot conclude the perusal of the six verses of this poem without having the reflection forced on our minds that,—

> Tho' foulness mid sunbeams all golden may shine,
> Yet foulness with sunbeams can never entwine. ·

There is an incongruity in the poet's admixture of lofty with debasing thoughts and expressions, which strikes readers of even moderately refined taste and judgment, so that while admitting without reservation that the poet's heart was in the right place, we cannot overlook the many failings in his treatment of the most profoundly solemn and serious subjects ; the high toned anthems sung by his muse at the altar of his Temple being mixed with discordant notes derived from the false and artificial mode of thought of his age.

It is among such unpromising materials that we have to seek for a selection of verses more or less devoted to Nature, and free from such poetical tricks and trifles and artificial imagery as those we have been compelled to notice in passing, for the purpose of giving a just idea in other respects of the peculiarities of these early sacred poems.

Herbert's poem, THE TEMPLE, is divided into *The Church-Porch* and *The Church.* On neglected " education" he very justly remarks, under the first of these titles :—

> Some till their ground, but let weeds choke their son :
> Some mark a partridge, never their child's fashion :
> Some ship them over, and the thing is done.

Of " contentment" he says :—

> For wealth without contentment, climbs a hill,
> To feel those tempests, which fly over ditches.

Of those who contemn " living by rule," he remarks, in a Negative application of Nature :—

> Houses are built by rule, and common-wealths.
> Entice the trusty sun, if that you can,
>   From his Ecliptic line ; beckon the sky.
> Who lives by rule then, keeps good company.

For *Easter* he sings :—

> I got me flowers to strew thy way;
> I got me boughs off many a tree :
> But thou wast up by break of day,
> And brought'st thy sweets along with thee.

> The Sun arising in the East,
> Though he give light, and th' East perfume ;
> If they should offer to contest
> With thy arising, they presume.
>
> Can there be any day but this,
> Though many Suns to shine endeavour ?
> We count three hundred, but we miss :
> There is but one, and that one ever.

The tenth following poem, entitled *Antiphon*, "Let all the world in every corner sing," has been partly quoted, page 7.

His poem on *Employment* supplies the verses :—

> If as a flower doth spread and die,
> Thou wouldst extend me to some good,
> Before I were by frost's extremity
> > Nipt in the bud ;
>
> The sweetness and the praise were thine ;
> But the extension and the room,
> Which in thy garland I should fill, were mine
> > At thy great doom.
>
> .   .   .   .
>
> All things are busy : only I
> Neither bring honey with the bees,
> Nor flowers to make that, nor the husbandry
> > To water these.
>
> I am no link in thy great chain,
> But all my company is as a weed.
> Lord, place me in thy consort ; give one strain
> > To my poor reed.

On the same subject he quaintly observes in another poem :—

> O that I were an Orange-tree,
> > That busy plant !
> Then should I ever laden be,
> > And never want
> Some fruit for him that dresseth me.

Passing over twenty-one poems, we come to that on *Sunday*, "O day most calm, most bright," in eight verses of seven lines each, already noticed at page 7.

Virtue, a poem of four verses, barely escapes being marred by one faulty couplet:—

> Sweet Day, so cool, so calm, so bright,
> The bridal of the earth and sky,
> The dew shall weep thy fall to-night;
>   For thou must die.
>
> Sweet Rose, whose hue angry and brave
> Bids the rash gazer wipe his eye,
> Thy root is ever in its grave,
>   And thou must die.
>
> Sweet Spring, full of sweet days and roses,
> A box where sweets compacted lie,
> My Music shows ye have your closes,
>   And all must die.
>
> Only a sweet and virtuous Soul,
> Like season'd timber, never gives;
> But though the whole world turn to a coal,
>   Then chiefly lives.

The above poem commences very like that on *Sunday*, "O day most calm, most bright!"

The poem on *Man* is less elevated in its style than might have been expected:—

> For man is everything,
> And more : He is a tree, yet bears no fruit;
> A beast, yet is, or should be more :
>
>   .   .   .   .
>
> For us the winds do blow;
> The earth doth rest, heaven move, and fountains flow :
> Nothing we see, but means our good,
> As our *delight*, or as our *treasure :*
>
>   .   .   .   .
>
>
> Oh, mighty love ! Man is one world, and hath
> Another to attend him.

But allusions made to the " house, parrots, cupboard of food, cabinet of pleasure, navigation, drink, meat, and ' so brave a palace,' " necessarily limit the quotable matter.

He sings, addressing *Life :*—

> I made a posie, while the day ran by.
> Here will I smell my remnant out, and tie
>   My life within this band.
> But Time did beckon to the flowers, and they
> By noon most cunningly did steal away,
>   And wither'd in my hand.

Charms and Knots, a collection of couplets concludes, as if imitated from Lucretius, when he notices the deceptive appearance of puddles, that :—

> In shallow waters heav'n doth show :

Herbert, adding, however :—

> But who drinks on, to hell may go.

In a quaintly written piece, consisting of six verses, entitled *The Quip*, the "merry world" is represented as "all in sport to jeer at me :"—

> First, Beauty crept into a Rose ;
> Which when I pluck'd not, Sir, said she,
> Tell me, I pray, whose hands are those ?
> *But thou shalt answer, Lord, for me.*

"Then money came," followed by "brave glory," also "quick wit and conversation," each receiving the same rebuff, in the answer, "I am thine."

On *Business* we have the inquiry and reply :—

> Canst be idle ? canst thou play,
> Foolish soul, who sinn'd to-day?
>
> Rivers run, and springs each one
> Know their home, and get them gone :
> Hast thou tears, or hast thou none ?
>
> If, poor soul, thou hast no tears,
> Would thou hadst no faults or fears !
> Who hath these, those ills forbears.
>
> Winds still work : it is their plot,
> Be the season cold or hot :
> Hast thou sighs, or hast thou not ?

The remainder of this poem is of a more fanciful and artificial turn ; indeed it rarely happens that we meet with one of his poems free from objectionable phrases, lines, or verses of what appears to our present taste mere turgidity and affectation.

In treating of *Providence*, he says :—

> Shall I write,
> And not of Thee, *through whom my fingers bend*
> *To hold my quill?*

And goes on to say, speaking of man :—

> And made him *secretary* of Thy praise.

Negatively alluding to Nature, he proceeds :—

> Beasts fain would sing ; birds ditty to their notes ;
> Trees would be tuning on their native lute
> To thy renown : but all their hands and throats
> Are brought to Man, while they are lame and mute.

Of the thirty-eight stanzas composing this poem two are all we can select, so peculiarly quaint are the thoughts and language throughout, mingling spirit, love, tempests, children, cupboard, meat, flies, seasons, creatures, beef, sheep, herbs, metals, poisons, clothes, rain, hymns ; all of which come in for their share of comment. In the twelfth verse he remarks :—

> Tempests are calm to thee, they know thy hand,
> And hold it fast, as children do their father's,
> Which cry and follow. Thou hast made poor sand
> Check the proud sea, even when it swells and gathers.

We next proceed to a short poem on *Peace* :—

> Sweet Peace, where dost thou dwell ? I humbly crave,
> Let me once know.
> I sought thee in a secret cave,
> And ask'd, if Peace were there.
> A hollow wind did seem to answer, No :
> Go seek elsewhere.

Slight allusions are next made to Nature, but they possess more ingenuity and taste than usual ; first, " a rainbow," then " a garden," thirdly an " old man," followed by the story of a Prince of Salem.

In *Man's Medley*, he treats of man's spiritual welfare thus :—

> Hark how the birds do sing,
> And woods do ring.
> All creatures have their joy, and Man hath his.
> Yet, if we rightly measure,
> Man's joy and pleasure
> Rather hereafter, than in present, is.

We now pass over upwards of thirty pages before we arrive at any poem of a sufficiently distinctive character to connect itself with the object of this essay, but the specimen we then meet with is sufficiently brief and curious to give entire ; it is intended to express sorrow in a sincere Christian spirit, but it will be found difficult to refrain from indulging in a good-humoured smile at its conceits. The subject is *Grief*, thus expressed :—

> O who will give me Tears ? Come, all ye springs,
> Dwell in my head and eyes: come clouds and rain :
> My grief hath need of all the watery things,
> That Nature hath produced. Let every vein
> Suck up a river to supply mine eyes,
> My weary weeping eyes too dry for me,
> Unless they get new conduits, new supplies,
> To bear them out, and with my state agree.
> What are two shallow fords, two little spouts
> Of a less world ? The greater is but small,
> A narrow cupboard for my griefs and doubts,
> Which want provision in the midst of all.
> Verses, ye are too fine a thing, too wise
> For my rough sorrows : cease, be dumb and mute,
> Give up your feet and running to mine eyes,
> And keep your measures for some lover's lute,
> Whose grief allows him music and a rhyme :
> For mine excludes both measure, tune, and time.
> Alas, my God !

His version of the 23rd *Psalm*, " The God of Love my

Shepherd is," in six verses of four lines each, is so unexceptionable that we cannot pass it without notice, although
its only lines connected figuratively with Nature are :—

> He leads me to the tender grass,
> Where I both feed and rest ;
> Then to the streams that gently pass ;
> In both I have the best.

His poem, *The Rose*, has little reference to Nature,
but its versification is much more easy and flowing than
most of the specimens we have had to deal with; for
example :—

> Press me not to take more pleasure
> In this world of sugar'd lies,
> And to use a larger measure
> Than my strict, yet welcome size.
>
> First, there is no pleasure here :
> Colour'd griefs, indeed there are,
> Blushing woes, that look as clear,
> As if they could beauty spare.
>
> Or if such deceits there be,
> Such delights I meant to say ;
> There are no such things to me,
> Who have pass'd my right away.
>
> But I will not much oppose
> Unto what you now advise :
> Only take this gentle Rose,
> And therein my answer lies.

The true poetry of the subject really ends here, for the
concluding four verses introduce us to the Rose as a
medicinal plant; and the ready answer comes, " But I
health, not physic choose."

In a poem on *The Banquet*, or Sacrament, the breaking
of the bread is thus noticed :—

> But as Pomanders and wood
> Still are good,
> Yet being bruised are better scented ;

> God, to show how far his love
>   Could improve,
> Here, as broken, is presented.

Nature, in Herbert's poems, to adopt a common saying, is " conspicuous by its absence." There is so little beyond what is inferential, allusive, and merely verbal, that the little he can make of such scant materials gives no picturesqueness and but indifferently benefits his compositions.

IMAGINATION AND FANCY.

We shall have little to offer beyond what has been already stated in reference to evidences of Nature-Study derivable from these early sacred poems; but they mark an era, all the features of which command our attention. Taste in poetry, as in painting and in fashions, has its changes, regarded in a popular light. Herbert's poetry is replete with a peculiar style of imagination and fancy, and even that which approaches nearest to our sense of correctness and propriety in taste is not always unexceptionably so; nor can we at all times separate the good from that which is indifferent without destroying the sense of some of the couplets or verses. The classical allusion to the lofty old tree being destroyed by tempests that pass harmlessly over lowly shrubs, is *improved* by Herbert, page 163, who compares the want of " contentment" to one who " climbs a hill,"—

> To feel those tempests which fly over ditches.

His piece for *Easter* contains three excellent stanzas beginning :—

> I got me flowers to strew thy way,
> I got me boughs off many a tree :
> But thou wast up by break of day,
> And brought'st thy sweets along with thee.

Employment is another poem, page 164, possessing four most commendable verses, beginning :—

> If as a flower doth spread and die.

On the same subject, in another piece, he declines into wishing—

> O that I were an Orange-tree,

but with abundant godly wishes.

Virtue is depicted in four sweet verses, page 165, commencing :—

> Sweet Day, so cool, so calm, so bright,

the other verses having "sweet Rose—sweet Spring—virtuous soul.' Allied with these pleasant associations, occurs the fanciful line :—

> Thy root is ever in its grave.

Man is the topic of another poem. " He is a tree," also he is " a beast;" yet for him are displayed the heavens, earth, and fountains. He *is*—

> " One World, and hath
> Another to attend him."

He fitly compares *Life* to flowers, page 166 :—

> But Time did beckon to the flowers, and they
> By noon most cunningly did steal away.

We are reminded of Lucretius, whom he probably imitated in the couplet presenting the idea that shallow water on the ground, may yet present to our eyes the heavens above. To drink that water would not be drinking of heaven; on the contrary, the thirsty soul might encounter a direful doom :—

> In shallow waters heav'n doth show ;
> But who drinks on, to hell may go.

The fanciful title of *The Quip*, given to one of his pieces, page 166, might be extended to many others ; here—

> First, Beauty crept into a Rose.

But we have only selected one out of the six verses, each concluding, " *But thou shalt answer, Lord, for me.*"

The unpromising subject of *Business* is all alike poetical with the rest : two-thirds of it being exceedingly fantastic are omitted. There are some pleasing lines in four verses :—

> Rivers run, and springs each one
> Know their home, and get them gone.

One very quaint poem, page 167, entitled *Providence*, is in twenty-eight verses, combining all manner of conceits in thought and expression, so as to exclude all but two lines from our notice in this essay, the whole being as paradoxical as the poet himself. In the twelfth verse, however, he has made a happy allusion to that very common natural object "sand," which will come home to all who are acquainted with sandy districts, with their hills, mounds, extensive shores, and sand-banks :—

> Thou hast made poor sand
> Check the proud sea, even when it swells and gathers.

As a matter of Natural History our earth presents a very feeble object in *sand*, moved as it may be by every wind, carried hither and thither by every tempest, and yet in the course of time accumulating until it becomes as complete a barrier to the inroads of the sea as adamant.

In his search for *Peace* frequent, but slight allusions, are made to Nature by the poet, as in his appeal to " A hollow wind," and among others—man, garden, and the rainbow. Also in *Man's Medley*, page 168, the allusions are equally slight, in lines no more expressive than—

Hark how the birds do sing,
And woods do ring.

The reader has thus all picturesqueness and truth to Nature, left to his own unrestricted imagination. The very mention of " birds " or " woods " suffices, no doubt, to call up delightful associations in many minds, but small thanks are due to the poet who only thus *catalogues* a series of beautiful objects. Such poetry will ever be cold, hard, and dry, except perhaps to readers gifted with wonderfully powerful imagination and fancy : to whom the slightest hint may sometimes suffice to call up associations far more beautiful and brilliant than any of the poet's own most felicitous midsummer dreams.

To be amusing in tears, is not looked for under any circumstances, but how much less in pious poems! Herbert, however, is at no loss, whatever may be our estimate of his muse's sense of mourning. Writing on *Grief*, page 168, he calls to the " springs, clouds and rain, rivers," to aid his eyes in their overflowing. Grief thus expressed excites but little sympathy; and if our forefathers were genuinely affected by it (as for them it was written), we cannot feel flattered by the quality of their taste. Unquestionably, Herbert composed this piece to *Grief* in all sober earnestness ; for he could not otherwise have concluded it with—
" Alas, my God!"

The Rose, page 169, is a poem which by any other name would smell more sweet ; the flower is emblematic, without adding a single natural figure to the verses, which conclude with a reflection on its being a purgative physic!

We thus see how artificial may be the use of imagination and fancy, even where Nature is concerned; and how its very beauties may engender conceits in certain classes of minds not wanting in truly religious feeling. This style of metrical composition had thousands of admirers not only in Herbert's time, but likewise far into the following century, until, as we shall see, Dr. Watts largely contributed to a change in the character of sacred song.

Human Nature.

As connected with external Nature, our present section relating to mankind will be very limited indeed, as we have only three inferior examples to bring forward. In a long introductory poem, page 163, under the title of *The Church-Porch*, Herbert makes allusion to the education and bringing up of youth, observing:—

> Some till their ground, but let weeds choke their son.

But there is nothing further really noteworthy either for matter or treatment.

Employment, page 164, a poem in six verses, declares:—

> All things are busy : only I
> Neither bring honey with the bees,
> Nor flowers to make that, nor the husbandry
> To water these.

The last poem we shall notice, *Man's Medley*, relates to Man's spiritual welfare:—

> In soul he mounts and flies,
> In flesh he dies.

> He wears a stuff, whose thread is coarse and round,
>   But trimm'd with curious lace,
>   And should take place
> After the trimming, not the stuff and ground.

After this specimen of man-millinery comes the advice :—

> But as birds drink, and straight lift up their heads ;
>   So must he sip, and think
>   Of better drink,
> He may attain to, after he is dead.

To write thus in all seriousness about his own species, and above all upon sacred points of religion, presents such a motley figure of the great and little, that we feel doubtful how to receive poetry of this stamp, unless we attribute its faults to the age in which it was written, and not to any inconsistency chargeable to the poet, who followed, without forming or remodelling the taste of the times in which he lived.

RELIGIOUS, MEDITATIVE, &c.

As Herbert affords us but few specimens of Nature-Study in the poetry of *The Temple*, it is more observable in this instance than that of more productive poets, that single pieces often partake of two or more of the styles, we are commenting on ; thus, all that we have to consider here, have come under observation in a previous section, for a different object.

Among the poet's best pieces we find four verses addressed to *Virtue*, which appeal to many of Nature's most gratifying objects, as the day, earth, sky, dew, &c.

A poem of nine verses, page 165, containing reflections on *Man*, is not so commendable, as only three verses partly refer to Nature, although declaring " Man is everything," yet this lordly creation suggests thoughts not rising above his house, furniture, meat, drink, and other gross matters of artificial life, giving a very low tone to what is meant to be elevated and spiritual.

A poem of thirty-eight lines on *Business*, page 166, begins with the enquiry :—

> Canst be idle? canst thou play,
> Foolish soul, who sinn'd to-day ?

This would be deserving of considerable praise, were it not debased by the usual dead weight of odd, common-place allusions, such as :—

> If thou hast no sighs or groans,
> Would thou hadst no flesh and bones !

The twelfth, out of thirty-eight verses entitled *Providence*, page 167, describes the Almighty's power over tempests, the relations between which he compares to those of parent and child, for combined power, weakness, and dependence. The poet sings :—

> Man is the world's High Priest :—

but unfortunately the poet's *Temple* is, like this poem, a composition of very crude and heterogeneous materials— gems and rubble stone, metal and marl, pearls and puddle, rags and remnants are all worked in to supply rhyme or reason, with *naïve* adroitness and evident satisfaction.

He is more happy in the language of a short poem on *Peace*, which blessing he sought alternately in a cave, a garden, and elsewhere, only to find that it is not of earthly growth.

He has some fanciful reflections on Man under the title of *Man's Medley*, in which he almost puns to say :—

> Happy is he, whose Heart
> Hath found the Art
> To turn his double pains to double praise.

If anything could produce seriousness, surely sincere and unaffected *grief* should do so. But when the mourner speaks of his tearful eyes as, " two shallow fords, two little spouts," we hesitate to assent, and are not indisposed to smile at such a conceit, under such circumstances, for we find it difficult to associate sincerity with " whims and oddities."

The Rose offers another grotesque example of an antiquated meditative mood, transmitted through the medium of a Rose, represented as a purgative flower, for—

> What is fairer than a Rose ?
> What is sweeter ? yet it purgeth.

Another poem, the last we shall notice, is *The Banquet*, or Sacrament, which is suitably grave and solemn. Herbert very poetically introduces those sweet-smelling vegetable products, which—

> Yet being bruis'd are better scented;

in allusion to the buffetings Christ endured at the hands of his wickedly blind, and bigoted tormentors.

In closing our remarks on this section of our subject we would direct attention to those words of Herbert, in which he refers to " true beauty :" they occur in the fifth verse of his poem *The Forerunners :*—

> True Beauty dwells on high : ours is a flame
> But borrowed thence to light us thither,
> Beauty and beauteous words should go together.

" To the pure, all things are pure," and so, doubtless, it was in Herbert's case, but he was most certainly a stranger to the full sense of the last line of the above triplet ; it might rather be said of his style that, he considered goodness could not be degraded by the language in which it was clothed, but that it threw a halo of beauty even upon dust-heaps and offal, silvering them as doth the moon, its own beams the while abiding untainted.

It is because he is so artificial in his modes of figurative expression, that we find little in his works traceable to Nature's loveliness. If he names the rose, the orange-tree, or vine, we have them presented to us as either in a summer house, garden plot, or bouquet; and his mental vision takes in no landscapes, he merely sees the single rock, hill, sand-bank, ocean, river, or stream. He is a town and country poet; and has a taste for cabinets, cupboards, and millinery. When witty it is in puns, anagrams, quips, and quibbles, or grotesque associations. And yet withal he is vehement in praise of religious duties and moral excellencies; he is a fervent and devout Christian in all he does, though he is often liable to be misunderstood if too rigorously inter-preted: so discordant is the language which he frequently introduces in the midst of beautiful poetry. It would appear as though in striving to be pleasant and agreeable to the popular ear, in addressing the multitude on un-popular topics, he had purposed to draw them into Christ's fold, by appearing among them in as much as he could possibly assume of their own character, habits, and tone of conversation. He has a fling at the Pope, con-doles with kings, is pleasant among youth and lovers, measures lace with haberdashers, talks after the fashion of tailors and drapers, treats of carpentry, architecture, mer-chandize, and business generally; but never forgets that he is a missionary among fallen and degraded mankind;

offering to all alike the best counsel for obtaining forgiveness of their sins and a state of everlasting rest and
enjoyment in exchange for the troubles and mishaps of
their present lives.   He discourses almost recklessly on all
subjects but religion ; there he is always serious, even
when in his outer garb he appears to bear anything but the
clerical character.   Such is Herbert, an illustrious but
unequal poet, who unfortunately wrote too much, and
blotted too little.

ESSAY III.

DR. ISAAC WATTS.

18th century.

"To lift us from this abject, to sublime;
This flux to permanent; this dark, to day;
This foul, to pure; this turbid, to serene;
This mean, to mighty."——

Young.

ESSAY III.

On the Advance made in Nature-Study in the 18th Century, as shown in the Sacred Poems of Dr. Isaac Watts.

In selecting Dr. Isaac Watts as the representative hymn-writer of the Eighteenth Century, we are guided as much by the character of his sacred poetry, as by its wide-spread reputation. It might be supposed that the palm of celebrity was equally divided between him and Charles Wesley, who is said to have composed 7000 psalms and hymns, as already shown, however, (page 27), he is greatly inferior on the one point to which these essays are mainly directed : that of Nature-Study. But we have also such poets as Doddridge, Cowper, and Barbauld, each deservedly claiming attention, and yet after all, each must give way to him when variety, quantity, and importance of production are separately taken into consideration. It is from no party feeling, but on the contrary, from a sincere conviction that Watts has done more than any sacred poet previous to Keble to establish a bond between Christianity and Nature in numerous characteristics; thereby creating those pleasing and devotional associations, which justify our esteeming the universe and all its inhabitants and products, as forming one great Book of Nature, in which all may read lessons of grave instruction and profitable entertainment.

Isaac Watts was born in 1674, and died in 1748, being 74 years of age. His works collected in eight volumes octavo, were published in 1812, and contain a biography of him, together with numerous sermons, evangelical discourses, essays, a treatise on logic, psalms, hymns, and miscellaneous prose and poetical pieces. Among his essays there is one " On the improvement of Psalmody," and among his minor poems, a collection entitled *Horæ Lyricæ*, of which a large portion is dedicated " To Devotion and Piety." This latter work we have selected for our present purpose. In the preface to it he strongly advocates the employment of a more graceful and ornamental style than that of Sternhold, and censures the prevalent opinion that a loftier manner was to be devoted exclusively to profane and debasing compositions. He cites passages from the Bible in support of his advocacy of a strain which he conceives is not " too airy for worship," observing,—" 'Tis strange, that persons that have the Bible in their hands, should be led away by thoughtless prejudices, to so wild and harsh an opinion. Let me entreat them not to indulge this sour, this censorious humour too far, lest the sacred Writers fall under the lash of their unlimited and unguarded reproaches." He supports his arguments by referring to the bold metaphors and surprising and strange images employed in the Bible, even beyond anything adopted by profane authors. The length of his address affords sufficient evidence that when he wrote, in 1709, he well knew the extent and nature of the prejudices he might expect to meet with in the religious world. He states, in reference to the work we are about to analyse, that it was intended to have formed a part of the collection of hymns then in its second edition, but was ultimately kept separate because, as the poet says,—"I found some expressions that were not suited to the plainest capacity, and the metaphors are too bold to please the weaker Christian, therefore, I have allotted them a place here."

The author very candidly and fully examines the characteristics of his poems in a variety of lights, but never, even in the remotest manner, alludes to any ideas drawn immediately from the pure fount of Nature. He principally derives his inspiration from the Scriptures, but at the same time he is well read in, and much indebted to Homer, Virgil, Pindar, Horace, Pythagoras, Hesiod, Juvenal, and other classic authors; and names with approval Dryden, Otway, Congreve, Cowley, Blackmore, and other English writers, as well as Boileau, Corneille, and Racine among the French; and we may, therefore, safely infer that, like most other poets, he has unconsciously appropriated a certain peculiarity with regard to ideas associated with Nature which, while he found something similar in profane poems, yet nevertheless struck a kindred chord in his own breast, arising from a strong, inherent love of Nature, although expression was given to them almost unconsciously, or at least without any regulated principle in the construction and arrangement of design. Something struck him as beautiful, and appropriate for introduction into sacred song, and that something, without any precise consideration, he accordingly employed, unaware that the great master of the same peculiarity in the language of metrical compositions was Shakspeare, whom he never names, and to whom it might then, perhaps, have been indecorous to allude, the age appearing to have been so formal, sour, and precise, in these matters.

Watts was thirty-five years of age at the time when these poems were published, and we shall find they contain a more full and vigorous employment of language and metaphorical expressions impressed with Nature, than do his collected hymns, or the works of previous hymn writers. Thus we see that in proportion as his style in this one particular underwent this desirable modification, so, in like manner, the study of his lyric poems may have infused a similar spirit into other poets on whom the charms, grandeur, and wonders of Nature were not altogether lost, although found to be next to useless as literary aids; for Egyptian hieroglyphics do not contain so large an unlocked history of pre-historic Man, as does the world of Nature of applicable but unused stores of mental treasure. So true is it that to the multitude of mankind the saying applies—"Eyes ye have, but see not; ears ye have, but hear not."

1. The first poem is *Worshipping with Fear*; in which, allusive to The Creator, it is said :—

> A wreath of light'ning arms his crown,
> But love adorns it still.

. . . .

The ninth and last verse is :—

> Created powers, how weak they be !
> How short their praises fall !
> So much akin to nothing we,
> And Thou th' Eternal All.

2. *Divine Judgments* is a poem of six verses, varying from nine to twenty lines each; they record the terrors of winter, gales, drought, storms, and floods :—

> 'Tis by a warrant from His hand
>   The gentler gales are bound to sleep :
> The North wind blusters, and assumes command
>   Over the desert and the deep ;
>   Old Boreas with his freezing pow'rs
> Turns the earth iron, makes the ocean glass,
> Arrests the dancing riv'lets as they pass,
>   And chains them moveless to their shores ;
> The grazing ox lows to the gelid skies,
> Walks o'er the marble meads with withering eyes,
> Walks o'er the solid lakes, snuffs up the wind, and dies.

We have next a dread picture of a Polar winter :—

>   Fly to the polar world, my song,
> And mourn the pilgrims there (a wretched throng !)
>   Seized and bound in rigid chains,
> A troop of statues on the Russian plains,
> And life stands frozen in the purple veins.

>   .   .   .   .

>   Dress thee in steel to meet His wrath ;
>   His sharp artillery from the North
> Shall pierce thee to the soul, and shake thy mortal frame.
>   Sublime on Winter's rugged wings
>   He rides in arms along the sky,
> And scatters fate on swains and kings ;
>   And flocks and herds, and nations die ;

>   .   .   .   .

Then follows drought :—

>   The mischiefs that infest the earth,
> When the dog-star fires the realms on high,
>   Drought and diseases, the cruel dearth,
> Are but the flashes of the wrathful eye
>   From the incens'd Divinity.

>   .   .   .   .

>   The verdant fields are burnt to dust,
>   The sun has drunk the channels dry,
>   And all the air is death.

Lastly storms and floods :—

>   Hail, whirlwinds, hurricanes, and floods
>   That all the leafy standards strip,
>   And bear down with a mighty sweep
> The riches of the fields, and honours of the woods ;

> Storms that ravage o'er the deep,
> And bury millions in the waves :
> Earthquakes, that in midnight-sleep
> Turn cities into heaps, and make our beds our graves.

3. *Heaven and Earth* is the title of a short didactic poem, in which youth is admonished that :—

> The rills of pleasure never run sincere ;
>   (Earth has no unpolluted spring)
> From the curs'd soil some dang'rous taint they bear ;
> So roses grow on thorns, and honey wears a sting.
>
> In vain we seek a heaven below the sky ;
>   The world has false but flatt'ring charms :
> Its distant joys show big in our esteem,
> But lessen still as they draw near the eye ;
>   In our embrace the visions die,
>   And when we grasp the airy forms
>   We lose the pleasing dream.
>
> Earth, with her scenes of gay delight,
> Is but a landskip rudely drawn,
> With glaring colours, and false light ;
> Distance commends it to the sight,
>   For fools to gaze upon.

4. *Felicity above*, a poem of five verses, concludes :—

> Take me, URIEL, on thy wings,
> And stretch and soar away.

5. A poem of ten verses depicts GOD's *Dominion and Decrees* :—

> Th' Almighty Voice bid ancient night
>   Her endless realms resign,
> And lo, ten thousand globes of light
>   In fields of azure shine.
>
> He spake; the sun obedient stood,
>   And held the falling day ;
> Old Jordan backward drives his flood,
>   And disappoints the sea.
>
> Lord of the armies of the sky,
>   He marshals all the stars ;
> Red comets lift their banners high,
>   And wide proclaim his wars.

6. Of *The Creator and Creatures* he sings :—

> GOD is a name my soul adores,
>   Th' ALMIGHTY THREE, th' ETERNAL ONE ;
>
> .   .   .   .
>
> Thy voice produc'd the seas and spheres,
> Bid the waves roar, and planets shine ;
> But nothing like thy Self appears,
> Through all these spacious works of thine.
>
> Still restless nature dies and grows;
> From change to change the creatures run :
> Thy being no succession knows,
> And all thy vast designs are one :
>
> A glance of thine runs through the globes,
> Rules the bright worlds, and moves their frame :
> Broad sheets of light compose thy robes;
> Thy guards are form'd of living flame.

7. The hymn GOD *Glorious*, has the verse :—

> Those mighty orbs proclaim Thy power,
>   Their motions speak Thy skill !
> And on the wings of every hour,
>   We read Thy patience still.

8. As an example of the Negative employment of natural objects, we have his paraphrase of the 148th Psalm.* *The universal* HALLELUJAH, thus :—

---

* As the 148th Psalm supplies the matter for the three versions in paragraphs, 8, 10, and 20, it may interest the reader to have before him the following extract from the original:—

1. Praise ye the Lord.—
2. Praise ye Him, all His angels :—
3. Praise ye Him, sun and moon: praise ye Him all ye stars of light.
4. Praise Him, ye heavens of heavens, and ye waters that be above the heavens.
5. Let them praise the name of the Lord :—
7. Praise the Lord from the earth, ye dragons, and all deeps:
8. Fire and hail; snow and vapours; stormy wind fulfilling His word:
9. Mountains, and all hills; fruitful trees, and all cedars:
10. Beasts, and all cattle ; creeping things, and all flying fowl :
11. Kings of the earth, and all people ; princes, and all judges of the earth;
12. Both young men, and maidens ; old men, and children:
13. Let them praise the name of the Lord :—

Praise ye the Lord with joyful tongue,
  Ye powers that guard His throne ;

    .   .   .   .

Shine to His praise, ye crystal skies,
  The floor of His abode,

    .   .   .   .

Thou restless globe of golden light,
  Whose beams create our days,
Join with the silver queen of night,
  To own your borrow'd rays,

    .   .   .   .

Winds, ye shall bear His name aloud
  Through the ethereal blue,
For when His chariot is a cloud,
  He makes His wheels of you.

Thunder and hail, and fires and storms,
  The troops of His command,
Appear in all your dreadful forms,
  And speak His awful hand.

Shout to the LORD, ye surging seas,
  In your eternal roar ;
Let wave to wave resound His praise,
  And shore reply to shore;

While monsters sporting on the flood,
  In scaly silver shine,
Speak terribly their Maker-GOD,
  And lash the foaming brine.

But gentler things shall tune His name,
  To softer notes than these,
Young zephyrs breathing o'er the stream,
  Or whispering through the trees.

Wave your tall heads, ye lofty pines,
  To him that bid you grow,
Sweet clusters, bend the fruitful vines
  On every thankful bough.

Let the shrill birds His honour raise,
  And climb the morning sky:
While groveling beasts attempt His praise
  In hoarser harmony.

9. Another, but less effective Negative illustration is afforded by his poem *The Law given at* Sinai, in the 6th verse :—

> His chariot was a pitchy cloud,
> The wheels beset with burning gems;
> The winds in harness with the flames
>   Flew o'er th' ethereal road :
> Down through His magazines He past
> Of hail and ice, and fleecy snow,
> Swift roll'd the triumph, and as fast
> Did hail, and ice, in melted rivers flow.
>
> The day was mingled with the night,
>   His feet on solid darkness trod,
> His radiant eyes proclaim'd the God,
>   And scatter'd dreadful light ;
> He breath'd, and sulphur ran, a fiery stream :
> He spoke, and (though with unknown speed He came)
> Chid the slow tempest, and the lagging flame.

In the 8th verse he checks his ardent muse with the following reflections :—

> Forbear, young muse, forbear ;
> The flow'ry things that poets say,
> The little arts of *simile*
>   Are vain and useless here ;
> Nor shall the burning hills of old
>   With *Sinai* be compar'd,
> Nor all that lying *Greece* has told,
>   Or learned *Rome* has heard;
>   *Ætna* shall be nam'd no more,
> *Ætna* the torch of *Sicily ;*
> Not half so high
> Her lightnings fly.

10. In a Negative application similar to that in the preceding psalm is the poem *Sun, Moon, and Stars, praise ye the* Lord; omitting the last three verses :—

> Fairest of all the lights above,
> Thou Sun, whose beams adorn the spheres,
> And with unwearied swiftness move,
> To form the circles of our years ;

Praise the Creator of the skies,
That dress'd thine orb in golden rays :
Or may the sun forget to rise,
If he forget his Maker's praise.

Thou reigning beauty of the night,
Fair queen of silence, silver Moon,
Whose gentle beams, and borrow'd light,
Are softer rivals of the noon ;

Arise, and to that sov'reign Pow'r
Waxing and waning honours pay,
Who bid thee rule the dusky hour,
And half supply the absent day.

Ye twinkling Stars, who gild the skies,
When darkness has its curtains drawn,
Who keep your watch, with wakeful eyes,
When business, cares, and day are gone :

Proclaim the glories of your LORD,
Dispers'd through all the heav'nly street
Whose boundless treasures can afford
So rich a pavement for his feet.

11. The following piece entitled *Sincere Praise*, taking the 2nd, 3rd, and 4th verses, is simply meditative :—

Nature in ev'ry dress,
Her humble homage pays,
And finds a thousand ways t' express
Thine undissembled praise.

In native white and red
The rose and lily stand,
And free from pride, their beauties spread,
To show thy skilful hand.

The lark mounts up the sky,
With unambitious song,
And bears her Maker's praise on high
Upon her artless tongue.

12. And the annexed piece is *A song to creating wisdom.* It is divided into five parts ; the last two verses of Part 1st are :—

Thy hand how wide it spread the sky ?
How glorious to behold ?
Ting'd with a blue of heavenly dye,
And starr'd with sparkling gold.

> There Thou hast bid the globes of light,
>   Their endless circles run;
> There the pale planet rules the night,
>   And day obeys the sun.

13. Then follows the 2nd Part, commencing :—

> Downward I turn my wond'ring eyes
>   On clouds and storms below,
> Those under regions of the skies
>   Thy num'rous glories show.
>
> The noisy winds stand ready there
>   Thy orders to obey,
> With sounding wings they sweep the air,
>   To make thy chariot way.
>
> There, like a trumpet loud and strong,
>   Thy thunder shakes our coast;
> While the red lightnings wave along,
>   The banners of thine host.
>
> On the thin air, without a prop,
>   Hang fruitful show'rs around:
> At Thy command they sink, and drop
>   Their fatness on the ground.

14. Succeeded by the 3rd Part, omitting the first verse :—

> How did His wondrous skill array
>   Your fields in charming green;
> A thousand herbs His art display,
>   A thousand flowers between!
>
> Tall oaks for future navies grow,
>   Fair Albion's best defence,
> While corn and vines rejoice below,
>   Those luxuries of sense.
>
> The bleating flocks His pasture feeds:
>   And herds of larger size,
> That bellow through the Lindian meads,
>   His bounteous hand supplies.

15. Next follows the 4th Part :—

> We see the Thames caress the shores,
>   He guides her silver flood:
> While angry Severn swells and roars,
>   Yet hears her ruler, GOD.

> The rolling mountains of the deep
>   Observe His strong command;
> His breath can raise the billows steep,
>   Or sink them to the sand.
>
> Amidst Thy wat'ry kingdoms, LORD,
>   The finny nations play,
> And scaly monsters, at Thy word,
>   Rush through the Northern sea.

16. And the 5th Part, omitting the last verse :—

> Thy glories blaze all nature round,
>   And strike the gazing sight,
> Through skies, and seas, and solid ground,
>   With terror and delight.
>
> Infinite strength, and equal skill,
>   Shine through the worlds abroad,
> Our souls with vast amazement fill,
>   And speak the builder GOD.

17. The same reflective spirit pervades the poem, GOD's *Absolute Dominion*, of which we give the first, second, and part of the third verses :—

> Lord, when my thoughtful soul surveys
>   Fire, air and earth, and stars and seas,
>   I call them all Thy slaves;
> Commission'd by my Father's will,
> Poisons shall cure, or balms shall kill;
>   Vernal suns, or Zephyr's breath,
> May burn or blast the plants to death
>   That sharp December saves;
>   What can winds or planets boast
>   But a precarious pow'r ?
> The sun is all in darkness lost,
> Frost shall be fire, and fire be frost,
>   When He appoints the hour.
>
> Lo, the Norwegians near the polar sky,
>   Chafe their frozen limbs with snow,
>   Their frozen limbs awake and glow,
>   The vital flame, touch'd with a strange supply,
> Rekindles, for the GOD of life is nigh:
> He bids the vital flood in wonted circles flow.
>   Cold steel exposed to Northern air,
> Drinks the meridian fury of the midnight Bear,
>   And burns the unwary stranger there.

.   .   .   .

The fate of Shadrach, Meshach, and Abednego, calls forth the comment :—

> I see the furnace blaze with rage
> Sevenfold: I see amidst the flame
> Three Hebrews of immortal name;
> They move, they walk across the burning stage
> Unhurt, and fearless, while the tyrant stood
>   A statue; fear congeal'd his blood:
>   Nor did the raging element dare
>   Attempt their garments, or their hair;
> It knew the LORD of nature there.
> Nature compell'd by a superior cause,
>   Now breaks her own eternal laws,
>   Now seems to break them, and obeys
>   Her sov'reign King in different ways.
>   Father, how bright Thy glories shine!
>   How broad Thy kingdom, how divine!
> Nature, and miracle, and fate, and chance are Thine.

18. In *Condescending Grace*, the following lines are effectively imaginative : —

> When the Eternal bows the skies,
>   To visit earthly things,
>
> .   .   .   .
>
> He bids His awful chariot roll
>   Far downwards from the skies,
> To visit every humble soul,
>   With pleasure in His eyes.
>
> .   .   .   .

19. Addressing *The Infinite*, the poet solicits power to "raise a lofty song to our Eternal King." We omit the first three verses, and commence :—

> Thine essence is a vast abyss,
>   Which angels cannot sound,
> An ocean of infinities
>   Where all our thoughts are drown'd.
>
> The mysteries of creation lie
>   Beneath enlighten'd minds,
> Thoughts can ascend above the sky,
>   And fly before the winds.
>
> Reason may grasp the massy hills,
>   And stretch from pole to pole,
> But half Thy name our spirit fills,
>   And overloads our soul.

> In vain our haughty reason swells,
> For nothing's found in Thee,
> But boundless inconceivables,
> And vast eternity.

20. We have a third piece applying to the 148th Psalm, 10th verse, composed of the three following verses :—

> Sweet flocks, whose soft enamel'd wing
> Swiftly and gently cleave the sky;
> Whose charming notes address the Spring
>   With an artless harmony;
>   Lovely minstrels of the field,
>   Who in leafy shadows sit,
>   And your wondrous structures build,
> Awake your tuneful voices with the dawning light ;
> To Nature's God your first devotions pay.

>   .   .   .   .

> Serpents, who o'er the meadows slide,
> And wear upon your shining back
> Num'rous ranks of gaudy pride,
> Which thousand mingling colours make;
>   Let the fierce glances of your eyes
>   Rebate their baleful fire:
> In harmless play twist and unfold
> The volumes of your scaly gold:
> That rich embroidery of your gay attire,
>   Proclaims your Maker kind and wise.

> Insects and mites, of mean degree,
> That swarm in myriads o'er the land,
> Moulded by wisdom's artful hand,
> And curl'd and painted with a various dye;
>   In your innumerable forms
>   Praise Him that wears th' ethereal crown.

>   .   .   .   .

21. The wisdom, power, and goodness of the Creator are set forth in *The Comparison and Complaint* :—

> Infinite Power, eternal Lord,
>   How sovereign is thy hand!
> All nature rose t'obey Thy word,
>   And moves at Thy command.

> With steady course Thy shining sun
>   Keeps his appointed way;
> And all the hours obedient run,
>   The circle of the day.

> The raging fire, the stormy sea,
> Perform Thine awful will,
> And every beast and every tree,
> Thy great designs fulfil.

The argument follows, that man should with equal fidelity perform his part.

22. The Almighty's supremacy is further set forth in the song, GOD *Supreme and Self-sufficient*, from which we exclude only the last verse and part of the first :—

> What is our God, or what His name,
>
> .   .   .   .
>
> The spacious worlds of heavenly light,
> Compar'd with Him how short they fall ?
> They are too dark, and He too bright,
> Nothing are they, and GOD is all.
>
> He spoke the wondrous word, and lo,
> Creation rose at His command:
> Whirlwinds and seas their limits know,
> Bound in the hollow of His hand.
>
> There rests the earth, there roll the spheres,
> There nature leans, and feels her prop :
> But His own self-sufficience bears
> The weight of His own glories up.
>
> The tide of creatures ebbs and flows,
> Measuring their changes by the moon;
> No ebb His sea of glory knows;
> His age is one eternal noon.

23. In the poem, *Looking Upward*, the poet soars from earth to heaven ; his powers of imagination are shown in the first three out of five verses :—

> The heavens invite mine eye,
> The stars salute me round;
> Father, I blush, I mourn to lie
> Thus grovelling on the ground.
>
> My warmer spirits move,
> And make attempts to fly;
> I wish aloud for wings of love
> To raise me swift and high.

> Beyond those crystal vaults,
> And all their sparkling balls;
> They're but the porches to Thy courts,
> And paintings on Thy walls.

24. The address to *The* God *of Thunder* is not descriptive, and displays but little imagination, its simple element
is the artillery of heaven in full force of action :—

> O the immense, th' amazing height,
> The boundless grandeur of our God,
>
> .　　　.　　　.　　　.
>
> He speaks; and lo, all nature shakes,
> Heav'n's everlasting pillars bow;
> He rends the clouds with hideous cracks,
> And shoots His fiery arrows through.
>
> Well, let the nations start and fly
> At the blue lightning's lurid glare.
>
> .　　　.　　　.　　　.
>
> Let noise and flame confound the skies,
> And drown the spacious realms below;
> Yet will we sing the thunder's praise,
> And send our loud Hosannas through.
>
> .　　　.　　　.　　　.
>
> Thus shall the God our Saviour come,
> And lightnings round His chariot play;
> Ye lightnings, fly to make Him room,
> Ye glorious storms prepare His way.

25. We shall give the entire poem, *Fire, Air, Earth and
Sea, praise ye the Lord*, being the fourth of the kind among
these Lyric Pieces; but it generalizes more, and is therefore capable of bolder treatment, with grander effect :—

> Earth, thou great footstool of our God
> Who reigns on high; ——
>
> .　　　.　　　.
>
> Fire, thou swift herald of His face,
> Whose glorious rage at His command,
> 　　Levels a palace with the sand,
> Blending the lofty spires in ruin with the base:
> 　　Ye heav'nly flames, that singe the air,
> 　　Artillery of a jealous God,

> Bright arrows that His sounding quivers bear
>   To scatter deaths abroad ;
> Lightnings, adore the sovereign arm that flings
> His vengeance, and your fires upon the heads of kings.
>
>   Thou vital element, the Air,
>   Whose boundless magazines of breath
>   Our fainting flame of life repair,
> And save the bubble Man from the cold arms of death;
>   And ye whose vital moisture yields
>   Life's purple stream a fresh supply;
> Sweet Waters wandering through the flow'ry fields,
>   Or dropping from the sky;
> Confess the pow'r whose all-sufficient name
> Nor needs your aid to build, or to support our frame.
>
>   Now the rude air, with noisy force,
>   Beats up and swells the angry sea,
>   They join to make our lives a prey,
>   And sweep the sailor's hopes away,
> Vain hopes, to reach their kindred on the shores !
>   Lo, the wild seas and surging waves
>   Gape hideous in a thousand graves :
> Be still, ye floods, and know your bounds of sand,
>   Ye storms adore your Master's hand;
> The winds are in His fist, the waves at His command.
>
>   From the eternal emptiness
>   His fruitful word by secret springs
>   Drew the whole harmony of things.
>   That forms this noble universe:
>   Old Nothing knew His pow'rful hand,
> Scarce had He spoke His full command,
> Fire, Air, and Earth, and Sea heard the creating call,
> And leap from empty Nothing to His bounteous All;
>   And still they dance and still obey
> The orders they receiv'd the great creation-day.

26 *The Farewell*, in five verses, only offers us the single couplet :—

> Thou mighty mole-hill, Earth, farewell !
> Angels aspiring " leave the Globe for ants to dwell."

27. The first half of the hymn entitled *Sovereignty and Grace*, draws largely upon the imagination, to grasp as far as possible some remote conception of the Almighty's infinite power and glory :—

> The LORD! how fearful is His name !
> How wide is His command?
> Nature, with all her moving frame,
> Rests on His mighty hand.
>
> Immortal glory forms His throne,
> And light His awful robe:
> Whilst with a smile, or with a frown,
> He manages the globe.
>
> A word of His almighty breath
> Can swell or sink the seas:
> Build the vast empires of the earth,
> Or break them as He please.

28. Passing at least twelve pages of these poems without notice, we come to the one, *Breathing towards the heavenly Country*, imitated from Casimire, 1st Book, 19th Ode :—

> The beauty of my native land
> Immortal love aspires ;
>
> There glides the moon her shining way,
> And shoots my heart through with a silver ray,
> Upward my heart aspires:
> A thousand lamps of golden light
> Hung high, in vaulted azure, charm my sight:
>
> Must ye for ever walk the ethereal round,
> For ever see the mourner lie
> An exile of the sky,
> A prisoner of the ground !
> Descend some shining servants from on high,
> Build me a hasty tomb ;
> A grassy turf will raise my head ;
> The neighbouring lilies dress my bed;
> And shed a cheap perfume.

29. *Desiring to Love* CHRIST, is a poem worthy of Herbert, for its peculiar quaintness of expression, but out of seven, only the first two verses must suffice by way of example :—

> Come, let me love; or, is thy mind
> Harden'd to stone, or froze to ice ?
> I see the blessed Fair One bend
> And stoop t' embrace me from the skies !

> O! 'tis a thought would melt a rock,
> And make a heart of iron move,
> That those sweet lips, that heavenly look,
> Should seek and wish a mortal love!

30. In a similar strain is his *Meditation in a Grove*, after the fashion of an amorous love ditty, concluding with wounding every tree to "carve our passion on the bark." Another poem, *Mutual Love stronger than Death*, ends with the fanciful couplet:—

> So billow after billow rolls
> To kiss the shore, and die.

31. Omitting no less than sixteen poems, we at length find five verses in the sacred song, *Come, Lord* JESUS; commencing at the second :—

> Our months are ages of delay,
> And slowly every minute wears :
> Fly, wingèd time, and roll away
> These tedious rounds of sluggish years.
>
> Ye heav'nly gates, loose all your chains,
> Let the eternal pillars bow;
> Blest SAVIOUR, cleave the starry plains,
> And make the crystal mountains flow.
>
> O for a shout of violent joys
> To join the trumpet's thund'ring sound !
> The angel herald shakes the skies,
> Awakes the graves and tears the ground.
>
> .   .   .   .   .
>
> Our airy feet with unknown flight
> Swift as the motions of desire,
> Run up the hills of heavenly light,
> And leave the welt'ring world in fire.

Watts' Lyric Poems end here, so far as they are "Sacred to Devotion and Piety;" his other pieces to Honour, Friendship, and the Memory of the Dead, do not demand our present attention.

As regards Nature-Study, Watts' *Horæ Lyricæ* affords more and freer examples than are to be found in the usual selections collected from his Hymns. Indeed, he often condescends to be puerile and occasionally fantastic in his adoption of figures drawn directly from Nature, which gives the impression of their being first and unpolished draughts. It does not, at least, accord with our present taste, for example, he represents the stars to " wink and beckon with their amorous fires ;" but, in truth, a galaxy of light puts in the shade all such slight scratches and roughnesses. It is, however, a critical weakness to look for, and to single out the smallest blemishes of genius, as astronomers are wont to dilate on a few dark spots in the sun.

The preceding selected extracts we shall now proceed to group and examine collectively ; commencing with :—

1. Description.

We find in these poems but little in illustration of mere Descriptive Poetry, and they would, therefore, have supplied earlier critics with the observation that Watts displayed but a slight acquaintance with Nature. As thus limited, few of our early poets can be rated as lovers of and expounders of Nature. But in our critique we take a wider range, and can trace to what extent a poet is alive to Nature's beauties and influences beyond what appears in his works as merely descriptive poetry in word-painted scenery. In paragraph No. 2, pictures of winter, drought, storms, and floods are highly wrought ; in 15, allusion is made to the Thames and the Severn ; in 17, we find the opposites of a Norwegian winter, and the fiery furnace prepared for destroying three righteous Hebrews, graphically pourtrayed and strikingly contrasted; while in 25, the four elements constituting the material world are pleasingly described.

2 AND 3. SIMILES, ETC.

We notice, as peculiar, the absence of Similes, and we find only one approach to a proverbial expression, which occurs in the 3rd paragraph—

—— Roses grow on thorns, and honey wears a sting.

And so it is with our pleasures, as all experience proves.

By a verse in the 9th paragraph, we find the poet would curb his muse, " Forbear !" he exclaims :—

> The flow'ry things that poets say,
> The little arts of *simile*.

—which may, probably, account for the absence of that mode of figurative expression throughout these poems, as just remarked.

4. IMAGINATION AND FANCY.

The poet has displayed more grace and imagination in his psalms than in his hymns, and frequently with considerable effect. Of the Creator he says, in the 1st paragraph :—

> A wreath of lightning arms His crown,
> But love adorns it still.

In the 3rd, he has somewhat imitated Shakspeare perhaps, in the line :—

> The rills of pleasure never run sincere.

It is much the same with the " course of true love."

The poet, in the 4th paragraph, appeals to Uriel, on whose wings he would fain soar to heaven.

Paragraphs 5, 6, 12, 13, and 14, to 17, contain various specimens distinguishable for a moderate share of imaginative effect, but no more than seems required to render them poetical, referring, as they do, to various features of Creation, and God's dominion over all. The poet is infinitely more elevated in tone in the 18th paragraph, in which occurs the couplet :—

> When the eternal bows the skies,
> To visit earthly things.

In the next paragraph appear his verses on *The Infinite*, but they are not equal to the subject, nor, indeed, to the poet's usual command of thought and diction. Paragraphs 20 to 24, are but slightly noticeable for the successful display of imaginative effect; and 25 is little if at all superior, although the subject is that of the four elemental constituents of the globe. From the latter we have omitted the following, as relating more to ART than to NATURE. The first verse alludes to the Earth, as :—

> Our house, our parent, and our nurse ;
> Mighty stage of mortal scenes,
> Drest with strong and gay machines,
> Hung with golden lamps around ;
> (And flow'ry carpets spread the ground)
> Thou bulky globe, prodigious mass,
> That hangs unpillared in an empty space !

The 26th paragraph has the fanciful line :—

> Thou mighty mole-hill, Earth, farewell !

And the 27th generalizes where human effort fails to find sufficiently figurative and expressive language to depict the magnitude and might of the great Architect of the Universe. The poet, declaring that "fearful is His name," imagines that Nature—

> Rests on His mighty hand.

That His throne is "immortal glory,"—

> And light His awful robe.

So far this is at once both a fine and a feeble effort ; but beyond this it is as it were a mere painting of the lily, or gilding refined gold. It is as true that what can be written in words cannot probably be depicted by the most skilful painter, as that the mind may attain to heights of intelligence which baffle the power of the most practised pen to commit to writing.

5. HUMAN NATURE.

In the poem, paragraph 3, we have only one phase of Human Nature set before us,—the character of Youth; all others are implied, but without distinct features, in general references to either saints or sinners.

6. RELIGIOUS, MORAL, MEDITATIVE.

Except so far as Nature-Study is concerned, it may be stated with truth that all Watts' poems are either religious, or moral and meditative, expressive of sentiment and feeling. We have, however, only to give prominence to such pieces as are expressly illustrative of their composition in drawing from and being more or less indebted to Nature in the broadest possible acceptation of the term. In the 1st paragraph we observe the poet's admirable adaptation of a figure due to "Lightning," and afterwards to the weakness of "created powers," and man himself—

> So much akin to nothing we.

The poem named *Divine Judgments*, 2nd paragraph, describes the terrors of Winter severities, Floods, Drought, and Storms, each in tragic contrast, associated with attendant evils, powerful enough to—

> Turn cities into heaps, and make our beds our graves.

The 3rd paragraph contains abundant matter both for censure and commendation, relating to *Heaven and Earth*, for—

> Earth has no unpolluted spring.

Nothing but—

Distance commends it to the sight,
For fools to gaze upon.

As another poet sings,—"Distance lends enchantment to the view."

Sincere Praise, 11th paragraph, alludes to—

Nature in every dress.

but names only "red and white;" in short, it is about the most unambitious of the poet's lyric productions.

The five parts into which *A song to creating wisdom* is divided are designed in a truly pious and reflective spirit ; they draw a graphic, pleasing, and instructive picture of the heavens, the earth, and its products and embellishments. Their Creator's pity for his creatures, " we see, adore, and love." Of the same character is the next piece, entitled God's *absolute dominion.*

The song, 21st paragraph, demands that man's fidelity in the service of his Maker should be equal with that shown by all earth's elements, products, and creatures.

The paragraphs 24, containing the poem *The* God *of Thunder ;* and 25, the elements *Fire, Air, &c.* are of a mixed composition, more or less meditative in their composition. From this source flows the song :—

The Lord, how fearful is His name !

in the 27th paragraph. And the same may be declared of the 28th paragraph, *Breathing towards the heavenly country,* and the next, *Desiring to love Christ ;* but none of them present any striking feature for special comment.

We proceed, lastly, to examine this poet's use of—

7. Negative Views of Nature.

Watts is generally far from deficient in the employment of this figure, which gives a distinctive character to his sacred poems, as compared with other compositions of the same or an earlier period of literary history. We have only marked four examples, and these are originated by Scripture texts, and are consequently without originality, except in the mode of their treatment ; three are different versions of the 148th Psalm, the first, in the 8th paragraph, exclaiming :—

> Shout to the Lord, ye surging seas
> In your eternal roar.

He also calls on " monsters sporting on the flood," with " young zephyrs ;" and proceeds : —

> Let the shrill birds His honour raise,
> And climb the morning sky ;
> While groveling beasts attempt His praise -
> In hoarser harmony.

The 10th paragraph contains a second version from the same source. It calls on " ye twinkling stars" to—

> Proclaim the glories of your Lord.

The 20th paragraph concludes the series, with *Flying fowl, and creeping things, praise ye the* Lord :—

> Sweet flocks, whose soft enamel'd wing
> Swift and gently cleave the sky;
>
> .   .   .   .
>
> To Nature's God your first devotions pay.

Nor does he omit " serpents, who o'er the meadows slide ;" nay, nor even—

> Insects and mites, of mean degree,
> That swarm in myriads o'er the land.

Returning to the 9th paragraph, we have there the poem on *The Law given at* Sinai, in which occurs the line referring to the presence of the Almighty :—

> His feet on solid darkness trod,

which, although singularly non-natural, is, nevertheless, highly figurative and almost magically expressive of that spiritual sovereignty, of which it is difficult to convey even a slight conception.

Whatever defects we may find in Watts, as a sacred poet, he is superior to many of his predecessors. His Preface to the *Horæ Lyricæ* makes it clear that he was acutely aware of the dearth of life and vigour in most of the sacred poems of his own and earlier times, and as Wesley said of Music, so Watts thought of Poetry, that the Muse should not be degraded from her divine station to promote only profane and debasing subjects. He points to classical usage, and Scripture language, and thence draws the conclusion that no subject is too serious or solemn to be adorned by every attribute of taste and knowledge; and we have in his own example the clearest evidence of his high aspirations. If he occasionally fell short of his aim, he at least did so with perfect freedom from the censure of trifling; he never condescended to anagrams, emblems, quips, and paradoxes. Such trifles had been admitted, approved, and were constantly being imitated by verse makers, who were proud of such conceited conceptions as a fitting dress for their most serious thoughts.

We find, therefore, more variety in Watts's poems; he appears to have left no style untried, and even endeavoured to produce a kind of sacred ballad. He has bestowed more pains than almost any previous hymn writer and versifier of the Psalms, to let no opportunity escape for sublime descriptions, and consequently his versions of the Psalms stand conspicuous among poems of that class.

ESSAY IV.

JOHN KEBLE,

19TH CENTURY.

And this our life, exempt from public haunt,
Finds tongues in trees, books in the running brooks,
Sermons in stones, and good in everything.

SHAKSPEARE.

See the bliss Heaven could on all bestow !
Which who but feels can taste, but thinks can know.

. . . . . .

Slave to no sect, who takes no private road,
But looks through Nature up to Nature's God.

POPE.

ESSAY IV.

ON THE ENLARGED AND REFINED STATE OF NATURE-STUDY, AS EVIDENCED IN THE SACRED POETRY OF JOHN KEBLE.

THE nineteenth century, so far as regards naturalistic poetry, has been less remarkable in the general character of its sacred poets, than in the special excellencies of him whom we have selected as the representative poet of the age in this particular department ; and whose example, bearing this distinction, cannot fail to have a powerful influence on the poetry of the future. He was born in 1792, and died in 1866, aged 74 years. His " Christian Year" was first published in 1827, and has gone through nearly 150 editions. His home descriptions appear to relate principally to the scenery common to Burthorpe, and also to the parish of East Leech ; but although he gives many graphic descriptions of the East, his knowledge appears to have been derived not from travel but from reading, conversation, and pictorial representations of regions otherwise quite foreign to him. An elaborate criticism on his poetry appeared in the *British Quarterly Review* for 1867, which differs widely from the views expressed in the present essay, for we are there informed that,—"There is a tendency in poets of Keble's order to exalt Nature above man"; as if "man" were *not* a part of "Nature." Then again Keble is the "interpreter of Nature," and "He sees glimpses of the infinite meaning of her various and changeful moods"; neither of which can we discover; nor does the critic favour us with a single "interpretation," or a single instance of any "glimpse of the infinite meaning" seen by the poet, to enlighten us with respect to what we are to understand by these apparently meaningless assertions. That the poet is a "student of her many mysteries," and that he is profoundly devout and humble in his investigations of Nature we willingly admit to be fully proved by a large portion of our selected examples; but no where has that study resulted in a single "interpretation," or the slightest evidence of the poet having seen in any one instance "the infinite meaning of her (Nature's) various and changeful moods." Keble is stated to have combined "the best teachings of Wordsworth and Coleridge, *their* insight into Nature's meaning and message;" a sentence which conveys no appreciable meaning; for it is assumed that Nature has a "meaning and message," but it is overlooked that in whatever sense that statement is to be taken, no two poets agree in their individual "insight," but each has a personal insight (so to speak), according with his own mental constitution. This yearning to deify insensate matter will, and can only decline, with the establishment of healthier and more correct views and estimates of Nature: taking Nature as a whole, animate and inanimate, intellectual or instinctive, vegetative or inorganic.

These in their entirety are Nature. How severally to *interpret* them, attain to their *meaning*, or *message* (if they have any), or obtain any *insight* whatever into Nature's arcana has never yet, we fear, been the favoured lot of any poet, past or present. Philosophy may superficially and partially interpret Nature, but the poet never can do so, because it is not his province.

A notice of Sacred Poetry in connection with Nature-Study, as exemplified in the psalms and hymns composed by English Poets, would be very imperfect indeed, without a fuller account than we have yet given of Keble's poetry ; we therefore propose, in continuation, to examine the construction of such of the poems in his " Christian Year,"* as principally relate to Nature.

1. The work opens with the hymn to *Morning.*‡

> Hues of the rich unfolding morn,†
> That, ere the glorious sun be born,
> By some soft touch invisible
> Around his path are taught to swell;—
> Thou rustling breeze so fresh and gay,
> That dancest forth at opening day,
> And brushing by with joyous wing,
> Wakenest each little leaf to sing;—
> Ye fragrant clouds of dewy steam,
> By which deep grove and tangled stream
> Pay, for soft rains in season given,
> Their tribute to the genial heaven:—

Thirteen verses follow in a different strain.

2. The next hymn is addressed to *Evening.*‡

---

* The tenth edition, 12mo. Oxford, 1833.

† See Cecil F. Alexander, page 79.
> " The roseate hues of early dawn,
> The brightness of the day."

‡ As already noticed in the First Essay, page 55, Keble's hymns for *Morning,* and *Evening,* are quoted in " The Book of Praise ;" except four introductory verses to the first, and two introductory ones to the second of these poems.

> 'Tis gone, that bright and orbèd blaze,
> Fast fading from our wistful gaze;
> Yon mantling cloud has hid from sight
> The last faint pulse of quivering light.
>
> In darkness and in weariness
> The traveller on his way must press,
> No gleam to watch on tree or tower,
> Whiling away the lonesome hour.

The concluding ten verses refer to and apply this natural opening sketch.

3. The poem for *Advent Sunday* has but few such lines as :—

> Up from your beds of sloth for shame,
> Speed to the eastern mount like flame,
>
> And fast beside the olive-border'd way
>
> Full many a soft green isle appears:
>
> When withering blasts of error swept the sky,
>
> On shelter'd nooks of Palestine !

4. *The Second Sunday in Advent* calls forth :—

> Not till the freezing blast is still,
> Till freely leaps the sparkling rill,
> And gales sweep soft from summer skies,
> As o'er a sleeping infant's eyes
> A mother's kiss; ere calls like these,
> No sunny gleam awakes the trees,
> Nor dare the tender flowrets show
> Their bosoms to th' uncertain glow.

Then follows the application to the Church, in a tone of encouragement couched in the figurative style, to which we shall proceed specially to direct attention. Thus in the second verse :—

> Why then, in sad and wintry time,
> Her heavens all dark with doubt and crime,
> Why lifts the Church her drooping head,
> As though her evil hour were fled ?

The poet then asks :—

> Is she less wise than leaves in spring,
> Or birds that cower with folded wing?

as though he would suggest,—for the leaves appear in their proper season, and the birds prepare for the coming storm, or other misadventure: and further, " the Church " " sees the world is waxing old," as declared in Esdras.

> By tempests, earthquakes, and by wars,
> By rushing waves and falling stars,
>
> .   .   .   .   .
>
> Not surer does each tender gem,
> Set in the fig-tree's polish'd stem,
> Foreshew the summer season bland,
> Than these dread signs thy mighty hand.

The concluding three verses urge the necessity of striving "To lead on earth an angel's life," in a tone and manner suitable to the gravity of the occasion.

5. The *Third Sunday* commences :—

> What went ye out to see
> O'er the rude sandy lea,
> Where stately Jordan flows by many a palm,
> Or where Gennesaret's wave
> Delights the flowers to lave,
> That o'er her western slope breathe airs of balm?
>
> All through the summer night,
> Those blossoms red and bright*
> Spread their soft breasts, unheeding, to the breeze,
> Like hermits watching still
> Around the sacred hill,
> Where erst our Saviour watch'd upon his knees.
>
> The Paschal moon above
>
> .   .   .   .
>
> Below, the lake's still face
> Sleeps sweetly in th' embrace
> - Of mountains terrass'd high with mossy stone.
>
> .   .   .   .

---

* In a note, this is stated to refer to Rhododendrons, said to clothe the western bank down to the water's edge.

Wandering so wild and vain,
To count the reeds that tremble in the wind,
On listless dalliance bound,
Like children gazing round,
Who on God's works no seal of Godhead find.

. . . .

Or choose thee out a cell
In Kedron's storied dell,
Beside the springs of Love, that never die,
Among the olives kneel
The chill night-blast to feel,
And watch the Moon that saw thy Master's agony.

6. The *Fourth Sunday* might be mistaken for a part of Tennyson's *In Memoriam;* it begins:—

Of the bright things in earth and air
How little can the heart embrace !
Soft shades and gleaming lights are there —
I know it well, but cannot trace.

Mine eye unworthy seems to read
One page of Nature's beauteous book:
It lies before me, fair outspread—
I only cast a wistful look.

I cannot paint to Memory's eye
The scene, the glance, I dearest love—
Unchang'd themselves, in me they die,
Or faint, or false, their shadows prove.

The remaining twelve verses afford a happy application of the foregoing lines.

7. We have already, in the First Essay, page 57, commented on the poem here assigned to *Christmas Day*, commencing :—" What sudden blaze of song."

8. From the poem for *St. Stephen's Day*, we select the first verse :—

As rays around the source of light
Stream upward ere he glow in sight,
And watching by his future flight
Set the clear heavens on fire;
So on the King of Martyrs wait
Three chosen bands, in royal state—

—alluding to St. Stephen, St. John, and the Holy Innocents in the presence of our Saviour ; but the foregoing comparison, however poetical, is neither clear, nor quite consistent.　We merely quote the verse, however, for the sake of the first four naturalistic lines.

9. We only find one verse, namely the fourth, in the poem for *St. John's Day* :—

> Gales from Heaven, if so He will,
> Sweeter melodies can wake
> On the lonely mountain rill
> Than the meeting waters make.

10. In the fifth verse of the poem, *The Holy Innocents*, allusion is made to unconscious childhood :—

> Like infants sporting on the shore,
> That tremble not at Ocean's boundless roar.

11. The poem for the *First Sunday after Christmas*, in the second verse, refers to the sun, moon and stars as :—

> ———— wanderers of the sky.

And of Joshua's commanding the sun to stand still, and its having "returned ten degrees," the poet observes in the third verse :—

> And backward force the waves of Time,
> That now so swift and silent bear
> Our restless bark from year to year ;

Then of hopes, vows, and prayers it is remarked :—

> These, and such faint half waking dreams,
> Like stormy lights on mountain streams,
> Wavering and broken all, athwart the conscience glare.

Of our Father, " Lover of our souls," it is declared :—

> Thou seek'st to warn us, not confound,
> Thy showers would pierce the harden'd ground,
> And win it to give out its brightness and perfume.

But alas !—

> Time's waters will not ebb, nor stay.

12. *The Circumcision* :—this poem, in the sixth verse, affords the figure :—

> Now of thy love we deem
> As of an ocean vast,
> Mounting in tides against the stream
> Of ages gone and past.

The following appeal in the twelfth verse comes unexpectedly, and is quoted more for its peculiarity in this place than its being strictly adapted for our purpose generally :—

> Would'st thou a Poet be ?
> And would thy dull heart fain
> Borrow of Israel's minstrelsy
> One high enraptur'd strain ?
>
> Come here thy soul to tune,
> Here set thy feeble chant,
> Here, if at all beneath the moon,
> Is holy David's haunt.

Of the " child of tears," it is inquired :—

> And seems it hard, thy vernal years
> Few vernal joys can shew?

And he is advised to " sow in holy fear ;"—

> So life a winter's morn may prove
> To a bright endless year.

13. On a text, for the *Second Sunday after Christmas*, from Isaiah—" When the poor and needy seek water,"—it is observed in the second verse :—

> Nor knew an angel form was nigh
> To show soft waters gushing by
> And dewy shadows mild.

As " with Moses' rod"—

> Out of the dry unfathom'd deep
> Of sands, that lie in lifeless sleep,
> Save when the scorching whirlwinds heap
> Their waves in rude alarm.

Even when—

> —— on the traveller's listless way
> Rises and sets th' unchanging day,
> No cloud in heaven to slake its ray,
> On earth no sheltering bower.

Though we may be fainting in the wilderness, Israel's
God will be there :—

> To turn the bitter pool
> Into a bright and breezy lake,
>   The throbbing brow to cool :
>
> .   .   .   .
>
> The scent of water far away
>   Upon the breeze is flung :
> The desert pelican to-day
>   Securely leaves her young.
>
> .   .   .   .
>
> To Thee we turn, our last and first,
>   Our Sun and soothing Moon.
>
> From darkness, here, and dreariness
>   We ask not full repose,
>
> .   .   .   .
>
> Is not the pilgrim's toil o'erpaid
> By the clear rill and palmy shade ?
> And see we not. up Earth's dark glade,
>   The gate of Heaven unclose ?

14. For *The Epiphany*, the poem commences figuratively :—

> Star of the East, how sweet art Thou,
>   Seen in Life's early morning sky,
> Ere yet a cloud has dimm'd the brow,
>   While yet we gaze with childish eye.

As in old age " our childhood's star" may again arise :—

> Will not the long-forgotten glow
>   Of mingled joy and awe return,
> When stars above or flowers below
>   First made our infant spirits burn ?

15. We now pass to the poem for the *First Sunday after
Epiphany* :—

> Lessons sweet of Spring returning,
>   Welcome to the thoughtful heart !
>
> .   .   .   .
>
> Sweet the lengthening April day,
> While with you the soul is free,
> Ranging wild o'er hill and lea,
>
> .   .   .   .

> Every leaf in every nook,
> Every wave in every brook.
> Chanting with a solemn voice
> Minds us —.
>
>   .   .   .   .
>
> Needs no show of mountain hoary,
>   Winding shore or deepening glen,
> Where the landscape in its glory
>   Teaches truth to wandering men:
>
>   .   .   .   .
>
> See the soft green willow springing
>   Where the waters gently pass,
> Every way her free arms flinging
>   O'er the moist and reedy grass.
> Long ere winter blasts are fled,
> See her tipp'd with vernal red,
> And her kindly flower display'd
> Ere her leaf can cast a shade.
>
>   .   .   .   .
>
> If, the quiet brooklet leaving,
>   Up the stony vale I wind,
> Haply half in fancy grieving
>   For the shades I leave behind,
> By the dusty wayside drear,
> Nightingales with joyous cheer
> Sing, my sadness to reprove,
> Gladlier than in cultur'd grove.
>
> Where the thickest boughs are twining
>   Of the greenest darkest tree,
> There they plunge, the light declining—
>   All may hear, but none may see.
>
>   .   .   .   .

16. The poem for the *Second Sunday* touches on Human Nature:—

> The heart of childhood is all mirth:
>   We frolic to and fro
> As free and blithe, as if on earth
>   Were no such thing as woe.

Sixteen verses follow, recommending a Christian course of life.

17. Another for the *Third Sunday* opens with :—

> I mark'd a rainbow in the north,
>   What time the wild autumnal sun
> From his dark veil at noon look'd forth,
>   As glorying in his course half done,

> Flinging soft radiance far and wide
> Over the dusky heaven and bleak hill-side.

. . . . .

The third verse proceeds :—

> Light flashes in the gloomiest sky,
> And Music in the dullest plain.
> For there the lark is soaring high
> Over her flat and leafless reign,
> And chanting in so blithe a tone,
> It shames the weary heart to feel itself alone.

This is applied and moralised on throughout the remaining nine verses. In the fifth verse occurs the simile referring to " Christian worth," which—

> May dwell, unseen by all but Heaven,
> Like diamond blazing in the mine.

18. The hymn for the *Fourth Sunday* commences :—

> They know th' Almighty's power,
> Who, waken'd by the rushing midnight shower,
> Watch for the fitful breeze
> To howl and chafe amid the bending trees,
> Watch for the still white gleam
> To bathe the landscape in a fiery stream,
> Touching the tremulous eye with sense of light
> Too rapid and too pure for all but angel sight.

Six verses follow referring to the "storms within," and pointing to the only means of deliverance.

19. *Fifth Sunday after Epiphany.* In this poem the Lord is addressed as :—

> Thou whose soft showers distil
> On ocean waste or rock,
> Free as on Hermón hill.

20. The fourth verse of the poem for the *Sixth Sunday after Epiphany*, commenting on those which precede it, alludes to the fond fancies of the lover :—

> So, have I seen some tender flower
> Priz'd above all the vernal bower,

> Shelter'd beneath the coolest shade,
> Embosom'd in the greenest glade,
> So frail a gem, it scarce may bear
> The playful touch of evening air;
> When hardier grown we love it less,
> And trust it from our sight, not needing our caress.
>
> And wherefore is the sweet spring tide
> Worth all the changeful year beside?
> The last-born babe, why lies its part
> Deep in the mother's inmost heart?
> But that the LORD and source of love
> Would have the weakest ever prove
> Our tenderest care.——

Of our dreams of Heaven, the poet declares, in reply to the inquiry—" What is the heaven we idly dream?"—

> The self-deceiver's dreary theme,
> A cloudless sun that softly shines,
> Bright maidens and unfailing vines,
> The warrior's pride, the hunter's mirth,
> Poor fragments all of this low earth:
> Such as in sleep would hardly soothe
> A soul that once had tasted of immortal Truth.

Then in immediate contrast to this gross conception of heavenly bliss, comes :—

> What is the Heaven our God bestows?
> No prophet yet, nor Angel knows;
> Was never yet created eye
> Could see across Eternity;
> Not seraph's wing for ever soaring
> Can pass the flight of souls adoring,
> That nearer still and nearer grow
> To th' unapproachéd LORD, once made for them so low.

The self-accused :—

> —— live and die: their names decay,
> Their fragrance passes quite away;
> Like violets in the freezing blast
> No vernal steam * around they cast.

---

* See page 213, for " dewy steam."

21. The poem for *Septuagesima Sunday* has already been quoted and fully examined in the First Essay, page 56.

22. *Sexagesima Sunday.*   As in the Garden of Eden :—

> The sentence is gone forth, the ground is curs'd:
>   Yet mingled with the penal shower
>   Some drops of balm in every bower
> Steal down like April dews, that softest fall and first.

23. The poem dedicated to *Quinquagesima Sunday*, on the text from *Genesis*, " I do set my bow in the cloud," strongly reminds us of Herbert's address to *Peace*, " Sweet Peace, where dost thou dwell? "   He inquires of the " Rainbow," etc. ; and it really may have suggested the following :—

> Sweet Dove ! the softest, steadiest plume
>   In all the sunbright sky,
> Brightening in ever-changeful bloom
>   As breezes change on high ;—
>
> Sweet Leaf ! the pledge of peace and mirth,
>
> .   .   .   .   .
>
> Sweet Rainbow ! pride of summer days,
>   High set at Heaven's command,
> Though into drear and dusky haze
>   Thou melt on either hand ;—
>
> .   .   .   .   .
>
> Not blither, after showers, the Lark
>   Mounts up with glistening wing.

24. The second stanza of the piece for *Ash Wednesday*, begins :—

> The loving eye that watches thine
>   Close as the air that wraps thee round.

The following is a beautiful address to those who mourn, heavily oppressed with grief :—

> Nor fear lest sympathy should fail—
>   Hast thou not seen, in night-hours drear,
> When racking thoughts the heart assail,
>   The glimmering stars by turns appear,
> And from th' eternal home above
>   With silent news of mercy steal ?
> So angels pause on tasks of love, .
>   To look where sorrowing sinners kneel.

25. For the *First Sunday in Lent*, the third verse of the poem alludes to the destruction of Zoar :—

> Ah, wherefore gleam those upland slopes so fair ?
> And why, through every woodland arch,
> Swells yon bright vale, as Eden rich and rare,
> Where Jordan winds his stately march ;
> If all must be forsaken, ruin'd all,
> If God have planted but to burn ?—

The concluding verse gives a picture of home :—

> Sweet is the smile of home ; the mutual look
> When hearts are of each other sure ;
> Sweet all the joys that crowd the household nook,
> The haunt of all affections pure.

26. For the *Second Sunday in Lent*, is a hymn of fourteen verses, from the first of which we take the following simile :—

> Where tears of penance come too late for grace,
> As on th' uprooted flower the genial rain.

27. *Third Sunday in Lent.* This poem, commencing, "See Lucifer like lightning fall," does not offer much matter for comment. " Where Abraham fed his flocks " is mentioned as,—

> A land that drinks the rain of heaven at will,
> Whose waters kiss the feet of many a vine-clad hill.

The Israelites :—

> Oft as they watch'd, at thoughtful eve,
> A gale from bowers of balm
> Sweep o'er the billowy corn, and heave
> The tresses of the palm,
> Just as the lingering Sun had touch'd with gold,
> Far o'er the cedar shade, some tower of giants old.

The conquered " Heathens " leave behind them,—

> The limpid wells, the orchards green
> Left ready for the spoil,

> The household stores untouch'd, the roses bright
> Wreath'd o'er the cottage walls in garlands of delight.

Alluding to the Pagan poets of Greece, the poet remarks, respecting their effusions, that their legends awake "a vision blest :"—

> As little children lisp, and tell of Heaven,
> So thoughts beyond their thought to those high Bards were given.

The concluding verse we quote entire for its beauty :—

> There's not a strain to Memory dear,*
> Nor flower in classic grove,
> There's not a sweet note warbled here,
> But minds us of Thy Love.
> O Lord, our Lord, and spoiler of our foes,
> There is no light but thine : with Thee all beauty glows.

28. The poem for the *Fourth Sunday* commences :—

> When Nature tries her finest touch,
> Weaving her vernal wreath,
> Mark ye, how close she veils her round,
> Not to be trac'd by sight or sound,
> Nor soil'd by ruder breath?
>
> Who ever saw the earliest rose
> First open her sweet breast ?
> Or, when the summer sun goes down,
> The first soft star in evening's crown
> Light up her gleaming crest ?

This leads the author to reflect and moralize on that other flower—"Love, the last best gift of Heaven." The first line of the first verse may have been suggested by Burns' allusion to "Auld Nature" that,—

> Her 'prentice han' she tried on man.

29. The second verse of the poem for the *Fifth Sunday in Lent*, thus relates the miracle of the burning bush :—

> Far seen across the sandy wild,
> Where, like a solitary child,
> He thoughtless roam'd and free,

---

* A note here makes reference to Burns' Works, i. 293, Dr. Currie's edition.

> One towering thorn* was wrapt in flame—
> Bright without blaze it went and came :
> 　Who would not turn and see?
>
> Along the mountain ledges green
> The scatter'd sheep at will may glean
> 　The Desert's spicy stores:

　·　　　　·　　　　·　　　　·

30. *Sunday next before Easter*, (*Palm Sunday*), the poem opens with an impressive and persuasive address to all Christian Poets :—

> Ye whose hearts are beating high
> With the pulse of Poesy,
> Heirs of more than royal race,
> Fram'd by Heaven's peculiar grace,
> God's own work to do on earth,
> 　(If the word be not too bold,)
> Giving virtue a new birth,
> 　And a life that ne'er grows old—
>
> Sovereign masters of all hearts !
> Know ye, who hath set your parts ?
> He who gave you breath to sing,
> By whose strength ye sweep the string,
> He hath chosen you, to lead
> 　His Hosannas here below;—
> Mount, and claim your glorious meed;
> 　Linger not with sin and woe.

Should they fail to respond to this call, then :—

> Stars, His guiding hand that own,
> Flowers, that grow beneath our feet,
> 　Stones in earth's dark womb that rest,
> High and low in choir shall meet,
> 　Ere His name shall be unblest.

And should minstrels be supine, still wanting in their mission :—

> Then waken into sound divine
> The very pavement of Thy shrine,
> Till we, like Heaven's star-sprinkled floor,
> Faintly give back what we adore.

---

* A note explains this to be " Sench," said to be a sort of Acacia.

> Childlike though the voices be,
>   And untunable the parts,
> Thou wilt own the minstrelsy,
>   If it flow from childlike hearts.

31. The poem for the *Monday before Easter*, has for its text —" Doubtless Thou art our Father." He is " Our Father," through every adversity of life, even although :—

> The fragrance of our old paternal fields
> May be forgotten ; and the time may come
>   When the babe's kiss no sense of pleasure yields
> Even to the doting mother.

It is the common lot of Human Nature that :—

> There are who sigh that no fond heart is theirs,
>   None loves them best.

God's light shines impartially on the evil and the good in His world :—

> Thus sunbeams pour alike their glorious tide
>   To light up worlds, or wake an insect's mirth:
> They shine and shine with unexhausted store—

The memory of ransomed spirits was brought to our Lord's mind's eye during the two nights and days in the Garden of Gethsemane, even "in His hour of agony." On this the poet apostrophizes,—

> Ye vaulted cells, where martyr'd seers of old
>   Far in the rocky walls of Sion sleep,
> Green terraces and archéd fountains cold,
>   Where lies the cypress shade so still and deep,
> Dear sacred haunts of glory and of woe,
> Help us, one hour, to trace His musings high and low.

His " unearthly thoughts have passed from earth away : "—

> And fast as evening sunbeams from the sea

have also passed his footsteps " in Sion's deep decay."

In vain we indulge in repining, and in vain fancies :—
> So dreams the heart self-flattering, fondly dreams.

The light that streams from His " dear name : "—
> —— shines, a pale kind star in winter's sky.

32, 33. *Tuesday before Easter*, " Christ refusing the wine ; " and *Wednesday before Easter*, " Christ in the Garden ; " are of that solemn and sacred character which demands a severe rather than an embellished tone of treatment ; and consequently they afford no specific figures beyond those found in the Scripture narrative.

34. The poet, in commemorating the *Thursday before Easter*, desires to possess the fervour and power of Daniel, to pray for " God's new Israel," sunk low though " flourishing to sight as fair as Sion ;" adding :—

> 'Tis true, nor winter stays thy growth,
>   Nor torrid summer's sickly smile ;
> The flashing billows of the south
>   Break not upon so lone an isle,
> But thou, rich vine, art grafted there,
> The fruit of death or life to bear.
>
> .   .   .   .   .
>
> Oh! grief to think, that grapes of gall
>   Should cluster round thine healthiest shoot !
> .   .   .   .   .

The Resurrection is suggested in the couplet :—

> So when th' Archangel's word is spoken
> And Death's deep trance for ever broken.

35. The fourth verse of the poem for *Good Friday* has the figure :—

> —— Love, the flower that closes up for fear
> When rude and selfish spirits breathe too near.

The next verse has the reflection on mourners looking to the Cross :—

> Then like a long-forgotten strain
>   Comes sweeping o'er the heart forlorn
> What sunshine hours had taught in vain
>   Of JESUS suffering shame and scorn.

36, 37. Passing over *Easter Eve*, which only affords an unsuggestive dirge, we note the following couplet of the first verse of the poem for *Easter Day :*—

> Oh! day of days ! shall hearts set free
> No "minstrel rapture" find for Thee ?

The words in inverted commas are found in Sir Walter Scott's " Lay of the Last Minstrel :"—

> "For him no minstrel raptures swell."

The third and fourth lines are metaphorical :—

> Thou art the Sun of other days,
> They shine by giving back Thy rays.

38. For *Monday in Easter Week*, we have the poem :—

> Go up and watch the new-born rill
>   Just trickling from its mossy bed,
>   Streaking the heath-clad hill
>   With a bright emerald thread.
>
> Canst thou her bold career foretel,
>   What rocks she shall o'erleap or rend,
>   How far in Ocean's swell
>   Her freshening billows send ?
>
> Perchance that little brook shall flow
>   The bulwark of some mighty realm.
>   .   .   .   .
>
> Or canst thou guess, how far away
>   Some sister nymph, beside her urn
>   Reclining night and day,
>   Mid reeds and mountain fern,
>
> Nurses her store, with thine to blend
>   When many a moor and glen are past,
>   Then in the wide sea end
>   Their spotless lives at last ?

In conclusion the poet asks "even so, the course of prayer, who knows ?"

39. For the *Tuesday in Easter Week*, we have the much admired address "To the Snow-drop."

> Thou first-born of the year's delight,
>   Pride of the dewy glade,
> In vernal green and virgin white,
>   Thy vestal robes, array'd ;

'Tis not because thy drooping form
  Sinks graceful on its nest,
When chilly shades from gathering storm
  Affright thy tender breast;

Nor for yon river islet wild
  Beneath the willow spray,
Where like the ringlets of a child,
  Thou weav'st thy circle gay ;

'Tis not for these I love thee dear—
  Thy shy averted smiles
To Fancy bode a joyous year,
  One of Life's fairy isles.

They twinkle in the wintry moon,
  And cheer th' ungenial day,
And tell us, all will glisten soon
  As green and bright as they.

Is there a heart, that loves the Spring,
  Their witness can refuse?

.   .   .   .   .

" Yet mortals doubt" all heavenly news. But we confess
we see no connection between these five verses, and the
nine that follow; the first relate to the earliest flower of
spring, the remainder to " wandering" and " faithless
hearts," advised to seek guidance.

40. In the hymn for the *First Sunday after Easter*—
" First Father of the holy seed,"—lines occur that are
characteristic of the poetry of " The Christian Year," for
they come unexpectedly, and where most other hymnists
would have taken their key from the opening lines of the
poem. Thus the third verse begins :—

For oft, when summer leaves were bright,
And every flower was bath'd in light,
  In sunshine moments past.

And the eleventh and last verse runs thus :—

O joys, that sweetest in decay,
Fall not, like wither'd leaves, away,

> But with the silent breath
> Of violets drooping one by one,
> Soon as their fragrant task is done,
> Are wafted high in death!

41. *Second Sunday after Easter;* the poet imaginatively describes—

> In outline dim and vast
> Their fearful shadows cast
> The giant forms of empires on their way
> To ruin.

Balaam, who "fain would curse" the Israelites, is represented as being so abstracted, and so intent on observing the fate of empires, that :—

> No sun or star so bright
> In all the world of light—

could draw to heaven his downward eye; yet meanwhile :—

> Lo, from yon argent field,
>
> One gentle star glides down, on earth to dwell.
>
> A token of wild war,
>
> But close to us it gleams,
> Its soothing lustre streams
> Around our home's green walls, and on our churchway path.

" He watch'd his sorceries dark and dread :"—

> He watch'd till morning's ray
> On lake and meadow lay,
> And willow-shaded streams, that silent sweep
> Around——

42. The *Third Sunday's* hymn opens with :—

> Well may I guess and feel
> Why Autumn should be sad ;
> But vernal airs should sorrow heal,
> Spring should be gay and glad
> Yet as along this violet bank I rove :
> The languid sweetness seems to choke my breath,
> I sit me down beside the hazel grove,
> And sigh, and half could wish my weariness were death.

> Like a bright veering cloud
>   Grey blossoms twinkle there,
> Warbles around a busy crowd
>   Of larks in purest air.

The fourth verse affords a happy touch of Human Nature:—

> Mysterious to all thought
>   A mother's prime of bliss,
> When to her eager lips is brought
>   Her infant's thrilling kiss.
> O never shall it set, the sacred light
>   Which dawns that moment on her tender gaze,
> In the eternal distance blending bright
> Her darling's hope and hers, for love and joy and praise.

43. *Fourth Sunday after Easter*. In reference to Human Nature, we have here :—

> The watchful mother tarries nigh
> Though sleep have clos'd her infant's eye,
> For should he wake, and find her gone,
> She knows she could not bear his moan.

Suppliants are represented awaiting the monarch " to aid :"—

> The splendours of his crowning day.

Looking homewards :—

> The everlasting gates again
> Roll back, and, lo ! a royal train—
> From the far depth of light once more
> The floods of glory earth-ward pour :
> They part like shower-drops in mid air,
>   But ne'er so soft fell noon-tide shower,
> Nor evening rainbow gleam'd so fair
>   To weary swains in parchéd bower.

All which is very sweet, smooth, and mellifluous, but wanting in that sublimity of treatment which the subject naturally suggests.

44. The hymn for the *Fifth Sunday*, commences—" Now is there solemn pause in earth and heaven;" and the second only, out of twelve verses, can be quoted as an example of Nature-Study :—

> Deep is the silence as of summer noon,
>   When a soft shower
>   Will trickle soon,
> A gracious rain, freshening the weary bower—
>   O sweetly then far off is heard
>   The clear note of some lonely bird.

45. The hymn for *Ascension Day* begins :—

> Soft cloud, that while the breeze of May
> Chants her glad matins in the leafy arch,
>   Draw'st thy bright veil across the heavenly way.

But this strain is not sustained in the ten succeeding verses. The sixth verse, however, happily alludes to space in the triplet :—

> The sun and every vassal star,
> All space, beyond the soar of Angel wings,
>   Wait on His word.

46. To the *Sunday after Ascension* the poet has devoted thirteen verses, from which we quote the first two :—

> The Earth that in her genial breast
> Makes for the down a kindly nest,
> Where wafted by the warm south-west
>   It floats at pleasure,
> Yields, thankful, of her very best,
>   To nurse her treasure :
>
> True to her trust, tree, herb, or reed,
> She renders for each scatter'd seed,
> And to her Lord, with duteous heed
>   Gives large increase :
> Thus year by year she works unfeed,
>   And will not cease.

47. The poem for *Whit Sunday* has reference to the text from the *Acts* relating to the meeting of the Apostles when "they were filled with the Holy Ghost ;" and as might be expected, we find little in it concerning Nature beyond words and single lines. So far this poem forms a useful study, being as remote as possible from the *descriptive* style. Of old, God "came down from Heaven, in power and wrath :"

> Before His feet the clouds were riven,
>   Half darkness and half flame :
> Around the trembling mountain's base
>   The prostrate people lay ;
>   A day of wrath, ———
>   A dim and dreadful day.

His second coming was " in power and love,"—

>   Softer than gale at morning prime
>   Hover'd his holy Dove.

On Sinai the fires rushed,—

>   In sudden torrents dread,

>   .   .   .   .

>   Like arrows went those lightnings forth
>   Wing'd with the sinner's doom.

48. The poem for *Monday in Whitsun-week* has for its text that portion of *Genesis* referring to the interrupted building of the City of Babylon. It commences :—

>   Since all that is not heav'n must fade,
>   Light be the hand of Ruin laid
>   Upon the home I love :
>   With lulling spell let soft Decay
>   Steal on, and spare the giant sway,
>   The crash of tower and grove.

>   Far opening down some woodland deep
>   In their own quiet glade should sleep
>   The relics dear to thought,
>   And wild-flower wreaths from side to side
>   Their waving tracery hang, to hide
>   What ruthless Time has wrought.

>   Such are the visions green and sweet
>   That o'er the wistful fancy fleet
>   In Asia's sea-like plain,
>   Where slowly, round his isles of sand,
>   Euphrates through the lonely land
>   Winds towards the pearly main.

>   Slumber is there, but not of rest ;
>   There her forlorn and weary nest
>   The famish'd hawk has found,
>   The wild dog howls at fall of night,
>   The serpent's rustling coils affright
>   The traveller on his round.

> What shapeless form, half lost on high,
> Half seen against the evening sky,
>   Seems like a ghost to glide,
> And watch, from Babel's crumbling heap,
> Where in her shadow, fast asleep,
>   Lies fall'n imperial Pride ?
>
> With half-clos'd eye a lion there
> Is basking in his noontide lair,
>   Or prowls in twilight gloom.

    .   .   .   .

49. The poem for *Tuesday in Whitsun-week* is addressed to Candidates for Ordination, and has only very remote references to Nature, such as :—

> Lord, in Thy field I work all day.

The pastor's flock are " wilful, wandering sheep." Through the " weary course he runs," he becomes like him who,—

> All powerless and benighted seems.

50. For *Trinity Sunday* we have a poem a little, but not much more indebted to Nature. The poet alludes to the Creator's " mercy's ocean wide," and seeks,—

> To search the deepening mystery,
> The wonders of Thy sea and sky.

The poet muses on entering the church, and approaching the shrine :—

> As travellers on some woodland height,
> When wintry suns are gleaming bright,
> Lose in arch'd glades their tangled sight ;—
>
> By glimpses such as dreamers love
> Through her grey veil the leafless grove
> Shews where the distant shadows rove ;—
>
> Such trembling joy the soul o'er-awes
> As nearer to Thy shrine she draws ;—

    .   .   .   .

> The busy world a thousand ways
> Is hurrying by, nor ever stays
> To catch a note of Thy dear praise.

    .   .   .   .

> Alas ! for her Thy opening flowers
> Unheeded breathe to summer showers,
> Unheard the music of Thy bowers.

51. *First Sunday after Trinity.* This poem opens with the enquiry :—

> Where is the land with milk and honey flowing ?
>
>   .   .   .   .   .   .
>
> Here over shatter'd walls dank weeds are growing,
> And blood and fire have run in mingled stream ;
> Like oaks and cedars all around
> The giant corses strew the ground.
>
>   .   .   .
>
> These are not scenes for pastoral dance at even,
> For moonlight rovings in the fragrant glades,
> Soft slumbers in the open eye of heaven,
> And all the listless joy of summer shades.
>
>   .   .   .   .   .

Then follows another enquiry, figuratively expressed :—

> Where is the sweet repose of hearts repenting,
> The deep calm sky, the sunshine of the soul ?
>
>   .   .   .   .   .
>
> ———— Our path of glory
> By many a cloud is darkened and unblest :
> And daily as we downward glide,
> Life's ebbing stream on either side
> Shows at each turn some mouldering hope or joy,
> The Man seems following still the funeral of the Boy.
>
>   .   .   .   .   .

These verses close with the appeal :—

> Touch our chill'd hearts with vernal smile,
> Our wintry course do Thou beguile.

52. *Second Sunday after Trinity.* The poem begins :—

> The clouds that wrap the setting sun
>   When Autumn's softest gleams are ending,
> Where all bright hues together run
>   In sweet confusion blending :—
> Why, as we watch their floating wreath,
> Seem they the breath of life to breathe ?
> To Fancy's eye their motions prove
> They mantle round the Sun for love.

> When up some woodland dale we catch
>   The many twinkling smile* of Ocean,
> Or with pleas'd ear bewilder'd watch
>   His chime of restless motion ;
> Still as the surging waves retire
> They seem to gasp with strong desire,
> Such signs of love old Ocean gives,
> We cannot choose but think he lives.
>
> .   .   .   .
>
> But he, whose heart will bound to mark
>   The full bright burst of summer morn,
> Loves too each little dewy spark
>   By leaf or floweret worn :
> Cheap forms, and common hues, 'tis true,
> Through the bright shower-drop meet his view ;
> The colouring may be of this earth ;
> The lustre comes of heavenly birth.
>
> .   .   .   .

Human nature is sketched in the lines :—

> No distance breaks the tie of blood ;
>   Brothers are brothers evermore ;
>
> .   .   .   .
>
> Wild thoughts within, bad men without,
> All evil spirits round about,
> Are banded in unblest device,
> To spoil Love's earthly paradise.

53. In the poem for the *Third Sunday after Trinity*, the first three verses give a phase of Human Nature seeking seclusion :—

> O, hateful spell of Sin ! when friends are nigh,
>   To make stern Memory tell her tale unsought,
> And raise accusing shades of hours gone by,
>   To come between us and all kindly thought !
>
> Chill'd at her touch, the self-reproaching soul
>   Flies from the heart and home she dearest loves
> To where lone mountains tower, or billows roll,
>   Or to your endless depth, ye solemn groves.
>
> In vain : the averted cheek in loneliest dell
>   Is conscious of a gaze it cannot bear,
> The leaves that rustle near us seem to tell
>   Our heart's sad secret to the silent air.

---

* A note states this to be imitated from Æschylus.

Nor is the dream untrue ; for all around
  The heavens are watching with their thousand eyes,[*]
We cannot pass our guardian angel's bound,
  Resign'd or sullen, he will hear our sighs.

He in the mazes of the budding wood
  Is near, and mourns to see our thankless glance
Dwell coldly, where the fresh green earth is strew'd
  With the first flowers that lead the vernal dance.

In wasteful bounty shower'd, they smile unseen,
  Unseen by man—but what if purer sprights
By moonlight o'er their dewy bosoms lean
  To adore the Father of all gentle lights ?

54. For the *Fourth Sunday after Trinity* we have a poem of twenty-three verses, commencing with :—

It was not then a poet's dream,
  An idle vaunt of song,
Such as beneath the moon's soft gleam
  On vacant fancies throng ;

Which bids us see in heaven and earth
  In all fair things around,
Strong yearnings for a blest new birth
  With sinless glories crowned ;

Which bids us hear,

   .   .   .   .

When dewy eve her curtain draws
  Over the day's turmoil,
In the low chant of wakeful birds,
  In the deep weltering flood,
In whispering leaves,[†] these solemn words—
  " God made us all for good."

All true, all faultless, all in tune,
  Creation's wondrous choir
Open'd in mystic unison
  To last till time expire.

   .   .   .   .

---

[*] See the hymn by John Hunt, page 78.
    And stars bedecked the skies,
  That seemed Creation's thousand eyes.

[†] See page 240, No. 55: " Or whispering palm-leaves," &c.

But Man, and—

> Man only mars the sweet accord.

The advance of Night is beautifully expressed :—

> But when eve's silent foot-fall steals
>   Along the eastern sky,
> And one by one to earth reveals
>   Those purer fires on high,
>
> When one by one each human sound
>   Dies on the awful ear,
> Then Nature's voice no more is drown'd,
>   She speaks and we must hear.

The next verse, the eleventh, suggests :—

> Then pours she on the Christian heart
>   That warning still and deep,
> At which high spirits of old would start
>   Even from their Pagan sleep.

—but what the "warning" is which "Nature" thus "pours on the Christian heart," on this approach of Night —"eve's silent foot-fall," is left entirely to the reader's imagination. This peculiarity in many of these poems gives them a singular obscurity, which the reader often attributes rather to his own ignorance than to the poet's neglecting more definitely to express the sentiments which he designs to convey to all minds, to the weak equally with the wise. Sacred poetry above all other kinds, ought to be as free as possible from indications of haste, for if the reader feel bewildered, his further perusal of a poem must end in disappointment; the thread of the argument being once broken, all that follows becomes incoherent and inconclusive. And we have little doubt that to this very circumstance may fairly be attributed the want of entire satisfaction which we have frequently heard expressed by readers who rank above the average standard of compo-

tency to form an opinion of the general excellence or deficiency of compositions, although unable to discover the
precise source of their dissatisfaction.

55. *Fifth Sunday after Trinity;* the text here given
is from St. Luke's Gospel,—"We have toiled all the
night," and relates to the repeated efforts of the anxious
fishermen; applying this, the poet proceeds to depict the
following sea-piece :—

> For not upon a tranquil lake
>   Our pleasant task we ply,
> Where all along our glistening wake
>   The softest moonbeams lie;
>
> Where rippling wave and dashing oar
>   Our midnight chant attend,
> Or whispering palm-leaves* from the shore
>   With midnight silence blend.

It is Man's Nature to desire peace, but :—

> Sweet thoughts of peace, ye may not last:
>   Too soon some ruder sound
> Calls us from where ye soar so fast
>   Back to our earthly round.
>
>   .   .   .   .
>
> Full many a dreary anxious hour
>   We watch our nets alone
> In drenching spray, and driving shower,
>   And hear the night-bird's moan.

56. The poem for the *Sixth Sunday after Trinity* gives
a sketch of Human Nature, in which the Conscience-
stricken sinner is thus set before us :—

> When bitter thoughts, of conscience born,
>   With sinners wake at morn
> When from our restless couch we start,
>   With fever'd lips and wither'd heart,
> Where is the spell to charm those mists away,
> And make new morning in that darksome day ?

---

* See page 238, No 54, " In whispering leaves," &c.

One draught of spring's delicious air,
One steadfast thought, that GOD is there.

57. The Feast in the Wilderness is set forth in the
poem for the *Seventh Sunday after Trinity*, in a style well
worthy of attentive perusal :—

> Go not away, thou weary soul:
> Heaven has in store a precious dole
> Here on Bethsaida's cold and darksome height,
> Where over rocks and sands arise
> Proud Sirion in the northern skies,
> And Tabor's lonely peak, 'twixt thee and noonday light.
>
> And far below, Gennesaret's main
> Spreads many a mile of liquid plain,
> (Though all seem gather'd in one eager bound,)
> Then narrowing cleaves yon palmy lea,
> Towards that deep sulphureous sea,
> Where five proud cities lie, by one dire sentence drown'd.
>
> .   .   .   .
>
> ———— the guests are gone,
> And over all that upland lone
> The breeze of eve sweeps wildly as of old—
> But far unlike the former dreams,
> The heart's sweet moonlight softly gleams
> Upon life's varied view, so joyless erst and cold.
>
> As mountain travellers in the night,
> When heaven by fits is dark and bright,
> Pause listening on the silent heath, and hear
> Nor trampling hoof nor tinkling bell,
> Then bolder scale the rugged fell.
>
> .   .   .   .
>
> So when the tones of rapture gay
> On the lorn ear die quite away,
> The lonely world seems lifted nearer heaven;
> Seen daily, yet unmark'd before,
> Earth's common paths are strewed all o'er
> With flowers of pensive hope, the wreath of man forgiven.
>
> The low sweet tones of Nature's lyre
> No more on listless ears expire,

> Nor vainly smiles along the shady way
>   The primrose in her vernal nest,
>   Nor unlamented sink to rest,
> Sweet roses one by one,* nor autumn leaves decay.
>
>   .   .   .
>
>   There's not a star the heaven can show,
>
>   .   .   .   .
>
> But feeds with solace kind the willing soul—
>   Men love us, or they need our love;
>   Freely they own, or heedless prove
> The curse of lawless hearts, the joy of self-control.

58. For the *Eighth Sunday after Trinity*, the fifth verse is as follows :—

> Thou know'st how hard to hurry by,
> Where on the lonely woodland road
>   Beneath the moonlight sky
>   The festal warblings flow'd.

59. In the first verse for the *Ninth Sunday after Trinity* we find :—

> While underneath each awful arch of green,
> On every mountain top.————

And the next verse has the line :—

> Where all around on mountain, sand and sky,

are traces of " God's chariot wheels."

60. A poem of six verses of eight lines each, dedicated to the *Tenth Sunday after Trinity*, the subject being Christ's weeping over Jerusalem, is unusually scant of references to Nature :—

> Why doth my Saviour weep
>   At sight of Sion's bowers ?
> Shows it not fair from yonder steep,
>   Her gorgeous crown of towers?

61. We can only appropriate the second verse from the poem for the *Eleventh Sunday after Trinity* :—

---

* In the 40th paragraph of this Essay, page 281, we have quoted,—
     " Violets drooping one by one," &c.
And in the 54th, page 239, occur the two lines:—" And one by one
to earth reveals," and—" When one by one each human sound."

> Is this a time for moonlight dreams
> Of love and home by mazy streams,
> For Fancy with her shadowy toys,
> Aerial hopes and pensive joys,
> While souls are wandering far and wide,
> And curses swarm on every side ?

62. The fourth verse of the poem for the *Twelfth Sunday after Trinity*, is one referring to Human Nature in a state of hardened disbelief :—

> The deaf may hear the Saviour's voice,
>   The fetter'd tongue its chain may break;
> But the deaf heart, the dumb by choice,
>   The laggard soul, that will not wake,
> The guilt that scorns to be forgiven ;—
> These baffle e'en the spells of heaven.

The author mentions allusive to earth :—

> The vex'd pulse of this feverish world.

The sixth verse concludes :—

> Weak eyes on darkness dare not gaze,
> It dazzles like the noon-day blaze ;
> But He who sees God's face may brook
> On the true face of Sin to look.

These lines perplex our philosophy, " weak eyes " generally finding relief in " darkness ;" and we certainly never heard of eyes pained or " dazzled " by it, as by " noon-day blaze."

63. The poem for the *Thirteenth Sunday after Trinity* is so entirely deficient in allusions to Nature that we shall omit it altogether. It refers to Moses on the Mount, and contains twenty-one verses of four lines each.

64. The *Fourteenth Sunday after Trinity* has a poem in the second verse of which we find an allusion to the weakness of Human Nature, as exemplified in the conduct of nine out of the ten cleansed lepers. When in sore trouble :—

Then from afar on God we cry ;
But should the mist of woe roll by,
Not showers across an April sky
    Drift, when the storm is o'er,
Faster than those false drops and few
Fleet from the heart, a worthless dew.

65. The poem for the *Fifteenth Sunday* has the text—
" Consider the lilies of the field, how they grow," and proceeds :—

Sweet nurslings of the vernal skies,
    Bath'd in soft airs, and fed with dew,
What more than magic in you lies,
    To fill the heart's fond view ?
In childhood's sports, companions gay,
In sorrow, on Life's downward way,
How soothing ! in our last decay
    Memorials prompt and true.

Relics ye are of Eden's bowers,
    As pure, as fragrant, and as fair,
As when ye crown'd the sunshine hours
    Of happy wanderers there.
Fall'n all beside—the world of life,
How is it stain'd with fear and strife !
In Reason's world what storms are rife,
    What passions range and glare !

But cheerful and unchang'd the while
.   Your first and perfect form ye show,
The same that won Eve's matron smile
    In the world's opening glow.
The stars of Heaven a course are taught
Too high above our human thought;—
Ye may be found if ye are sought,
    And as we gaze, we know.

Ye dwell beside our paths and homes,
    Our paths of sin, our homes of sorrow,
And guilty man, where'er he roams,
    Your innocent mirth may borrow.
The birds of air before us fleet,
They cannot brook our shame to meet—
But we may taste your solace sweet
    And come again to-morrow.

Ye fearless in your nests abide—
    Nor may we scorn, too proudly wise,
Your silent lessons, undescried
    By all but lowly eyes:

> For ye could draw th' admiring gaze
> Of Him who worlds and hearts surveys :
> Your order wild, your fragrant maze,
>   He taught us how to prize.

The next verse concludes very paradoxically :—

> Ye felt your Maker's smile that hour,
>   As when He paus'd and own'd you good ;
> His blessing on earth's primal bower,
>   Ye felt it all renew'd.
> What care ye now, if winter's storm
> Sweep ruthless o'er each silken form ?
> Christ's blessing at your heart is warm,
>   Ye fear no vexing mood.

The transition from the flower to consider the state of fallen Human Nature follows as a consequence :—

> Alas ! of thousand bosoms kind,
>   That daily court you and caress,
> How few the happy secret find
>   Of your calm loveliness !
>   .   ,   .   .
> Go sleep like closing flowers at night.

66. The *Sixteenth Sunday after Trinity* offers a poem affording us only the observation that Human Nature is constantly subject to " woe :"—

> In Life's long sickness evermore
>   Our thoughts are tossing to and fro :
> We change our posture o'er and o'er,
>   But cannot rest, nor cheat our woe.

The tenth verse alludes figuratively to returning "wanderers :"—

> So wanderers ever fond and true
>   Look homeward through the evening sky,
> Without a streak of Heaven's soft blue
>   To aid Affection's dreaming eye.

67. *Nineteenth Sunday after Trinity.* The Seventeenth, and the Eighteenth Sunday are barren of allusions to Nature.

In the first verse of the poem for the Nineteenth we meet with the following couplet :—

> When fade all earthly flowers and bays.
> When summer friends are gone and fled.

"The martyrs liv'd,"—the three cast into the fiery furnace, for the " angel came "—

> To make the rushing fire-flood seem
> Like summer breeze by woodland stream.

The poet offers a picture of parental solicitude, in the seventh verse :—

> The Father, who his vigil keeps
> By the sad couch whence hope hath flown,
> Watching the eye where reason sleeps.

68. The hymn for the *Twentieth Sunday* deals with the grand and sublime in Nature, commencing :—

> Where is thy favour'd haunt, eternal Voice,
> The region of thy choice,
> Where, undisturb'd by sin and earth, the soul
> Owns thine entire control ?—
> 'Tis on the mountain's summit dark and high,
> When storms are hurrying by :
> 'Tis 'mid the strong foundations of the earth,
> Where torrents have their birth.
>
> No sounds of worldly toil ascending there,
> Mar the full burst of prayer ;
> Lone Nature feels that she may freely breathe,
> And round us and beneath
> Are heard her sacred tones : the fitful sweep
> Of winds across the steep,
> Through wither'd bents—romantic note and clear,
> Meet for a hermit's ear,—
>
> The wheeling kite's wild solitary cry,
> And, scarcely heard so high,
> The dashing waters when the air is still,
> From many a torrent rill
> That winds unseen beneath the shaggy fell,
> Track'd by the blue mist well ;
> Such sounds as make deep silence in the heart,
> For Thought to do her part.

69. Tranquil and very different is the next scene, opening to us the *Twenty-first Sunday* :—

> The morning mist is clear'd away,
> Yet still the face of Heaven is grey,
> Nor yet th' autumnal breeze has stirr'd the grove,
> Faded yet full, a paler green
> Skirts soberly the tranquil scene,
> The red-breast warbles round this leafy cove.

A verse which leads to reflections on, and associations with the red-breast's " cheerful tender strain."

70. In the poem for the *Twenty-second Sunday*, Human Nature is associated with external Nature :—

> What liberty so glad and gay,
>   As where the mountain boy,
> Reckless of regions far away,
>   A prisoner lives in joy?
>
> The dreary sounds of crowded earth,
>   The cries of camp or town,
> Never untun'd his lonely mirth,
>   Nor drew his visions down.
>
> The snow-clad peaks of rosy light
>   That meet his morning view,
> The thwarting cliffs that bound his sight,
>   They bound his fancy too.
>
> Two ways alone his roving eye
>   For aye may onward go,
> Or in the azure deep on high,
>   Or darksome mere below.
>
> O blest restraint! more blessed range !
>   Too soon the happy child
> His nook of homely thought will change
>   For life's seducing wild.

71. This sketch is followed for the *Twenty-third Sunday*, by a bright sunset scene, with appropriate reflections on its likeness to " decaying life :"—

> Red o'er the forest peers the setting sun,
>   The line of yellow light dies fast away
> That crown'd the eastern copse: and chill and dun
>   Falls on the moor the brief November day.

> Now the tir'd hunter winds a parting note,
>   And Echo bids good-night from every glade!
> Yet wait awhile, and see the calm leaves float
>   Each to his rest beneath their parent shade.

.   .   .   .

Allusive to man's " slow creeping on cold earth," as contrasted with the soul's flight to heaven, the poet sings of the former, compared with man's attempts,—" breezes laugh to scorn,"—

> Our puny speed, and birds, and clouds in Heaven,
>   And fish, like living shafts that pierce the main,
> And stars that shoot through freezing air at even—
>   Who but would follow, might he break his chain?
>
> And thou shalt break it soon; the groveling worm
>   Shall find his wings, and soar as fast and free
> As his transfigur'd Lord with lightning form
>   And snowy vest—such grace He won for thee.

72. For the *Twenty-fourth Sunday after Trinity*, the poet has taken his text from Proverbs—" The heart knoweth his own bitterness," and this leads to reflections affecting Human Nature :—

> Why should we faint, and fear to live alone,
>   Since all alone, so Heaven has will'd, we die,*
> Nor even the tenderest heart, and next our own,
>   Knows half the reasons why we smile and sigh?
>
> Each in his hidden sphere of joy or woe
>   Our hermit spirits dwell, and range apart,
> Our eyes see all around in gloom or glow—
>   Hues of their own, fresh borrow'd from the heart.

" If hearts" in perfect sympathy were a feature of earth, man would seek no higher home; nor, if we had insight into the " bosom's night," of " rude bad thoughts," should we be content with earth :—

> Who would not shun the dreary uncouth place?
>   As if, fond leaning where her infant slept,
> A mother's arm a serpent should embrace:
>   So might we friendless live, and die unwept.

---

* A note informs us that this idea is suggested by Pascal.

Here as before we notice a strange obscurity in the poet's figurative expression, affording another occasion of mistiness; for where a figure presents multiplied aspects, the reader is perplexed to ascertain which one of them the poet had in his mind, and was desirous should be understood by the reader.

73. For the *Twenty-fifth Sunday,* we are presented with a brilliant sun-rise :—

> The bright hair'd morn is glowing
>   O'er emerald meadows gay,
> With many a clear gem strowing
>   The early shepherd's way,
> Ye gentle elves, by Fancy seen
>   Stealing away with night
> To slumber in your leafy screen,
>   Tread more than airy light.
>
> And see what joyous greeting
>   The sun through Heaven has shed,
> Though fast yon shower be fleeting,
>   His beams have faster sped.
> For, lo ! above the western haze
>   High towers the rainbow arch
> In solid span of purest rays :
>   How stately is its march!
>
> Pride of the dewy morning !
>   The swain's experienc'd eye
> From thee takes timely warning,
>   Nor trusts the gorgeous sky :
> For well he knows, such dawnings gay
>   Bring noons of storm and shower,
> And travellers linger on the way
>   Beside the sheltering bower.

74. The hymn for the *Sunday next before Advent,* opens with the solemn lines :—

> Will God indeed with fragments bear,
> Snatch'd late from the decaying year ?
> Or can the Saviour's blood endear
>   The dregs of a polluted life ?

  AN ESSAY ON

When down th' o'erwhelming current tost,
Just ere he sink for ever lost,
The sailor's untried arms are cross'd
In agonizing prayer, will Ocean cease her strife?

The Laws of Nature are inexorable, unchangeable; neither for youth nor age, for saint or sinner, will "Ocean cease her strife."

75. For *St. Andrew's Day*, the hymn opens with a phase of Human Nature :—

When brothers part for manhood's race,
  What gift may most endearing prove
To keep fond memory in her place,
  And certify a brother's love ?

'Tis true, bright hours together told,
  And blissful dreams in secret shar'd,
Serene or solemn, gay or bold,
  Shall last in fancy unimpair'd.

Even round the death-bed of the good
  Such dear remembrances will hover,
And haunt us with no vexing mood
  When all the cares of earth are over.

76 *The Conversion of St. Paul* has suggested the following picturesque sketch :—

The midday sun, with fiercest glare,
Broods o'er the hazy, twinkling air ;
  Along the level sand
The palm-tree's shade unwavering lies,
Just as thy towers, Damascus, rise
  To greet yon wearied band.

The leader of that martial crew
Seems bent some mighty deed to do,
  So steadily he speeds,
With lips firm clos'd and fixed eye,
Like warrior when the fight is nigh,
  Nor talk nor landscape heeds.

77. For *St. Philip and St. James's Day*, we have the poem commencing :—

Dear is the morning gale of spring,
  And dear th' autumnal eve;
But few delights can summer bring
  A Poet's crown to wear.

Her bowers are mute, her fountains dry,
   And ever Fancy's wing
Speeds from beneath her cloudless sky,
   To autumn or to spring.

Sweet is the infant's waking smile,
   And sweet the old man's rest—
But middle age by no fond wile,
   No soothing calm is blest.

Still in the world's hot restless gleam
   She plies her weary task,
While vainly for some pleasant dream
   Her wandering glances ask.

78. The poem for *St. John Baptist's Day* is replete with allusions to Nature, in a figurative sense :—

Twice in her season of decay
The fallen Church hath felt Elijah's eye
   Dart from the wild its piercing ray :
Not keener burns, in the chill morning sky,
   The herald star,
   Whose torch afar
Shadows and boding night-birds fly.

   Star of our morn,
   Who yet unborn
Didst guide our hope, where Christ should rise.

   Love draws a cloud
   From you to shroud
Rebellion's mystery here below.

   And since we see, and not afar,
The twilight of the great and dreadful day,
   Why linger, till Elijah's car
Stoop from the clouds ?————

79. In the poem for *St. Bartholomew* we have a natural optical effect described as produced by artificial means ; for the " mirror " may be a polished stone, metal, glass, or water :—

Hold up thy mirror to the sun,
   And thou shalt need an eagle's gaze,
So perfectly the polished stone
   Gives back the glory of his rays :

> Turn it, and it shall paint as true
>   The soft green of the vernal earth,
> And each small flower of bashful hue,
>   That closest hides its lowly birth.
>
> .   .   .   .
>
> Nathanael
>
> .   .   .   .
>
> In his own pleasant fig-tree's shade,
>   Which by his household fountain grew,
>
> .   .   .   .
>
> God's witnesses, a glorious host,
>   Compass Him daily like a cloud.
>
> .   .   .   .

80. We glean but little from the poem for *St. Matthew*;
it commences :—

> Ye hermits   .   .   .
>   The nearest heaven on earth,
> Who talk with God in shadowy glades,
>   Free from rude care and mirth ;
> To whom some viewless teacher brings
> The secret lore of rural things,
> The moral of each fleeting cloud and gale,
> The whispers from above, that haunt the twilight vale :
>
> Say, when in pity ye have gaz'd
>   On the wreath'd smoke afar,
> That o'er some town, like mist upraiz'd,
>   Hung hiding sun and star.
> Then as ye turn'd your weary eye
> To the green earth and open sky,
> Were ye not fain to doubt how Faith could dwell
> Amid that dreary glare, in this world's citadel ?
>
> But Love's a flower* that will not die
>   For lack of leafy screen,
> And Christian Hope can cheer the eye
>   That ne'er saw vernal green ;
> Then be ye sure that Love can bless
> Even in this crowded loneliness,
> Where ever-moving myriads seem to say,
> Go—thou art nought to us, nor we to thee—away !

---

* Coleridge has—" Flowers are lovely ; Love is flower-like."

> There are in this loud stunning tide
>   Of human care and crime ;
> With whom the melodies abide
>   Of th' everlasting chime ;
> Who carry music in their heart
> Through dusky lane and wrangling mart,
> Plying their daily task with busier feet,
> Because their secret souls a holy strain repeat.
>
> .   .   .   .
>
> The tide of sun-rise swells,
> Till tower, and dome, ———
> Are mantled with a golden cloud.

81. *St. Michael and all Angels*, has suggested the dignified poem commencing :—

> Ye stars that round the Sun of righteousness
>   In glorious order roll,
>
> .   .   .   .
>
> Ye eagle spirits, that build in light divine,
>   Oh ! think of us to-day,
> Faint warblers of this earth, that would combine
> Our trembling notes with your accepted lay.
>
> Your amarant wreaths were earn'd ; and homeward all,
>   Flush'd with victorious might,
> Ye might have sped to keep high festival,
>   And revel in the light ;
>
> But meeting us,   .   .   .
>
> .   .   .   .   .
> Ye turned to help us in th' unequal fray.———

" Ye "—who came thronging " all space " to adore at the birth of Christ :—

> As if the stars should leave
> Their stations in the far ethereal wild,
> And round the sun a radiant circle weave.

82. For *St. Luke* we have a poem of twenty verses, the first two being :—

> Two clouds before the summer gale
>   In equal race fleet o'er the sky :
> Two flowers, when wintry blasts assail
>   Together pine, together die.

> But two capricious human hearts—
> No sage's rod may track their ways,
> No eye pursue their lawless starts
> Along their wild self-chosen maze.
>
>   .   .   .   .

83. The poem for *St. Simon and St. Jude*, consisting of thirteen verses of four lines each, represents the Lord's "gracious care" to send some cheerful spirit to tend the "saddened heart that once was gay," when—

> Cheerful as soaring lark, and mild
>   As evening blackbird's full-ton'd lay,
> When the relenting sun has smil'd
>   Bright through a whole December day.
> These are the tones to brace and cheer
>   The lonely watcher of the fold,
> When nights are dark, and foemen near,
>   When visions fade and hearts grow cold.
> How timely then a comrade's song
>   Comes floating on the mountain air,
> And bids thee yet be bold and strong—
>   Fancy may die, but Faith is there.

84. For *All Saints' Day* the poem opens with a wintry scene, commencing :—

> Why blow'st thou not, thou wintry wind,[*]
>   Now every leaf is brown and sere,
> And idly droops, to thee resign'd
>   The fading chaplet of the year ?
> Yet wears the pure aerial sky
> Her summer veil, half drawn on high,
> Of silvery haze, and dark and still,
> The shadows sleep on every slanting hill.
> How quiet shows the woodland scene !
>   Each flower and tree, its duty done,
> Reposing in decay serene,
>   Like weary men when age is won,
> Such calm old age, as conscience pure
> And self-commanding hearts ensure,
> Waiting their summons to the sky,
> Content to live, but not afraid to die.

---

[*] "Blow, blow, thou winter wind."—*Shakspeare.*

If we had but foresight we might perchance see :—

.   .   .   .

> The four strong winds of Heaven fast bound,
> Their downward sweep a moment staid
> On ocean cove and forest glade,
> Till the last flower of autumn shed
> Her funeral odours on her dying bed.

.   .   .   .

An allusion to Famine and War is not so clear,—

> As bloodhounds hush their baying wild
> To wanton with some fearless child,
> So Famine waits, and War with greedy eyes,
> Till some repenting heart be ready for the skies.

85. The poem entitled *Catechism*, has verses touching Human Nature ; the infant mind is thus expressed :—

> Oh ! say not, dream not, heavenly notes
>   To childish ears are vain,
> That the young mind at random floats,
>   And cannot reach the strain.
>
> Dim or unheard, the words may fall,
>   And yet the heaven-taught mind
> May learn the sacred air, and all
>   The harmony unwind.

.   .   .   .

> ———— —— pleas'd to mark
>   Our rude essays of love,
> Faint as the pipe of wakening lark,
>   Heard by some twilight grove :

Children—

> Like spring-flowers in their best array,
>   All silence and all smiles.
>
> Save that each little voice in turn
>   Some glorious truth proclaims,
> What sages would have died to learn,
>   Now taught by cottage dames.

86. For *Confirmation*, the poem commences :—

> The shadow of the Almighty's cloud
>   Calm on the tents of Israel lay,

.   .   .   .

The warriors should prove—

> Steady and pure as stars that beam
>   In middle heaven, all mist above,
> Seen deepest in the frozen stream :—
>   Such is their high courageous love.
>
> And soft as pure, and warm as bright,
>   They brood upon life's peaceful hour,
> As if the Dove that guides their flight
>   Shook from her plumes a downy shower.
>
> Spirit of might———
>   Now leading on the wars of God,
> Now to green isles of shade and dew
>   Turning the waste Thy people trod.

87. On *Matrimony*, the poem contains in the second verse a rather dark, metaphorical allusion to Love, prefigured as a bird, to express " wedded Love," awaiting and obtaining Divine approval :—

> We cower before th' heart-searching eye
>   In rapture as in pain ;
> Even wedded Love, till Thou be nigh,
>   Dares not believe her gain :
> Then in the air she fearless springs,
> The breath of Heaven beneath her wings,
> And leaves her woodnote wild,* and sings
>   A tun'd and measur'd strain.

88. *Visitation and Communion of the Sick.* This poem opens with :—

> O Youth and Joy, your airy tread
> Too lightly springs by Sorrow's bed.
> Your keen eyeglances are too bright,
> Too restless for a sick man's sight,
> Farewell: for one short life we part :

Death—

> Once more I came : the silent room
> Was veil'd in sadly-soothing gloom,

---

* Milton in his *L'Allegro*, has the well-known lines,—

> Or sweetest Shakspeare, Fancy's child,
> Warble his native wood-notes wild.

> And ready for her last abode
> The pale form like a lily shew'd,
> By virgin fingers duly spread,
> And priz'd for love of summer fled.
> The light from those soft-smiling eyes
> Had fleeted to its parent skies.

89. The hymn for the *Burial of the Dead* opens thus :—

> Who says, the wan autumnal sun
>   Beams with too faint a smile
> To light up Nature's face again,
> And, though the year be on the wane,
>   With thoughts of spring the heart beguile ?
>
> Waft him, thou soft September breeze,
>   And gently lay him down
> Within some circling woodland wall,
> Where bright leaves, reddening ere they fall,
>   Wave gaily o'er the waters brown.
>
> And let some graceful arch be there
>   With wreathed mullions proud,
> With burnish'd ivy for its screen,
> And moss, that glows as fresh and green
>   As though beneath an April cloud.——

> .   .   .   .

We here give the third verse, and (with a view to preserve the sense) without omitting the portion belonging to Art, which names " arch"—and " mullions."

90. KEBLE's Poem, *Forms of Prayer to be used at Sea*, consists of five verses, eight lines each, the first being :—

> The shower of moonlight falls as still and clear
>   Upon the desert main,
> As where sweet flowers some pastoral garden cheer
>   With fragrance after rain :
> The wild winds rustle in the piping shrouds,
>   As in the quivering trees :
> Like summer fields, beneath the shadowy clouds
>   The yielding waters darken in the breeze.

· We thus bring to a close our selections of Naturalistic Poetry chosen from ninety out of the one hundred and nine poems in Tʜᴇ Cʜʀɪꜱᴛɪᴀɴ Yᴇᴀʀ: "Thoughts in Verse for the Sundays and Holydays throughout the Year," but containing also others for special ordinances of the Church, Matrimony, Baptism, Confirmation, &c. We have seldom stayed to make any other than some very pointed observation, and it, therefore, now becomes necessary to go over the whole in detail under the several heads following, in order to obtain a concentrated view of each peculiar feature in these poems, so far as the same has any reference to Universal Nature, either external or internal, material or mental.

The foregoing selections we shall now proceed to group under the heads of:—1. Description; 2. Figurative language generally; 8. Similes; 4. Imagination and Fancy; 5. Human Nature; 6. Religious, Moral and Meditative expression of sentiments and feeling; and 7. Negative views of Nature. We commence with:—

1. Dᴇꜱᴄʀɪᴘᴛɪᴏɴ.

The sacred poems of Keble abound in descriptive poetry. It is observed in a critical notice of his work in the *British Quarterly Review*, 1807, that he "was more than a word-painter of landscapes;" and the reviewer endeavours to make it appear that Keble "beheld Nature as a parable, rich with eternal truth, and attempted to expound the intimate connection of human emotion with the transient or more permanent beauties displayed in the material world;" but this latter as a distinguishing characteristic of his poetry is not proved by the examples before us: and we believe we have omitted none that his poems afford." As the statement indicates original research and application, it cannot surely include adaptations from Scripture texts, and imitations from ancient and modern poets. In this respect the assertion thus advanced is absolutely unsupported; and this we venture to state, without conceiving it at all derogatory to the poet's fame to assign him a true instead of a false position in this respect. His many excellencies and beauties require none of the false glitter of fulsome laudation to set off their intrinsic worth.

The first two poems are respectively descriptive of *Morning*, page 213 :—

Hues of the rich unfolding morn,

comprised in three introductory verses; and of *Evening* :—

'Tis gone, that bright and orbed blaze,

delineated in two stanzas. If we omit these prefatory verses the rest do not suffer, but remain more strictly hymn-like in their character. Indeed, it is peculiar to Keble's poems in the *Christian Year*, that one, two, or more verses may be thus extruded without disadvantage.

His ability in description often appears in single lines, as on page 214 :—

And fast beside the olive-border'd way,

.   .   .   .

Full many a soft green isle appears ;

.   .   .   .

On shelter'd nooks of Palestine !

Eight lines, page 214, relate that :—

Not till the freezing blast is still,

s 2

and other autumnal appearnuces set in, will—

> —— the tender flowerets show
> Their bosoms to th' uncertain glow.

We are presented with an Eastern scene, page 215 :—

> Where stately Jordan flows by many a palm,

contained in five verses beautifully descriptive of flowers and balmy air ; the moon, lakes, mountains, and dells.

At page 216, occurs a figurative allusion, leading to a description of early dawn :—

> As rays around the source of light
> Stream upward ere he glow in sight.

Keble is generally very happy in such allusions to Nature, and they possess all the vigour that might be expected to accrue from actual observation working on a sensitive poetical temperament. In an Eastern sketch of this nature, page 218, he refers to the desert, as :—

> —— the dry unfathom'd deep
> Of sands, that lie in lifeless sleep.

The notice of this dreary wilderness, and its pilgrim traveller, comprises seven verses, all more or less descriptive.

Nearly five verses commencing on page 219, are occupied with a picturesque description of Spring—:

> Sweet the lengthening April day,
>
> .　　　.　　　.　　　.
>
> Ranging wild o'er hill and lea.

We have here the leafy nook, willow, and reedy grass ; the brooklet, grove, and nightingale ;—altogether affording a delicious foretaste of rustic sounds and scenery.

A storm of thunder and rain is graphically sketched, page 221,—" the rushing midnight shower," and " fitful breeze "—

> To howl and chafe amid the bending trees,

concluding with " the fiery stream " of the vivid lightning. Very different are the two verses, page 221, delicately depicting the lover's fond fancies :—

> So have I seen some tender flower
> Priz'd above all the vernal bower.

Remarking on the destruction of Zoar, page 224, the poet imagines the Eastern scene before him :—

> Ah wherefore gleam those upland slopes so fair ?
>
> .　　.　　.　　.　　　.
> If all must be forsaken, ruin'd all.

The poem for the *Third Sunday in Lent*, presents but a brief outline referring to the land where " Abraham fed his flocks :"—

> A land that drinks the rain of heaven at will ;

and " oft as they watched" would—

> A gale from bowers of balm
> Sweep o'er the billowy corn, and heave
> The tresses of the palm.
>
> .　　.　　.　　.
> The limpid wells, the orchards green.

—A truly luscious pictorial realization of Fancy's sketch.

The poet has graced his picture of " the sandy wild," page 236, by introducing—

> Along the mountain ledges green
> The scatter'd sheep at will may glean
> The Desert's spicy stores.

The Garden of Gethsemane, page 227, suggests—

> Ye vaulted cells where martyr'd seers of old
>   Far in the rocky walls of Sion sleep,

with their " terraces, fountains, and cypress shade."

A pleasing mountain sketch, page 229, occurs in the verse :—

> Go up and watch the new-born rill
>   Just trickling from its mossy bed,
>   Streaking the heath-clad hill
>   With a bright emerald thread :

—perhaps the spring-head of waters on their way to merge " in Ocean's swell :"—

> Perchance that little brook shall flow
>   The bulwark of some mighty realm.

This is all sunshine and beauty, compounded of the merest matters of fact, in a method of which Keble was a decided master; that is, making the most of Nature's commonest and ever-present features.

One of the poems for *Easter Week* is addressed to *The Snow-drop*, page 229; we quote only the first of six verses :—

> Thou first-born of the year's delight,
>   Pride of the dewy glade,
> In vernal green and virgin white,
>   Thy vestal robes, array'd.

Balaam, page 231 :—

> He watch'd till morning's ray
> On lake and meadow lay,
> And willow-shaded streams, that silent sweep
> Around ———

Allusive to Eastern ruins, page 234, the poet pictures a scene :—

> Far opening down some woodland deep
> In their own quiet glade should sleep
>   The relics dear to thought,
> And wild-flower wreaths from side to side
> Their waving tracery hang, to hide
>   What ruthless Time has wrought.

Three verses follow, equally deserving of notice, relating to the sandy desert :—

———— Asia's sea-like plain.

A " woodland height," page 235, is drawn :—

When wintry suns are gleaming bright,

.   .   .

———— the leafless grove
Shows where the distant shadows rove.

" Israel among the ruins of Canaan," page 236, leads to the description :—

Here over shatter'd walls dank weeds are growing,
And blood and fire have run in mingled stream ;
Like oaks and cedars all around
The giant corses strew the ground.

Autumn is thus depicted, page 236 :—

The clouds that wrap the setting sun
When Autumn's softest gleams are ending,
Where all bright hues together run
In sweet confusion blending.

.   .   .   .

When up some woodland dale we catch
The many twinkling smile of ocean.

This ocean scene is extended ; and the next line opens with three highly descriptive verses :—

The full bright burst of summer morn.

" The Fishermen of Bethsaida," who labour on no " tranquil lake," form the subject of the poem, page 240 :—

Where rippling wave and dashing oar
Our midnight chant attend.

.   .   .   .

Full many a dreary anxious hour
We watch our nets alone
In drenching spray, and driving shower,
And hear the night-bird's moan.

A sketch is given of Bethsaida, page 241 :—

> Here on Bethsaida's cold and darksome height,
>   Where over rocks and sands arise
>   Proud Sirion in the northern skies,
> And Tabor's lonely peak, 'twixt thee and noon-day light,
>   And far below, Gennesaret's main
>   Spreads many a mile of liquid plain.

The approach of night-fall is suggested by :—

>   The low sweet tones of Nature's lyre
>   No more on listless ears expire,
> Nor vainly smiles along the shady way
>   The primrose in her vernal nest,
>   Nor unlamented sink to rest
> Sweet roses one by one, nor autumn leaves decay.

A mountain forest, page 242, is seen :—

>   While underneath each awful arch of green,
>   On every mountain top.——

A view of Jerusalem, page 242, is spoken of as :—

>   Shows it not fair from yonder steep,
>   Her gorgeous crown of towers?

The only poem in *The Christian Year* that distinctly treats of the sublime in Nature's scenery is the one for the *Twentieth Sunday after Trinity*, page 246, and it is certainly very majestic throughout the three verses, commencing :—

>   Where is thy favour'd haunt, eternal Voice,
>   The region of thy choice ?

The reply is that—" 'Tis on the mountain's summit,—'mid the strong foundations of the earth,"—and nought heard but—" the fitful sweep of winds,—or the kite's wild solitary cry,—the dashing waters,"—

>   Such sounds as make deep silence in the heart,
>   For Thought to do her part.

There is an awful grandeur in all this lonely and lofty assemblage of rude, rough, ungenial scenes of rifted rocks and solitary streams and passes amid the wailing winds, and the wild shriek of birds of prey; but its tone is not in unison with the poet's own nature, which sought out rather the pleasing and beautiful than the sublime of scenery, and hence arises the scarcity of delineations of this character.

Approaching Autumn is described, page 247 :—

> The morning mist is clear'd away,
> Yet still the face of Heaven is grey,
>
> .   .   .   .
>
> The red-breast warbles round this leafy cove.

The " Mountain boy," page 247, dwelling amid mountain scenery, gives occasion to make reflections on both :—

> The snow-clad peaks of rosy light
>   That meet his morning view,
> The thwarting cliffs that bound his sight,
>   They bound his fancy too.

A " sun-set," or sun-rise, was the poet's delight, as well for itself, as for the associations with human life, it naturally called forth; of the former, page 247, he sings :—

> Red o'er the forest peers the setting sun,
>   The line of yellow light dies fast away
> That crown'd the eastern copse : and chill and dun
>   Falls on the moor the brief November day.

This is quite Turneresque, there is such close attention to light, and colour, and shade,—marking time, place, and season with faithful exactitude.

The poet's descriptive powers are further exemplified in this poem, page 248, by his account of the huntsman, echo, the fall of the leaf, the speed of clouds, birds, fish,—

> And stars that shoot through freezing air at even.

But we now come to a bright, sunny piece, such a one as the poet loved to paint, and one that has been much and deservedly admired. It is adopted for the *Twenty-fifth Sunday after Trinity*, its subject being " The two rainbows," and is, as usual, made the vehicle for reflections, which, in this instance, have reference to human life in contrast with the circumstances attending the morning and the evening rainbow :—

> The bright hair'd morn is glowing
>   O'er emerald meadows gay,
> With many a clear gem strowing
>   The early shepherd's way.

The morning rainbow is addressed as :—

> Pride of the dewy morning !

But the shepherd knows that it only portends :—

> —— noons of storm and shower.

We have next to contemplate an Eastern scene, page 250 :—

> The midday sun, with fiercest glare,
> Broods o'er the hazy, twinkling air ;
>   Along the level sand
> The palm-tree's shade unwavering lies,
> Just as thy towers, Damascus, rise.

And somewhat similar is the poem for *St. Matthew*, page 258 :—

> The tide of sun-rise swells,
> Till tower, and dome,——
> Are mantled with a golden cloud.

In contrast to this we have a calm, but wintry day described, page 254 :—

> Yet wears the pure aerial sky
> Her summer veil, half drawn on high,
> Of silvery haze, and dark and still
> The shadows sleep on every slanting hill.
>
> How quiet shows the woodland scene !
>   Each flower and tree, its duty done,
> Reposing in decay serene,
>   Like weary men when age is won.

Autumn presents us with another phase of our Seasons, page 257 :—

> Who says, the wan autumnal sun
>   Beams with too faint a smile
> To light up Nature's face again,
> And, though the year be on the wane,
>   With thoughts of spring the heart beguile ?

In a sea-piece, the moonlight is supposed to be falling upon the wide ocean, " the desert main :"

> The wild winds rustle in the piping shrouds,
>   As in the quivering trees :
> Like summer fields, beneath the shadowy clouds
>   The yielding waters darken in the breeze.

The Nature-Student's first aim is the achievement of powerful and effective Description. From the earliest to the latest examples, we find among all poets abundant illustrations, and to these we strongly recommend attention for the matter of their subjects, and their several modes of treatment. But this is, after all, a very elementary department of Nature-Study, and if it went no further, its object would be poor and insufficient indeed. There is more of the physical than the mental required to become a good descriptive poet ; so much depends on the eye, that we have not hesitated to call the writer confined to this single pursuit, a poet artist.

2. Figurative Language generally.

In this department we incur the risk of repeating examples of similes, and of the purely imaginative and fanciful in poetical expression ; whatever does not strictly appertain to the latter, it is proposed to bring together in the present section.　For instance, we have in the poem for *Advent Sunday*, page 214, such a line as :—

> When withering blasts of error swept the sky,

language entirely metaphorical, and yet not purely imaginative.　So again, page 214, the lines :—

> Why then, in sad and wintry time,
> Her heavens all dark with doubt and crime,

are applied to the drooping state of the Church.　Keble is rich in this peculiar and particular application of Nature's aspects in the material world to express sentiments in relation to Christian life and conduct.　To attain to full fruition in this respect was no doubt the great aim of his study as a divine and a poet ; and maintaining the same style and strain he doubtless expressed what he sensibly felt personally when he penned the stanzas, page 215 :—

> Of the bright things in earth and air
> How little can the heart embrace !
> Soft shades and gleaming lights are there—
> I know it well, but cannot trace.

" Nature's beauteous book," ever before him, won his ardent attention ; he found it to be a wondrous and most mysterious tome ; it had not one alone, or only two, but many readings, and multitudinous meanings, affirming and contradicting, yet proving nothing under man's " interpretation."　Are earth, fire, and water among our greatest blessings ?　Are they not also devouring, tormenting, and destructive elements ?　Is air a delicious delicacy ? Yet do not its component parts combine the deleterious with a life compound ?　Is nature alike to all eyes and understandings ; to the wise alike with the wicked, to the philosopher alike with the poet ?

Alluding to Joshua, and the sun's becoming stationary,
page 217, Keble has the line:—

> And backward force the waves of Time.

And in concluding the next poem, page 218, occurs:—

> So life a winter's morn may prove
> To a bright endless year.

Trust in the Saviour, is thus expressed, page 219:—

> To Thee we turn, our last and first
> Our Sun and soothing Moon.

And again, in the next poem, page 219 :—

> Star of the East, how sweet art Thou,
> Seen in Life's early morning sky,
> Ere yet a cloud has dimm'd the brow,
> While yet we gaze with childish eye.

Of the self-deceived, page 222, we are warned :—

> They live and die : their names decay,
> Their fragrance passes quite away.

The poem, page 223, for *Quinquagesima Sunday*, metaphorically applies—"Sweet Dove, Sweet Leaf, Sweet
Rainbow !"

A light is figuratively spoken of, page 227, as streaming
from the Saviour's name on the Cross :—

> It shines, a pale kind star in winter's sky.

Allusive to Sion, page 228, where the "billows of the
south" break on no isle more lone :—

> But thou, rich vine, art grafted there,
> The fruit of death or life to bear.
>
> Oh ! grief to think, that grapes of gall
> Should cluster round thine healthiest shoot !

Of our Saviour, page 229, the poet sings :—

> Thou art the Sun of other days,
> They shine by giving back Thy rays.

An imaginary pageant is depicted, page 231, in the lines :—

> In outline dim and vast
> Their fearful shadows cast
> The giant forms of empires on their way
> To ruin :———

To Balaam and mankind revealed, page 231 :—

> Lo from yon argent field
>
> .   .   .   .
>
> One gentle star glides down, on earth to dwell.

Describing Sinai, page 234 :—

> Like arrows went those lightnings forth,
> Wing'd with the sinner's doom.

The weak Pastor, page 235, declares :—

> " Lord, in Thy field I work all day."

Appealing to the Creator, page 235, the poet seeks :—

> To search the deepening mystery,
> The wonders of Thy sea and sky.

The poem for the *First Sunday after Trinity*, page 236, has the inquiry :—

> Where is the sweet repose of hearts repenting,
> The deep calm sky, the sunshine of the soul ?

The fourth verse of this poem, page 236, sounds the Christian's " war-note," declaring :—

> ——— But our path of glory
> By many a cloud is darken'd and unblest :
> And daily as we downward glide,
> Life's ebbing stream on either side
> Shows at each turn some mouldering hope or joy,
> The Man seems following still the funeral of the Boy.

The fifth and last verse, closes with the lines :—

> Touch our chill'd hearts with vernal smile,
> Our wintry course do Thou beguile.

The universal benevolence of the Creator is expressed on page 241 :—

Earth's common paths are strewn all o'er
With flowers of pensive hope, the wreath of man forgiven.

The poem for *St. John Baptist's Day*, page 251, may be referred to for displays of figurative language, but they would be too lengthy for repetition, and are not very clear in detached passages.

The seasons are compared to the life of Man; and winter to his period of decay, page 254, Nature then reposing :—

Like weary men when age is won,
Such calm old age as conscience pure
And self-commanding hearts ensure,
Waiting their summons to the sky.

In this department the Nature-Student at once enters upon a new field of observation, a mountain is something more than a mere mass of inert matter; and vegetation and animal life present entirely different features to his mind than those required for simply describing those external appearances that meet the eye in his everyday experience. For our present purpose we have now to learn how to apply objects significantly for mental purposes, in appeals to the mind's eye, and not to the mere organ of vision, with which faculty we may be keenly blest: although blind to all the beauteous and intellectual semblances and associations in which Nature is profusely prolific.

3. SIMILES.

There is a singular scarcity of similes in most of our sacred poets, but this is more remarkable in the case of

such a poet as Keble. The presence of similes affords at
least one decided example of originality, when not borrowed
from other sources and merely remodelled.

The slothful are urged, page 214, to—

> Speed to the eastern mount like flame.

Listless travellers in an Eastern clime, page 216, are no
better, but more—

> Like children gazing round,
> Who on God's works no seal of Godhead find.

There are two views of Nature,—Nature as a whole ;
and, the objects of Nature singly. As a whole we have no
difficulty in conceiving the amazing power and insight, and
goodness of the Creator. But if we come to judge between
clime and clime, man and man, the infinite variety of
natural products ; our earth, its waters, and the planetary
system, we are at once lost in wonder, love, and admiration.
This so-called " book," is far more than even a combined
Laboratory, Library, and Museum ; for there is, besides,
a mysterious current of intellect and instinct in active
operation, enveloping and influencing this amazing universe
of mind and matter.

God's love is spoken of, page 218 :—

> As of an ocean vast,
> Mounting in tides against the stream
> Of ages gone and past.

Cheering as is the light of day and the song of birds,
yet still more so is " the soft gleam of Christian worth,"
page 221, a sentiment illustrated from the fact in Nature
that :—

> Light flashes in the gloomiest sky,
> And Music in the dullest plain.

The self-accused die forgotten, page 222 :—

> Their fragrance passes quite away ;
> Like violets in the freezing blast
> No vernal steam around they cast.

There is a singularity here in the expression "vernal steam," somewhat similar to that on page 213, "dewy steam."

"Tears of penance" are alluded to, page 224, when coming "too late for grace :"—

> As on th' uprooted flower the genial rain.

This appears to be original, and is certainly happily chosen.

The passage of thought, page 227, is expressed as, rapid,—

> And fast as evening sunbeams from the sea.

The fires on Sinai, page 234, rushed forth :—

> Like arrows ———
> Wing'd with the sinner's doom.

Speed is variously exemplified, from its slowness on earth to the soul's flight to heaven ; even the breeze laughing to scorn all man's puny efforts, page 248 :—

> And fish, like living shafts that pierce the main,
> And stars that shoot through freezing air at even.

Even Famine and War wait for their prey, page 255 :—

> As bloodhounds hush their baying wild
> To wanton with some fearless child.

We see in the applications the poet makes of Nature indisputable evidence of his power or weakness. It is no praise, but absolute censure, to claim for a poet any excellence he neither possesses nor attempts to display ; and we have already noticed the singular deficiency of Keble in this department of Nature-Study.

4. Imagination and Fancy.

There is some delicious painting in the portraiture of
Morning, page 213, " Hues of the rich unfolding morn," but
as appertaining more to the imaginative, we find :—

> Thou rustling breeze, so fresh and gay,
> That dancest forth at opening day.

And again :—

> Ye fragrant clouds of dewy steam,

precursors of "soft rains."

In the poem for the *Sixth Sunday after Epiphany*, the
10th verse has the epithet "vernal steam," while here the
poet employs " dewy steam," as noticed page 278.

The mildest zephyrs, page 214, delicately appear :—

> As o'er a sleeping infant's eyes
> A mother's hiss :—

Yet the while—

> No sunny gleam awakes the trees,

and all verdure shrinks from appearing before the " uncer-
tain glow" of April skies ; hence arises the inquiry respecting the drooping Church :—

> Is she less wise than leaves in spring,

which advance with the progress of the summer season.

Of the Eastern flowers expanding at night, page 215, it
is said they :—

> Spread their soft breasts, unheeding, to the breeze.

The Eastern wanderer is advised ·to seek a cell in
Kedron :—

> And watch the Moon that saw thy Master's agony.

The poet sings of " earth and air," that :—

> Soft shades and gleaming lights are there,

—indicative of perplexing sights, and signs, and mysteries innumerable.

Suggestive of the music of winds and waters, page 217, the poet hints :—

> Gales from Heaven, if so He will,
>   Sweeter melodies can make
> On the lonely mountain rill
>   Than the meeting waters make.

Joshua's commanding the sun to stand still, introduces into the poem, page 217, such expressions as—" go wanderers of the sky,"—" the waves of Time," and dreams—

> Like stormy lights on mountain streams,
> Wavering and broken all, athwart the conscience glare.

Again :—

> Time's waters will not ebb, nor stray.

God's " love" is compared to the " ocean :" page 218,—

> Mounting in tides against the stream
>   Of ages gone and past.

" To reap in love," we are advised to " sow in holy fear :"—

> So life a winter's morn may prove
>   To a bright endless year.

Mental gloom and dulness are admonished, page 221, that :—

> Light flashes in the gloomiest sky,
> And music in the dullest plain.

Much in Nature escapes the attention of the unobservant eye and mind of the mere versifier; as regards rain, he would see little beyond a wide-spread downfall, and it would never occur to make any distinction, such as that which we meet with at page 221, where the Lord is addressed :—

> Thou, whose soft showers distil
> On ocean waste or rock,
>   Free as on Hermon hill.

For the *Sixth Sunday after Epiphany*, we find a poem, page 222, strongly marked by imagination and fancy, in treating of the passion of love, and its high flown fancies, aided in the description by allusions to flowers and glades, and to tender youth and maturer age. The favourite flower :—

> So frail a gem, it scarce may bear
> The playful touch of evening air ;
> When hardier grown we love it less,
> And trust it from our sight, not needing our caress.

The Poet alludes to those who listlessly dream of such a heaven as—

> A cloudless sun that softly shines,
> Bright maidens and unfailing vines.

The self-accused are said to die :—

> Like violets in the freezing blast.

But this is one of those comparisons which is simply ornamental, without having the merit of accuracy or point.

Notwithstanding the ground being cursed, page 223, through Adam's offence, mercy's showers,—

> Steal down* like April dews, that softest fall and first.

The poem, page 223, is not remarkable for any particularly felicitous use of the " Dove, Leaf, Rainbow, or Lark." It begins :—

> Sweet Dove ! the softest, steadiest plume
> In all the sun-bright sky,
> Brightening in ever-changeful bloom
> As breezes change on high.

The next poem is deservedly distinguishable for the couplet :—

---

* The 6th verse of the poem for *Septuagesima Sunday*, has the couplet:—

> The dew of Heaven is like thy grace,
> It steals in silence down.

> The loving eye that watches thine
> Close as the air that wraps thee round—

This is truly admirable and most poetical.

For the *Third Sunday in Lent*, page 224, the poem has the line :—

> Whose waters kiss the feet of many a vine-clad hill.

The innocence of infancy is not a little heightened by the chosen moment of their babble, thus, page 225:—

> As little children lisp, and tell of Heaven.

The force of association with scenery is applied to the Eastern pilgrim :—

> There's not a strain to Memory dear,
>   Nor flower in classic grove,
> There's not a sweet note warbled here,
>   But minds us of Thy Love.

The mysterious workings of Nature are alluded to, page 225, and the inquiry is suggested :

> When Nature tries her finest touch,
>   Weaving her vernal wreath,
> Mark ye, how close she veils her round,
> Not to be traced by sight or sound,
>   Nor soil'd by ruder breath ?

Goethe was wont to express a desire to detect Nature in the act, in the progressive course of some new development. It is true that Nature has many secrets, and works many marvels in secret; but it is equally true that its investigator, man, is abundantly ignorant. How much does Nature perform openly and daily before our eyes, of which man is as ignorant as he is of her sublimest mysteries. Some little he can read in Nature's book, and most assuredly it is *little* indeed.

The idea of the Sun shining on the evil and the good

without distinction has been variously modified, and among others by Keble, page 227, as follows:

> Thus sunbeams pour alike their glorious tide
>   To light up worlds, or wake an insect's mirth:
> They shine and shine with unexhausted store——

Here Nature-Study steps in most advantageously and conspicuously to assist the poet in eliminating novel views of consequences dependant on Nature's laws and pheno-mena; and particularly in this department of the playful and pleasing efforts of all-powerful imaginative fancy. The results are to a certain degree as plain and conspicuous as can possibly be conceived, and yet they do not occur as matters for common observation. Thus there is little to notice in the melting snow, or the fact of a shadow cast before us, until a Burns, or a Campbell turns some such simple fact to advantage by means of an agreeable associa-tion with past friendships, or coming events.

Allusive to Sion, page 228, in "her height of pride," a flourishing isle, the poet declares:—

> 'Tis true, nor winter stays thy growth,
>   Nor torrid summer's sickly smile;

but now:—

> The flashing billows of the south
>   Break not upon so lone an isle.

"Love," page 228, is figured as:—

> —— the flower* that closes up for fear
> When rude and selfish spirits breathe too near.

The Snowdrop is addressed, page 229, as the "first-born of the year's delight," and as being loved, but—

---

* Coleridge, in his poem, *Youth and Age*, has the line—"Flowers are lovely; Love is flower-like."

> 'Tis not because thy drooping form
>   Sinks graceful on its nest,
> When chilly shades from gathering storm
>   Affright thy tender breast;

but rather because—

> Thy shy averted smiles
> To Fancy bode a joyous year.

The brightness of summer is vividly expressed, page 230, in the line—

> And every flower was bath'd in light.

There are joys that fall not "like wither'd leaves," page 231, but like the passage—

> Of violets drooping one by one,
> Soon as their fragrant task is done,
>   Are wafted high in death !

The whole of the poem for the *Second Sunday after Easter* is highly imaginative. It opens with an artistic sketch allusive to the prophet Balaam on his mission to curse the Israelites :—

> O for a sculptor's hand,
> That thou might'st take thy stand,
> Thy wild hair floating to the eastern breeze,
>   Thy tranc'd yet open gaze
>   Fix'd on the desert haze,
> As one who deep in heaven some airy pageant sees.

The pageant, page 231, follows ; "giant forms of empires :"—

> In outline dim and vast
> Their fearful shadows cast.

Pleasing rural silence is very happily impressed on the reader, page 233, in the lines :

> Deep is the silence as of summer noon,
>   When a soft shower
>   Will trickle soon,
> A gracious rain, freshening the weary bower—
>   O sweetly then far off is heard
>   The clear note of some lonely bird.

As a stretch of the imagination a good idea of the infinity of heavenly space is conveyed, page 233, in the couplet :—

> The sun and every vassal star,
> All space, beyond the soar of Angel wings.

The poem for *Whit Sunday*, page 234, calls into exercise the highest efforts of imagination and fancy, representing the Creator, as :—

> Before His feet the clouds were riven,
> Half darkness and half flame.

But the poem closes in a more subdued strain, when :—

> Softer than gale at morning prime
> Hover'd His holy Dove.

The poet prays, page 234, that decay may fall lightly on his loved home :—

> Such are the visions green and sweet
> That o'er the wistful fancy fleet.

Here "green and sweet" do not contrast well, unless we take them to mean "green" and pleasant.

Of Asia the poet sings :—

> Euphrates through the lonely land
> Winds towards the pearly main.

The desert is well described, page 234 :—

> Slumber is there, but not of rest ;
> There her forlorn and weary nest
> The famish'd hawk has found.

The unsearchable riches of the Almighty mind are figuratively and judiciously expressed, page 235, as :—

> To search the deepening mystery,
> The wonders of Thy sea and sky.

The heedlessness and apathy of "the busy world" are alluded to in the triplet, page 235 :—

> Alas ! for her Thy opening flowers
> Unheeded breathe to summer showers,
> Unheard the music of Thy bowers.

The poet sums up "the listless joys of summer shades,"
page 236, as :—

> —— pastoral dance at even,
> — moonlight rovings in the fragrant glades,
> Soft slumbers in the open eye of heaven.*

Of autumnal clouds the muse declares :—

> To Fancy's eye † their motions prove
> They mantle round the Sun for love.

Ocean's waves and "chime of restless motion," suggest,
page 237 :—

> Such signs of love old Ocean gives,
> We cannot choose but think he lives.

Of Autumn's dewy morn, a very lovely sketch is given
in the verse :—

> But he, whose breast will bound to mark
>   The full bright burst of summer morn,
> Loves too each little dewy spark
>   By leaf or flow'ret worn :
> Cheap forms, and common hues, 'tis true,
> Through the bright shower-drop meet his view;
> The colouring may be of this earth ;
> The lustre comes of heavenly birth.

This is a delicate and pleasing flight of imagination, and
one that must strikingly affect the true Nature-Student,
who can see and feel beyond the harsh, crude realities of
this working-day life, and perceive realities reaching beyond
the common powers of observation inherited by the unre-
fined sensibilities of poor feeble human nature unaided
by culture, and unblest with more than an ordinary share of

---

* Shakspeare has, in *King John,*—" To seek the beauteous eye of
heaven to garnish ;"—and in *King Richard II.,*—" All places that the
eye of heaven visits."
  † Gray in his poem, *The Progress of Poesy,* has :—
  " Bright-eyed Fancy, hovering o'er."

intellectual intelligence, however physically gifted with thews and sinews, to prove that in all other respects " a man's a man for a' that."

The conscience, stricken with a sense of error, yet desirous of concealment, is thus described, page 287 :—

> The averted cheek in loneliest dell
>   Is conscious of a gaze it cannot bear,
> The leaves that rustle near us seem to tell
>   Our heart's sad secret to the silent air.

Then as to the impossibility of secrecy :—

> Nor is the dream untrue : for all around
>   The heavens are watching with their thousand eyes,
> We cannot pass our guardian angel's bound,
>   Resign'd or sullen, he will hear our sighs.

Keble never allows any opportunity to escape of introducing some floral design, so even here he avails himself of the opportunity to notice the early flowers of Spring, "that lead the vernal dance :"—

> In wasteful bounty shower'd, they smile unseen,
>   Unseen by man ——

" Unseen," if we follow the poet who has depicted the subject of his poem " in loneliest dell," and we may assume that the wild flowers of the forest were floating in his imagination, and led to this natural observation on the heedlessness and neglect of the common frequenters of our fields and forests, to whom " a primrose" is but " a primrose ;" for eyes have they, but they see not.

The poet, on the contrary, as noticed page 233 :—

> When dewy eve her curtain draws
>   Over the day's turmoil,

hears much to awaken his Fancy :—

> In the low chant of wakeful birds,
>   In the deep weltering flood,
> In whispering leaves, ——

and " all Creation's wondrous choir."

An Eastern midnight sea-piece, page 238, suggests among other sounds that of " whispering palm-leaves," blending with the silence.

Nightfall is expressed, page 241, by the negative statements that :—

> The low sweet tones of Nature's lyre
> No more on listless ears expire.

" Nor vainly smiles "—" the primrose "—

> Nor unlamented sink to rest
> Sweet roses one by one. ———

More serious claims demand from the poet, page 243, some other course than :—

> ——— Fancy with her shadowy toys,
> Aerial hopes and pensive joys.

Public excitement, page 243, is well expressed by :—

> The vex'd pulse of this feverish world.

" Consider the lilies of the field, how they grow," is the poem allotted to the *Fifteenth Sunday after Trinity*, page 244 : —

> Sweet nurslings of the vernal skies,
> Bath'd in soft air, and fed with dew,
> What more than magic in you lies
> To fill the heart's fond view ?

The whole poem, consisting of seven verses of eight lines each, is a well sustained effort in the exercise of imagination and fancy. " The Flowers of the Field " we have always with us, but not so " the stars of Heaven," and even :—

> The birds of air before us fleet.

But the flowers :—

> Ye fearless in your nests abide.

Describing mountain scenery, the poet exclaims, page 246 :—

> Where is thy favour'd haunt, eternal Voice?

It is amid the lofty peaks, with storm and flood :—

> Such sounds as make deep silence in the heart,
> For Thought to do her part.

The mountaineer's experience is limited, page 247, seldom reaching beyond " his morning's view :"—

> The thwarting cliffs that bound his sight,
> They bound his Fancy too.

A November sunset, page 248, suggests :—

> And Echo bids good-night from every glade !

A morning sunrise, page 249, disturbs some fairy revel :—

> Ye gentle elves, by Fancy seen
> Stealing away with night
> To slumber in your leafy screen,
> Tread more than airy light.

A rainbow appears—

> In solid span of purest rays ;
> How stately is its march !

" Solid" and " march" seem rather to clash here, as substitutes to express *vivid* and *vanish*.

Poetic licence scarcely extends to paradox, and that Keble is often dark, and even paradoxical, must be admitted by his warmest admirers; what, for example, is there more unfavourable to poesy in the Summer Season than in any other season of the year? How are we to reconcile the two verses, page 250 :—

> Dear is the morning gale of Spring,
> And dear th' autumnal eve;
> *But few delights can summer bring*
> A Poet's crown to weave.

> *Her bowers are mute, her fountains dry,*
>   And even Fancy's wing
> Speeds from beneath her cloudless sky,
>   To Autumn or to Spring.

This transfers us to the Deserts of Arabia, or a Summer all Dog Days, rather than to the sweet Summer Season of which our own Thomson has sung so cheerily.

The poem for *St. John Baptist's Day*, page 251, displays much imagination and fancy, but cannot be easily abridged to advantage.

The properties of the mirror to reflect the sun, as well as the fruitful earth, page 251, are given in the poem for St. Bartholomew. The third verse destroys the illusion :—

> Our mirror is a blessed book.

From a naturalistic point of view all continuity is here broken, and the mind refuses to admit the remotest analogy, although upheld by three consecutive verses. A mirror shows anything and everything presented to it, but not so a book; the one is indefinite in its exhibitions, the other definite and limited; the mirror is ever-changing, while the book is fixed and unaltered.

The poem for *St. Matthew*, page 252, opens with an address to the "hermits," who are taught :—

> The moral of each fleeting cloud and gale,
> The whispers from above, that haunt the twilight vale.

The poet declares that :—

> —— Love's a flower that will not die
> For lack of leafy screen,

but may dwell in thronged and smoky cities and towns,

> Even in this crowded loneliness.

The next poem, page 253, begins :—

> Ye stars that round the Sun of righteousness
> In glorious order roll,
>
> .   .   .   .   .
>
> Ye eagle spirits, that build in light divine,
> Oh ! think of us to-day.

The throng of Angels is described :—

> As if the stars should leave
> Their stations in the far ethereal wild,
> And round the sun a radiant circle weave.

A pleasant tone pervades the poem for *St. Simon and St. Jude*, page 254 :—

> Cheerful as soaring lark, and mild
> As evening blackbird's full-ton'd lay,
> When the relenting sun has smil'd
> Bright through a whole December day.

A wintry sketch opens the next poem :—

> Why blow'st thou not, thou wintry wind,
> Now every leaf is brown and sere?

And the succeeding verse begins :

> How quiet shows the woodland scene !
>
> .   .   .   .   .
>
> Like weary men when age is won.

The final close of summer is represented in the lines :—

> Till the last flower of autumn shed
> Her funeral odours on her dying bed.

This is followed, page 256, by the poem for *Confirmation*, which urges that Christian warriors should prove :—

> Steady and pure as stars that beam
> In middle heaven ———

Paragraph 83, the poem opens with :—

> O Youth and Joy, your airy tread
> Too lightly springs by Sorrow's bed.

A verse of the poem for the *Burial of the Dead*, page 257, utters the wish :—

> —— let some graceful arch be there
> With wreathed mullions proud,
> With burnish'd ivy for its screen.

The ocean by moonlight is fancifully sketched :—

> The shower of moonlight falls as still and clear
> Upon the desert main,
> As where sweet flowers some pastoral garden cheer
> With fragrance after rain.

There is not much point in the comparison next made, that—

> Like summer fields, beneath the shadowy clouds
> The yielding waters darken in the breeze.

Shadow is all the same whether it falls on the solid earth or the yielding waters, with the only difference that on water it is often attended with a deep blue, or purple appearance, but on the earth is invariably gray, or black.

Nature-Study stands pre-eminent in the promotion of imagination and fancy. Much may be done without such study, just as now and then we learn of some self-taught statuary, painter, musician, or mechanic. Observing what others have done, we may, by adopting a similar course, elicit from Nature itself many unobserved, yet noteworthy facts. But we must have Nature before our eyes ; we must systematise it, otherwise instead of being a volume, it will be a chaotic mass, most unmanageable in its matter and proportions. The primary object of Nature-Study is, or should be, the enlargement of our powers of imagination and the scope of our fancy. We find the rule for executing this in the examples left us by our predecessors; we find the materials in and around us, which we grasp or miss, according as we study or neglect the plenteous bounty of Nature. If the Natural Philosopher has barely scratched the surface of the globe in his investigations of its external crust, as we would scratch the rind of an orange; we may say with still greater truth, in reference to the Poet, that his labour and inquiry have yet to begin. He has planned much but executed little; at all events, a large field of investigation still awaits the zealous Nature-Student. We have in this section adduced many examples from Keble's poems, but they afford no prominent marks to distinguish them for novelty of design and execution; as a whole they are rather to be commended as good and above censure, than as being distinguished for any superiority.

5. Human Nature.

We observe the usual deficiency in these poems which marks kindred productions, so far as respects characteristics of Human Nature in various grades of society. This is perhaps more remarkable in the present instance, because the sacred poetry of *The Christian Year* frequently admits of picturesque description. But it deals only with mankind at large, or singly, as man, woman, or infant, saint or sinner; and few passions come into play beyond devotion, love, hatred, or callousness. But our examples will best illustrate and make clear this absence of individuality.

The poem for *The Holy Innocents*, page 217, alludes to our Saviour blessing little children, and their unconsciousness of His awful presence, and proceeds to say that they :—

> On th' everlasting Parent sweetly smil'd,
> (Like infants sporting on the shore,
> That tremble not at Ocean's boundless roar.)

Of those who are conscience-stricken, we are assured, page 217, that their "half-waking dreams" of hopes, vows, and prayers :—

> Like stormy lights on mountain streams,
> Wavering and broken all, athwart the conscience glare.

The twelfth verse of the poem for *The Circumcision*, page 218, commences :—

> Wouldst thou a Poet be?
>
> .   .   .   .
>
> Come here thy soul to tune,
> Here set thy feeble chant.

The fourteenth verse begins with the inquiry :—

> Art thou a child of tears
> Cradled in care and woe?

and proceeds :—

> If thou would'st reap in love,
> First sow in holy fear:
> So life a winter's morn may prove
> To a bright endless year.

Man's heedlessness, page 220, is compared to the levity of childhood :—

> The heart of childhood is all mirth ;
> We frolic to and fro.

"Storms within" the human breast are similar to those without, page 221, that,

> —howl and chafe amid the bending trees.

The Lover's fond fancies are delicately sketched, page 222, and a tender instructive lesson is given for the avoidance of self-deception, and gross estimates of man's *summum bonum.*

The mother's care over her offspring leads to the inquiry :—

> The last-born babe, why lies its part
> Deep in the mother's inmost heart ?
> But that the Lord and source of love
> Would have His weakest ever prove
> Our tenderest care ——

We have gross, sensual dreams of Heaven, but :—

> What is the Heaven our God bestows ?
> No prophet yet, no Angel knows.

The innocence of childhood is shown, page 225, as displayed in simple talk on a lofty subject :—

> As little children lisp, and tell of Heaven.

Nothing human can be purer or more transparent and charming than such infantile lispings; and their sayings are not always inappropriate. A girl of the tenderest age, overhearing a conversation regarding the Trinity, replied with enthusiasm—"O I think I understand, it is like having *three* lighted candles in this room, and yet only *one* light !"

The wanderer in the desert, where " He thoughtless roam'd and free," is compared, page 225, to " a solitary child."

Of poets framed to do " God's own work " on earth, Keble sings, page 226 :—

> Sovereign masters of all hearts !
> Know ye, who hath set your parts ?
>
> He hath chosen you to lead
> 　His Hosannas here below ;—
> Mount and claim your glorious meed ;
> 　Linger not with sin and woe.

The time may come, page 227 :—

> When the babe's kiss no sense of pleasure yields
> Even to the doting mother : ———

Man seeks the respect and love of his fellow-creatures, and yet :—

> There are who sigh that no fond heart is theirs,
> None loves them best ———

A mother's passionate attachment to her offspring, page 232, is touchingly illustrated by :—

> A mother's prime of bliss,
> When to her eager lips is brought
> Her infant's thrilling kiss.

And again, on occasion of sleeping, page 232:—

> The watchful mother tarries nigh,
> Though sleep hath closed her infant's eye,

for waking " she could not bear his moan."

Of the multitude, as being negligent of public worship, page 235, it is said :—

> The busy world a thousand ways
> Is hurrying by, nor ever stays
> To catch a note of Thy dear praise.

Human Nature is seldom individualized, it is generally masses of mankind that are alluded to, thus, page 236 :—

> Life's ebbing stream on either side
> Shows at each turn some mouldering hope or joy,
> The Man seems following still the funeral of the Boy.

In the poem for the *Second Sunday after Trinity*, page 237, occurs the peculiar couplet :—

> No distance breaks the tie of blood ;
> Brothers are brothers evermore.

And in the last verse but one of the same poem the evil-disposed are thus spoken of :—

> Wild thoughts within, bad men without,
> All evil spirits round about,
> Are banded in unblest device
> To spoil Love's earthly paradise.

The next poem, page 237, describes another phase of the baseness of the human heart :—

> O hateful spell of Sin ! when friends are nigh,
>   To make stern Memory tell her tale unsought,
> And raise accusing shades of hours gone by,
>   To come between us and all kindly thought !

The following verse recounts the natural desire on the part of the " self-reproaching soul " to discover some deep dark dell of perfect seclusion ; to find which she :—

> Flies from the heart and home she dearest loves
>   To where lone mountains tower, or billows roll,
> Or to your endless depth, ye solemn groves.

The poem, page 239, exhibits a felicitous picture of rural harmony, but while :—

> All hymn Thy glory, Lord, aright,
>
> Man only mars the sweet accord.

Discomfort rather than peace proves to be the common lot of humanity, thus, page 240 :—

> Sweet thoughts of peace, ye may not last :
>   Too soon some ruder sound
> Calls us from where ye soar so fast
>   Back to our earthly round.

In a somewhat similar strain is the next poem composed, page 240 :—

> When bitter thoughts, of conscience born,
>   With sinners wake at morn,
> When from our restless couch we start,
>   With fever'd lips and wither'd heart,
> Where is the spell to charm those mists away,
> And make new morning in that darksome day ?

Human Nature is generalized, page 244, and we learn of it in the abstract :—

> ———— The world of life,
> How is it stained with fear and strife !
> In Reason's world what storms are rife,
> What passions range and glare !

And again :—

> Alas ! of thousand bosoms kind,
>   That daily court you and caress,
> How few the happy secret find,
>   Of your [the lilies] calm loveliness.

The " Mountain boy " rejoicing in his liberty, " glad and gay," and although a lonely, yet a mirthful prisoner, is described, page 247, as the creature of surrounding circumstances :—

> The snow-clad peaks of rosy light
>   That meet his morning view,
> The thwarting cliffs that bound his sight,
>   They bound his fancy too.
>
> .   .   .   .
>
> Too soon the happy child
> His nook of homely thought will change
> For life's seducing wild.

In reference to " our hermit spirits," page 248, the poet inquires :—

> Why should we faint, and fear to live alone,
>   Since all alone, so Heaven has will'd, we die ?

On souvenirs, as between brothers in token of fond remembrances, page 250, we meet with the lines :—

> When brothers part for manhood's race,
>   What gift may most endearing prove
> To keep fond memory in her place,
>   And certify a brother's love ?

The leader of a " martial crew," page 250, is represented :—

> With lips firm clos'd and fixed eye,
> Like warrior when the fight is nigh,
> .Nor talk nor landscape heeds.

Of youth and middle age, page 251, it is declared :—

> Sweet is the infant's waking smile,
> And sweet the old man's rest—
> But middle age by no fond wile,
> No soothing calm is blest.

Surely this is sufficiently paradoxical? How can it be that "middle age *by no fond wile, no soothing calm is blest ?*"

The love of music may pervade all classes, even in " dusky lane and wrangling mart," page 253, for :—

> There are in this loud stunning tide
> Of human care and crime,
> With whom the melodies abide
> Of th' everlasting chime.

" Clouds" may move, or " flowers" grow and die in unison, page 254 :—

> But two capricious human hearts—
> No sage's rod may track their ways,
> No eye pursue their lawless starts
> Along their wild self-chosen maze.

Winter being significant of the Seasons having completed their round of duty, the same periodic course is applied to the progress of man's life, page 254 :—

> Like weary men when age is won,

who with their conscience clear of offence are :—

> Content to live, but not afraid to die.

Arguing in favour of infant education, page 255, particularly in singing, the poet proceeds :—

> Oh ! say not, dream not, heavenly notes
> To childish ears are vain,
> That the young mind at random floats,
> And cannot reach the strain.

They are :—

> Like spring-flowers in their best array,
> All silence and all smiles.

And there is now taught in our dame-schools :—

> What sages would have died to learn.

Commencing with " Youth and Joy," the scene at length changes, and the visitor to the sick-room, page 256, exclaims :—

> Once more I came : the silent room
> Was veil'd in sadly-soothing gloom,
> And ready for her last abode
> The pale form like a lily shew'd,
>
> The light from those soft-smiling eyes
> Had fleeted to its parent skies.

Dramatic effect is not generally to be sought for in sacred poems. We mostly find in them allusions to infancy, youth, relationship, and some few phases of life, but not in much variety. Man's present and future state are variously treated, as are also some few passions and sentiments, but there is little of individual character. Whatever affects man under any circumstances, however, belongs to the present department of our selections, as distinguished from characteristics which relate to the brute, or animate creation generally.

6. Religious, Moral, Meditative Expressions of Sentiment and Feeling.

The weary traveller, page 214, when night is approaching has his attention awakened by every passing incident, and lonely indeed must be his way when he has—

> No gleam to watch on tree or tower,
> Whiling away the lonesome hour.

The poet alludes to the Church, page 214:—

> —— —— in sad and wintry time,
> Her heavens all dark with doubt and crime.

That the world is waxing old, as declared by Esdras, page 215, is shown:—

> By tempests, earthquakes, and by wars,
> By rushing waves and falling stars.

Addressing the Lord, page 217, as "Lover of our souls," the poet writes:—

> Thou seek'st to warn us, not confound,
> Thy showers would pierce the harden'd ground.

In the wilderness, page 219, the pilgrims declare:—

> From darkness here, and dreariness
> We ask not full repose.
>
>   .   .   .   .
>
> Is not the pilgrim's toil o'erpaid
> By the clear rill and palmy shade?
> And see we not, up Earth's dark glade,
> The gate of Heaven unclose?

In a retrospect of early life, page 219, the inquiry is made:—

> Will not the long-forgotten glow
> Of mingled joy and awe return,
> When stars above or flowers below
> First made our infant spirits burn?

"I mark'd a rainbow in the north," sings the poet, page 220, and thence in a meditative mood moralizes on the lights and shadows of human experience:—

> Brighter than rainbow in the north,
> More cheery than the matin lark,
> Is the soft gleam of Christian worth,
> Which on some holy house we mark.

So again, page 221, the natural aspect of a storm of wind, rain, and lightning, is metaphorically applied to the "storms within" the troubled breast.

Heaven, as imagined by worldly-minded men, page 222, and as Scripturally understood, is set forth ; the first as :—

> The self-deceiver's dreary theme ;

the other, as :—

> —— the Heaven our God bestows.

Although the ground was cursed for Adam's fall, page 223 :—

> Yet mingled with the penal shower,
> Some drops of balm in every bower
> Steal down like April dews ——.

The poem, page 223, refers to the Rainbow, and concludes :—

> God, by His bow, vouchsafes to write
>   This truth in Heaven above ;
> As every lovely hue is Light
>   So every grace is Love.

Mourners are feelingly addressed, page 223, in the poem for *Ash Wednesday* :—

> Hast thou not seen, in night-hours drear,
> When racking thoughts the heart assail,
>   The glimmering stars by turns appear,
> And from th' eternal home above
>   With silent news of mercy steal ?
> So Angels pause on tasks of love,
>   To look where sorrowing sinners kneel.

A domestic scene is drawn, page 224, on the old theme :—

> Sweet is the smile of home ; the mutual look
> When hearts are of each other sure.

The poem for the *Third Sunday in Lent*, page 224, offers the reflection that each association with melody, flowers, songs of birds, " minds us of thy Love :"—

> O Lord, our Lord, and spoiler of our foes,
> There is no light but Thine : with Thee all beauty glows.

Remarking on the secresy and mystery of Nature's operations, page 225, the poet proceeds :—

> Who ever saw the earliest rose
>   First open her sweet breast ?
> Or, when the summer sun goes down,
> The first soft star in evening's crown
>   Light up her gleaming crest ?

" But there's a sweeter flower,"—" A brighter star :"—

> 'Tis Love, the last best gift of Heaven ;
>   Love gentle, holy, pure :
> But tenderer than a dove's soft eye,
> The searching sun, the open sky,
>   She never could endure.

Christian poets are advised, page 226, to do service in promoting " God's own work " on earth :—

> Giving virtue a new birth,
>   And a life that ne'er grows old.

The mountain stream is described, page 229, making its way to the Ocean :—

> Perchance that little brook shall flow
>   The bulwark of some mighty realm.

And such is the course of prayer and good works.

The beautiful poem on *The Snow Drop*, page 230, after describing the flower, asks :—

> Is there a heart, that loves the Spring,
>   Their witness can refuse ?

Seeking worldly pleasure before more serious employ-ments, is represented, page 230, as occurring :—

> —— When summer leaves were bright,
> And every flower was bath'd in light,
>   In sunshine moments past.

The Christian's death-bed is referred to, page 230, in the lines :—

> O joys, that sweetest in decay,
> Fall not, like wither'd leaves away,

> But with the silent breath
> Of violets ————
> Soon as their fragrant task is done,
> Are wafted high in death !

The earth is represented, page 233 :—

> True to her trust, tree, herb, or reed,
> She renders for each scatter'd seed.

Not so "these barren hearts of ours," for "nought we yield." Christians are warned, page 236 :—

> ———— Our path of glory
> By many a cloud is darken'd and unblest.

A very pleasing poem for the *Third Sunday after Trinity*, page 237, has for its subject —" Comfort for sinners, in the presence of the good." It consists of ten verses of four lines each. The fifth verse, referring to " our guardian angel," is somewhat paradoxical in stating :—

> He in the mazes of the budding wood
> Is near, and mourns to see our thankless glance
> Dwell coldly, where the fresh green earth is strew'd
> With the first flowers that lead the vernal dance.

To some extent this may perhaps illustrate the text— " There is joy in the presence of the angels of God over one sinner that repenteth ;" but the repentant sinner is surely the least likely person to regard Nature's "wasteful bounty" in the " budding wood ;" or a guardian angel to be mindful of such giving up of earthly for heavenly meditations, except as matter for rejoicing.

With the same experience as the Fishermen of Bethsaida, page 240, we may all exclaim :—

> Sweet thoughts of peace, ye may not last.

The cry has been, is, and ever will be universal.

The "bitter thoughts," and mental pangs of conscious sinners are vividly depicted, page 240 :—

> When from our restless couch we start,
> With fever'd lips and wither'd heart.

To be quelled only by :—

> One steadfast thought, that God is there.

The muse declares, page 243, it is no time for gaiety and frivolity :—

> While souls are wandering far and wide,
> And curses swarm on every side.

The deaf and dumb may attend to Divine instruction, page 243 :—

> But the deaf heart, the dumb by choice,
>   The laggard soul, that will not wake,
> The guilt that scorns to be forgiven ;—
> These baffle e'en the spells of heaven.

Of ten lepers cleansed only one returned to give God thanks, page 244, and thus it is with us after affliction :—

> —— should the mist of woe roll by,
> Not showers across an April sky
>   Drift, when the storm is o'er,
> Faster than these false drops and few
> Fleet from the heart, a worthless dew.

The poem of *The Flowers of the Field*, offers many pleasant reminiscences, page 244, such as :—

> In childhood's sports, companions gay,
> In sorrow, on Life's downward way,
> How soothing ! in our last decay
>   Memorials prompt and true.

The woe and restlessness of human nature are feelingly described, page 245 :—

> In Life's long sickness evermore
>   Our thoughts are tossing to and fro :
> We change our posture o'er and o'er,
> But cannot rest, nor cheat our woe.

The Christian is never deserted, never wholly alone ; page 246, not even :—

> When fade all earthly flowers and bays,
>   When summer friends are gone and fled.

The strong influence of grand mountainous scenery on

the mind is graphically expressed in the poem for the *Twentieth Sunday after Trinity*, page 246, which assembles objects of great sublimity, and then observes, in reference to the gloomy rocks and rushing waters :—

> Such sounds as make deep silence in the heart,
> For Thought to do her part.

Analogous to this influence of scenery on the mind is the limited experience of the " Mountain boy," page 247 :—

> The thwarting cliffs that bound his sight,
> They bound his fancy too.

He is thus, as it were, physically and mentally hemmed in and bounded by his narrow sphere : as by a " blest restraint ;" but once cast on the wide world :—

> His nook of homely thought will change
> For life's seducing wild.

Of death and the soul's flight to heaven, page 248, the poet sings :—

> And thou shalt break it soon ; the groveling worm
> Shall find his wings, and soar as fast and free
> As his transfigur'd Lord.——

In favour of a secluded hermit-life, the poet observes :—

> Why should we faint, and fear to live alone,
> Since all alone, so Heaven has will'd, we die.

Logically examined, we naturally inquire, but is it also the will of Heaven for man " to live alone ?" The Scriptures, most assuredly, do not speak approvingly of a life of " single blessedness."

A solemn hymn for *Sunday next before Advent*, page 249, has self-examination for its object :—

> Will God indeed with fragments bear,
> Snatch'd late from the decaying year ?

" The decaying year" of human life ; the " fragments" of a life of dissipation or obdurate indifference ; the sinner :—

> Just ere he sink for ever lost.

But the application is more especially addressed to the mariner whose life is passed on a sea of peril, Nature's unswerving laws being hinted at in the inquiry—" Will Ocean cease her strife?" No, not for sailor, saint, or sinner. Nature is no " respecter of persons."

Perhaps, as critically treated, it would have been better to speak of " Ocean," in reference to " his," and not " her strife," as more Neptunian.

The gifts of friends and relations, particularly brothers, page 250, are alluded to as keeping " fond memory in her place," and being ever more or less present to the mind : —

> Even round the death-bed of the good
> Such dear remembrances will hover,
> And haunt us with no vexing mood
> When all the cares of earth are over.

City and town life, with all their gloom and mercenary traffic, as exhibited page 252, is a life not without solace :—

> And Christian Hope can cheer the eye
> That ne'er saw vernal green ;
> Then be ye sure that Love can bless
> Even in this crowded loneliness.

Man's capriciousness is represented, page 254, as greater than that of two fleeting clouds, or two kindred flowers :—

> But two capricious human hearts—
> No sage's rod may track their ways.

There is much for serious reflection, page 254, as life is on the wane, in the sentiment :—

> Content to live, but not afraid to die.

" Content," as not wishing premature decease.

7. NEGATIVE VIEWS OF NATURE.

The first poem, addressed to *Morning*, has in the second verse an allusion to the fresh, rustling breeze :—

> That dancest forth at opening day,
> And brushing by with joyous wing,
> Waken'st each little leaf to sing.

The last line of the first verse in the next poem, *Evening*, represents the fading away of the sunset as :—

> The last faint pulse of quivering light.

But this may or may not be taken as properly coming under the designation of being negative.

We have to pass over no less than twenty-seven poems before we meet with another specimen to offer in this department, so rare are the evidences of negative views of Nature in these as in most modern poems.

The miracle of the Burning Bush is depicted, page 225, as :—

> One towering thorn was wrapt in flame—
> Bright without blaze it went and came.

In the poem for *Palm Sunday*, page 225, a general call is made on those " whose hearts are beating high " with poetical impulse to assist in promoting " God's own work " on earth, and who are chosen to lead :—

> His Hosannas here below.
>
> .   .   .   .
>
> But if ye should hold your peace,
> Deem not that the song would cease—
> Angels round His glory-throne,
> Stars, His guiding hand that own,

> Flowers, that grow beneath our feet,
>   Stones* in earth's dark womb that rest,
> High and low in choir shall meet,
>   Ere His Name shall be unblest.

" The Deaf and Dumb " are the subject of a poem for the *Twelfth Sunday after Trinity*, page 248, in which the fourth verse records that :—

> The deaf may hear the Saviour's voice,
>   The fetter'd tongue its chain may break ;
> But the deaf heart, the dumb by choice,

are irreclaimable even by " the spells of heaven."

The poem on *The Flowers of the Field*, page 244, has in the fourth line of the fourth verse, a singular expression, among others, in praise of the flowers for various qualities :—

> And guilty man, where e'er he roams,
>   Your innocent mirth may borrow.

Now certainly nothing can be more out of character than " mirth " as applied to any flowers whatever, although we admit the license of " smiling meads " and even " smiling flowers," but we should as soon think of singing flowers as of mirthful ones.

A dark text from the *Revelations*, leads to a poem of not the most lucid character, in seven verses of eight lines each, for *All Saints' Day ;* the third verse commencing :—

> Sure if our eyes were purg'd to trace
>   God's unseen armies hovering round,
> We should behold by angel's grace,
>   The four strong winds of Heaven fast bound.

---

* This poem having for its text that passage from *St. Luke*—" I tell you that, if these should hold their peace, the stones would immediately cry out."

And in consequence :—

> Their downward sweep a moment staid
> On ocean cove and forest glade.

This, as a non-natural illustration, is by no means striking, but we give it more from the scarcity of examples than from seeing in it any particular excellence. Indeed, none of the foregoing can lay claim to originality except in expression.

The 10th chapter of "NATURE-STUDY, as applicable to poetry and eloquence," is specially devoted to this subject, which thus renders it unnecessary to enter upon details on the present occasion. It is not all poetry that will admit of even the occasional employment of this figure, but the examples occurring in *The Christian Year* are singularly deficient in character and vigour, which we cannot attribute in every instance to the nature of the subjects; as, if used, it would have contributed considerably to enhance the solemnity and grandeur of many of the Poems.

CONCLUSION.—The preponderance of examples cited is in favour of *Description* and *Imagination and Fancy;* and the fewest are afforded by *Negative Views of Nature*. Examined, therefore, from a naturalistic point of view, Keble stands prominent in Descriptive Poetry, which Nature-Study teaches is the department of oldest date and practice, and requires more of the artistic eye of the painter, than the mental acuteness of the metaphysician. High wrought, perfect, and graphic description is deserving of unbounded praise; and it has attained various degrees of excellence in modern times and among particular classes of poets. Poet-artists, word-painters, rank according to general merit and particular subjects, just as we have portrait and flower, marine and landscape, cattle and still-life painters. Burns was less descriptive than Scott, and Wordsworth was more diffuse than Thomson. With many poets description is closely studied, being a main object; with others, as with Burns, Byron, Keats, and Shelley, it is sketchy, because it is a mere accessory and not a principal feature.

As a descriptive poet Keble shines in all that is light, pleasant, and cheerful; he seldom rises to the sublime, or descends to the sombre side of nature. His delight is in :—

Hues of the rich unfolding morn.

He has rainbows, but no thunderstorms or earthquakes ;—

The tide of sun-rise swells,

but ocean never wrecks and whelms a single ship or sailor. All is flowery, fragrant, and bespangled with dew, shining in sunbeams, or silvered by moonlight :—

How quiet shows the woodland scene !

Even summer, as being too hot and arid, is excluded from the poet's portfolio :—

But few delights can summer bring,

Her bowers are mute, her fountains dry.

Although he describes, it is questionable whether description was a primary consideration with him; he may now and then have seen in it a suitable vehicle for introducing, conveying and commenting on, certain doctrinal points, and religious and moral sentiments; he certainly never disconnects them. As thus viewed he would not study variety, but appropriateness to his subject. Thus the seasons of the year assimilate well with phases of human life. We have our youth and age, our spring and winter, our sunshine and shade, our growth and death. We are fruitful or barren, we are as grass or as the green bay-tree, we aspire like the eagle, or grovel like brutes. What is there in man, his condition, and aspirations that has not its immediate or remote analogy in Nature, although not in Nature alone? Some have claimed for our poet an insight into and an interpretation of Nature peculiarly his own, but without adducing proof of such assumption; nor can we trace any evidence to authorise such an opinion. His being the one or the other would be an argument in favour of originality in some particular direction. His intense love of Nature, almost amounting to adoration, we are prepared to admit; but beyond this he does not advance a single step. His performances are unexceptionable in so many points of view that we excuse the want of novelty here, evident imitation there, and something approaching to feebleness in another quarter, so long as a general impression remains that there is much to praise, little to condemn, and the greater part to commend. He is never harsh, never sensibly incongruous, never offends the most delicate taste, and always conveys an impression of having excelled where many might have failed; and, no other sacred poet has expounded scriptural and moral truths to the reading public in anything approaching such fascinating metrical strains of long sustained sweetness and harmony.

His style is far from being rich in any novelty of Figurative language in general; and he is remarkably deficient in Similes derived from Nature; hence arises the paucity of our illustrations in these divisions of our subject.

x 2

But he overflows with imagination and fancy of a quiet, placid, soothing character, born of zephyrs, clouds, dew-drops, rising and setting suns, stars, and moonlight; each of the seasons suggests pleasant dreams, aided by flowers and fruits; animate and inanimate Nature supply—

> The low sweet tones of Nature's lyre,

or rise to describe mountain cliffs and "the desert main." All is sunny, delicious, and in sweet harmony; all is beauty and loveliness, with but an April shower, or a quickly passing storm to disturb the general serenity of the scenery.

Keble has indulged to a greater extent than is usual in sacred poems, so nearly allied to hymns, in depicting human characters, as—the poet, the conscience-stricken sinner, the self-accused, the mother, travellers and wanderers, relations, the mountaineer; with the passions of love, man's youth and age, and life and death. And closely associated with man's varied career are numerous Religious, Moral, and Meditative expressions of sentiment and feeling, constituting the most meritorious and vital portion of *The Christian Year*, of which let the critic speak as he may in other respects, yet it is undoubtedly here that we must look for the distinguishing excellencies of this work, and therefrom account for its extraordinary popularity with the religious world. It is more than probable that its composition was suggested by *The Temple*, 1683; and the "Sacred Poems and Pious Ejaculations," by Henry Vaughan, 1654; and with these before him, Keble could not only see the superiority of Vaughan's compositions, as compared with Herbert's, but must have felt assured of the possibility of excelling both, if it were only by avoiding the vicious taste that permitted an assemblage of the most uncouth with the most sacred subjects. In the department just alluded to, Keble strains every effort, and spares no pains to present whatever he has to offer in the way of instruction, comment, advice, or reflection, in the most polished manner possible. He did not go the length that Herbert allowed his muse, as declared in his poem of *The Forerunners:*—

> So, *Thou art still my God*, be out of fear,
> He will be pleased with that ditty ;
> And if I please Him, I write fine and witty.

There is much to be said in argument on both sides, but nothing can be said in favour of the poet who does not put forth all his strength in fulfilling his stewardship. Nothing in Nature is done carelessly, heedlessly, or rudely, from the mightiest mass to the minutest object. Man can but do his best, and having done all he will still accuse his imperfections ; but he need not therefore abandon the attempt as worthless in the eyes of his fellow men. Watts wisely lamented that profaneness had taken possession of the best music and poetry, and prudently sought to redeem them by wedding them to Sacred Song. Herbert chose the rusticity of his period, and suffers the consequences in this more refined age. Keble, without prescribing rules, or promising reforms ; simply gives us the one, and ably practises the other throughout his volume.

It is putting a poet's compositions to a severe test to try them " one by one" in the critical crucible, expecting to bring them out seven times purified ! We acknowledge freely the one-sided views taken in the present instance, our strictures being limited to such portions only as are confessedly indebted in a greater or less degree to immediate or borrowed draughts from universal Nature: that is, Nature in its most unrestricted and unconfined sense of relating to all and everything that is not strictly Art, or in other words—the work of man. But we trust we have not failed in our principal design, which is to open up to authors and readers a new field of investigation, which, the more it is cultivated, the more will it tend to ennoble literary, and particularly poetical compositions, as well as to enlarge and improve the critical taste of the reading public.

" On a first glance through its pages, the volume commends itself as containing a numerous collection of quotations from our best poets under distinct headings, and these selections alone would give the work a value to any writer or thinker. The systematic arrangement of ideas must be as useful to the poet-student as to any other, and such might find assistance in Mr. Dircks' suggestions."—*Coventry Herald and Free Press.*

" Dr. Dircks quotes largely from the critical writings of great authorities in literature, and arranges under several heads descriptive passages from the poets. The idea is a good one, and the book is suggestive."—*The Daily News.*

" The author of this valuable work has sought, by systematizing the study of Nature, and by stimulating his readers with quotations from the works of our poets, to lead the mind to a reverential contemplation of the grand and mysterious objects of the universe. We may, with truth, say that he has collected together in one volume some of the most valuable and stimulating products of the mind of man, which cannot fail to assist the reader in his study of the great and wonderful book of Nature."—*The Devon Weekly Times.*

" This work is carefully written, and appears to be well-arranged, while the great abundance and variety of the illustrations quoted from a great number of sources show the author to be a man deeply read in poetry. The beauty of these selections almost tempts one to dip here and there as erratically as the honey-bee seems to do, when winging from flower to flower. Certain as she is of finding something pleasant in whatever flower she visits, so we are in opening at any page. It is a work worthy of being placed alongside of Lord Kames' ' Elements of Criticism,' and we may hope that through its study our authors may elicit new and correct ideas from the vast field of Nature lying unbounded before our view."—*Dorset County Express.*

" We quite agree with Dr. Dircks, that all poets are more or less susceptible of the impressions of the natural world. For there never was and there never could be a poet who could look with mere indifference on the beauty and majesty of the visible creation, with its ever-shifting scenery of rain and storm, and sunshine, and its strange emotional influences over the human heart."—*The Dublin Review.* (*January.*)

" Externally it is a very handsome volume ; and, internally, from its prefatory chapter at least, a very promising one, both to poets and their readers ; but especially to those of the former who seek to extend their knowledge of the powers and the promptings of ' The Mighty Mother.' To such, it is at once a storehouse and a beacon ; showing, by numerous examples, how far the study of Nature has already resulted favourably in art development ; and also warning the student from appropriating the thoughts and images of his predecessors. It will be valuable also to the poetical CRITIC, by enabling him, in common with the poets, to judge to what extent Nature has hitherto been consulted and studied by the latter ; and with what differences of style and treatment her boundless stores have been used."—*The Durham County Advertiser.*

" Mr. Dircks deals fully with the subject, and shows how far the study has been carried, how it has been used by poets, concocters of proverbs, and others ; and in what way it has been misused, abused, and misapplied. The author gives copious specimens from the works of ancient and modern writers, in order to point out to the student how far they have succeeded in drawing analogies from natural objects. In this he evinces a critical taste, sound judgment, and a clear discernment of imperfections, caused either by the absence of poetical inspiration or from a merely superficial knowledge of the art of applying similitudes. The student of Nature will find this volume a valuable aid towards the attainment of that ideal of perfection which Professor Dircks considers within the reach of the talented."—*The Essex Telegraph.*

" The book is exceedingly interesting and instructive. We are not aware that the subject has ever before been passed under review in so complete and exhaustive a manner. To have amassed so many apposite illustrations under each heading indicates also wide reading and much good taste."—*The Globe.*

" The most casual glance through the volume makes manifest the experience, research, study, and labour expended in its production ; and closer perusal shows that these four items have been made the happy substratum of chapters teeming with matter of the widest interest. We heartily commend Mr. Dircks' book to our readers."—*The Gloucestershire Chronicle.*

" Certain it is that this work displays no little thought, much research, and a keen appreciation of Nature's loveliness and perfection."—*The Hampshire Independent.*

" Mr. Dircks has gathered together a very charming collection of extracts from our poets to illustrate the various chapters, and having analyzed them, has arrived at certain results, touching in his way on many interesting questions, such as the scientific blunders of the poets."—*The Hereford Mercury.*

" Its scheme (the work now before us) is original, its object practical, it does not profess to make its readers poets, but it will give many a new train of thought ; it will quicken the imagination by a proper direction of the powers of observation, and thoughtful readers will enjoy many a country stroll the more, and find food for reflection in nature's works. It is almost microscopic in its glance into the studies and methods of study of eminent poets, but, above all, it teaches its readers to become able critics to appreciate the true beauties of poetry from the false lure of mere word pomp, by showing that metaphor to be true, must follow nature itself. The style (of the work) is concise, regular, and flowing."—*The Kentish Observer.*

" Mr. Dircks has explored his library to some purpose. Whatever English Literature has to offer in the way of poetry has been laid under tribute to furnish him with illustrations for his theories. In this age of rapid writing, when we have barely time to glance for ideas at contemporary authors, it is pleasant to meet with a man who has not only read widely and wisely, but is accurate enough in remembering what he has read to be enabled to spread before us a really splendid mélange of his acquisitions—we had almost said erudition."—*The Leader.*

" Mr. Dircks leads his reader along the flowery paths of poetry, to show by his many quotations the source of the beauties contained therein. The volume is one the perusal of which will prove very gratifying."—*Leicester Advertiser.*

" We are induced to give a lengthened notice of this work rather in connection with the fact of the author being a civil engineer, than from finding in it anything bearing on scientific or ordinary practical results. Mr. Dircks' is a critical work, yet not so as regards the various classes, and the composition of poetry; but solely on the matter of how Nature has been studied hitherto by poets, as evidenced in their own productions ; and ascertaining the method of that study. A careful perusal of his opening essay, or preface, lays bare the whole case in a most lucid and satisfactory manner. The work is dedicated, by permission, to the Right Hon. Lord Houghton; and as a first attempt to unravel a very important and interesting subject, we esteem it to be well deserving of public patronage."—*The Mining Journal.*

" The mind may evolve ideas in ceaseless round, but unless he who begets the thoughts knows also how to set them in array to the best advantage, his fertility of creation will render him but small service. Professor Dircks takes great pains to point this out, and his book will afford an abundance of matter for reflection, whilst the examples quoted cannot fail to inform the reader of defects and beauties in composition, of which he was never before cognizant."—*The Merthyr Express.*

" By great research and labour, and the exercise of a keenly critical mind, our author has gathered together and systematically arranged so many examples of the manner in which Nature has been treated by various writers that his work may well serve, as he intends it, as a sort of grammar on the subject—serviceable alike to the student and the critic."—*The Norfolk Chronicle and Norwich Gazette.*

" The admirable work, entitled ' Nature-Study,' is from the able pen of Mr. Dircks, who has executed his task with a research and talent rarely to be met with. We can confidently recommend this work to our readers, having ourselves derived much pleasure and instruction from its perusal."—*North Wales Chronicle.*

" Mr. Dircks, who is already familiarly known by his biographies of the Marquis of Worcester, and of Samuel Hartlib, has in the book before us entered into a very different and more speculative field of study ; and his views are advocated very earnestly, [and the reader will be] pleased with the cento of exquisite passages from the poets by which they are illustrated."—*Notes and Queries.*

" The subject is a large and important one, and Dr. Dircks possesses in a rare degree many of the qualities necessary for its full elucidation. His illustrations are drawn from science, art, poetry, and philosophy, and the extent of his scholarship and erudition is only equalled by the earnest and reverent spirit which pervades every page of his elaborate work."—*Oxford Chronicle and Berks and Bucks Gazette.*

" Dr. Dircks has evidently bestowed much labour on the handsome volume before us ; and has selected an immense number of quotations from writers, in both prose and verse, to illustrate at the same time the prevalence and the advantages of Nature-Study. Here is no flashy essay or sensational fiction, but a grammar on the subject of Nature-Study, than which no earthly study can be more interesting or more profitable to man. We feel quite certain that Mr. Dircks does not in the least over-estimate the results of the adoption of his method, and to what he claims may be safely added the mental discipline involved, and the pleasure which would necessarily accompany the study. As a whole, we have nothing but praise for Mr. Dircks' work, and our opinion of it will be tersely expressed by saying that, it will find its place on our bookshelves beside the kindred works of Harris, and Horne Tooke."—*The Peterborough Advertiser.*

" Here we have the profound man of science entering the domain of fancy, and essaying to discuss the very cases in which our knowledge of poetry exists. *Nature-Study* is certainly a most extraordinary book, pregnant with thought, no doubt calculated to enlarge our ideas of the fundamentals of poetry, in relation to the study of external Nature. As a mental exercise, we can recommend no better volume."—*The Rochdale Observer.*

" The few quotations which we copy, from among the many hundreds which the Author gives, indicate, however, ability to describe, pourtray, picture what exists in Nature—master-pieces indeed.
" Every facility should be afforded for the sale of such a delightful book as this is."—*The Rugby Advertiser.*

" The author sets out by noticing the various attempts that have been made to reduce the study of Nature to a proper system, and endeavours to show the crudeness of the methods of study, of which there has been any information obtainable. Altogether there is much that is profitable to be obtained by a perusal of this excellent work."—*The Rugby Gazette.*

" Reviewing our own remarks, we must pronounce a very favourable opinion on the result of Mr. Dircks' thought and labour. The task, on his own showing, is difficult, of reducing ' the art' in which he treats to system. The last chapter is more practical than all the others ; indeed, the preceding ones are more elucidatory of the elements of poetic art ;

as an aid, the author is entitled to our best thanks."—*The Stratford-upon-Avon Chronicle.*

. " With a view to assisting the course of study, the author has selected a large number of poetical illustrations, in which Nature in its various moods and aspects is written about by our best poets. This forms a valuable and attractive collection of poetry, to which the author's pertinent and judicious comments give an additional interest."—*Sunderland and Durham County Herald.*

" Mr. Dircks' Nature-Study is an excellent *Gradus ad Parnassum.* He is evidently fond of his subject, and has taken great pains. He has read a large number of books, and has collected a great mass of material. His industry is most praiseworthy, and his taste correct."—*Westminster Review.*

" We have not space for extracts, but we would remark that we concur with the author in his estimate of many parts of Tennyson's beautiful, but obscure poem, ' In Memoriam.' In conclusion, we would state that we have derived much pleasure and instruction from the perusal of Mr. Dircks' work."—*The Wiltshire County Mirror.*

" This is a volume of rare value, and its production has entailed on its talented author no ordinary amount of labour, and evinces a thorough knowledge of the writings of our poets. There is an admirably arranged index, not only of subjects, but also of authors, quoted in the work. This is no made-up book. It is a deeply reflective publication, written by a man who thoroughly knows his subjects, and under whose guidance the student will acquire an assistance which he will find truly valuable. We must add that the work is dedicated, by permission, to Lord Houghton."—*Yorkshire Gazette.*

One Volume, cloth, crown 8vo. with Portrait, price 3s 6d.

NATURE-STUDY,

SECOND EDITION.

EDINBURGH: W. P. NIMMO.

OPINIONS OF THE PRESS.

" For originality of conception, and the importance and interest of its matter, this work may justly be said to stand alone. Its tendency is to prove and establish the fact of there being little or connection between the objects of poetry and those of science in this study of external nature. His process of investigation developes a beautiful and well-ordered system, having the practice of all poets, whether ancient or modern, for its authority. It is no vague guess-work, but on actual examples illustrative of the subject and its peculiar arrangement that Dr. Dircks establishes his system. Chapter X, ' On Negative Views of Nature,' we commend to the reader's special notice."—*The Aberdeen Free Press*, 17th February, 1871.

" Mr. Dircks, in his admirable work, lays down a course of study—very common-sense like—which, if followed, will unquestionably assist the student in no small degree in his search after the beautiful. In perusing the elegant selections from the poets, the reader is charmed with the scholarly way in which the poetry of the different 'masters' is criticized. Taken altogether, 'Nature-Study' is an important addition to English Literature. It is an able work, worthy of the author—who is by no means new to fame—in which the tyro may read and understand, while the erudite will also find ample food for thought and contemplation."

Aberdeen Herald, 8 April.

" Dr. Dircks' work is essentially, as he modestly styles it, ' a grammar on the subject of Nature-Study.' It is a grammar that does much credit to his acute observation, his critical discrimination, and his powers of long-continued devotion to a study from which he could scarcely hope immediate fame or emolument."—*Brechin Advertiser*, 22 August.

" Dr. Dircks—Nature-Study, 2nd edition—renders his meaning clear and intelligible to all, and so sets forth the beauties of his theory, that it is impossible to avoid catching some measure of his enthusiasm with respect to the advantages to be derived from a systematic study of Nature : a system [as he states] well-grounded, unexceptional, and universal."—*City Press* (London), 21st January.

" The author, with a power of erudition which strikes one more and more forcibly at almost every page, amasses a large collection of illustrative examples of species of nature-study, pursued solely by natural instinct, or talent, or genius, or through the interposition of a direct inspiration. These are put forward as the result of a mental process wholly without system ; and the aim of succeeding chapters is to reduce the elements of this process, so to speak, to a systematic and progressive form of study. We commend this book to all well-read, cultivated, and contemplative minds, as a storehouse of pleasant and instructive information, and which they are not likely to have met with before."

Doncaster Chronicle, 27 January.

" The point of resemblance which we find in it [Nature-Study] to the previous works of the same author, is in the power of research displayed, which gives great value to Dr. Dircks' ' Life of the Marquis of Worcester,' and which here also appears to advantage ; the illustrative quotations which are made being taken from a vast variety of sources, and manifesting an extensive knowledge of literature, and especially English literature. His book contains much sound and suggestive criticism ; whilst his evident appreciation of the beauties of poetry, and his extensive acquaintance with that department of literature, make it pleasant to follow him from one topic to another, and to compare along with him the productions of different authors."

Edinburgh Courant, 12th February.

"'Nature-Study' has been so well appreciated by the public as to reach a second edition. We have been delighted with the perusal of this excellent and instructive book, which, besides pertinent remarks and rules for the study of Nature, contains a collection of the richest and most precious gems of literature, well selected and tastefully arranged."

Fife Herald, 2 February.

"Mr. Dircks has endeavoured to show, by carefully selected examples, the ways in which Nature has affected poetic minds at different times and under varied circumstances. He shows too that the fears entertained that the progress of Science would rob Nature of half its charms have no real foundation. The best evidence which we can lay before our readers of the value of this able and instructive work is to be found in the fact that the copy before us is one of a second edition."

Galway Express, 21 January.

"All that books can communicate of 'Nature-Study,' Dr. Dircks has laid before his readers in a concise, well-arranged, and lucid form, but—what is of infinitely more importance—his work is eminently calculated to lead them to think, compare, and reason for themselves; we deem the author a public benefactor, and wish him heartily all the success he merits."—*Guernsey Mail and Telegraph*, 21 March.

"This book forms a curious monogram on the study of Nature. It may attract the readers by the rich array it presents of poetical quotations, especially of those finer passages which constitute the great, humanizing texts of literature. The book itself, is exceedingly well got up in typography and arrangement; and it is dedicated to Lord Houghton."—*The Hawick Advertiser*, 26 February.

"We have perused this work with more than common interest. Mr. Dircks has looked deep into the subject, and must have spent some years in gathering materials for his treatise. His book abounds with much valuable thought and acute observation and suggestion; and no reader who has paid any attention to the subject treated of can fail of making additions to his knowledge by means of this treatise."

The Inverness Advertiser, 24 February.

"The fact that two editions have been called for of Mr. Dircks' 'Nature-Study,' speaks well of a treatise on the 'Art of attaining those excellencies in poetry and eloquence which are mainly dependent on the manifold influences of Universal Nature.'"

Leamington Courier, 26 January.

"We hail with pleasure the truly original criticisms of one who is well-read and self-reliant upon poets and writers whom the world has always sworn by. Mr. Dircks is a thoughtful, and often an incisive critic of poets. We illustrate Mr. Dircks's critical ability by a quotation which hits Mr. Tennyson very hard, but not harder than he deserves. The quality of his writing has originality, power, and pertinence, such as is not often presented to us."—*The Manchester Guardian*, 29 March.

II.

One Volume 8vo. of 650 pages, with Steel Engravings of two unpublished Portraits, and 45 Wood Engravings, price 24*s*.

THE LIFE, TIMES, AND SCIENTIFIC LABOURS

OF

EDWARD SOMERSET,

SIXTH EARL AND SECOND

MARQUIS OF WORCESTER,

To which is added

A REPRINT OF HIS CENTURY OF INVENTIONS (1663), WITH A COMMENTARY THEREON.

" A monument raised late, it is true, but not too late, to a great and modest genius. A national biography which illustrates and elevates our ideas of the past, and a contribution which the world will recognise to the European History of Science."—*Dublin University Magazine*, September 1865.

" A work which displays a high order of literary ability, careful antiquarian research, much ingenuity, and withal thorough honesty of purpose. [Lord Worcester's] life, told as Mr. Dircks has told it, is one of much interest. Here we have an elaborate—although of course not a completely exhaustive—account of his life ; at any rate the most complete account of him ever likely to be written—a work filled with abundant evidence of the most painstaking research, a work written in a generous and sympathising spirit, and with every attribute of conscientiousness."—*Engineering*, 5th Jan. 1866.

" The production of this volume is no common achievement ; Mr Dircks has undertaken to write the life of a man about whom the public know very little. He has, we think, collected some curious information, and established the claim of the Marquis to be the first constructor of a steam-engine. The reprint of the celebrated *Century of Inventions* adds greatly to the interest of the volume."—*The Spectator*, 14th Sept. 1867.

III.

One Volume, 8vo., price 21*s.*, only 100 copies printed,

WORCESTERIANA;

A COLLECTION OF

BIOGRAPHICAL AND OTHER NOTICES, ALPHABETICALLY ARRANGED, RELATING TO EDWARD SOMERSET, SECOND

MARQUIS OF WORCESTER,

AND HIS IMMEDIATE FAMILY CONNECTIONS; WITH OCCASIONAL NOTES.

"The present volume is, as it were, a supplement [to Mr. Dircks' *Life of th Marquis of Worcester*]. It contains what the French call ' pièces justificatives,' on which that biography was founded ; and such other materials connected with the history of Lord Worcester's family and his invention of the steam-engine as will prevent, as far as possible, a repetition of the gross errors hitherto promulgated on these subjects."— *Notes and Queries, February 3, 1866.*

IV.

One Volume, crown 8vo., price 3*s* 6*d,*

A BIOGRAPHICAL MEMOIR

OF

SAMUEL HARTLIB,

MILTON'S FAMILIAR FRIEND,

With Bibliographical Notices of Works published by him ; and a reprint of his Pamphlet, entitled, "AN INVENTION OF ENGINES OF MOTION."

" Mr. Dircks' is the first careful attempt to make posterity his (Hartlib's) friend."—*The Examiner,* 18th February, 1865.

"A scholar-like little monograph, giving all the information that can be given about a man whose name occurs in the correspondence of almost every eminent literary or scientific person of the time of the Commonwealth."—*The Spectator,* 20th May.

V.

Two Volumes, crown 8vo., with engravings, price 10*s* 6*d.* each.

PERPETUUM MOBILE;

OR, HISTORY OF THE SEARCH FOR SELF-MOTIVE POWER FROM THE 13TH TO THE 19TH CENTURY.

First and Second Series.

WITH AN INTRODUCTORY ESSAY.

VI.

One Volume, crown 8vo., with portrait, price 3s 6d,

CONTRIBUTION TOWARDS A HISTORY

OF

ELECTRO-METALLURGY,

·ESTABLISHING THE ORIGIN OF THE ART.

VII.

One Volume, crown 8vo., with engravings, price 2s,

OPTICAL ILLUSIONS: THE GHOST!

AS PRODUCED IN THE SPECTRE DRAMA,

Popularly illustrating the marvellous optical illusions obtained by the apparatus called the Dircksian Phantasmagoria.

VIII.

One Volume, crown 8vo., with two portraits, price 4s,

INVENTORS AND INVENTIONS,

IN THREE PARTS.

I. The Philosophy of Invention. II. The Rights and Wrongs of Inventors, Legally and Politically Examined. III. Early Inventors' Inventories of Secret Inventions, employed from the 13th to the 17th Century, in substitution of Letters Patent.

IX.

One Volume, crown 8vo., cloth, price 3s,

SCIENTIFIC STUDIES;

TWO POPULAR LECTURES, DELIVERED 1864 AND 1869.

1. The Life of the Marquis of Worcester; and 2. Chimeras of Science.

X.

One Volume, 8vo., cloth, 4s,

PATENTS AND PATENT LAW,

IN THREE PARTS.

1. So-called Patent Monopoly; 2. Statistics of Inventions; and 3. Policy of a Patent Law, etc.